Hoopi
Shoopi
Donna

Also by Suzanne Strempek Shea

Selling the Lite of Heaven

Hoopi Shoopi Donna

Suzanne Strempek Shea

POCKET BOOKS
New York   London   Toronto   Sydney   Tokyo   Singapore

POCKET BOOKS, a division of Simon & Schuster Inc.
1230 Avenue of the Americas, New York, NY 10020

Copyright © 1996 by Suzanne Strempek Shea

Shea, Suzanne Strempek.
   Hoopi, shoopi Donna / by Suzanne Strempek Shea.
     p.   cm.
   ISBN 0-671-53544-7
   I. Title.
   PS3569.H39126H66   1996   96-33676
   813'.54—dc20   CIP

First Pocket Books hardcover printing June 1996

10 9 8 7 6 5 4 3 2 1

Printed in the U.S.A.

This is for Tommy Shea,
my husband and my greatest gift.

Acknowledgments

I am very grateful to all who have supported my writing.

For all their unfailing help, I send special thanks to my agent, Ann Rittenberg; my publicist, Amy Greeman; my friend Elinor Lipman; my mother, Julia (Milewski) Strempek; and the constant St. Jude.

For their initial faith in my work, I once again thank Mary Anne Sacco, Jane Rosenman and Donna Ng.

Hoopi
Shoopi
Donna

Chapter

1

Winkie Papuga started the whole thing.

He just had to go and say it to me one more time, almost like he was underlining, then he let go of my hand, blew his nose, stepped off the porch, got into his car, rattled over the bridge, unlocked his apartment, took out his teeth, settled onto his daybed, clicked to the "Wheel of Fortune" and went on, I guess, with the rest of all the little actions that would make up the whole entire remainder of his life, not ever once knowing what he had done to mine.

No, he probably never ever gave it a second thought how, right after telling me how my father had been like a brother to him, then correcting how that wasn't exactly right because he couldn't really stand any of his brothers—no, he said firmly, Adam Milewski had been more like the kind of brother he wished his real brothers would have been, had they not been such SOBs (that expression meaning nothing against his own loving and dearly departed mother, of course, I had to be sure)—right after that, to change the subject, because if he went on he was going to start crying over how if my father

truly had been his brother then he might have had at least one
relative who would want to spend time with him in his old
age, Winkie Papuga added, without even taking one breath to
make it clear that now we were talking about something totally
different:

"You ever play the accordion anymore?"

That day, people asked me (like I would have known) did we
have them remove my father's gold teeth because what good
were those or any other such valuables going to do him down
there? Didn't we think they had colored his mustache a little
too darkly? Who put that hammer and that sausage funnel in
there with him? How much was the casket, and somebody
took a picture of it, didn't they? Who was going to get all of his
record albums? Did anybody get a chance to say at least a few
words to him at the very end—and, if they did, what were
they? So there was nothing too strange about Winkie, too,
asking me something odd, or something that went way back,
many, many years previous to this day, about a subject that
had no connection to it at all. And because of that I didn't need
a second to answer him, no, I no longer play the accordion,
and I haven't picked up the thing since the eighth grade. I
decided to skip reminding him of the details, how in the space
of a couple of months, my world went flying off in a direction
you couldn't find on any map, no matter how big a magnifying
glass you held up to it—how I out of nowhere got stuck with a
little sister, got run over by a diaper truck, and got a real huge
hate for the father I once had loved like nothing or no one else.

Instead of telling Winkie all that, I just said, "The accident.
Remember?" To help him recall, I pointed to the right shoulder
that, even many years after what happened, still makes
cracking noises if I move it a certain way. I brought it to that
position just then, pulling my hand up and back like I was
going to hitchhike or put my thumb on the low C on the
keyboard, and from under the shoulder pad of the blazer that
was the only black piece of clothing I was able to come up with
in my closet, and that made me look, I thought, like a hostess
at a Steak & Brew, came the snap of the noise that always
sounds painful to others but never actually hurts me one bit.

Winkie, who, I remember, brought to my house once I got

home from the hospital a case of Moxie and a carton of blue-and-white-striped paper straws with little bendable elbows, winced and whispered, "Oh, yeah," and landed his eyes on the spot next to me, where two pitted aluminum screws kept the top hinge of the front storm door in place.

"Too bad," he said solemnly. "For all them years, your father used to say to me again and again, 'You know, Winkie, if she keeps on with it, she could . . .'" He stopped and looked at me right here, well aware that I knew the rest. Everybody in the world—at least everybody in the world around here—knew the rest of that sentence, because when I was a kid, and when my father was feeling in a certain mood, he would say to anybody who would listen to him go on and on, "If she keeps on with it, she could start her own all-girl polka band like the one I saw that time in Chicopee . . ."

Winkie smiled at me, and, so why not, we finished it together: "the one that makes a killing at weddings."

Then he laughed, and I found I somehow was able to as well, though not as hard as he was, and I couldn't help but take the guy around the shoulders and hug him fiercely like I was getting ready for someone to try to pull him away from me. I smelled camphor and Aqua Velva, but mostly what was coming into my head was how his was the height and size and heft of my father. This is how he had felt, way back when we actually did hug, and I would never feel that ever again. So I held on for maybe longer than Winkie was used to, if he was accustomed to any of this sort of thing at all, and he eventually pushed me away. But he did so slowly and kindly, and only so I could clearly hear him say:

"You know, he loved when you made the music."

I smiled as much as I could and said that I knew, because I did. For nearly eight years straight, from the first grade on, my favorite thing in the world was playing the accordion. Mostly, I must add, my favorite thing was playing it for my father. It was the main way we talked, though no words as you would recognize them ever were used.

I was not one of those kids who had to be screamed at about how much the lessons cost and how the thing is never used and what a waste it was to buy it and it would be better off on the front lawn with a "for sale" sign stuck to it because surely there had to be thousands of kids out there who would jump at the chance to have music lessons. Nobody had to promise me desserts, or a puppy if I practiced one hour a day for a year. Nobody had to make a chart to hang on the refrigerator and paste metallic stars on each of the days I did my scales and went over the next few new bars. I, too, loved when I made the music, and I practiced willingly and without reminder for one hour of each and every day of the week, just after supper was over and everything was put away, from 6:30 to 7:30, dragging an armless chair from the table to the center of the kitchen, unfolding my metal music stand under the plastic glow-in-the-dark cross braided to the string of the ceiling light, then lugging the heavy black case from my bedroom closet, pulling on the beautiful, shining instrument, unsnapping the bellows, and playing over and over my father's many favorite polkas and obereks and mazureks and waltzes, one after another, stopping only to get another book or to flip the page from "You Are Teasing Me, My Darling," to "Wait for Me, Haniu," moving my fingers easily along the keys and the buttons with what Mrs. Dranka proudly pointed out to anyone who stopped by The Melody Academy during my weekly lesson was "a rare grace."

And for each of those hours of each of those days of each those nearly eight years of practicing, my father would sit at the head of the table, a silver rosary crawling through his left hand, a Camel glowing in his right one, smiling half at me and half past me, to (here I've always had to imagine because I never got the nerve to ask and he never told me) the place he came from, some world that must have had music like that playing everywhere, old-country versions of "Pretty Maryśka" and "When It's Evening" and the Polish national anthem flowing out of every house and tree and lake and cloud the whole day long. My father was somewhere else for that one hour with me, and it wasn't within five thousand miles of that kitchen table. And if I've ever known any one thing for certain in my whole entire life, it was that right then, I was making him truly happy.

I heard Winkie say "Too bad you didn't keep on with it," and that brought me zooming back through the great space separating that kitchen and this front door, one narrow hallway apart, really, but thousands of miles from that pure time to this day so unbelievable and sad.

"Yeah," I answered, though I arrived back in the present without any opportunity to give a thought to whether or not I agreed with him. "Too bad."

Winkie went on, shaking his head and moving his hands together and apart as if he were playing something himself, but he got drowned out suddenly as she cracked that laugh and I could see, over the heads of the circle of admirers that Cioci Urszula and John the Barber were straining to edge their way into, my sister's hands flying up, fingers spaced and poised as graceful as a figure skater's, as she sighed loudly, "But that was my father for you!"

The people around her made the "aaaahh" sounds you hear when gifts are opened at a baby shower, like whatever story she just presented was the sweetest thing they'd ever seen. She might as well have just unwrapped the cuddliest, smallest, palest yellow terry cloth lamb, its eyes embroidered on so it held not even the remotest danger of a loose button that could be sucked down a windpipe. Then Millie Banach embraced my sister, and Peter Chmura patted her head, and Joe Miarecki told my sister he'd yet to hear a man go on about a daughter the way her father always had gone on about her.

Winkie Papuga must have seen me watching all that because he poked me a little in the arm, then harder, and harder again, until I finally turned. His eyes searched my face for a second or two, stopping with sadness, I saw, on the familiarity he found in the arc of my eyebrows and at the higher right side of my mouth. And he said to me again, "When you made the music, I never saw nobody so proud." Then he let go of my hand, blew his nose, and stepped off the porch.

At that point, I must admit, I did not know myself what Winkie had done right there. I had dishes to clear and keys and pocketbooks to locate, doggie bags to wrap, a toilet paper roll to refill, promises to make that, yes, I really would stop by someday, and nosy people to assure that, yes, I knew I eventually would find the right guy, and that, yes, I, too, had seen the sign announcing that the AmVets had started a pitch league for singles and was offering a free mixed drink to each person who registered. Getting everybody out of my house seemed to take about nine years, and in the end I was left alone with the silence and the empty folding chairs and the scattered TV tables and the icebox full of leftovers and the wilting red rose pulled for me from the casket blanket, and I went off to my own teeth and bed and television program, getting dragged into an ominous setup to a tragic true-life rescue story about boys who were playing with gasoline and a barbecue grill, and I did not even attempt to close my eyes until the kids—the actual kids who were the subject of the story—appeared as I was certain they would, in real life, at the end of the program, pointing their bandages into the camera as they warned others not to be as stupid as they had been.

If you want to know exactly, it would be two weeks and one day before Winkie Papuga's words to me would work their way down to the level where I would hear them in my head, at around four in the morning, coming in so clearly that I would think he somehow had gotten into the house and up the stairs and over to my room and next to my ear. But there was no one there when my eyes popped open, only the dark and the sound of his words running like the Conrail engine that right at the same time was barreling down the tracks laid six feet from my bedroom wall, bound for somewhere that you would not know about unless you were that engineer right now pulling on the horn, telling everybody to get out of your way.

You have a trip to make.

There is somewhere you have to go.

And you are driving.

I gave my notice three and a half hours later, my first and last day back at the factory.

"Donna, Donna, I'm so very sorry—so very sorry." Mr. Newbury began to chant this sadly the minute he saw me in his doorway. He came forward with his hand extended, and

6

instead of my own I pushed into his palm the folded-up letter I had handwritten on a legal pad back when it still was dark:

I will be leaving my job. This is my two-week notice, but since I have three weeks and three and a half days of vacation coming, this will be my last day.

He looked at it for quite a while, as if reading two sentences would take that much time. So I added, to make sure he understood and, maybe, to make it all that more real for me, "I mean I won't be working here. Even today. And not ever again."

Then I took a step, backward, toward the door—a silly thing to do. What was I thinking—that I was such an important part of this place that Mr. Newbury might lunge at me and hold me captive until I changed my mind?

He only said "Donna—" and stopped at the one word, then scratched at his ear and squinted, "—I don't mean to . . . it's not my business . . . but, sometimes, at times like these, we make decisions . . .

"I made it," I interrupted in a small voice, trying to be polite, trying to look at his vacation-tanned raisin of a face more than I was looking at his shiny brown shoes, all perfect as you would see in a store window, except for the fraying end of one lace. "Mr. Newbury. I've made the decision. . . . Thank you, you've been very good to me all these years. Do I need to sign anything?"

He stared at me thoughtfully for a couple of seconds, and whatever he saw must have convinced him I truly wanted out. He left the room to bring back a form that called for too much information, and, sighing a little, he told me to write only my name where he'd made the letter X. He assured me he would have the rest of it typed out later on by somebody, so I needn't worry about having to come back. A copy, and my remaining paychecks, would be mailed to my home. Obviously, Mr. Newbury said, I felt I had to leave, that my mind was set, and he wouldn't keep me from whatever it was I was going to do. But, he said, I should know there always would be a place for me, as there had been for, what was it? (here he counted on his

7

fingers) sixteen years already?—a span of time during which, it now occurred to me, if you had been born at the beginning, you now would be nearly old enough to drive and nearly of legal age to do all sorts of things across the entire country.

After making that generous offer, Mr. Newbury left a lengthy space in the conversation, and most likely here he was creating an opportunity for me to confide in him, to fill him in about the plans that were making me quit so abruptly—as if I could actually tell people at all right now, and as if when they heard, they wouldn't think I really had gone off the deep end. But, you know, I wouldn't blame them for thinking that way, even though to me it makes perfect sense that when you love somebody too much, even though to simply look at the two of you in the many recent years nobody would have guessed that, and you lose him forever in an instant right out of the clear blue sky without your getting a chance to set things straight with him, you go and decide to quit your job and tell everyone you're going to try something different, something you'd always wanted to do, something that might have made that one person happy if you had done it when he was around to see. You say to everyone that now you see how short and how unpredictable life is, and that now is the time for that change.

Usually in such cases, according to what I read in the paper, distraught people will say something like that and then, instead of opening the soft-serve ice cream stand they'd been talking about, or spending more time with their kids, the next thing they do is go off and kill themselves. In my case, I certainly was distraught, and I certainly was going to do something different. But I skipped right over the part where I was supposed to have gone off and hung myself in the sand pit behind the fire station. I had no choice. I could not be dead and still be the leader of an all-girl polka band.

Chapter

2

*I*t was only because she had landed far ahead of me, clear across the street, her body draped almost neatly over the rounded top of the Kajkas' proudly hand-clipped golden privets like a cleaning rag you might have stretched out there to dry in the sun, that everybody figured Betty had been trying to save my life.

They had no choice but to suppose. We victims were of no help with providing an explanation, and the guy who had done all this to us knew nothing more than that he had the sun in his eyes. Plus, our town was small, and that was way back, in 1973, so there were no big, modern, expensive investigative teams to be called in, no regional accident specialists to be consulted, no computerized gizmos to roll out of some van that might be called an Emergency Mobile Incident Scene Unit to photograph and measure and walk back and forth in front of the place where the path from the river met up with Norbell Street, at the site of the exact spot where I pounded out of the trees frightened and sniffling, my accordion wheezing and flopping against me with every step, Betty screaming on my heels, and I almost went right into the street, only I spotted the truck from the Healthy Delivery Diaper Service flying down the hill so awfully fast, swerving even, sounding its normally joyful tooting horn in what suddenly was a threatening blast, the coronated plastic baby mascot stuck to the roof frozen in fear, the guy in the driver's seat bouncing and shouting something and waving and looking terrified, and I stopped so sharply at the curb that my only copy of the sheet music for "The Sweet, Sweet Bobby Polka" fell from my hand and blew into the road, and I heard Betty yell something as she threw herself toward the paper just as the truck came into the corner of my eye and got bigger and bigger until, just as I tried with all I had to grab for the end of her sweater and swing her out of the way, there is nothing more to remember, until that first sound of Mrs. Frydryk reciting the *Zdrowaś Marya*, and the feeling of somebody lifting my accordion off my face, and the first thing I saw being the blurry diaper man leaning over me in his pink-and-blue coveralls, folding his hands and mumbling to me how "They're gonna kill me. I just know it—and I didn't see anything. Really . . . it was the truck!" and the second thing I saw, my father, racing down the hill at me and screaming "Monkey!" in a horrified tone of voice I'd never before heard from him, but running straight past me and over to that old doll that lay flopped on top of the row of bushes.

You could say the flashing lights, and the screaming people, and the prayer words recited around sobs, and the man shooting photos I tried to cover myself from but found I couldn't move my arms, and the instant my father used my pet name on somebody else couldn't have been a more literal way to say to me that the fine and dear life you had been blessed with is over and done with, good-bye, amen. But I would have to say it only comes close. The real, true moment for all that (though even if you were there and observed it, you would not have been able to tell this at the time) came on a still late summer night six months earlier. The night I found out I was getting a sister.

I had made it happily and just fine for fourteen years without one, mostly because for me it was honest and true what they say about not really missing what you never have known, and because it was as if I had two sisters anyway, in Carolyn Lyszko and Theresa Zych, two very different girls from two very different houses on my street with whom I did most of the things I imagined I would have done with them had we all come from the same set of parents.

Carolyn's home was only four to the left of mine as you went out my front door. Hanging over the steep corner of River and Pulaski, it was a tiny, white, shuttered and awninged Cape that gave up to Lyszko & Son Vegetables and Fruits what most people would have used as their front room. In the shoebox spaces upstairs, the parents, Raymond and Jennie, raised Carolyn and her sister Marilyn (though born three and a half years apart, they had been given the twin names their mother had held in her head since childhood) and their brother, Ray Jr., feeding them the finest selections from the two back shelves marked "Less Than Perfect, But Perfectly Good!" But there had to have been some kind of beneficial vitamins and nutrients left in all those shriveling tangelos and rusting icebergs and bendable potatoes because the Lyszko kids turned out to be absolutely breathtaking, lean and strong with flawless skin, intense blue eyes, and golden-blond hair that seemed lit from within. People from milk commercials. The amazing thing was, they did not realize their good fortune and acted like they had nothing over the rest of us people who simply looked normal, or worse.

Theresa, on the other hand, was nothing much to behold, but she thought just the opposite—and often put those thoughts into words. She was what my mother would call brash, and, my mother added, that attitude came from Theresa's having no real mother figure, no one to teach her to be ladylike. "If her father ever got the nerve to marry again, she would have turned out a different girl—I just know it right here," she would tell me, pounding at the place on her chest where you would draw the heart.

I know it had been talked about around town how Mitchell Zych once had his sights set on somebody, but he never seemed to have done anything about it other than phone "Freddie Brozek's Polka Explosion" the first Sunday of each month and request that "Lass With Lips Like Red Berries" be sent out to "someone special, I hope she knows who she is." Maybe if he had done a little more, like make sure that she indeed knew who she was and that, if she did, that she knew who he was, there might have been someone like a mother there—at least another female to do and say and explain the things a girl needs as her life goes along. But there was no female on the farm that was behind the polka park that was across the street from my house—no human female, that is— only the holsteins and the chickens and the couple of Nubian goats and Theresa's father and Theresa's brothers, Teddy and Winston, the first named for her father's father and the second named for her mother's bad habit. Neither could remember anything about the grandfather, but both boys four and five when she left, long could see in their minds, exact as a photograph, the snake of cigarette smoke that followed their mother everywhere, including out the door as she bumped her huge leather suitcase down the front porch stairs that one last time, saying sorry, she tried, she really did, but this just was not the life for her.

Theresa was an infant baby when all that happened, one so small that you could have left her lying on the floor all day and she would have been right there in the same exact spot once you decided to come on back. Theresa herself had no recollection of her mother, but, if she had wanted to, she could have seen her every time she looked in the mirror—her same good amounts of coarse black hair overtaking the same small round face cut this same way by the same long straight nose and that same way by the same slitty green eyes and the same pair of thin lips. Had she sought professional help for all those feelings she stuffed away about Mrs. Zych's taking off like that, Theresa could have sent some psychotherapist around the world, first-class. But, as far as I knew, they never came out, not even to the cows. And somewhere in her head she turned the whole situation into one big yardstick she set next to everyone who was her age. "So you needed two parents? Just look how well I'm doing with only one."

The three of us got along great most days, spending our spare hours in the silly play that filled so much of the first

fourteen years of my life, a string of thousands of days that
were so far from any trouble or worry or concern I shouldn't
even have taken the time to learn how to spell those words.

We tied the goats to our wagons and led them on parades
down the street. We held fingernail-growing races, and, as we
saw on a TV commercial, we soaked our cuticles in Palmolive
Dishwashing Liquid twice a week until my mother began to
think she was going crazy with her bottle emptying so fast. We
hid in the mountain laurel along the riverbank, having just
escaped from the orphanage and the dogs sent looking for us.
We picked rocks and, certain they held gold, hammered the
shiniest ones to smithereens on the concrete slab in the
backyard that held Babci's Blessed Virgin Mary statue. When
we were still small enough to fit in the space between my
parents' divan and the wall, we met there once a month to pay
our nickel dues for membership in the Hedgehog Club we
titled for an animal we'd never seen but whose name we loved.
We made up codes to be sent by flashlight across a pitch-black
field, and alphabets that could be deciphered only when held
up to a mirror, upside down. On sleep-overs, we danced in our
underwear to the music of Herman's Hermits. We decorated
what we called a hippie room in a corner of Theresa's
basement, hanging up curtains of plastic beads and pictures of
Paul Revere and the Raiders, and, when her father wasn't
around, we lit sticks of incense and candles stuck into the neck
of a Scope bottle Carolyn picked from the trash basket in her
bathroom. We sat there, on the floor, and argued not over war
or the establishment, but important stuff like who would get to
marry Philip Grybosz and his mile-long eyelashes, and what
would be the first, middle, and confirmation names of the boy
quadruplets and girl quadruplets he and the one of us who
would be his wife would have and raise. We began and ended
so many days walking to and from school, even dressed
sisterly, alike in our red-and-green-and-white plaid jumpers
and our pigtails, which we pronounced "picktails," ending not
just with regular rubber bands but woven with thick white
satin ribbons. And we practiced our music together, outdoors,
even, once in a while, at the side yard of the Lyszkos' store, or
high on one of Theresa's fields, or on the beach at the river.

All that began when our parents signed us up for polka music lessons the month we entered first grade in 1964, the very same point in time that Mrs. Dranka's nephew joined her in business, and, in an attempt to attract enough students to keep the both of them busy, she decided to hold her first lesson sale. The lessons were taken by most kids in our town, which I used to figure had to have more Polish people than probably Poland itself, and where the tiny row of shops on Main Street thrived largely due to the traffic drawn by The Melody Academy, which, other than weird Mr. Lawson's mildewy basement with its four noisy dehumidifiers whining at high speed, was the only place for miles where you could learn to play music of any kind at all.

It was my mother who spotted the announcement for the lessons, and she was the one who cut it out and paper-clipped it to the wall calendar in the pantry. With a spare seam ripper, she trimmed so neatly around the dramatic photograph of a square-faced woman staring soberly from beneath a beehive hairdo, wearing some dark dress with a high neck and holding an elaborate accordion.

"Music has filled my life with happiness and culture," read the quote in large type next to the woman's head. "Let me share that happiness with you or your child. Please visit The Melody Academy's special registration night."

Another line gave the address and telephone number, followed by one that told you refreshments would be served, then by a whole column listing the instruments taught throughout owner Sophie Dranka's twenty-three years in business. There were checkmarks printed next to each one, as if the woman with the hairdo (that had to be Sophie) had gone through the ad herself and had marked, yes, I teach accordion, and, yes, the piano, too. And that's right—clarinet, flute, and all string instruments.

I really think I might have ended up picking the accordion on its looks alone—simply because of how, instead of an instrument, it could have been a treasure chest that, if you hit the right buttons in the correct order, would click open to reveal the piles of riches that in picture books you always see pirates running their sharp and greedy hooks through. The one Mrs. Dranka had on display on a chair on the night of her open house was blood colored, with silver and gold and mother-of-pearl outlines and accents. The main body was done in some kind of plastic, but it appeared to be more like glass pressed over folds of deep red velvet. You just couldn't help but touch it, and that's what my father did, slowly running his hand down the bass buttons and then standing back and folding his arms and continuing to take it all in like it was some famous work of art he'd bought a ticket and stood in line all afternoon to have the chance to admire. I walked past him, to where Carolyn was thinking that the clarinet might be fun, and helpful, too, because she had snakes in the stone wall in her backyard and maybe she could use the thing to call them out so her father could take their heads off with his hoe. Next to her, Theresa was telling her father she wanted a guitar because she always saw at least one in the cowboy movies she loved. Back over at the accordion, my mother was sipping a cup of pink punch and, with her new glasses, was reading a price list for lessons and instruments. Mrs. Dranka had picked up the accordion and was playing "Clock on the Wall" very patiently to a little boy who was poking his finger into the bellows every time they opened. My father, a half smile on his face, slowly closed his eyes. His foot began to tap the floor gently. I watched him and watched him, and then I walked over and tugged at his shirt. "I'll practice it every day," I promised him, and, oh, the look he gave me.

"Donna," is all he said, slowly and incredulously, though, knowing him, I knew he meant much, much more. I knew that I might as well have just informed him he had been named the king of the world.

Babci demanded to pay for my lessons, so I can say truly that she had a lot to do with this. Coming up with the $1.25 every week was her duty, she pointed out, as the grandmother, and, she would add if you gave her the time, it also was her duty as the woman who had raised my father by herself for all but the first eight months of his life in this country, having no choice but to do so alone after her husband came out of the woods that day with that one bad mushroom looking so normal among the others piled there in his basket.

Babci was the one who was left on this earth to see that my father practiced his English and that he kept busy and that he didn't fall in with the wrong bunch of boys. She was the one who checked his homework even though she had little idea what it was supposed to say. The one who signed him up for the Young Men's Polish Association's baseball team, then sat in the stands and French-knotted the borders of eighteen linen napkins while her son sat on the bench his whole first season with the Red and White Sox. The one who registered him for altar boys, then, for the first time in her life, parked herself way, way up in the front of the church, in the first pew actually, and recited who knows how many litanies of thanksgiving for the beloved boy on the other side of the communion rail, the handsome boy, the wonderful boy, the good boy who, in all those years, had to be beaten with the strop only once, when Babci found a nip of vodka shoved into one of his bedroom slippers early on in his first year here in his new country.

That last part shouldn't give the impression that Babci was mean. Because she was just the opposite. But she was not one to put up with any crap from anybody—especially from someone she had waited so long for and had yearned for so greatly. My father was the end result of twenty-two years of novenas Babci could count making beginning back in Zakopane, at the side of the featherbed in the tiny attic room in her parents' home, where, for the five months between their marriage and their leaving the country, she and Jasiu silently got to know one another, often with a rooster napping on the headboard. She prayed her novenas on the floor beneath the pitching hammock that she got sick in all the way to America, in the packed train car that took them up to the jobs in western Massachusetts, and on her knees in the mud in front of the Blessed Virgin Mary statue they set in the backyard of their first apartment here on River Street. But each month, then each year, came and went with Babci imploring the help of a different saint by tacking his or her medal to the wall above her pillow, and without any of them being so kind as to send her even the most fragile or hopeless infant—until her forty-first birthday, when Jasiu placed on her dinnerplate the simple one-page letter of reply from his younger brother, and she began to shake so much she had to be given half a juice glass of blackberry brandy, which she emptied in one swig, then told Jasiu to forget about dinner, and she ran upstairs to dig out of the cedar closet all those baby blankets she'd crocheted so long ago. By hand, Babci sewed them together in that one night, the hopping bunnies and the three kites and the sleeping green dog ending up linked large enough to cover the guest room queen-sized bed that soon would cradle the fourteen-year-old boy being sent off to live with the uncle who had offered to adopt any niece or nephew who was available and who would pay for the ticket here and bring the child up with all the advantages Americans have but yet don't know it.

Bone-thin, tall, silent, bushy-haired, and with a panicked look about him, the boy was shocked and miserable when he arrived, but Babci and Jasiu were understanding—wouldn't you be at least a little bit off-kilter after being torn from your family and your home? But he eventually changed his tune. Forget democracy, convertibles, supermarkets. Adam Milewski was in heaven over indoor plumbing. And once he learned the words to express gratitude, he always said them to his new parents in triplet: "Thenk you, thenk you, thenk you," his appreciation being that great for every little thing.

Babci called my father Adam, pronouncing it "Oddom," but more often she called him "son," and once in a while her childhood name for him: *"Dar."* She would say that softly, with the *r* running on like there was a whole long chorus line of them. The word means gift.

He called her *Matka*, the same exact thing he must have called his original mother, and I wondered, when it first occurred to me, was that strange for him? When he wanted to make her laugh, he called Babci *"piękna,"* which means beautiful. But he wasn't kidding. For as long as I knew her, Babci was something to see, both looks-wise and inside, too, with an oblong face that without any help from any cosmetics had cheeks shaded that same mauve everybody these days is decorating their bedrooms in. Her hair was long and white, but I never saw it loose during the day, just always wound in a neat circle of braids at the back of her head, tight and fixed in the shape of a pillbox hat. She was maybe five feet tall, and her body was the kind of round that made the belt on any of her outfits just an accent that lay on top of the fabric, not something that actually functioned to pull a garment in and around a waist, as she had none to define. She wore a long-line bra, a twenty-four-hour girdle, a garter belt, hoisery, clunky black high heels, and a colorful floral dress every single day, and every single day affixed a religious pin to her collar—a gold Virgin Mary medal set into a rosebud, a silver cross encircled by fake diamonds, a mother-of-pearl dove of peace, or the one her mother gave to her the day Jasiu decided to quit the salt mine and announced he was taking his nineteen-year-old bride to America—the small image of poor burned and battered Our Lady of Czestochowa, painted on an oval of wood. When things began to get really confusing for me, Babci gave me that one, laying her hand on my shoulder and saying I should remember my faith. But at that point, I didn't have it in me to remember to take the thing off my shirt before throwing it in the laundry the night of the day she pinned it to me. Years later, I still have in my jewelry box the rusted piece of metal that was the finding, and the cracked lump of wood on which you can still make out the painting of a knowing eye, a holy cheek, and the deep scar across it.

Every morning that the weather was favorable, Babci walked down the street into the center of town to pick up the things she might need, hauling behind her the wheeled, wire cart that would hold the sack of flour and the jar of cloves from Tenczar's Superette, the box of flesh-toned stockings from Wojcik's, the lamb chops and the *kiszka* blood sausage and the greasy pound of lard from the butcher shop, and the package of rock candy from Lis's Corner Spa. She moved along quickly and happily, usually humming some church song, nodding hello to everybody she passed, saying a prayer in her head whenever she saw someone she thought could use one, spreading her general good nature around her as she walked, like you're supposed to when you distribute grass seed onto new loam, in a wide, sweeping circle as you move along, making sure not to miss even the smallest spot. And if you did happen to skip over one part, well you tried your best, and what more ever could be asked of you?

Huntley and Brinkley and their dark theme song would tell her different every night at 7 P.M., but the America that Babci knew was not going to hell in a handbasket. Sure, you might see some kids hanging around the common who could use a haircut and a kick in the pants to get a job, and once in a while there went that big van with the rainbow striping in which that young couple and their barking dogs lived parked deep in the woods beynd the Kokoszkas' smokehouse, but take away the modern automobiles at the curb and that row of men's magazines in the brown paper sleeves behind the drugstore cash register, and, to Babci, the town would look just about the same as it had when she got here in the tough time that was 1931. It looked even better, she was proud to point out, when you approached her home, the beige duplex at 74 River Street that she and Jasiu initially rented the left half of from the manager at St. Stan's, then took over as landlords when he moved to New Britain three years later, then bought in late 1949, when the guy's widow was looking to unload the place, never having liked it anyway, with all those trains running so close to the house the men in the coal car could see you in the bathtub if you didn't remember to pull the shade.

Adam scraped and painted the house every few summers, and regularly fed and trimmed and otherwise tended to the shrubbery and trees and flowers that Babci and Jasiu, then Babci and Jasiu and Adam, then Babci and Adam alone, had planted, one every other weekend each summer, now mature and full and lush and throwing forth more blossoms that you'd ever have enough vases for. Babci herself still maintained a small garden next to the tracks, but a while back had cut her vegetable plants down to only Big Boy tomatoes and an early bed of carrots and radishes, relying instead on going down to the Lyszkos', or on Mr. Grzywna to roll the rest to her door every summer Tuesday and Thursday morning in his rattling pickup that moved down the street about two miles an hour while he stuck his head out the window and yelled what he had to offer: potatoes, tomatoes, broccoliiii. She would flag him down with a little wave, make her selections, pay with the change from her apron pocket, then do her household chores and bake a rye bread all before the rest of us even got started on our day. She broke only to head downstreet and, later, to kneel for the Angelus at noon and to have tea and a little sandwich of some sort before spending all afternoon on our supper—starting the soup, slicing the vegetables, mixing or roasting or basting the main course, icing the dessert, everything—the works—made up from scratch and passed through the little doorway my father had cut between her pantry and ours. All of it would come together while "The Edge of Night" and the other of her programs blared from the living room so loudly that my mother needed only to keep the picture lit on her set on the other side of the wall on the other side of the house from which Babci had kicked out the Ratusz brothers in 1956 so the newlyweds could live inexpensively and so Adam could live only a few feet away, where Babci could keep an eye on him and his new wife, who seemed like a nice enough girl, except her parents hadn't had the decency to pass their language on to her. Babci would have to use English with Helen, something she hated to have to do in her own home. But, for Adam, she would. After all, things like that were a mother's duty.

My own mother's duty was to be my mother, my father's wife, and to sew things. And back when she had only my father and me to worry about, she was really very good at all three.

She would be seated at her black iron Singer Stitchmaster by the time I left for school every day, wearing a pink smock that she'd given many pockets for her measuring tape and notepad and chalk and thimbles, and, in a much more productive version of infant Theresa at the time her mother split, my mother could be found in the exact same spot when I returned at the end of the school day, but with an entire stack of completed work ready to show off to us. She many times simply made repairs at people's armpits or crotches, but a lot of her work was to start from nothing to make a whole dress or even a lined and detailed winter coat out of the material and the pattern someone had picked out for their special outfit for their special day—for their Sweet Sixteen party or for their shower or for their wedding or for their anniversary, or for their being photographed by the newspaper, as Mrs. Siok was, for a front-page story on how she and her husband, who ran the bank, went and named their first baby Penny.

Ours was not a fancy town, but there were enough people around who were aware of my mother's talent and who would want her to sew them something. Even curtains and table-cloths sometimes, and once a nineteen-piece trousseau complete with silk underthings and little pouches in which to store them when you didn't have them on or when they weren't in the hamper, and another time, a gold-and-green satin blanket for somebody's showhorse, and once, just once, a red-white-and-blue banner, long enough to stretch across the front of a house, on which she had been paid to stitch foot-tall letters that spelled out "Welcome Back You Old Coot."

My mother sewed every single piece of clothing I ever wore as a kid, from the baby ones on up, from the underwear on out, and my mother's only regret about sending me to school at Sts. Peter and Paul was my having to wear the same old plaid jumper, white blouse, red bow tie, green knee socks, black shoes, red blazer, and red beanie every single day, rather than getting to select from all the wonderful school clothes she would have loved to have made for me. She compensated for that loss by sewing the most fashionable and extensive after-school wardrobe ever seen or worn, most of it made from the remnants of fabric she was allowed to keep from most of her jobs.

I played in the sandbox in suspendered shorts of blue cotton printed with small yellow shovels and starfish, underneath, a blue T-shirt with sleeves edged in the same shovel design. I climbed trees in denim coveralls, the knees of which she'd appliquéd with apes swinging from branch to branch, and a fat bunch of bananas bright yellow on the front. For my time working in the garden, she whipped together in one hour a floppy white canvas hat and hand-painted alternating rabbits and lettuces along the brim. When I helped Babci in the kitchen, I had a huge chef's hat and apron hanging and waiting for me in the broom closet. For the day my father showed me how to ride a two-wheeler, there were little knickers and a neckerchief, in fluorescent orange for safety's sake. If I went to work with him in the garage, on went the gray jumpsuit and matching service station cap, my name stitched in red script on each. There even was an outfit for studying— khaki culottes that allowed for curling up on the couch, and a matching khaki vest with a row of pockets and slots that held pencils and a tiny notebook and a large rectangle of pink eraser. The blouse to go with it was white and, with indelible ink and high hopes, she had rubber-stamped it all over with red, yellow, and blue *A*-plusses.

When I entered first grade, my mother became the official costumer for all plays and Name Day celebrations and holiday productions held there. She cranked out dozens of sets of angel wings for Christmas and Easter productions, bending a closetful of wire hangers as their bones, and, thanks to her, the Three Kings, if they wished, could have six changes of wardrobe during Midnight Mass. She stitched peaked caps from starched white cotton and, down in the cellar, formed clog-shaped papier-mâché shoe covers for the "I'm a Little Dutch Girl" number in one United Nations Day pageant. For three straight days just before my fourth-grade spring festival, she tied together grass skirts from old bamboo porch shades and turned our TV screen to static as she sewed eighteen identical aloha shirts of fabric on which happy people waved as they surfed past erupting volcanoes and buttons shaped like ukeleles. When the nuns decided to illustrate the story of Father Kulpa's Fiftieth Name Day celebration, my mother made a Statue of Liberty outfit from the old celadon curtains that once hung in the living room and that she'd kept out of the boxes of clothes and things we sent to Poland twice a year, just knowing they would come in handy one day. To illustrate the pastor's arrival here as a little boy, six or seven of us, dressed in drab immigrant clothes my mother had detailed with neat patches and hemmed rips, piled into a cardboard steamship and shuffled it past the drapery landmark, while Tony Besko, credited in the program as "Beloved Father, age five," repeated annoyingly, *"Już jesteśmy tam?* ("Are we there yet?")

I won every Halloween contest I ever entered, and, dressed as Cleopatra the Queen of the Nile complete with paper barge and rubber asp, or as a rainbow trout, a tossed salad, or the Leaning Tower of Pisa, I politely collected savings bonds, bowling passes, unabridged dictionaries, fish and chips vouchers, a pickle jar full of pennies, numerous sporting goods, and, when I was seven, the great honor of flipping the switch on Jesus' electric halo at the nativity scene on the town common.

My mother forever was running a tape measure from my shoulder to my wrist, or holding different colors of fabric against my face and hair, or having me turn and turn while she watched the way a skirt would hang and flow at this new length. I did not need a Barbie doll—I was one myself, minus the comic-book shape and the trademark embossed on the behind. I was played with as much, if not more, and I ate up the attention like it was something I needed to survive, not knowing then how much, for me at least, that was exactly the case.

My mother's mother had taught her how to sew, and she did that mostly by ripping apart anything my mother made some progress on and telling her to do it over correctly in the small overheated corner bedroom in which I slept the couple times a year we would get over to Worcester. My mother's parents, a complete and living set of a Babci and a Dziadziu, were pleasant to me but were usually too busy to come out to visit us, as they had all they could do to keep up with the demand for the draperies they made for a living on huge tables in their basement, wearing pincushions held to their wrists by elastic and listening to Bob Steele on talk radio out of Hartford.

They employed my Uncle Joe, who grinned a lot more than he ever talked, and his quiet well-postured wife, Urszula, who wore a tailored skirt and blazer even when installing on a ladder, and they got a lot of work out of my Uncle Abie, who was great with hems and who was full of energy and who lived at home so he really had no excuse not to be downstairs most of his waking hours. Another nice guy, Walter somebody, who was not a relative, drove the delivery van, for some reason called me Speed, and always shared his glass jar of unstained pistachio nuts with me when we did visit.

My mother sewed for the business while she was growing up, but believed she wouldn't be in it forever. She held the dream of becoming a big-time fashion designer, and that set the course of her life. However, she landed not on Seventh

Avenue, working for somebody who by now might have his name on bed sheets and chocolates and deodorant, but on the other side of Wanda Milewski's bedroom wall, all because her semiformal lawn party ensemble of white dotted-swiss skirt, blouson, vest, beret and handbag was selected by her Clothes Friends 4-H Club as its entry in the 1954 Regional Showcase— the same event at which my father, one building away, was exhibiting an enormous and totally unflawed head of Purple Edge cabbage that appeared to be rolling on its way to at least statewide notoriety.

He was sneaking a cigarette behind the vegetable pavilion the morning he caught sight of my mother for the first time, as she was waiting in a line of well-dressed girls milling at the door to a barn marked by a tacked-up paper sign that read "Homemaking, Ages 14–16," adjusting her beret in the mirror of an empty but still smelly rendering truck before going in for her turn on the runway. The dark and straight hair that ended in a soft flip, the angled stick of Avon Be My Valentine Red she nervously touched to her lips a third time, the way she blessed herself when a name was called and it must have been hers because she looked startled and then queasy and then, in a swish of confidence scraped together from somewhere, she disappeared into the building—all this made him catch his breath.

She was so absolutely lovely, you had to see her for yourself to really understand. But to give an idea, he would say, when he talked about that, how my mother appeared to him to be something like those beautiful girls who so joyously jumped around in matching skirts and sweaters at the sidelines of the basketball games. But when the boy who was to be my father would go up to them to express his admiration, they would only sneer. This one, in her white heaven costume, he knew, would never do anything like that. She would never laugh at him or tell him to get lost or call him a DP or just plain ignore him, and it was true that she did none of those things when she came flying out of the barn, a thin applause trailing her as she snatched off her hat, her eyes down, running to where she didn't know, just far from those people who had pointed out bluntly and none too quietly that an invisible zipper would have made all the difference—away from them and almost right smack into the tall, thin, gentle-looking boy who stood in the dirt yard holding out to her with both arms the huge vegetable he had just run in and grabbed from the stand with the state judges only two heads away from examining it, their blue ribbon out and ready for hanging from one of its flawless outer leafs, and he was saying to her: "For you. You. The most perfect."

As it had been since the day after his high school graduation, when dead Jasiu's good friend Winkie Papuga picked him up just after sunrise for his first shift at Blue Ribbon Meats, my father's job was to put on a lab coat and a shower cap and stuff *kielbasi*, firmly packing miles of hog casings from 6 A.M. to 3 P.M., then come home, drink two Budweisers, and head straight to more work: in warm weather mowing our lawn and those of at least two old ladies down the street, yanking chickweed and other unwanted things from the garden and mixing whatever he pulled out into the worm pile behind the garage, sliding under the car on a little wheeled contraption he built himself and changing the oil or fooling with something in the engine that you couldn't reach simply by lifting the hood, planting a morning glory at each utility pole on the street at night so nobody would know he was the one who'd put it there, repairing the porch railing so it didn't wobble when you sat on it even though you weren't supposed to, and when he was done with it all, smoking and boasting about the Red Sox over the stone wall to Johnny Frydryk. In the cold weather, he'd shovel for us and the same old ladies he mowed for, he'd fix chair legs or paint the pantry or build shelving in the cellar for all the things Babci had canned. He'd read library books about home projects, then build me a rocking horse or a sandbox or a set of flat wooden ducks—a mother and three babies, all set on four-inch spikes that he stuck into the backyard when the ground thawed—or he'd craft for my mother a small red wooden Ferris wheel to give to her on Valentine's Day, each seat the exact size for an expensive-looking imported bonbon or sachet to sit. All year round, whenever he had the chance, he'd play his polka records, mostly 78s as thick as dinnerplates and cared for as gently as Babci kept her one precious set of china.

From far across the room, I knew the artists by their record labels: the blue Karo, the red Mercury, the maroon Dana and Stella. Okeh was orange, Columbia could be red or green. The black RCA Victor had the picture of the dog. Most had belonged to dead Jasiu and dated from the early thirties, back when Chicopee turned out not only Uniroyal tires but big-time polka musicians like Jan Robak, and Al "Cocoa" Czelusniak and his Gaytime Orchestra.

Gene Wisniewski and his Harmony Bells, Chet Dragon, Joe Lazarz, Pete Anop, Johnny Menko, Wesoly Bolek, and Bob Szymanski. Peter Uryga and his Motor City Orchestra, Walt Solek, the Malach Brothers, Spike Haskell and the Jolly Millers, Six Fat Dutchmen, Frankie Yankovic and the Yanks. Eddie Siwicki and his Golden Bells Orchestra, Chet Ososki and his Blue Diamond Orchestra. Stan Wolowic and the Polka Chips, Ed "Wimpy" Swierad and his Aristocrats, and "King of the Polkas" Brunon Kryger and his International Orchestra. They all lived in our home.

Many of these people he'd actually seen in person, some of them back when nobody but their mothers knew their names, playing in somebody's garage or cellar or barn. My father's collection of music and signatures was so great and so legendary that local polka dj's often asked my father to appear on their shows and share his knowledge about the artists he collected, something he found quite funny.

"They always say, 'Come and tell us about some of these men,'" he'd boast. "I say, 'The only thing I can tell you is some of them are dead.'"

In our home, my father was his own disc jockey. He'd shout into the kitchen that Victor Zembruski's *"Wiejska Dziewczyna"*—the one about the pretty country girl—was being played just for my mother, even though she had grown up in the city. Frank Wojnarowski's *"Jedzie* Boat" was my Babci's favorite and usually began the night's music. Anything by the great accordionists—Lou Prohut of Lou Prohut and the Polka Rounders, Whitey Bernard of Whitey Bernard and his

Three Kings Orchestra, Stas of Stas and the Connecticut Twins, Frankie Gubala and his Polka Fun Boys—was dedicated to me.

We'd sing, we'd dance, and when he'd had enough, we'd help my father put each of the records back into their sleeves, back into the case he'd organized alphabetically, from the "Alycja, My Love" oberek to the old *"Życie Jest Trudne"* waltz that detailed, in three-quarter time, the truth I had yet to learn back when the words were simply something to sing mindlessly as you washed the supper dishes: "Life Is Hard."

Each of the records was buffed carefully with an old diaper before and after its ride on the turntable, and my father never used the phonograph arm that would have allowed for multiple numbers to be played but that could have harmed the precious discs that put him in the best of moods. But then, at that time he normally had only good moods to begin with— another thing that made everybody crazy about him. You couldn't help but be. For starters, many people said he looked something like the adorable Cookie on "77 Sunset Strip"— shiny brown hair dense and rippled, and he used Vaseline to keep it up and back off the thin, heart-shaped face that, like the rest of his six feet and two inches, wore not an ounce of extra fat. He had that one gold tooth that you could see—the third one over on the top left as you were looking at him—and when he laughed hard enough that his head tilted back, two other ones normally out of view would shine the same metal. His left shoulder was decorated with a small tattoo of a Polish eagle—a white, crowned bird on a shield of red, its wings outspread—but even if he'd had enough muscle on him, he could never make even one feather ruffle on command. The only other physically distinguishing thing about him was a modest mustache— not one of those odd, thin ones from the old movies, and not one that was too bushy or that got in the way of his eating. In the bathroom cabinet he kept a tiny mustache comb that, once I was tall enough to discover it was there, hung on a cup hook behind the Old Spice, I sometimes used on my eyebrows.

But it was not his looks that would make you notice my father, and certainly not anything he said, as he never really said too much to anybody. You only needed to watch what he did. How except for the cigarettes and a very good memory for any occasion on which he had been done wrong, he had no bad habits that I knew of. He did play the numbers once a week, but there was nothing you could say about that because he made his picks with religion in mind, claiming 1 for the one God, 3 for the Holy Trinity, 4 for the four evangelists, 7 for the number of days it took to create the heavens and the earth, 12 for the number of disciples, and 33 for Jesus' age when they stuck him up on the cross.

And every Sunday morning after the 7 A.M. mass, he would drive Babci and my mother and me over to Jasiu's grave, bringing along a watering can for the summer flower pot, or a fresh bunch of laurel when it was too cold for things to grow. He always knelt to pray at what he knew was the end of the plot, respectfully never stepping on the area that was exactly over where Jasiu lay. Then, arm in arm, if the weather allowed, he would circle with Babci through the rest of the cemetery, each week nodding attentively for the billionth time to her same stories, about how this one had died from blood poisoning and how this one looked like the pope and how that one really had always loved this one and isn't it something how they are now only one stone away from each other for eternity—but with his wife between them?

Once he began his working life, my father regularly sent packages to his original family in Poland, cleverly hiding dollar bills in gifts so they wouldn't be stolen when the officials inspected the boxes. He was pretty confident that whoever would be checking the mail might not think to unscrew the ballpoint pen or fully unfold the right-hand cuff of the old pair of trousers or undo the lamination on the prayer card, but he was absolutely certain his father would do so once he got the package safely inside his house. My own father never would speak of such things, but my mother told me many times how those dollar bills added up after a while, and how my Poland Babci and Dziadziu went shopping with them at the Black Market, a place I imagined to be a version of Lis's, only painted in drab colors and odd enough in inventory to offer the many things she told me they were able to buy there over the years: oranges and one time a pineapple, plate glass, a set of rubber tires for the hay cart, vitamins, peppermints, Levi's. It sounded like the only thing the market didn't carry was plane tickets, because neither Polish Babci and Dziadziu nor any of their eight children ever bought any and came to visit. American Babci bristled whenever I would ask anything about that.

"*This* is your father's home now," she would say so sternly I would think maybe somebody else had sneaked into her skin. "*This* is his family."

I was sorry to have gotten her angry, but I was glad about what she had said, that this was the place he was staying, that we officially were his, as I wouldn't have wanted it any other way—especially on every summer Sunday up through my fourteenth year, when, the minute he heard the first few notes to the tune that Ignacy Ulatowski helped make so famous— the one with the chorus that is spelled "*Hupaj Siupaj Dana*," but sounds like "Hoopi Shoopi Donna"—my father would take a break from tending bar across the street at Pulaski Park, the place known to all as the Polka Capitol of New England, and would go to find me down the hill goofing off with the kids and would take me and spin me around the dance floor under the corrugated metal roof on which red letters larger than the tallest man told the world "We Love Our Polka Fans." Still in his white apron, he would scoop me up, and he would spin us so fast I feared I would go flying off into the coals of the chicken barbecue pit. But my father always held me tightly enough to keep that from happening, and we both went on to loop around the floor, making those whooping noises when we bumped into the couples we knew, singing along, all of us swirling in a sea of dancers and perfume and sweat and Miller High Life, thinking of nothing but the music, shuffling exactly over the cornmealed floor and making sure to end each dance in front of whoever was the day's bandleader, bowing to him at the end of the song in gratitude for this wonderful music here in this wonderful country.

So considering how good we all had it here, I guess it only made sense that once he had a whole bunch of his own kids, my father's poor younger brother Czesław, for whom his parents never had been lucky enough to locate another couple of infertile relatives, sooner or later would try to make one of his children as fortunate as his own brother once had been. For one whole year Stryj Czesław wrote lots more and lots longer than his usual Easter and Christmas postcards, and every one of these extra notes was filled with one more holy picture and one more hint about how little Elżbieta Józefa, nearly six and the youngest of the half a dozen girls on the farm, probably never would amount to much because of the family's dire straits. Though I didn't know what they contained even after my father had read them and had stacked them next to the pile of bills on the shelf above the kitchen sink, I think I counted eight of the letters received over that one summer and up to that one Sunday night—the night of my fourteenth birthday— when, once he probably thought I was long ago in bed, my father, armed with a black-and-white photograph of the grinning, scraggly-haired kid in a frayed rag of a dress, finally found the courage to sit down and talk to my mother.

I was in bed, but I was still awake under the sheet using three pairs of glow-in-the-dark rosaries to light up the first chapter of the Trixie Belden book Walter had sent me as a gift along with a package of nuts, when through the heating grate that I had come to leave open year-round for its eavesdropping value, I found out something a whole lot more shocking than the mystery that Trixie and her gang were uncovering at the moss-covered mansion.

"But you know . . . it's expensive—if it wasn't, we would have had more kids," my mother was saying quickly, at a level that was somewhere between talking and whispering, and at a pace that told anyone who really knew her that she was quite nervous.

"A child needs things . . . and we only make so much money . . . and it is a lot of responsibility, looking after somebody else's . . . We're lucky to be here, to be living so cheaply . . . lucky that your aunt wants us here. She could be getting good money for this side of the house—you know?"

"I know. I know," my father answered. "But she is small yet. We will be able to do this—I will make every effort to do what I can to help you." He stopped for a few moments and looked at my mother, then he slowly said: "There are some things in this life that must be done, and there can be no escaping them."

And now, on the floor with my nose to the grate, I watched as he smiled the smile both he and I knew she couldn't resist, and he brought from his pocket the photograph of the needy little girl who, according to his brother, had only a doll's left leg to play with, the other body segments having been dismembered and distributed among her five sisters.

My mother put her hand to her face as she examined the blurry image for a long time, and then she finally told my father she would think about it, which, he knew, since this was her way, meant she would come to him later with the answer he wanted to hear. Instantly he dropped to his knees and kissed her wedding band over and over, in between each of his "Thenk you. Thenk you. Thenk yous."

I looked away from them to the Jesus statue on my night table. He had his hand up in a position that looked like he was saying, "Hey you shouldn't be doing that," and he was right. I shouldn't have been wasting any more time snooping. I should have been thinking of exactly what was happening here, of why I was shuddering suddenly, even though it wouldn't be cold in the house for another month.

Out the window, across the street, the long strings of yellow bug lights glowed along the edge of the polka pavilion like an electric rosary, one big enough, I was certain, to fit the hands of God. They had been plugged in back when it started to get dark, back when you still could count the rows of cars stretching from the street and across the ballfield to the bandstand, back when you still could make out the couples bobbing on the dance floor and waving their hankies high above their heads, back when my father had just returned from the park, had taken a bath, and still was honing into the medicine cabinet mirror his pitch about the girl, back when my only concern about the future was how often I would be allowed to wear the Muguet du Bois that Mr. and Mrs. Lyszko had Carolyn bring over to me along with a note reading "Happy Birthday to a girl with a lot of sense, but no scents!"

Now I sniffed at the lilies of the valley blooming a little too wildly on my wrist, and I leaned against the low windowsill two stories above the street and wondered what it would all be like, to have this girl as a sister. To have a sister at all— something that seldom had crossed my mind, popping up only at odd times like once in a while when Mr. Zych would sound the bell next to the back door of the farmhouse, and Theresa would have to run home and leave whatever it was we had been busy and having fun with, and I would feel a sadness as I wanted her to stay—maybe not forever, but for a few more hours at least. Now I was going to know that, how it would be to have someone here all the time and for years even, someone who would never have to go home for supper, who would stand next to me as we washed our hands at the kitchen sink, who would follow my lead as we brought the serving plates to the table, who would become another link in the perfect circle of four that every night held hands and asked God's blessing over this food and this family. My mind flew: Where were they going to keep her? What was she going to wear? What would she do every day? What would we do together? I was spinning with all I now knew, though I wasn't yet supposed to know a thing.

"And we hope you'll join us next Sunday, when Bob Hundenski and the Corsairs will be here for your listening and dancing pleasure. On behalf of St. Stanislaus Lyceum, thank you—*dziękuje.*"

Master of Ceremonies Mitch Moskal said that, I knew, though I couldn't see this exactly from way up in my room, then handed the silver microphone back to Laughing Richie and Jolly Marcia and their orchestra, who all led the crowd in "God Bless America," then, to a sharp drumroll, asked every-one to join in a song for the homeland, *"Boże Cós Polskę."* Knowing well what was coming up, the crowd would begin the song ahead of the band, asking God to save the land that even those who'd never been there figured had to be wonderful— isn't that where all this great music got its start?

When things that made no sense happened, Babci would tell me that God has His reasons, and that as things progress, the answers to all the whys I am asking will be revealed. In some cases, like when I wanted to know the reasons behind such hard things as how the Kostek girl could be a nurse away in the war for all that time and make it out okay, but then come home and trip off the railroad bridge while fishing and land on her head in the river and now they don't know if she will be able to walk again, Babci would also tell me we will not understand fully until we get to heaven and everything is explained, and I imagined that would be like when the astronauts come back, there's always a spokesman in a suit standing in front of all those microphones, and he knows the answers to any question that's asked, and you are there in a crowd yelling the things that bugged you all your life: "Whatever happened to that Kennedy half-dollar I brought in for history then left in my desk during recess then never saw again?" "What's on the other side of the stars?" "Where did my mother run off to?" "What was I really supposed to have done with my life, anyway?"

But while this girl coming from Poland seemed to me a pretty crazy and out of the blue thing. It could not be a hard thing like that, something you needed a big explanation for. How could she be, I asked myself. She was just a little kid. I looked down through the grate again, which you could not fault me for because, except for the times that Carolyn had us stay over on her screen porch, I normally made the last thing I saw before I closed my eyes the sight through the crosshatched metalwork, and that was usually of my parents, sitting close on the couch, maybe my mother's head on my father's shoulder as she sketched some piece of clothing so ornate you would have to be running a country to ever even for one second consider wearing it, and he was twirling one of her flippy curls as he read up on how to build us a wishing well with a handle you could crank to raise or lower the bucket, or a barbecue pit you could decorate with your family's initial done in a contrasting color of brick, and the sound of Babci's TV next door was muffled by the wall, and all this was best on the nights that rain was hitting the window, or snow was out there making no sound but you knew it was falling and covering everything, and a train had just passed the house, and the noise of it was getting farther and farther away, and everything was still once again, and I felt here we are all safe and all in the same place and there is nothing but good here, and I didn't have to look back fifty years later and know how lucky I had been—I knew it at that very point, how, down to my new pink nightgown with the number 14s my mother cross-stitched in light blue satin floss on each collar point, I had it the best of anybody in the world. And it came to me that I half wanted to share all of that with one hundred little kids from some other country who had nothing to call their own, and that I half wanted to keep all this to myself forever, or for as long as it could last.

Chapter

3

$\mathscr{I}$t took a good four hours to drive to John F. Kennedy International Airport, and another half hour to find the terminal after we got sidetracked when my father decided to make a stop at a church right on the airport grounds that a guy at Blue Ribbon told him had as its altar a statue of Mary levitating above a propeller.

We all knelt at the communion rail, I the only one between my parents for the very last time, and we prayed silently for our private needs. I asked to be a wonderful sister, something I felt well on my way to, mostly because people, once they found out what was going to happen, told me that's what I was going to be. And I had no reason not to believe them. Because of my snooping, I knew exactly what my parents were going to talk about when, three weeks after they made their decision, they drove me on a Wednesday night for an ice cream cone at the Double D in Ludlow, a place we usually visited only on weekends, and we parked far away from the ordering window, at the last picnic table, and they sat me down with my banana split and told me God had picked us out to do something incredibly special.

I took the news very well. In order not to give myself away, I had rehearsed many nights in the mirror, complete with large eye movements, the response of, "Really? Oh boy . . . I mean girl!" I thought saying that might sound cute and be memorable, so in the years to come my parents might laugh as they recalled my exact words when asked by people to tell the story of how they informed me I was getting this little sister.

My parents did laugh, and then they said they were certain I would be so great about all this. And that's exactly what my mother told all our relatives after we returned and she got on the phone, free to make the announcement aloud now that it had been broken to me, and eager to add, since they liked my suggestion, that the girl would be nicknamed Betty (after my favorite character in "The Flintstones"—though I didn't tell them this because I didn't know if they would like my choice not being after a saint or something). I don't know when and where Babci had learned about this whole thing, but by the time we got back to the house, she had the Maytag churning and was down in the cellar humming the song about the mountain men and feeding into the wringer all the tiny little matching tops and pants and skirts I nearly had forgotten ever wearing.

The bronze big toe of Mary's bronze right foot dangled dangerously close to one of the three blades ready to whirl into action just below, but the Mother of God didn't seem concerned. She just floated calmly there on the wall, her hands folded, her head tilted down, as with great concentration she listened in on what we all had to say. I had progressed from sisterly prayers to lay some more Our Fathers on my annual request for a Christmas horse when, out of nowhere, and I still can't tell you from where though I've had a lot of time since then to think about it and all I can come up with is maybe I have some type of psychic ability, I suddenly felt my brain coming pretty close to asking that all of what was about to happen would be some mistake—a joke, maybe—that perhaps Stryj Czesław and Stryjanka Józefa had the kind of sense of humor to make all this up. That maybe with all those dollar bills my father sent to the family over the years they were living high on the hog way over there, and maybe they didn't have even one single kid, never mind six. Maybe we would get to the airline terminal to find not a girl but maybe the man Czesław himself, smoking a cigar and wearing big rings, shouting, "Hello! Good joke! Ha! I just wanted to see your face, brother—that's all!" But I didn't even think past that, and neither did I pray for a plane crash—though it came pretty close to being put into words in my mind. I don't know. Suddenly it all frightened me, and I had a wave of not liking anything that was happening. Still, there was no way I could hope this little kid would die. Not at that point in my life, anyway.

My first in-person sight of Betty was of her being led through a door marked "Customs," clutching a filthy rubber leg, and the hand of an airline stewardess. She was tiny, and certainly cute, and was wearing a faded corduroy jumper that once had been royal blue, a thick buttoned-up brown knit cardigan stuffed underneath it, dingy white knee socks, and a pair of high black rubber boots that were clean but very scuffed. Her yellow hair was pinned in a messy crown of braids that must have started getting loose and frizzy somewhere over the North Sea, and her skin was the most blinding shade of pale I had only seen only once before, that time Eddie Kopanski left a box of millipedes in Sister Lucentia's pencil drawer.

Before the moment I spotted Betty, I always had thought they made up those pathetic-looking kids in the magazine ads that ask people to send money to a foreign country every month so someone can eat or afford soap. I was aware, from my religion book photographs of people in ripped clothing mobbing CARE workers for their chance to dip old tin cans in a cauldron of watery soup, that there were those lots, lots, lots worse off than me. But I never had the occasion to see one of them in real life until Betty came shuffling toward us warily, the gray eyes that were set dead center in her little donut face darting from one of us to the next, stalling for a second on me, then settling up and to my left, on my father, over to my mother for a bit, then slowly back to my father. I followed her stare and looked at him, how his eyes got real wide and how his mouth opened like the way in books they say it does when you are truly amazed about something. His arm left my shoulder, and he made the four or five giant steps forward, stopping short, suddenly, and crouching to her height I guess so as not to scare her more then she was. But that couldn't have happened, I knew from her face. She recognized family when she saw it, and right here in front of her it was.

"Stryj Ojciec!" she whispered in awe, hardly being able to get out the words for Uncle Father, her smile so big and getting in the way of her speech. Then, and Shirley Temple couldn't have done it as well, she jumped to hug him, and they were just hanging on to each other, the stewardess standing above them using the shiny red-white-and-blue neckerchief that matched her suit and cap to blot the makeup pooling beneath her eyes.

My mother had moved into the space my father had vacated between us, and she and I did nothing but watch the other two, their heads so close as in low tones my father whispered things to the girl in their language. From where I stood I caught only pieces: "Beautiful" and "airplane." "Tired." "Happy." "Food." "Home." "Toilet." And "Beautiful" again. The girl nodded a few times, shook her head once or twice, but was saying no words back to him, except for calling him Uncle Father one more time. I don't know how long it was—probably not even a few minutes only—but it seemed like it took my father a long while to stand up and take Betty by the hand and bring her the few feet over to us.

She first looked up at my mother, who, compared to the toothless and haggard image I had in my mind of worked-almost-to-death Stryjanka Józefa, must have looked to the girl like some kind of fairy book princess—even more so in the winter-white Jackie Kennedy-type suit she had lined with pearl-colored silk and had painstakingly hand-embroidered with delicate silver-thread snowflakes just for this meeting. Betty slowly took her all in, then stuck her hand into the pocket on the bib of her jumper and brought out two smooth sticks, crossed and tied together with a couple rounds of old brown string.

"*Krzyż Święty, Stryjanka Matka,*" Betty said in a very small voice, one so tiny my mother didn't catch it. She bent at the waist and said to the girl, "What?—I mean . . ." She looked to my father for the words.

"It's '*co*'—'what' is '*co*,'" he said nervously. "She said, 'Holy cross,' and she says it's for 'Aunt Mother.' Aunt Mother! Isn't she something?" Now he was the one pushing at tears.

My mother gently took the sticks from Betty's hand and thanked her, even curtsying like the kid was an official of some kind. There was an awkward moment, like we all knew something was missing, then my mother leaned down again and gave her a stiff but warm version of the kind of hug you would expect a nice mother eventually would.

When they let go of each other, it was my turn, but it became apparent that an introduction wasn't going to be necessary. Betty walked the one step over from my mother and stared straight into my center, like I had a magic pendant or something hanging there that was hypnotizing her. She didn't do anything else or say anything for a second, then she suddenly grabbed me around the waist and began to sob like someone had just killed everybody she knew.

"*Siostra!*" she bawled into the front of my church coat.

You guessed it: "Sister."

Betty rode out of the terminal and out to our car high upon my father's shoulders. He sang to her the song about the four crazy frogs, the one I hadn't heard probably since I was that small. On every one of the words that meant four, he'd jump high, and she'd laugh like nothing had ever been so funny. "More!" she'd plead to him in their language when he ran out of verses.

My mother and I walked behind them, holding hands because we never had separated after she had taken mine as we crossed the busy street between the building and the parking lot. It confused me that my mother had seemed somewhat odd with Betty. That, unlike you might think she would, she hadn't swooped down as soon as she could have and kissed her cue ball of a face until there was nothing left to it. That she hadn't unveiled an entire Polish vocabulary she secretly might have been studying when nobody was home in preparation for all this, maybe having traded a couple of Sunday dresses for vocabulary lessons with Steffia Krolik down the street. That she didn't sob and sniffle about how now her life was complete with two girls to take care of. I squeezed my mother's hand, just to check her mood, but she didn't do anything back to answer me. She simply kept her steady walking pace, her eyes straight ahead on my father and Betty, her other hand holding on to the small cotton parcel that was the girl's only piece of luggage, if you could even call it that. The size of two shoeboxes stacked one on the other, it was a lumpy bundle more than it was anything like a suitcase, anything with any construction—no zippers or lids or snaps or hinges or locks or wheels—almost what could be considered a pillow of a thing. Betty's mother, I guessed it to have been, had covered the contents with white cotton cloth, then had sewn it secure (though rather messily compared to the fine stitchery I was used to seeing in my own home), and had written my father's name and address on it real big, in the same kind of squiggly penmanship he used. I wondered what was inside it. More sticks? It probably was just more of those ugly clothes she was wearing. I was glad my mother, who had been reluctant to sew anything for the kid until she had an idea of her size, went and had half a closet full of my old intricately matching things repaired and ironed and hanging ready for her to wear the minute we got home, before she actually let Betty out loose in a town where people knew us. People who didn't know us already were staring, but probably mostly because my father's voice had gotten a lot louder, and he was hopping from car to car with the kid jouncing and screaming delightedly as he counted each one of his long steps.

"Isn't the car around here somewhere?" I was getting impatient, but it was mostly because I was hungry. It was nearly two in the afternoon, and we hadn't eaten since the early morning, since my mother had passed me peanut butter and jelly spread on Ritz just after the billboard for the Warner bra factory outlet in Bridgeport.

My mother said, "It's a little farther. We'll be there in a minute," without even looking at me. She probably was in shock, I concluded. Like when people have been in an explosion but are not physically hurt and are just wandering around the disaster scene with big hollow looks on their faces, wondering what has just happened here and suddenly amazed how never before had it occurred to them that, without any warning, in an instant their lives could turn into something they are praying to wake up from. I had seen such people on the TV news, and add a few smudges of ash to her suit and my mother right then could have passed for one of them.

We caught up to them just as my father was placing the girl onto the backseat.

"Car," he was saying, dragging out the *r*. Then he got fancy: "au-to-mo-bile."

He pointed at the seat and said the word. Then he put his hand on the window and said it again. Betty just looked very tired and very happy and very white and didn't say anything back.

"You're going to confuse her, Adam," my mother whispered, giving him a little nudge. "You point to a window and say car, or automobile, and she's going to think that you call a window a car, not a window."

I snickered, thinking how it might be fun to get somebody all messed up like that. My father frowned at me, and I felt bad.

"That's just funny," I explained.

"Well, she doesn't know—she'll think you're laughing at her," he said, and in Polish quickly explained the situation to Betty, who responded only by pointing for her bag, which my mother placed squarely on her lap, the writing facing toward her in case she needed it that way for some reason. The girl reached in through a small slit in a seam and worked out a slice of squished-up rye bread, which she tore into quarters and began handing one to each of us.

"She brought her own food . . . ," my mother said, right to Betty, sounding as astonished as she appeared to be, and she slowly accepted her piece and nudged me to take mine from the girl, which I did, and I looked at the bread rougher and heavier than what I was used to, the crust a lot darker and thicker than Babci's, but still soft, like somebody had made it not too long ago. Something about that hit me, how in the short number of hours that this bread would still be considered fresh, Betty had gone from her home to here, from a horse and wagon on a dirt road to an airplane to the cushy backseat of a brand-new 1972 Chevy Chevelle, the car that, when my father eventually put it into reverse, caused her to take my hand and not let go until we stopped again, about an hour later, not too far into Connecticut, at a Howard Johnson's, for a lunch or supper, or whatever it was at that point in our mixed-up day.

For really the first time since I found out about her coming to join us, it all made me think what if *I* had been the one sent off somewhere so far away, to where I couldn't understand anybody, to where things were so different? How would my parents have broken the news to me, that I probably would never see them again in this life? What would I have thought of their decision? Wouldn't I have fought and screamed that I didn't care that we didn't have Sunday comics and Jell-O and elections? Wouldn't I have cried that I didn't want to leave them? I tried to imagine what Betty might have said to her parents when she had been given the word, when they showed her the airplane ticket my father had wired money over for. But I didn't know her well enough at that point to even venture a guess.

Overall, I had so little experience with small children that I might as well have been given a kitten or a gerbil or something else that was tiny and helpless and nothing like me, not even of my species or even from the same planet. Betty's hand might as well have been the paw of a dog that no one wanted, or of a space alien that had nothing in common with me, and here it was, edging up to the closest warm thing in the backseat, which was me, not knowing what was going to happen next, and not even having the right words to ask the question. I looked down at her stubby thumb half the size of my own and soon found myself feeling powerful and smart— and not just because of my size alone. I thought about all the things I could tell her and show her. I realized that it had been more than just something nice for them to say when grown-ups cautioned me about how important I would be to Betty—

like right at that moment, when I reached over and pushed down the lock on her door, certainly saving her from flying out onto the interstate at fifty miles an hour.

All the way to the restaurant, my father tossed questions back to Betty, looking at her in the rearview mirror more than he was looking at the road, but getting away with that without a complaint from my mother, who obviously did not want to make a first impression as one who was a nag.

"How is your father?"

"Your mother?"

"Your *dziadzius?*"

"Your *babcis?*"

He worked his way through the family, through Betty's many sisters, starting with Aniela, the eldest, who he knew to be good in art, continuing on through Dorota and her foot split last spring by the neighbor's plow, to Kasia, who he had been told prayed incessantly and circled the house on her knees three times daily and often spoke of entering the convent, then to Genia, who could not be pulled from the kitchen she loved to work in so much, down to Olisia, tall and scholarly and ten years old but now considered the baby of the family with Elżbieta gone for good to a place the rest of her family never would be able to imagine.

At the sound of the name Aniela, Betty jumped in her seat like she'd been given an electric jolt, and she quickly reached for her pack of stuff and went rummaging around in it again, as my father continued to inquire about the neighbors: the Pytkas, the Kuligs, the Wojtowiczs, the Zaluckis and the Pulas, and the Witkowskis, the Krzyzeks, the Skuras, the Janoszes and all their various interests and ailments—at least those they were having and suffering from when my father last saw them so long ago, as if Edziu Kuba's sore throat wouldn't have healed in the twenty-one years since. My father said he was curious, and if she didn't mind telling him:

"Do the Dobkas still keep the finest draft horses around?"

"Do the storks still nest in the dead tree next to the church?"

"Do you know of fat Jerzy Wilga, and a chubby kid he used to pal around with, now a man, of course?"

"And how about Pawel Bialowicz? Lived next to the miller's pond? Had two small bumps on the side of his left hand that were really sixth and seventh fingers?"

To each question, Betty would just give a little word for "good" or would shrug and would keep looking out the window, at things that I was sure, from my father's stories of his old home, she had never before seen, even in a dream she might have had when delirious with some illness: Buildings more than one story high. Huge and speeding tractor trailers. Long streets jam-packed with houses and not even the smallest space between them. Signs hanging and screaming messages over the road—one of them a cigar ad that had real smoke puffing from it. Long cars zooming past, containing people of colors other than our own. It was two days before Christmas, and many of the autos were stuffed with brightly wrapped packages piled on the knees of ladies wrapped in fur and wearing big shining earrings. One station wagon had a wreath tied to its back hatch. A taxi driver had woven a string of colored lights around his rear window. A garbage truck passed us, Santa waving from the driver's seat.

After a long time, in her little words and in her little voice, Betty finally answered my father all in a row that the farm was good and that the animals were good and that school was good. Government was good, too, she threw in, wherever that came from, and that made me realize Theresa's prediction had come true: We were going to be living with a Communist.

Betty was still at work, inside the bag. There couldn't have been that many things in there to go through, and finally, finally, she pulled her hand back out, holding a black-and-white photo of me—but not of me. It was of someone who looked exactly like me, who even was wearing my long watermelon head and my square shoulders and my dark braids and my U-shaped smile. She was seated straight and proud and serene on the back of a beautiful white horse that wore no saddle or bridle, only a rope around its neck, held by an unseen hand, if anybody was holding it there at all. The girl wore an old-looking dress with an apron over it and was barefoot. Yet, looking straight ahead at what had to be the fantastic things that lay ahead of her, she looked as elegant as any dressed-up person or movie star I'd ever seen. And the thing was, this was me, in another place, another world even, and, somehow, I had come out of Betty's bundle of stuff. I stared at the picture for so long you'd think I would have bored a hole in it.

"Aniela," Betty eventually whispered, leaning into me and smiling, and she pointed to the girl like she was some kind of celebrity that needed only the one name for identification. "Aniela."

Then she pointed to me and snuggled even closer, looking as at home and as content as if she'd known me for all her days.

"Food. Here," my father said, deeply and slowly, skipping any verbs and sounding like he was Tonto. He pointed ahead to the aqua-and-orange castle of a building as we finally turned off the highway and pulled to a stop in a space near a row of busy telephone booths.

Betty's eyes got wider than they'd been, and she squeezed my hand tighter than she had when that pickup had swerved in front of us and my father had blasted on the horn for a good long time instead of, I knew, muttering his usual Polish swear words, because now here was someone who knew exactly what he was saying. Obviously not aware she could get out the same door she'd come in through, Betty slid over the seat and followed me as I got out, and now she was holding on to a handful of my coat. I was getting crabby, my stomach making noises that could have been heard in Vermont. But I didn't complain. I only allowed her to hang on, and that photograph of us in the parking lot—of me holding my tongue and Betty holding my coat—is the one my father shot right there and got back from the drugstore weeks later and printed "My Two Girls" in pen on the top part of the white border and taped it to the frame of the dresser mirror on his side of the bedroom.

Up the Howard Johnson's walk, it was my mother and me following them once again, but now she was talking with some brightness in her voice and was praising me for my care of Betty in the backseat and was informing me that we all, each one of us, would have "many interesting days ahead," and that we all would have to be patient with what she called "this new situation."

"It'll be a big adjustment, but it's going to be so nice," she told me and, it seemed, herself. "A big family!"

A big family? I thought of the Iwanickis, who stuffed nine screaming kids, a couple of parents, a cockatiel, and a thousand-year-old uncle into their two bedrooms and the room most people use only for receiving relatives on Sunday afternoons. Had she forgotten about them? Now that was what you could rightly call a big family. When you came right down to it, ours—even with Babci thrown in—still was nothing but a handful of people who could all fit into a bathroom to live, if they had to.

"Four, please," my father answered very loudly when the waitress greeted us and asked him how many were in our party. And then he turned to my mother and me, looking very pleased.

"Four, Helen! We have to ask for four now!" He had picked Betty up, and he bent her thumb to have her fingers illustrate the number. "Look—she knows how to count already!"

Both of us nodded—it sure appeared that she did. Betty stared at her hand and seemed puzzled, then worked to free it. We all followed the waitress, whose nametag read Mary Ann and who wore a shiny orange-and-white polyester uniform and whose left calf bore a big blue vein shaped like a peace sign.

Betty cleaned her Old King Cole clam strip special clear down to the painting of him on the bottom of the sectioned plate, only to leave portions of it at a stop sign in Trumbull, in a Woolworth's parking lot in Meriden, behind the seesaw at a playground in Windsor Locks, in a trash can on the shore of the lake across from the Basketball Hall of Fame, and in a storm drain on the bridge at the bottom of our street.

After the first time, my mother sat between us in the back and yelled to my father to pull over each time Betty began to percolate. I felt sorry for the kid as the stops added up. I even put my hand on her hot little back at one point. But as time went on I couldn't help but curl up farther and farther into my corner, cracking the window for air, and finally I asked if I could crawl over into the front seat. The last time, we were forced to stop within yards of our home, and I slid nearly onto the floor of the car, as the head of the girl who from now on would be known as my sister hung from the car, visible for the first time in our town, gagging for all the world that I knew to see.

"This . . . home," my father said loudly as he tipped the directional signal and finally took the right into our driveway.

Betty, of course, didn't know what he said, so she just sat and stared into the back of the front seat, crushing to her mouth a wad of my mother's once-beautiful white silk scarf. My father shut off the car at the side door of the house, got out and stretched, then opened Betty's door and helped her onto the driveway. She reached toward the car floor for her parcel, then, wide-eyed, dragged out the word *"dom?"* for home, and my father said back, softly, *"tak,"* for yes. So she picked up her parcel bag and wobbled to the end of the driveway and stood in front of the garage door, her back to us.

None of us did anything but look at Betty, who appeared waiting to be parked somewhere. Finally my father jogged over and picked her up saying, no, no—this—this is home. He walked her up to the correct building and patted the beige asbestos shingle next to the door handle and took her hand to do the same.

Home, he repeated. Home. Home. Home. Home. And all of a sudden, it was so long ago and there was still-living Jasiu next to the shaking Adam, taking his hand and putting it up to the wall, to something solid, to the place where he had landed, where he would belong from now on. And the boy, and now the girl, together pronounced the word for it.

Chapter

4

*B*etty ate like somebody was going to be handing out prizes at the end of the meal.

After the first few days, I began to think that was the biggest reason she got sent here—she must have been too expensive for them to keep. Carolyn regularly brought over the bananas and the pink grapefruits the kid quickly became hooked on. Theresa came by, the first day with a bottle of the farm's whipping cream, and after that empty-handed, just to stare, and to whisper to me that people who were poor and skinny often had tapeworms. She went into great detail about how she once read that such things could be lured up from the stomach by setting a piece of raw hamburger on the tongue and several times tried to talk me into getting Betty to do that.

Babci was exhausted most of the time, getting up a whole hour and a half earlier than usual just to bake and fry and knead and mix and test with toothpicks the things she felt would make the girl feel at home: plates of plump and greasy *gołąbki*, heaps of crispy fried veal loaf, pigs feet in aspic, black bread soup, lot of beets, fresh mushrooms in sour cream, bowls of shimmering onion-covered *pierogi*, platters of *kielbasi* and *kiszki*, ham pudding, pot after pot of *kapusta* rich with shreds of pork, and, for dessert, airy mountains of powdered sugar-sprinkled *chrust* and almond *mazureks* and platters of plum cake.

Everything, and I mean everything, that was set before the girl disappeared. *"Dobry,"* she would proclaim happily with nearly every spoon- or forkful. Good.

We ordinarily had a couple of those kinds of dishes at each meal, but once Betty arrived, Babci stopped serving all the other great American things she had over the years come to add to her repertoire. Gone were the gooey lasagnas with the long strips of green and red peppers, the shepherd's pies and their tanned mashed-potato roofs, the circular hand-cut french fries mounded next to a lake of ketchup, the tiny daisy hams that went so well with buttered baby peas, the hamburger specials with thick slices of tomato, the spicy breaded frozen fish sticks stacked on the serving platter like cordwood, and, all for me, the occasional family-size can of Chef Boyardee Beefaroni. With the coming of Betty, our table overnight turned into something out of a travel brochure, all covered with vats and trays and casseroles containing strange stuff I'd never seen or even smelled before, and most coming complete with an old-country legend or some trick explained by Babci as she proudly served: Get the slice of cake containing the walnut, and you'll get a wish come true, or get the corncob missing part of a row of kernels, and you will end up with a spouse who is younger than you, or, even if you don't like it, take a bit of the charred and crusty end of the meat, so your hair will curl and the forces of the devil will bounce off. That sort of thing.

Whether it was done to make Betty feel more like she was at home or to make us feel like we were more like Betty was not made clear, but whatever the reason, this new menu got a grand start: The Christmas Eve *Wigilia* supper—loaded with dishes and rituals even on the holidays when you weren't taking in somebody right from Poland—was Betty's first real meal with us, served not even twenty-four hours after she walked in our house for the first time, took a seat at the kitchen table, stared fearfully at Babci wailing about if only Jasiu could see this precious baby, and conked out instantly, like somebody had unplugged her.

The first rule of Christmas Eve Day was that we were not supposed to sleep late—doing so would set a lazy tone for the coming year. That one was not hard for me, as I don't think I had closed my eyes for more than an hour all night. I sat back against the wall the whole time and watched Betty from my half of the twin bed set my parents had allowed me to pick out of the Sears catalog in concession for having to share my room. It was in the elegant French Provincial style I had admired in Haley Mills's city home in *The Parent Trap* and had the same glitzy gold paint accenting every squiggle and curve, drawer pull and leg. For some price that I only remember as ending with 99 cents, we each also got a matching white-and-gold nightstand with three drawers, two little white vase-shaped lamps for the tops, and were to share a long dresser that had a mirror and a little indentation for the pillow-topped white-and-gold stool you could sit on when you were in the mood to look at your reflection and fuss with yourself.

Earlier, I had taken a seat there and had watched my father watch my mother secure the covers one last time against dead-to-the-world Betty. My mother looked very tired. My father appeared at the same time both exhausted and ready to run around the neighborhood with happiness. I went over to get the view he looked to be greatly enjoying and saw only a circle of the center of Betty's face, the rest of her being nearly swallowed up by the bed linens over which Babci had spread a newly crocheted afghan embroidered to depict two little girls sheltered under a science fiction-sized red mushroom as they peered out at the raindrops. It was around two in the morning when, in the glow of the Porky Pig nightlight purchased by my father to ease the nighttime fears of a kid who my mother told me Stryj Czesław wrote was used to having real hogs tromping through her bedroom at all hours, I noticed one of the girls had a *B* stitched to the front of her pink pinafore, and that the other, identical but taller and with her arm around the shoulder of the younger one, wore a *D* on hers.

I can't recall many other realizations coming to me that night except that those two girls were supposed to be us, and that I was now officially somebody's sister, the one who was supposed to be taller and protective against the rain, and against the wolfish dog that barks from the Miareckis' porch, and against the dark that comes up so suddenly in late fall, and against the one deepest pothole in Crystal Lake that drops off without warning and that nobody ever has come up with a rope long enough to lower to its bottom, and against the kids who I knew were going to laugh and laugh at her as we all had laughed and laughed again and again at the scrawny Polish boy who lived with Nancy Zyla's family that one summer, making fun of him for a solid three months all just because he held his trousers up with both a belt and suspenders. I was the one with a *D* on her chest, just as Superman, who always comes through, has his *S*. I sat taller against the wall, the picture of Aniela that I'd stolen in the car placed next to me, and we both opened our eyes wider to watch for a reason to rescue Betty.

She made it through the night without my having to do anything at all for her, and, despite whatever Polish hour her own body clock was set at, Betty woke just before the American daylight came in the window.

There would be no eating until the first star came out, even though all those shining and glazed and raisin-dotted *babki* and strucels were made and ready, having been baked long before anyone else arose and went banging around and slamming doors or walking heavily or dropping something and making the dough fall. Overnight, magical foods had materialized everywhere—on the kitchen counters, on top of the refrigerator, replacing the toaster on the tea cart, even hidden in the sheaves of long yard grass that decorated the corners of the dining room to remind us of the harvest grains we would have been proud to have grown were we farmers back in Poland. The bundles would hang there until the end of the night's meal, when they would be untied and the candy pieces and little cakes inside would cascade over us in this land where you have so much extra to eat that you can use it for decorations.

Because she was the real thing, from the country in which all this stuff had been made up a long time ago, Betty knew better than I the rule about no breakfast or lunch that Christmas Eve Day—which actually was a good idea when you consider how her first American meal had gone over. So she didn't accept so much as a crumb of anything, even though Babci was willing to bend the custom due to Betty's ordeal the day before. Though I was starving, as I normally was several times a day, I didn't even ask if I, too, could be an exception. If this little Betty could stand it, so could I.

The nuns gave us the day off, and Babci and my mother wanted us girls out of the kitchen as much as possible, so I volunteered to make it my work to show Betty what our house was all about.

"What a good sister," Babci praised me, pinching my cheeks with her floured fingers.

"Nobody could have a better one," my mother told her, winking at me, and I proudly reached for Betty's hand.

Every corner and piece of furniture and rug and shelf I began to touch and name, as my father had done a little too much when Betty's joining us first had been decided on. With the goal of teaching us more of her language, he began to use only his Polish on me and my mother, right up to the windy Sunday when the grill, set too close to the back porch, started the stairs blazing, and my father kept yelling, "Fire! Get out of the house!"—but he did so in Polish, and neither of us understood him, and we stopped reading the funnies in the living room only when we heard a siren getting closer and noticed Babci through the window, jumping up and down in the street, waving the fire truck into our driveway.

Betty was a better student, paying lots more attention and trailing me attentively and without an extra sound except to repeat with her little accent what I was saying.

"Tebble," she would echo.

"Cherr."

"Rrrug."

"Telefeeshin."

We stopped at the telefeeshin for a long time, as I tried to explain what it was, then just decided to show her, standing with my back to the set and pulling the "on" knob that I was blocking from her, hoping to make her first sight of a TV program that much more magical, coming out of nowhere as it would be. And suddenly, blown from the white dot in the center of the green screen, there was Captain Kangaroo, sitting on his window seat, using round-edged scissors to cut a Christmas star from a piece of construction paper I imagined was yellow, reminding us to ask the help of an adult—he pronounced the word *ad*-ult—if we were too little to handle the job.

I waited for Betty's reaction to this man speaking to her from inside a box, his shears making rich chewing sounds as they worked their way through the thick paper. But she only stood there, hands behind her back, wearing the red-and-green checkered overalls I thought I could remember splashing eggnog on at Elaine Bigda's Christmas party way back when, and she looked at me and repeated "telefeeshin," plainly and without emotion, like it was only "spoon" or "door" or "water."

We climbed the stairs. Held the railing. Looked at my mother's counted cross-stitch sampler, which reminded us in gold thread that there but for the grace of God go I. We saw my parents' beds, and, again, our own, already made neat by Babci—something we should not expect to happen every day, we earlier had been warned. We looked in the closets and in the drawers, and I pointed to all the things that make up your daily outfit, though you might not realize their number until you actually stand there and say them separately: Underwear. Shirt. Vest. Blouse. Jumper. Pants. Shirt. Necktie. Blazer. Stocking. Gloves. Cap. Betty stood transfixed, like she didn't know you might need that many things in order simply to leave the house.

"Pents," she said. "Chairt." "Blesser." "Kep."

"Good," I told her, and I even patted her head. Touching her curls, washed this morning by my mother, was like touching air. I reached again, to make sure they were real, and Betty laughed, pointing to my own hair. I dangled a braid in her face.

"Hair," I said.

"Herr," she repeated, and we both laughed.

In my nightstand drawer, I showed her the baby food jar of pink sand that Frania Pytka from up the street had brought me from her college trip to Bermuda. Over my bed, I pointed to the frame holding the autograph of Marion Lush and each of his White Eagles. In the cigar box under my bed, I found her my two of the long hairs Joey Roman had pulled for each of us girls from the back of the moose found dead in the woods behind the school. I brought out the tiny picture of me and my father in a photo booth at Hampton Beach, taken back when I was four, the age at which I still believed him and still shrieked and cried when he was going somewhere and, just to get me going, he'd put his hat on and walk to the front door saying "Well I'm off to Africa!" I pointed to the little girl in the photograph, then I pointed to myself. Betty made the connection, her eyes widening.

I showed her my shelf of books, my alarm clock, my clear plastic coin purse, and, after emptying it out onto the bedspread, each of the different shapes of the money we here in America used. Then I showed her the calendar I had made on the day my parents and I visited the Double D, when I'd taken a piece of poster board and a ruler and had drawn a box for each day until the girl was to arrive. On the morning I showed it to her, each and every one of the four months of boxes was filled with a red X. It was finally full, I told Betty, but she had no way to know how amazing that was, never having seen how empty it had looked way back in September, when it seemed that many days would take forever to pass. So I slid it back under my bed, and I pointed out the window to the polka park, now still and sleeping under thick snow, only a line of dog tracks headed under the shelter. To Betty, it probably just looked like a house without walls. So that's when I took out my accordion from the closet, brought it out of its case, snapped it open, and pointed from it to the park, back and forth.

"That's what goes on there," I said, but she didn't pay attention to my gestures. She was just staring into the case, looking at it with the same look that I'd seen one night so long ago—the same expression my father had worn at Mrs. Dranka's open house, when he had stared at the same instrument, and I wanted what he wanted. She turned her head and looked at me, unbelieving, I interpreted, that such a thing could be mine. So I said proudly, and you might even call it showing off, but what did she know at that point, "Yes, it is mine, and what do you think of that?"

But Betty had no reply. So I shut the case with her still looking into it, and I slid it aside, and I led her downstairs and put on her boots and my little old blue coat with the sailor collar, and outside I showed her: Tree. And sidewalk. And sky. Snow. Driveway. Bird. Window. Johnny Frydryk. Shovel. Cold. And more cold. A train chugged past, and the engineer so high up in his little window sounded his horn when he saw us standing in the yard, and the sudden noise and the closeness of the whole thing sent Betty crashing into my side, full of fright.

"Train," I said to the girl, who shook as she pulled me back to the house.

My father came home just before dark, with his Christmas bonus: an extra day's pay and ten pounds of headcheese. He handed the envelope of money to my mother, and the stinking loaf to my grandmother.

"The first star is almost out," he called, signaling it was time to begin our feast.

I have two strong memories of that night. The first is how we ate and we ate and we ate: beginning with the soups—beet *barszcz* with tiny mushroom-filled dumplings, and a lighter one of creamed fish, then an almond soup of milk, honey, raisins, and rice. Then pickled herring. And the boiled potatoes with parsley. The green beans, and the cauliflower baked with breadcrumbs. After that, *pierogi* with their hidden fillings of sauerkraut, sautéed mushrooms, onions, sweet cabbage, prunes and cherries. Then the desserts of *blinczyki* cakes fried in oil, *pasteciki* tarts baked around fillings, ginger cakes, fruit compotes of apples, pears, peaches, plums, and the poppy-seed coffee cake. And, of course the *krupnik*—the holiday fire-vodka that came to life after months of being hidden in the dark in a huge jar behind the bundle of old *McCall's* in my parents' closet.

Prior to that Christmas I had only sniffed it, but that night my father announced he had had his first taste of *krupnik* at age fourteen, given by Jasiu, right here, in this house, at this table, and so would I. Neither my mother nor Babci protested out loud (though they put on serious looks for the first time that day, and Babci's eyes blinked suddenly at the sound of her lost husband's name on such a happy night), so my father took a fourth glass from the sideboard and poured me my share, and first they, then I, toasted: *"Nazdrowie!" "Sto lat!" "Wesołych Świąt!"* And it went down, heating me inch by inch, and I wondered who would want to make a habit of such a drink. But my father gave me another half a glass, and soon I got the idea. Then he brought down my accordion, and we all began singing: *"Niepojęte Dary,"* which told of the mysterious first-Christmas gifts, and *"Cieszmy Się,"* which invited everyone to rejoice, and we did, with Babci and Betty making up a little dance, then another, and my mother and father kissing, and, as if on cue, snow beginning to fall past the orange bulbs in the electric candles lighting our windows.

My father at one point started his Victrola and gently put down the needle on his 78 of *"Wśród Nocnej Ciszy"* by the chilling baritone Tadeusz Wronski, went over to the doorway to the living room, and looked at me sitting on the floor and untangling the lights we would loop around the tree, next to Betty, her bird mouth open, fallen asleep on the easy chair, and he stood there and broke into tears, his joy, he told us later after we all screamed what's the matter and woke and frightened the girl, being so great at that moment.

My father wept like I have yet to see anyone else do in the same manner, without his hands to his face, without his head down, and without covering his eyes. He cried unhidden, unashamed of how he might look or sound, leaning against the doorsill, his hands in his back pockets, as plain and as straightforward as he might have been if he were laughing instead. I wanted to look away, but I was unable to. Knowing him as I had day after day for my whole life, I watched him, and I thought back and tried to find a time when I was aware that maybe he had been missing something or had felt deprived in any way. That he had been without something he really needed or that he had to have something extra. I could not come up with anything, but obviously there had to have been something lacking, and most certainly lots of it. Because when he was able to again speak, my father told us with words spaced far apart and placed gently into the air like they were made of smoke:

"This is the happiest I have ever been in my life."

The second memory I kept from that Christmas Eve is of him and his joy, right there, and of the sudden sickening feeling, at that same moment, that I had failed him somewhere. Why hadn't he been that happy before this?

We had one whole week of my father on vacation and around with us for every single hour and so many leftovers and squishing everybody onto the couch to read stories and singing along to my music every night and playing the special Christmas albums and getting to stay up for Guy Lombardo's New Year's Eve special from the Waldorf-Astoria. One of my mother's magazines should have come to the house and photographed us with our decorations and our games and with our food and our jokes and our laughter, and we honestly could have told them we are not models hired to do this. This is really how we live.

And in what seemed like the time it takes to flip one of those magazine pages, it was over. I returned to school to finish up eighth grade, and Betty began grade one. On her first day, my mother delivered the girl to Sister Superior's office, and it wasn't ten minutes later that the school's eight other nuns were assembled there, summoned to meet the new student, but mostly to learn from Sister how they now would have first-class assistance with pronouncing the Polish in which the entire school sang and prayed and took one language class per week.

The nuns went crazy, clapping and praising God. They all had come from Polish families, back when they had families like the kind regular people do, but none of the sisters actually had been born in Poland.

"I went to Italy once," Sister Agnieszka said excitedly. "They brought me a pizza, and I asked 'What is this?'—it had an egg on it, if you can believe that! What we know as pizza here is nothing like the pizza there. I'm certain our Polish is laughable compared to what is spoken in Poland!"

She looked at my mother and lowered her voice. "There are many foreign language competitions throughout the year, and the only thing Sts. Peter and Paul's students return with are perfect attendance awards. Think of the things this girl can teach us! The inflections! The nuances of speech!"

Betty, unaware of her value, just smiled and fingered her doll leg, which she'd hidden in the pocket of her new uniform. My mother sat and took this in, and she should have realized something was wrong right then and there. Maybe she did, but she had not been raised to question nuns, so all she said was: "But, Sister, she'll learn English, right? As soon as she can? My family would very much appreciate it."

"Oh, she will," Sister Superior assured with a wave of her hand. "We will use little Betty as the basis for all sorts of new language programs. She will be the center of it. You and your family will be amazed!"

It turned out we were, but not in the manner you'd assume. The nuns didn't push Betty to learn even her alphabet. They just moved her between all eight classrooms all day like a traveling performer, making her recite her Polish poems, sing her Polish songs, go over her Polish days of the week and her Polish months of the year, her Polish kitchen utensils and her Polish geographical terms and her Polish body parts— whatever words she had to offer.

The nuns, of course, were beside themselves with enthusiasm, and the students loved Betty's visits, for she provided an hour out of the day just to stare into space, or doodle, or pass notes, with nothing required of them but to appear as if they were listening. The second week Betty was there, in anticipation of St. Valentine's Day, we even had an all-school assembly at which the kid was given a megaphone and was brought up on the stage, and we had to repeat after her the words to a love poem. And she was happy to do it. She had no idea what school was, so whatever was asked of her she did not see as unusual.

I should have kept my mouth shut, but I didn't like how Mark Kapinos and Tookie Borowiec made fun of Betty that one day, repeating the poem about the thorny red rose back to her in a perfect accent—but in her same teeny little pitch—until Sister Lugoria sneaked up on them with the croquet mallet she always kept under her desk. So I complained to my parents that after a month Betty wasn't doing anything in school that she hadn't known how to do before they signed her up. I didn't expect them to move Betty to another school, and of course they never would have—in my family you sooner would have grown a horn from your head than disconnect from anything having to do with the parish. The only option, my mother pointed out, was to hire a tutor, or to just continue with more of what my father and Babci already were doing: sitting with her as much as they could and teaching her English.

Because Dr. Anton had discovered that Betty's arches had fallen ages ago, and my father ended up having to take half a day off from work to drive to East Springfield and have the kid fitted for a pair of clunky orthopedic shoes that cost a whopping $63, paying somebody money to teach her was out of the question. So, "No more Polish. Everybody all English," was what my father knocked into the dining room table with the end of his butter knife at dinner that night.

"After you finish," he said to Betty, who was scooping a third helping of pickled herring onto her plate, "we study."

I was slicing off another disc of jellied cranberry sauce, to go with the turkey Babci had roasted with a huge onion stuck where its neck used to be and with its tail end facing east, all so that we would be free from laryngitis for the rest of the winter, when I realized what had been said. It might not have sounded like anything to you, and it might even make you laugh that I would make a big deal of it, but to me it was something. I could not remember a time my father had not been there while I practiced after supper. So I was not surprised by the great jump my heart made when I thought it would go by unmentioned. But, thankfully, that was not what happened. My father quickly turned and said to me apologetically, "Okay? I have to help the little one. Okay?"

"Sure," I answered, relieved he at least thought to say something.

"I'll listen," my mother offered, and she winked at me sweetly.

"But . . . what about Mrs. Conway?" This came from Babci.

"Oh—I forgot . . ." My mother trailed off, and she gave me one of those smiles where you look like you're mostly in pain.

I'd learned about this woman through the vent a week or so ago. Because a rich guy named Mr. Conway from Springfield had decided to run for state representative, his wife, a Mrs. Conway, had called to ask my mother if she made campaign wardrobes.

"I thought she meant banners, flags or buntings, or a cover for a podium—plain, basic things, just strips of cloths, really, and I was thinking about what a snap that would be—but she means an entire . . . custom . . . made . . . wardrobe," my mother said breathlessly when she returned from the phone call that had told her all that and she grabbed the stack of envelopes from my father's hands to get his attention. He had been going over the bills and had been chewing a pencil and he didn't look too happy, about the numbers he was looking at, or about being interrupted.

"She said Joan Kennedy has a designer in Boston, so she wants something like that—a designer from her husband's district. These could end up on the front page. Or even on television!"

My father smiled, but you would want more of a reaction after such news. And my mother had just the thing to get it: "She asked me if $250 would be enough for eight pieces— with her providing the fabric."

Now my father looked genuinely pleased. And he pulled my mother to him and he held onto her for a long time and he said things into her ear that I could only hear parts of. About money, "since the little one." And how he had been worried about paying for everything, "since the little one." But how he had been praying extra hard, "since the little one," and how it sounded like God had answered by having Mrs. Conway compliment the president of the hospital auxiliary on the beautiful eggplant chemise she wore to the Catholic Charities banquet and by having the president respond that, as often as she's able, she has a special thing designed by Helen.

"Just 'Helen'?" Mrs. Conway had asked.

"That's her business card, just 'Helen,' " the president had answered.

It was too good to be true—a designer with only one name—just like Joan Kennedy's Fiandaca. Mrs. Conway had begged the lady for our telephone number.

And now Mrs. Conway would be coming over to talk about how she did not want her generous bustline accentuated, and how all her life she felt she looked peaked in any shade of red, and I would be playing to no one.

"I'm sorry—but we can't pass this up," my mother said, after excitedly giving me a brief explanation of the agreement I already knew all about.

"Don't worry about it," I said simply, and I pretty much meant it. My playing for my father was a tradition, but a day's interruption wasn't going to mean the end of it—as far as I thought.

That first night, my mother and I were the only ones cleaning up from supper, as Babci, my father and Betty went into the living room to begin their "class" immediately after they got up from the table.

"What if Mr. Conway went on to become president of the country some day?" I asked my mother as I reached for another handful of silverware to dry. "We might be invited to the inauguration. You would have to make us all something new, in case we were to be photographed!"

She laughed. "You're jumping the gun a little. But I'm sure Mr. Conway will be happy to hear you have such faith in him."

"You never know," I told her, and she agreed that you never do.

"This could be the start of all sorts of things," she said. "But for now, this roasting pan is my first concern."

That was when the doorbell rang, and that was when my mother squeaked, "Oh, no! She's early!" and she yanked off her apron and checked her hair in the blackness of the kitchen window.

I peeked through the door to the dining room to get a look at Mrs. Conway, and she was pretty much what you might expect of a big shot: a snooty woman with a white-blond French twist who said, "How . . . are . . . you?" very loudly and very slowly to Babci and to my father, as if they couldn't understand English. To Betty, who was the one who had no idea what she was saying, Mrs. Conway went on and on, about how delightful this child is and what do you like to do, honey, as she touched the kid's cheek and mussed her hair, then she greeted my mother by her first name and asked her where her—and she used this exact word—"studio" was.

The two of them went up to my parents' bedroom, and I dragged a chair from the table to the center of the kitchen, unfolded my stand under the cross, went upstairs and got the accordion, then, with my father loudly assuring me as I passed through the living room that he would be listening, I went into the kitchen and turned to my lesson for the week and (this is truly how these things sometimes happen) played with few noticeable errors my latest assignment: a sad, dragging waltz titled "How Things Have Changed, My Dear."

The notes spilled out of me and across the table and right over to the spot where my father should have been lighting his second smoke and finishing the Apostle's Creed. They made it through that empty space and hit the wall and bounced across the room and through the crack in the kitchen door and across the dining room and off the waxed fruit centerpiece that I enjoyed sticking my fingernails into, and then traveled into the living room and over Babci's closed eyes and past the alphabet book on Betty's lap, and they found my father's ears, but all he was able to hear was the girl saying "Ah" over and over when she was supposed to be saying "A."

The next night, Mrs. Conway was returning to show my mother her many different pairs of footwear purchased especially for the campaign, and my father asked me quietly in private in the pantry if I wouldn't mind his missing another practice.

"Betty," he told me enthusiastically, "can recite up to C on her own!" And he didn't want to stop now. Plus, he confided that Babci wasn't of much help because she dozed off for most of the time, being so tired from all the extra work these past two months, you know, because of the little one, yet even though she was tired, Babci said she wanted to be there for Betty as she had been there for my father way back when he was trying to figure out what kind of language wouldn't need lines through its Ls and little hooks under its Es.

"You understand I must do this, don't you?" he asked me softly. I told him, yes, I understood.

The following night, my mother didn't come home until 9 P.M. after being in Springfield, walking through the fabric stores with Mrs. Conway all day. And they had another trip planned the next day for the same reason, but to somewhere near Framingham. Betty was up to E, though she often forgot C, and when she didn't, she pronounced it as Z instead.

It took less than one week for the job of cleaning up after supper to become mine alone. My mother was either with Mrs. Conway, was coming home from being with Mrs. Conway, Mrs. Conway was at our house, or my mother was up in her room sketching something for Mrs. Conway. Early on, it had been fun just to say the words *Mrs. Conway*, a name that sounded like something you might hear on a soap opera. We knew few people with what most other people might consider to be regular names, ones many families in this country have, ones that didn't look like someone put their hands in the wrong position on the typewriter. Those without a "ski" or a "icz," or Ls pronounced like Ws and Ws pronounced like Vs, Js like Ys and other Js like Is. Entire last names with just a single vowel to make them real words, an I or an A or a Y dropped in a jumble after someone threw the letters into the air. Brzoska. Dyrkacz. Mysliwy. Names that were like a sudden and abrupt noise: Sul. Haj. Wahl, Glod, Pyz. Names for which there were never enough space on employment forms, sweepstakes entries, rebate coupons. Matuszewszka. Zezulinska. Dziedzinski. Skorobohata. Andrzejewicz. And, sometimes, Milewski.

Conway was so different, exotic to me in its phoneticness, its two-syllable simplicity. Our state even had a town with that name, something I never could imagine being the case with my family. So I liked to drop it, especially around Theresa and Carolyn.

"I saw Mrs. Conway's husband's name on a bumper sticker," I'd say proudly.

Or, "Did you know people like Mrs. Conway keep all their shoes in clear plastic boxes?"

And, "According to my mother, Mrs. Conway's car has a button that makes the seat slide forward or back automatically, and a mirror in the sun visor that lights up at night in case you need to fix your makeup!"

The girls didn't react one way or the other to all this, and I eventually gave up even mentioning her. But that was mostly because I pretty quickly came to really dislike the woman, though we'd never met face-to-face. I knew only what I saw of her through the door crack, and how she treated the others, and how her perfume hurt something so high up in your nose you didn't even know anything could reach that far. And I knew she was taking over my mother, and my mother had yet to even get anywhere near her sewing machine.

In the living room, Betty had progressed up to G. And my father was apologizing to me every time I saw him, which was in the bit of time between when he came home and when we finished eating. I was learning three new songs, I told him, and he rubbed his hands together enthusiastically and said he couldn't wait to listen to them in person.

But that would have to wait, as would everything else, including the old ladies' snow and the peeling paint on the root cellar door and finally getting the huge Christmas star down from the roof of the garage. My father told us, after we'd finished an apple pie and my mother got the slice that contained the cranberry reminding her that even in something so sweet there can be something sour to have to take in, that he could not help but accept the extra job that was being advertised at the plant—of cleaning Blue Ribbon's famous smokers on weekends.

"I of course will still be able to make church—and the cemetery, of course," he told us over chicken soup one night, as Babci blessed herself and coldly muttered something in Polish about keeping the Lord's Day holy. "But after the cemetery, I will have to get going. I will try to return as soon as I am able."

My mother fiddled with her napkin.

"Everyone must make sacrifices in life," she said, more to the table than to any one of us in the room. "Look at Jesus."

Though I wouldn't have put this in the same category with being crucified, it was, I had to admit, something that hurt. What would happen to our winter Sundays of reading the papers and listening to the Bruins on the radio, our summer ones of eating our big meal on the porch, then going over to the park. What would happen to just being together? I'd considered all that already, because, I have to admit, the job was not a great and total surprise to me. It was just another thing I had heard something about, another thing whispered, another thing that I could collect only bits of, but another thing that ended with "since the little one."

I looked over at Betty, who was loudly sipping the last of her soup, oblivious to what she was causing. She finished the bowl and waited to be asked by Babci if she wanted more—a word the girl had fast caught on to—before nodding her head eagerly as if it were on a spring.

Theresa phoned the night that we all learned my father would be working each and every single day of the week. She had been home in bed with a cold for two days already and was in a bad mood and snapped, "Well, you'll still have one parent around, right?"

"Yes," I answered, defeated, but (though I did not bother to point this out to Theresa, who I think enjoyed blowing her nose into the phone longer than was really necessary) that was not entirely true: Mrs. Conway had my remaining one. And yes, Babci was still there, but these days only in the kitchen, then in the living room to snooze through Betty's English class, then in bed, her thick *pierzyna* and its millions of feathers flattening her to her mattress as she dreamed of ways to present some other kind of old-country legend about the color of beets.

So that was my winter, right there. And I have to say it was the first sad and lonely time I had ever known. And that's pretty funny when you think how we all never had been busier or had so many people in the house day in and day out.

Things just kept on this way, just kept getting crazier and crazier until our whole family became like that big metal carousel of mine that Babci had hauled down from the attic to amuse Betty, who was, I thought, a little old for such a thing. Even if she was, she seemed thrilled to sit with it and pump the red plastic clown hat on top until the whole thing whirled so fast it took off on its own across the kitchen tiles, and the individual paintings of all the circus creatures just blurred into one crazy band of color. But you knew they were still in there somewhere, the lion in its cage and the horse in its fancy traces and the clown on his tiny bicycle and the mother at her appointment and the babci at her stove and the little one in the living room with the father and his book when he wasn't working overtime at the plant, and the girl and her accordion and the dishes alone in the kitchen spinning in there, somehow, God juggling us all.

It wasn't just the inside of our house that was changing— things seemed to be whirling off everywhere I went. One day my girlfriend Karen Cieplak was her usual pious self, neatly printing the names of Jesus, Mary, and Joseph at the top of each of her test papers, drawing a small fat cross between each word, and spending all her recesses counting and elaborately logging the coins she collected for the missions each morning after class prayers—and the next day she was sneaking a copy of *The Godfather* off the bookmobile and marking dirty passages with snips of the red yarn with which she every day tied her single auburn braid.

She whispered only to us girls that there was something in her desk we ought to see, and we never learned exactly how this happened, but Father Kulpa found out somehow, and the next thing you know, Karen's mother was screaming and running up the school's front sidewalk in her high heels, and the boys were being herded off to the empty cafeteria to meet with Brother Mike, and Sister Superior was up at her podium telling us she would treat us girls like the adults we apparently were becoming, and she turned her back and asked those who did not look in Karen's desk that day to please leave the room as this does not pertain to them.

When she swung around to face the guilty, she was alone.

Beginning about two minutes after she opened the door to the hall and asked the group of us how dumb did we think she was, then yanked the earlobes of Vera Totowski, who dared to murmur an answer to that, Sister Superior's speech was as difficult to comprehend as the things we had read in the book—though at least with Sister we didn't have to look up any of the words. She spoke in terms we were familiar with:

"You could have been born a stick or a box," she said, stopping with a sniff and looking around the room, as whatever she had just said tried to sink its way into our brains.

"You could have been born a potato chip bag or a concrete mixer," she continued tersely, biting off every word. "But instead, you were born humans. Girl humans. And girl humans are different than boy humans. Obviously, with all that has been going on, the time has come for somebody to say that to you."

After that, she looked at the door, as if she were hoping somebody would come through it right then and there and save her from having to say another word, then all of a sudden she clapped her hands twice and instructed us to take out our English workbooks and turn to page 104.

I don't know what Brother Mike was discussing with the boys, whether it had any connection to all of what had been going on in the classroom, and whether it was any more or less cryptic that what we had been told, but Bobby Smola telephoned my house two days later and asked me out. Okay, it wasn't really out, like to a movie, but it was out of doors. To the river, specifically. There were what he called "neat ice things" formed around the rocks.

"Wouldn't you want to see them?" he asked, with the kind of desperation you would expect only from somebody who was getting paid for the number of people he could attract down there.

"I don't know," I said. And I didn't. I had seen ice things before, and plenty of neat ones, but never with Bobby—as if that would make them look any different. I'd never been anywhere with Bobby except for sitting in a classroom with him and thirty-one other kids every school day for eight years. He was a boy, after all, something that until recently I had no interest in. I only knew he had three sisters—one so old she already was in college, and two a little younger than he was, and that one of the younger ones wore a hearing aid—and I knew he lived in an old white house with Jed Clampett pillars out front, and I knew he was good in science and the clarinet, and, only since lately, I knew he had the power to drill this zinging thing right through my heart whenever I was anywhere near him.

Actually, I recently had begun mentioning Bobby Smola to my parents, dropping him into conversations, just to test the waters of what they might think of my talking about a boy. When my mother asked who had been down at the common one Saturday when some friends had been hanging around there, I listed Valerie Bogacz and Beverly Martowski and Tina Oliveira and a whole stack of other girls' names, then added "that nice Bobby Smola," even though he hadn't been there, but just to get her used to the name I hoped she'd very soon be saying often, as in "Call that nice Bobby Smola and ask him to dinner." Or "We're all going out, but why don't you ask that nice Bobby Smola to come and sit in the backyard with you." Stuff like that.

But my mother was fooling with some interfacing on a ringbearer's tiny white suit, and her question had been more one of those things you ask just to be polite, just to have something to fill up the air, and she really wouldn't have noticed if I'd said that Godzilla had shown up down there and started eating the swing set. Anyway, at least I'd said Bobby's name to her, once, out loud.

And it got easier the more I did it, tucking him into conversation, saying Bobby Smola this and Bobby Smola that, so often, I guess, that one Saturday morning my father suddenly asked me, "Why are you always talking about Bobby Smola?"

I was reading my horoscope and feeling cheated—"This morning may find you in the hot seat at an important business meeting" (I had no such meeting planned)—and was caught off guard. But I took a chance.

"You know—he's in my class."

"So are a million other kids," my mother said from inside the refrigerator she was emptying totally, all because she'd noticed one of the racks had a piece of something sticking to it.

"Well . . . he's nice . . . ," I offered.

"I bet," my mother said jokingly, like she knew what I was up to.

"Nobody likes a boy-crazy girl!" my father said abruptly. "You are only in grade school."

"But a teenager . . . ," reminded my mother, surprising me with her two cents, and, I think, having the same effect on my father. He looked over at her, then back at me. Then he narrowed his eyebrows and pointed his finger and said: "Just watch out—no funny business with the boys."

He looked at me and asked me if I had heard him.

"I did," I said. "I heard you." He got up from the table and put his hand on my shoulder as he passed, leaving some of his new aftershave there for the rest of the day.

I was a mostly obedient daughter, but the afternoon when Bobby called about the ice things, I tried to forget hearing my father's warning. God and he would have to forgive me: Something in me craved funny business—though I wasn't sure exactly what that was.

"I'd love to meet you there," I told Bobby.

"I'll be there after three-thirty," he said, his voice brightening. "Things there look their best just before sundown."

Betty was out on the driveway, giving her leg a ride on the sled, up and back, over and over, smiling and singing something I couldn't hear from inside but I assumed was not in English.

My mother had half an hour before Mrs. Conway would be coming for a fitting on the second of two box-pleated skirts she had ordered, and she was using the time for her weekly coupon search, a job that was all the more important these days considering the big appetite of the little one. She took a

pair of scissors and used the tips to scan each ad. Stewing beef
. . . aluminum siding . . . plowing . . . horse feed . . . last
chance to buy . . . half off with this coupon . . . She said these
words out loud, checking each ad, including the florist ones on
the page she regularly read to see how much older than her
were the people who had died in the past seven days.

"It says here that Feliksa Bys went at ninety-two," she told
me. "You can't ask for much more than that!"

Regina (Wadak) Poleszko was fifty-seven. That still seemed a
long way off, my mother said. Adolph Zombek had just turned
thirty-five. "I'll be that in a year," she said, shivering, but
pointed out that she felt better when she read further on how
he had expired after being kicked in the head by a mule.

"What are the chances of that?" she wondered with relief—
something, it suddenly occurred to me, though I don't know
why, Adolph Zombek might once have thought himself.

I went banging around the kitchen, hoping to distract my
mother and maybe get her to want to do something with me
that might be such fun she would call Mrs. Conway and
cancel, telling her something like, "I can't work with you
today—there are some things more important than money."

"Let's go through the buttons," I suggested. That was a job,
but one I loved, pouring her huge gallon jars of loose buttons
onto the table and finding mates that my mother would link
together with a piece of thread or a diaper pin. She paid me
two cents for every pair I could find, and we'd have races to see
who could find the most of one type.

But my mother didn't even look up and only asked, "Who
was on the phone?" and before I had a chance to make
something up that it had been someone other than Bobby
Smola, the doorbell rang, sparing me from lying and from
another sin I'd have to whisper to Father Kulpa at three o'clock
on Saturday afternoon, trying to be devout in cleansing my
soul, but being preoccupied the entire time, wondering if he
could see my face through the confessional screen as clearly as
I could make out his.

"Can you watch Betty, okay? Thanks a lot. I've got to get to
work." She said all this quickly, gave me a quick hug, and ran
off to answer the door.

"Wait!" I started to say, then let the word just float off into the pantry. What was I going to say? "Wait, I'm running off to meet Bobby"? I reluctantly dragged a chair over to the window and put my slippers up on the clanging radiator as I tried to think how I could get out of this. Outside, Betty picked her way over the ice, with the leg, which was now wearing a white ankle sock against the cold, sliding along behind her.

She was a happy kid, and I liked her enough. But there was some kind of wall in my feelings for her—they would stop just short of where they probably should have been. Like why didn't I put on my snow clothes and get out there and spin her around on the driveway so wildly that she would end up screaming bloody murder, then would plead something I would interpret as wouldn't I twirl her around again and again and again? I didn't go out there because I just didn't want to, that's why. If I really wanted to be honest with myself, I had been here first, and that arrangement had been as perfect as you could want it. There were enough people heaping kindness and love on Betty, and I figured she would not notice if I didn't add an extra ounce of mine. When I did think about it, it all came down to my not wanting to increase her joy and add to her fun any more than I was asked to. After all, I didn't see anybody doing that for me anymore.

This might have been a sin, though I didn't see it fitting into any of the Ten Commandments. There was "Honor your father and mother," but it stopped there. It sounded like God didn't really care what we did with our brothers and sisters, so I felt I was safe. Even so, I prayed the Act of Contrition every night, under the Penance Prayers on page 68 of the little missalette I had received from Babci on my First Communion Day, tucked inside a shiny white pocketbook that had a little compartment built especially for the book. I marked the prayer with that photo of Aniela that I had no choice but to swipe from Betty during the ride home from the airport, and after I prayed how sorry I was to have offended God through my ambivalence about Betty, I stared into the face of Aniela, who was alone in that field and was ready to ride off to wherever she wanted, having no little sister to mind or amuse. She had better things to do, as did I the day that Bobby called. Like homework, which included a special three-page illustrated report on the Huns and the Visigoths. And I soon would have to be helping with dinner. And I had to practice, a particularly difficult scale that was the first in a fat, red, illustrationless book full of them. Mrs. Dranka recently had been puzzled that for the first time since I'd been taking lessons from her, I'd become wooden in my playing, and she thought the answer would be to begin each practice with an exercise to loosen things up. They were not entire pieces—just the same four, boring rising and falling bars followed by four more that began with a higher note, and when I hit the end of the keyboard, I'd climb down back to the place where I'd started and do it all over again.

Thinking about all that work ahead of me, and sentenced to supervising Betty as she sat on my old wooden sled and chewed on an icicle she'd pulled from Johnny Frydryk's downspout, I felt more put upon than ever. My mother, or Babci—the adults—should have been the ones doing this. But they had other things to do, all because of Betty. Betty. Betty. Betty. Betty, whose name had to be the one said the most in this house in all the years this house had been here, and wasn't that something, considering she'd only lived with us for six weeks?

That's when I stood up.

I was not a child. I was not a stick or a box. I was a girl human. A teenaged girl human. And there was no reason I shouldn't have a date. That I shouldn't show up, materializing out of nowhere, as I'd daydreamed so often, with my accordion, to play and to sing for him the first piece of music I'd ever written in my life, a snappy polka titled "Sweet, Sweet Bobby," for Bobby Smola, who, other than our two minutes on the phone, never had said two words to me.

> "Sweet, sweet Bobby,
> neat, neat Bobby,
> no one else can beat my Bobby . . ."

I would play this for him and win his heart.

I ripped a long blank strip from the edge of the newspaper and wrote a note that said, "Gone Outside For 1 Minute.

Donna." How long would it take anyway, to run down to the river and back? I went to retrieve the accordion from my room, making it silently past my parents' bedroom door, where Mrs. Conway and my mother were sitting on her bed and chatting way more excitedly than you'd find believable in a discussion about clothing as they flipped through a stack of *Vogue*s and agreed that, for a more slenderizing look, Mrs. Conway should have only eight pleats in the skirt, not ten, like in this photograph here. Downstairs, I pulled on my boots and my ski jacket and looped my accordion over my shoulder. I spread a newspaper on the floor and called Betty into the house and told her to stay in the kitchen and on that paper and that Babci would be over here with the supper any minute. I opened the door to the dining room and yelled, "Betty's inside!" I felt cleared to go.

The kid stood dripping on the floor and squinting at me a little, trying to figure out what I was talking about. I removed her hat and gloves and unzipped her jacket. "Stay," I said, pretty sure she knew that word. I even put my hand out at her, like you would at a dog.

"Stay, Betty," I commanded. "I'll be right back. Stay."

I shut the door tightly behind me.

The snow was the frozen kind that was like walking across a big piecrust, your feet breaking through every so many steps. I crunched out through the backyard, over the tracks, through the woods, across Norbell Street, down the trail, and soon to the rocks, where Bobby Smola was sitting on a fallen tree, smoking a cigarette and staring at the river, which now was all Alps and Pyrenees and Rockies and Himalayas, all angles and forms and land masses, all golden suddenly. He had been telling the truth.

And when he heard the cracking of the twigs, he turned around and saw me and looked from my face to my accordion and back to my face. And he stood up and exhaled smoke and asked me, isn't this something, meaning the river, I guessed, and so I said it is. Sit over here, he told me, so I sat over there, where he had spread his coat over a part of the log, and he sat down next to me, to my left, not too close, and we didn't say anything for a while. Then he asked me what's that for, meaning the accordion, and I told him I have a surprise, and I unfolded the words and sat on a corner of the paper, and I began to play, and the notes were so high and bright and clear in the air that I was surprised the mountains before us didn't crack and slide into each other and leave nothing of any interest for anyone else to come down there and look at. I never got around to the lyrics. The music sounded just enough, I realized, and it was only me and Bobby, staring off into the formations, following the notes that disappeared inside of them.

Okay, so you might have been thinking that Bobby was going to laugh at me, coming down there like that and playing my music when nobody asked me to. But you would have been wrong. Bobby was wonderful and attentive and complimentary.

"That is so pretty," he said in a quiet voice, and genuinely, I should point out, like he couldn't help but comment after what he had heard.

"Do you want to hear more?" I asked, and my heart was pounding as he slid a few inches toward me, and, just like you know when it's going to happen on the soaps, I knew any second he was going to put his arm around me and set on my lips the kiss we had been halfway to in my dream the night before, the dream that died so violently when Betty went sleepwalking (I think) over to me and started beating me over the head with her leg.

It was Mark Kapinos and Tookie Borowiec who wrecked it in real life, their first snowball smacking Bobby on the center of his back, and we swung around to see them laughing and jeering and then sending another hit to Bobby, on the arm, and then, the one that hurt most, the one that went right into my keyboard.

"Run!" Bobby yelled, pulling a mound of snow toward himself for his artillery, so I did run, slipping at first, then catching my balance and heading back up the hill, some of their throws shooting past me and some of them finding me as I scrambled up the hill to where the path from the river met up with Norbell Street, where I pounded out of the trees running and sniffling, my accordion slippery wet and wheezing and flopping against me with every step. Suddenly out of nowhere there was Betty screaming and on my heels, and I almost went right into the street, only I spotted the diaper truck coming so awfully, awfully fast, and the words of my love for Bobby and the last minute of my life as I knew it flew from my grasp.

Chapter

5

The first thing I came around to making out was the flowers.

Daisies. White carnations. Pink roses. Purple gayfeather. Easter lilies, though it would be months to that holiday. So many flowers it would have taken Babci three summers to grow them all. They were everywhere, were all I could see, and in and among them were bows and shiny, spiky greenery. And a small card on a plastic harpoon. I worked to focus and make it out, and I finally could see the letters: H-E-R-O. I no sooner got to the o when I heard a lady's voice sneer, "Those aren't for her," and the entire garden was yanked from my view by somebody dressed all in white who swiftly carried them away and added them to a rainbow blur of what I soon figured out was a whole wall of not only daisies and carnations and lilies, but roses even, and birds of paradise and orchids.

"Gee! Does everybody love *you!*" the person in white cooed down to a bed that was all flat except for a small lump that looked to me to be only a pile of gauze.

"Why shouldn't they?" the other lady's voice asked. "Everybody loves a hero!"

The lump didn't say anything back. But I wanted to. I wanted to know what was going on. Where was I, and how did I get here, and why was everything so strange and scary? My entire body felt like only my knees had that time when I was at the end of the line playing crack-the-whip on Sasur's pond, and Tossy Sobieski all of a sudden just laughed and let go of my hand, and I smashed into a bench and landed with such force on a pile of hockey equipment that I even cracked the hard blade of one goalie stick. This time, I thought, something worse than that has happened. And at the same time, I felt I really didn't have to worry about it. A couple more odd scenes and sensations, and I would wake up from this nightmare, in my own room, and would know next time to skip the prune compote Babci had claimed would bring about sweet dreams.

So I didn't worry when I figured out I was lying on what looked to be a hospital bed. That I felt so bruised. That the exhausted-looking man snoring in the folding chair next to the flowers looked like my father would look if you marched him one thousand miles without ever stopping. That a hypodermic needle the size of the one I'd seen Mr. Zych's vet use on the steer was coming closer and closer to me.

I was correct that I would wake up, but rather than look over and see Betty kneeling at her bed, animatedly reciting her morning prayers with her hands stiffly folded and that holy-picture look on her face, I saw Betty flat on her back in a bed with high silver bars around it, her head wrapped in so many bandages she looked like the fortune teller at the Tri-County Fair who once shook her bracelets in Ewa Magiera's aunt's face and warned her against driving for one week. (She didn't, and nothing ever happened to her.) Betty's eyes were closed and bulged above huge purple and black circles, and there was a long white bandage taped around her little round chin. Glass bottles of liquids, some clear, one tinted brown, hung from tall metal trees at either side of her, and all kinds of hoses and tubes ran from them down to Betty, disappearing under the thin white blanket that covered the rest of her.

I was not in a cage, but on a large, hard bed, the top half of which tilted upward like the TV commercial electric beds that boast how they enable people to read at night without developing kinks in their necks. I had a short wall of bars on either side of my mattress, and my covers were drawn tightly around all of me, except for where they went under the sling that held my right arm and, oddly, a small spiral-bound notepad and the tiny kind of pencil they give you at the miniature golf course, the kind of pencil that—and I didn't realize it until that moment—was appropriate to be distributed at that kind of place, it being miniature, too.

I looked down at my left arm, and it seemed okay. But the hand was another thing. Everything but my last two fingers was wrapped up in white cloth, kind of like the surprise balls Lori Plotczik gave us as we left her tenth birthday party. When you started unrolling the crepe paper, a small toy or a coin would fall out every so often. With this, I wasn't sure what I'd find if I unwrapped it, though I prayed that whole fingers would appear sooner or later. There was a tube sticking into a square of gauze taped to the back of my hand, running from somewhere behind me and out of my sight. I went to move the left hand and found I could, and I brought it up and put it to my face, which was oddly stiff and, like a sack of potatoes, all lumpy and big, but I could feel nothing of what I was doing to it. I located a thick bandage at my hairline and another at the right side of my head. I tested. I moved both legs and all my toes, and they ached but seemed okay. I wanted to yell for an explanation. But no matter how I tried, I found myself unable to open my mouth.

Where Betty had her collection of flowers, my side of the room held only two beige metal chairs and a long window through which I saw snowflakes the size of cottonballs hurtling down the beam of a spotlight. A heating unit ran beneath the window, and there were several more stray vases of flowers set on that, their blooms shaking from the wave of warm air shooting up from the vents running beneath them.

This has to really be happening—right now, in real life, I told myself slowly, fearfully, and it was then that it occurred to me to try to figure out how I came to be there. Were there other people hurt, too? Were my parents and Babci lying in some other room, worse off than we were? I thought back as hard as I could, and I found Betty in the kitchen, standing on the newspaper, Dr. Murphy's health column, that day headlined "Buffalo Hump Syndrome Plagues Many," turning gray from the slush falling off her boots. I heard myself yelling, "Betty's inside!" and I could see Pappy Hanchett's frozen union suit waving stiffly on the line as I cut through his backyard. Then I could see myself grabbing Betty and pitching her toward the sidewalk in the hope she wouldn't get hit by something headed straight for us. In between the underwear and that terrifying moment there had to be more to the story, but it wasn't in my head that I could find. The only thing I knew for certain was that I obviously had saved a life. And when I realized that, something floated down over me—a warm and golden circle, the knowledge that I was now officially somebody's sister. The one who was supposed to be taller and protective against the rain, and against the wolf dog and against the dark and the things that are hidden beneath the surface of the lake. I forgot about my missing parents and Babci, even forgot about Betty—except for the fact she still was living, all because of me—and I lay satisfied in my bed. With a job well done and with a truth that I was certain not a lot of people ever get to know, I slept deeply.

Though my eyes were closed, the flash of light was bright enough to wake me. Of course I didn't know where I was at first, and tried to raise myself up, but couldn't. There were people scuffling over by the doorway at the foot of the next bed, and I could hear in the hall my father's voice as he shouted, "Get-et the *helr* out of here! Leave us alone! We have enough trouble!"

While all that was going on, I saw my mother enter the room slowly and stare at the bed I remembered was holding Betty, who'd yet to awaken as far as I knew. Then she looked over at me, and her face lit up when she met my eyes, and I moved my left hand up, and she ran over and threw her arms around me and hugged me and sobbed so close it hurt. She said my name again and again and again for quite some time, and I finally had to give her a shove in order to get a break.

She moved away, but not too far, and studied each part of me that she could see. I did the same, at her limp hair falling out of her wet black beret, at the scary paleness of her skin, at her tired eyes, red and teary. I pointed to my own face, to my arm, to my head. To Betty. My mother used her hanky and then pulled one of the chairs over to my side.

"Thank God you are alive . . . ," she managed to choke out, and I realized that was something I had forgotten to do, with all that had been going on.

"You will be all right," she assured me. "You know what's wrong? Did anybody talk to you yet?"

I shook my head that I didn't, that nobody had. So, sniffling, my mother was the one who told me the main damage, listing it like I imagined she had to over the phone to Worcester, to the nuns, to the girls, to who knows how many people. How the arm and its four breaks and the dislocated shoulder would have to remain in a sling for a month at least. How the fingers under the bandage were smashed up, but would be usable if I promised to do exercises once they healed. How I had a row of eighteen stitches in my head, probably some glass still in there—they would have to see—and I should not be alarmed if pieces started jutting out of my skin in the weeks to come. How my jaw was broken in five places and would be wired shut for a couple of months.

It was all too much, all too sudden and big, and I began to cry—though I didn't know how I was going to do such a thing, my mouth being all tied up as I now knew it to be. My sobs were little blasts that came out through my nose and made me sound like I was about to laugh instead. I pointed to Betty again with my little finger, suddenly desperate to know just how she was, and just what they had to sew up on her.

My mother shrugged sadly. "She's been like that since you got here yesterday," she said. "You were there. Imagine."

I tried to think about being there, wherever that was, the place this all had happened to us. I saw myself grabbing for the little sweater, I heard the horn. A chill went up my back even though the room was like an oven.

My mother stopped and looked quickly over at the door, and back at me. "I want you to know that I am not angry at you," she whispered. "Things happen. I understand how things can happen. I was a girl once, too, you know."

I didn't have a moment to decipher all that because right then my father and Babci came through the door. They stood at the foot of Betty's bed and blessed themselves and hung their heads. "Dad . . . ," I tried to say. It came out as something like "Ddddd," but it was enough to make him look up, and when he did he got the strangest look on his face, and he walked over to me very quickly.

"Are you all right?" he asked me coolly, and I nodded as best I could.

"Tell me," he said, bending down, straight into my eyes. "Why?" Then louder, "Why???"

I attempted to make the words, that I didn't know what he was talking about. But they only came out as mush.

"Look at her," he growled, pointing at Betty, and he started to shout, apparently not concerned about waking her up. "Look! Are you happy?"

That was a stupid question, but it is the kind you might ask in such situations, when you don't know what else to say.

My father went over to the window and stared out into the dark. He had on the overcoat my mother had made him for Christmas—gray wool herringbone with slit pockets hidden behind the fancy, flapped patch pockets in case he just wanted to jam his hands in from the cold without having to bother to unbutton anything. He touched a finger to the card on a ball of pastel carnations arranged in a footed glass to look like an ice cream sundae, a tiny red rose being the cherry on top and some brown moss spilling over the side, looking nothing like the hot fudge I was pretty sure it was supposed to represent. My father spoke to his reflection quietly, but my mother caught some of what he was saying in Polish. It was about me, and it was not nice.

And she warned: "Adam . . . She feels badly enough."

"What about the little one?" my father shot back. The words he used, all in one harsh shower, hard like stones, and hurting as much: irresponsible, crazy, disappointing. Was I happy now, he demanded to know.

I wasn't happy, to say the least, though I would be saying nothing, probably until the snow melted. All because of Betty. All because I had tried to save her. Okay, maybe I should have asked permission before leaving her alone. But I did leave a note, I did yell that she was there, and there had been grownups in the house when I left her behind. So I did something wrong. But nobody would have known that if Betty hadn't followed me, if she hadn't jumped into the road and forced me to go after her. And now I was in trouble, hated, injured, probably near death, and I would have to be using a bedpan.

I reached for the pad of paper inside the sling. Because I am not left-handed and didn't have much of that hand available anyway, it took me forever, but I made out the *S* that began the word that for me said it all. *Sorry.* Which I was, in many ways.

Chapter

6

$\mathcal{M}$aureen Browne, R.N., stopped at the McDonald's on Boston Road every day on her way to work just to buy me a strawberry milkshake. It was the only thing I would drink willingly, pushing the red-and-yellow straw way back between my left cheek and the end of my molars and sucking down the sicky-sweet stuff that had melted to the perfect gloppy state in her half-hour drive from Springfield. It was the one and only thing I looked forward to the whole day.

What about seeing my mother and father, you might ask. What about seeing Babci? My friends? Well, oddly enough, when you consider all the other people there are in the world, my parents and Babci were the only ones who ever showed up to see us, visiting steadily every night for the allotted 6 to 8 P.M. visiting hours. But it was not enjoyable. No games were brought in, no cards from friends were delivered, no magazines were stacked on the nightstand to help pass the time. No treats. No gossip. No nothing. The three of them just would float in somberly, moving at the pace you do when you approach the casket at a wake, and would stand around Betty's cage and stare at her like they expected her to do something besides lie there and sleep, which was all she had been doing for eight days in a row at the point I'm telling you about now.

Then they would shuffle over to me, one by one, first my weepy mother, then Babci, silent but with kind eyes, then last, and taking the longest to get to my side of the room, my father, also quiet, but with a look you could use to cut a hole in the side of a mountain. They would draw chairs up to my bed, and, facing Betty, we would all recite the rosary. Babci would place a string of beads in my left hand, and in my head I would say some of the words to the response parts, half-heartedly asking Our Father to forgive us our trespasses as we forgive those who trespass against us—as I was being trespassed on right here, right now, by my own family—but other than that I wouldn't really participate. I would mostly just sneak looks at the three of them, as they stared over at her, as they both prayed and seemed to hate me at the same time. It all would have made me sick, if I hadn't already been.

And come 8 P.M., Maureen Browne would poke her head in the door and would politely announce, "Sorry! Lights out!" and the three of them, long done with the rosary and largely silent for the ninety minutes ever since—except the few times when my mother or Babci would touch my hand and ask if I needed anything—slowly would get up and return the chairs back to where they'd found them, and my mother and Babci would kiss me good-night on the side of my dead face, then would pull on their heavy coats and would pause one more time over at Betty, where my father stood waiting, and Babci would hang one more scapular or holy medal or crucifix from one of her bars, and they would be gone.

That was the point in the night when I more than ever would wonder what was happening here. Still no mail being delivered to our room by cheery candy stripers, no Carolyn and Theresa popping in with comic books and news after school each day, no Mrs. Dranka with maybe a tape recording for me to listen to. I really loved Mrs. Dranka and just then got a big pang of loneliness for her, though it only had been a week or so since I last sat to her left and played "Janina" and she clasped her hands and looked to the ceiling and said, "I am so blessed to have a student who never, ever disappoints me."

My mother made some of Mrs. Dranka's clothes, and it always was a thrill for me to have something made of her odds and ends, a piece of her blue velvet jacket sewn into a collar for my winter coat, some silk from a shell—she loved fine things—made into a pocket flap, and once when she had my mother sew her a raincoat from that shiny "wet look" fabric, she overbought (on purpose, my mother always believed), and I got a coat of my own, free of charge, all because I was, she said, such a good student and such a good girl. The kind of girl she said she wished all her students were. Except for the boys, but you know what she meant. That they would all be like me.

What Mrs. Dranka did when she was not teaching or not in church—the two places I normally saw her—was a mystery to me. I knew she had a house, actually a cottage, at Lake Thompson, something her parents had built a long time ago, and I knew that she liked beauty aids. She regularly ordered Avon products from the mother of Billy Rolla, who often got his drum lessons for free in exchange for cuticle remover or cream bleach or bottles of the dramatic, dark nail polish that made you want to stare at Mrs. Dranka's graceful hands all the more. I knew some of her orders came with a surprise sample placed at the bottom of the bag by Mrs. Rolla. Why didn't she collect some of those lip balms and nail files and eyeliners and send them over to me, so I might have her to think of as I moisturized my left hand or erased the wrinkles that this whole experience was sure to bring about?

But there was no bag from Mrs. Dranka, no nothing from anybody. Actually, other than Jim Keene the orderly, carrying in the newest bunches of flowers for Betty, and the couple of doctors and nurses coming and going so businesslike throughout the day, mostly to wiggle Betty's limbs and ask me embarrassing questions about what they called voiding, there was no sign that there was anyone else in the world. It was as if the crash had spared Betty and me, but had disintegrated most everyone but the eight or so people I saw every day.

To take my mind off such things, I would reach for the

bedside table that had legs on only one side, allowing it to slide conveniently over my lap. A few days into all this, I had found out it contained a drawer that held a flip-up mirror, and I would set it up and study what had become of me, inventorying the black-and-purple-and-yellow skin, the bulging cheeks that made me look like I had never swallowed anything I had ever put in my mouth, the silver metal tabs that somehow had been pushed between each tooth and that held the ends of the small rubber bands crisscrossing up and down and clamping me shut and silent. One night I worked to lift up the bandage on my forehead and on the left side saw the start of the sharp lines of black threads holding together a long, fat, angry split that veered up into my hair. The whole thing was like being in a horror movie.

It was in that drawer that I kept my prayer book, which had been carried in by my mother, who whispered, "To bring you comfort," when she gave it to me. But what it really brought me was the picture of Aniela. And of that field, and the horse, and a calm place, up high, from where I could see for miles. The view I had was of nothing but wilderness, of wildflowers edging the grass on which the horse stood, and there were no people and no problems, nothing to have anybody hating me for, nothing to ask forgiveness for. In the mirror, my smile was gone. In the photo, it was righted and steady, as strong, smart, revered Aniela had nothing in the world to bother her.

The hospital I was in really was the first thing I had ever seen in my entire life. I had been born there, fourteen and a half years earlier, one floor above where I now lay, and I had shared the nursery, I would find out many years later, with the baby who would grow into the girl who did some drugs and then took a bolt cutter to all the locks on all the cages at the regional dog pound in Springfield. I can't speak for her, but I couldn't remember anything particular about the exact room we were in, though there was something familiar and comforting about the hospital's constant heat that warmed you into a state of laziness and that steadily dried out the floral arrangements that arrived two and three a day, even after we'd been there a few weeks. When we ran out of room for them all, my parents directed the nurses to send them to other rooms, and Nurse Durkin couldn't repeat enough times how, thanks to Betty, everyone in the entire hospital—even the ones who couldn't see or who were there to do nothing but die—had his or her own arrangement.

It figures Nurse Durkin would point that out. She paid me little attention, but loved Betty like crazy, always talking to her, patting her, playing with the one tuft of her yellow curls that was visible. Durkin knew three words of Polish and said them to the kid every one of the many times a day she had to come into our room. The words were *hungry, clock,* and *Thursday.* And I bet that if Betty could hear any of that being repeated to her so often, she probably worried that she had suffered brain damage.

That eighth night I was just plain scared and sad and confused and wanted to see another face, wanted to hear something other than the beeps and blips of the electronic devices that recorded Betty's state. So that eighth night I reached to ring for Maureen Browne. I had found out early in my stay that she liked to talk, and even though I wasn't contributing, we could get a pretty good conversation going. Every day I came to learn more about her. How she remembered being my age, because it was then that she had decided to become a nurse—mainly, she confided, because she loved the sound and the feel and the smell of a Band-Aid being opened.

Maureen Browne was nearly two years out of nursing school at UMass and, for about a week after graduation, had moved back in with her parents in West Springfield.

"Boy, did I miss seeing the river," she told me. "I can see the Connecticut—well I *could* see the Connecticut—right from my room—without even having to lift my head from the pillow," she'd tell me. "And I really, really missed my dog—Snoopy— a dachshund—everybody loves him, you can put a biscuit on his nose, and he'll drool and shake and go cross-eyed, but he'll leave it there until you say it's okay. Then he'll flip it off his nose, into the air, and he catches it and eats it in a second. I wish I could bring him in here for you."

But the hospital wouldn't have let her, and she didn't have

the dog anymore in the first place—it was back in the house with the view of the river, the house of Maureen's parents, whom she described as paranoid people who listened to so many news programs about the terrible state of the world that they left the house only for quick stops at the church and the bank and the grocery. They made her so crazy by asking every time she came in, "Have you been smoking dope?" "Is that dope I smell?" "Do you smell dope coming from somewhere?" that one day Maureen, who whispered that she wouldn't be able to afford dope until her college loan was paid in about fifty years, looked at the "Roommates Needed" section of the classifieds and found a whole brick house—but actually she ended up getting just one third of it—in Pine Point that was looking for another young woman to replace the one who had gone off to move in with her boyfriend. Not needing it where she was going, the girl, Barbara, left behind her bed, a rickety, antiquey black-veneered thing that Maureen slept in, settling into the well in the right-hand side of its mattress as easily as if she had created it over many, many years.

For roommates, Maureen got what the ad had described as "young professional women smokers"—two girls who turned out to be Gina Macero, who sold perfume at Steiger's downtown store and who, in jars under the counter, mixed the samples into different types in the hopes of creating an entire new scent someone would want to buy from her for a whole lot of money, and Sandy Flynn, a Certified Professional Secretary (she always added that title after her name whenever she signed anything), who worked in the administration office at the Forest Park Zoo and who once had to help chase a chimpanzee who'd escaped into the adjacent neighborhood and was found—though not by her—two blocks away, in a drugstore's toy aisle, swinging a plastic golf club with such concentration and skill that everyone just stood there and marveled at its ability.

Maureen liked the other girls, though she said her schedule prevented her from seeing much of them and from doing a lot of the things she had enjoyed doing with her college roommates. In school, she loved having the extra people around for meals, shopping, drinking, and dancing, and, especially, sharing long, drowsy Sundays spent in pajamas, making waffles, and watching old movies on a tiny rabbit-eared TV (Maureen now usually worked weekends so that kind of lounging was out). She had no other siblings even close to her age—in fact she had been a baby at the same time her five nieces and two nephews were—and said she had come to love how with roommates there always was somebody awake to tell your troubles to when something bothered you so much so late at night.

I was eager to learn what those troubles might be, because I bet they were wonderful and more exciting than anything I'd ever known. With Maureen, they would have to be. She was a lot of fun, cheery and neat, not too fat, not too skinny, always with her big red hair tied back in the same kind of bulky knot, always with a thick line of emerald penciled under her lower lashes, always with a smiley-face pin above her name tag, always getting enthused about something. In my mind I decided her dilemmas had to be more than things like getting called in to work on the night of a big date, or having a run in her fishnets. They had to be regarding boys. In her case, men.

The night before, she had let on to at least one interest, first coming into our room to routinely go through the thick pile of papers clamped to the board hanging from the end of Betty's cage, and ending up sitting at my side, poking at her cuticles with a fancy metal nail file imprinted with the name of some trademarked drug, describing to me how that afternoon she actually had sat down and split the last bowl of cafeteria tapioca with Dr. Young.

He was one of the three doctors—one for my mouth, one for my bones, Dr. Young for the rest of me—who appeared before me at unexpected intervals, and he was by far the most appealing: dark-skinned and with lambchop sideburns and with an English-Indian accent and with cologne that hung in the air long after he was gone off to repair someone else, that deep scent of spice rack/untamed wilderness so wondrous that it conquered for a short time the smell of the sharp ammonia cleaner slopped across the floor every other afternoon by a tiny, jumpsuited old man who tsk-tsk-ed when he worked around me and who sang animatedly in French to

Betty—even stopping to make some rhythmic hand movements that she didn't open her eyes to watch—while he mopped at the floor on her side of our room.

Maureen Browne explained to me that Dr. Young was involved with Betty and me because he had been the physician on duty in the emergency room when Betty and I had been wheeled in. We were his concern for life—or more accurately, for however long we remained hospitalized. And when he was gazing into my eyes, gently drawing my lids out of the way with his sensitive, fragrant fingertips, and blinding me with his little pen of a flashlight, I wanted to be kept there for eternity, feeling his warm hand on the part of my newly huge face that actually had some sensation left, hearing him tell me, "You gonna be okay, chickie," both thrilled and embarrassed by the realization that this was an adult man who, though I don't remember any of it, for sure had observed me in some state of helpless nakedness.

I could use another Dr. Young tidbit to get me through the next boring hour before I drifted off to another round of sleep. I already had collected some such info from Maureen: his car (a royal-blue Monte Carlo with black vinyl roof and a vanity plate that read DOCYNG), his license plate state (Virginia), and the fact that he skiied and had done so at Mount Snow one spring weekend and brought back the next workday a large boxed assortment of maple sugar candy that he left on the coffee table in the break room for everyone to enjoy. Maureen had picked out a larger piece shaped like a lumberjack and treasured it as a personal gift from the doctor, never eating it, instead keeping it on a shelf in her locker until it turned rock-hard and white at the edges and she finally wrapped it in a piece of Kleenex and threw it out for fear of it attracting ants into the sterile building.

Maureen said she knew that Dr. Young had at least one sister, because when somebody named Jeannie who works down in the cafeteria had come in before Christmas with a box of the leather barrettes she tools to pass the time until Johnny Carson comes on, Dr. Young had purchased two, saying he has a sister who wears her hair very long. Maureen also said she

overheard how he loves to bowl—candlepins, specifically—
when he has the time, and that he hoped someday to have a
lane in his basement, complete with an electronic ball return.

I yearned for more such information. But the nurse call box
with its one red button was gone from my side that eighth
night, fallen off the side of the bed, I guessed, when Babci had
leaned in to make sure my hand had made it to the first Our
Father bead right on schedule. I knew the call gizmo was
knotted around one of the slats on the side of the mattress, so I
went searching for it, sending my hand down the side of the
bed and far out of sight. I located a cord tied way down, almost
out of my reach, and I scratched with my two good fingers to
bring it up. But what my hand returned with was something I
hadn't seen before—some other control. "OFF" read the black
button. "ON" read the green one.

I pushed it on, not knowing or caring what to expect. I was
in a hospital—so what if this turned out to be something that
could electrocute me? And suddenly, the television set hanging from the ceiling by chains, the one my mother had told me
they couldn't afford to have hooked up, sprang to life. But just
my luck—it was public TV.

And it was the same stale little man, the one whom we all
had to sit and watch one night a few weeks back as he clumsily
moderated a debate between then-not-yet Representative
Conway and two other candidates, the one that Representative
Conway said regularly got sued for inserting way too many of
his own often harsh points of view into whatever topic he was
discussing on his local interest show. He was standing now in
front of a cardboard fireplace, pipe in hand, droning on and on
about the importance of us all contributing to the upcoming
fund-raiser, which would determine whether or not the children in our area would be able to benefit daily from a visit by
Mr. Rogers. The guy was as boring as the last time I'd seen
him, and I think he even wore the same dizzyingly checkered
sports coat, but watching him sure beat staring at the wall, or at
Betty, my other two options, which really amounted to about
the same thing. If nothing else, the TV was allowing me to see
somebody else, and to be assured that others existed outside

my closed, antiseptic circle. I was wondering how long I was going to be able to get away with the television before being found out, when the host shifted in his chair and brightened his tone.

"More tonight," the guy, Hoover Something-or-other or Something-or-other Hoover, said expressively, "about the little local girl whose act of selflessness might end up costing her her own life."

And there, filling the screen, was a huge picture of Betty's face, the way it used to look. Actually it was Betty from the picture of me and Betty in the Howard Johnson's parking lot. But they only showed her, looking confused, as she, I knew, hung on to my coat in what now seemed years ago rather than a couple of months back.

"You'll remember," the Hoover man prompted, "the tragic story of the little immigrant girl who saved the life of her new sister last week when she attempted to push her from the path of an oncoming out-of-control truck, its driver blinded by the setting sun. You'll recall how the love-struck elder girl had abandoned her baby-sitting duties and was running carelessly into the street after being discovered in a secret meeting with her boyfriend . . ."

All the air went out of me, I swear. He was talking about me. Oh, my God—me and Bobby . . .

"Well, when word got out about the heroism of this precious six-year-old who can barely speak English, who was sent here by a destitute family who feared she would not survive in their precarious household, who received for her lifesaving effort a blow so tremendous that she landed far across the street and now lies unconscious in Our Lady of Hope Hospital, the media"—here he got very dramatic, more, I should say, than he already was—"usually ready to pounce on anything and everything—adopted her as their own. And look, ladies and gentlemen. Over one week. What headlines . . ."

He picked up our local paper, the weekly *Penny Saver*, and slid a buffed fingernail along the long black headline: "Immigrant Tot Saves New Sister's Life." Below that was the same picture of Betty they'd already shown and a smaller shot of me, the one taken in school last September by the photographer who didn't notice or didn't care that the back part of my blouse collar accidentally was sticking up over my blazer. In between the two pictures was a small photo of a small truck, and of people standing next to it with their backs to the camera, looking down at what must have been me. Off to the right, nearly cut from the picture, nearly being stepped on by a man in snowmobile boots, was part of an accordion's keyboard.

The photo disappeared as Hoover unfolded the *Springfield Daily News*: "Sister's Selfless Act Moves Western Mass." There was a small headline in slanty type below it: "Diaper Deliverer Cleared in Crash."

And another story, Hoover noted, from our diocesan newsletter, *Flock Talk*. "Churches Begin Fund-raiser in Thanksgiving for Life Saved."

Another, from the Worcester paper: No story, only a photograph of Betty lying flat in her hospital bed, the one that had to have been taken by the person my father had yelled at in the hallway. In the background you could see part of what appeared to be me. Neither of us looked too good.

The man spoke as he held the page up to the camera, shaking it a little for emphasis:

"Imagine the heartbreak of a family who leaves the elder daughter to baby-sit, but the girl runs off to be with a boy, taking the younger child along—down to a raging, freezing river! But they can be grateful that at least one member of the family kept her wits about her: Through an extensive investigation, police have determined that little Betty was the hero."

Suddenly the screen showed a moving film of my house, the "All the Way With Conway" sign half covered by new snow, and a long line of people approaching our front door with frosted cakes and Reynolds-Wrapped bowls, stuffed animals, flowering plants and wrapped gifts. My mother, at the door, whiter and thinner than she'd ever looked. Carolyn in her school uniform, standing in the driveway, weeping out of control. Theresa, next to her, smiling and holding up to the camera a bottle of the family's milk. Babci shooing the reporters away, off the front walk, down the sidewalk, and the next thing you see is a bobbing shot of the inside of our garage, but somebody else's stuff filling it: A row of at least eight small, shiny bicycles, each complete with bells and baskets and matching plastic ribbons shooting from the end of each handlebar. A pink-and-white wooden playhouse with a working porch swing that an arm from an unseen body reached out to and demonstrated how well it could move back and forth. A large box with a label that showed it contained an elaborate jungle gym, its slide and its four different types of rides, its seesaw and glider all shaded by a tower with a happily striped canvas roof.

"All these are among the untold items that have been streaming into the Milewski household for little Betty," the man in the studio said, and he was in front of the camera again, this time holding a coffee can he jiggled so you could hear a couple of coins banging together inside.

"This station is joining in the effort to somehow show this little girl what America is all about. We urge you to send donations to the station—for the 'Thank You, Betty Fund,' that is." He gave the address and noted in a whisper that any money sent would not be tax deductible, but a break in taxes, he noted, was not the issue here. A life was, he said, pointing his pipe at us viewers as he requested, "No matter what your relationship with the Almighty, please ask him to spare our little Betty." Then, in what must be his trademark farewell, Hoover wished "A very, VERY, pleasant evening to you all." He took a seat in an easy chair next to the fireplace and relit his pipe as the studio lights slowly dimmed and a symphony began to play.

In those few minutes, it all began to make sense. No wonder they hated me! I'd gone to see Bobby, and not only that but they thought I brought Betty with me, there, to the river, where she could have slipped in and drowned. They must not have known I'd left her safe in the warm kitchen, they probably hadn't seen the note, must not have heard me yell I was leaving her there for them to watch.

They didn't know that I'd ordered Betty to stay, that she hadn't listened, that she instead had taken off on her own and had followed me, and now look what happened. They didn't know that she was the one who had done wrong, not me, really. They all saw me as the one who probably killed her, when I was the one who tried to save her. With how it looked to them, no wonder they couldn't stand to come near me.

But the worst thing was, I couldn't tell them any different, and Betty was of no help. Tears rolled down my big, fat, numb cheeks and splashed onto the plastic identification bracelet that offered a suggestion under the line for blood type. B POSITIVE, it urged me. But I just couldn't.

Maureen Browne stuck her head in the door two nature shows and one natural foods cooking program later.

"I thought I heard voices," she said, wagging a finger at me and exaggerating a threatening tone that it would be hard to imagine her using for real.

"Hey—you found the button, you sneak! No harm in that—just don't play it all the time, or they'll find out, and they'll start adding it on to your bill. And believe me—they don't give this away!"

I turned my head away, to the window, to outside, where there lived a whole town of people who I now knew thought I was some kind of irresponsible tramp.

"What's the matter?"

I didn't look at her, just pointed to the TV.

"It's no problem. You won't get in trouble."

I motioned some more, though how was she going to guess what I meant?

"What's wrong?" Her tone was genuine, and she came closer.

I took the pad from my sling and showed it to her, the words I'd been working on in the hours since I learned what people thought about me, what they were saying about me.

"Sorry, honey," she said. "Can't read it."

I pointed to each letter.

"I. Led?"

I shook my head.

"No. I Red?"

I grabbed it from her.

"I really wish I knew what you wanted," she said. I turned toward Betty, same old lumpy form, same old beeps from her monitors. Maureen Browne took the TV button, clicked it off, sending the cheerful, hefty woman in pioneer dress, with her mayonnaise jar full of sprouting mung beans, disappearing into blackness.

Maureen shoved the button somewhere far back under the mattress, out of sight.

"I won't tell if you don't," she said. I just looked at her frantically, right into her blue eyes, hoping she could catch one of my awful thoughts somehow and tell me it wasn't so bad. I beamed them into her brain, the news I just got, about what people were saying, about how awful it made me feel. I ached for somebody to tell me everything would be all right.

Whatever message, if any, she received from me, Maureen Browne said, "You want me to stick around for a while?"

I nodded, shaking, relieved, and she sat down and began to retie her shoes slowly, and she said, oh, she had a great story for me, about how Gina yesterday got to apply a spray of musk oil to the inner wrist of a celebrity who was looking for a new smell to go with her new wardrobe.

"You'll never believe this," Maureen Browne frothed. "It was the wife of that guy Conway! Ever heard of him?"

I worked all night on the word, in the soft beam of the nightlight, quitting and faking sleep when anyone looked in on us, or administered a needle, or jammed a thermometer you don't want to know where. I fell asleep, started up again, slept some more. I went over the lines again and again, scratching them into the paper. And by the morning I had two words that anyone who knew the English language could have made out:

I Tried.

My parents and Babci arrived the next day, carrying a large light blue cloth sack from which they pulled a statue of Our Lady, beautifully painted and with a golden metal halo behind her head, tiny crystals dangling from the end of each of its many points. They cleared Betty's nightstand of three vases and the wooden cross Nurse Durkin's husband had carved and set the statue on it so its gaze was fixed right on the girl's face. It was a special statue blessed at the Kościoł Mariacki in

Krakow, they told her, and would bring about good things for the faithful. So pray, they told her. But hurry up because we have to return it to church tonight so the next person on the list can take her home.

"She's looking better, Babci, don't you think?" my mother asked when she came over to me, taking off her gloves and putting down her purse.

Babci scrutinized me and nodded, then smiled. She didn't say much when she came to visit me. I figured out she had to be disappointed in me, but, being Babci, she was unable to be anything stronger than that.

My father remained at Betty's side, adjusting the statue so its powers could beam on target right into the little crumpled girl. He was no softer to me than he had been at the beginning of this, and I wondered if he knew how terrible that made me feel.

The other two got their chairs and sat down, took out their beads, and waited for my father to take his seat. My mother had to call him. "Adam." He turned a moment later and sat. When he did, I took the pad from my sling and waved it at them as much as I was able to.

"I didn't do anything wrong—she did!" I was screaming this in my head. "Look! Look at the words! 'I tried.'" The number 2 after that, then just mush—all I could manage—for "save her." "I tried to save her" it would have said if I had been able to make all those letters legible. But I couldn't. So they looked at the paper, then they looked at each other, but they didn't get it. They studied it again, then gave me their sad expressions, and it was so very disappointing. They had turned to Betty and begun their prayers, in the name of the Father and of the Son and of the Holy Spirit, heading into the first of the Five Sorrowful Mysteries, when something in me just froze up, and I decided: fine. Betty can tell them what happened when she's better. Then won't they feel bad! If that's what they want, if they want to think these terrible things about me, then that's what they can do. I will not try to tell them again.

Chapter

7

$\mathcal{I}$n my house, whenever somebody said the word "Wednesday," somebody else would add "Prince Spaghetti Day!" because the commercial in which Anthony's mother yelled for him so loudly that he could hear her ten blocks away told us over and again that's what that day was.

I don't know exactly who started it, but no matter how the word was used by someone in the family, the custom stuck. When I came home to announce that Sister Gallardia would be having her hammer toe operated on and we would be getting out of school early on Wednesday, my mother added, without even looking up from her machine, "Prince Spaghetti Day!" My father mentioned that he had asked Theresa's father to truck some manure over to the garden on Wednesday afternoon, and "Prince Spaghetti Day!" was what Babci replied. My mother hung up the phone and sniffled that Mrs. Izyk's sister had passed away and that the wake would be Wednesday. The rest of us just looked at each other, and she bawled "Prince Spaghetti Day" as she ran up to her room.

But when Doctor Young squeezed my good hand and

happily told my parents, "It looks like chickie can go home on Wednesday," nobody apparently felt like adding anything. So it was just plain old Wednesday when they brought me a paper bag containing my old cranberry bell-bottoms and a new white blouse my mother had given only one arm and a big, billowy, elasticized part on the other side that would accommodate my sling, and they set me in a wheelchair, and they rolled me past Betty, who was entering her third week of sleeping.

Maureen Browne came in earlier than she was required to and brought me two milkshakes and a greeting card that had a real though dried-up shamrock trapped under cellophane on the front. Under the words "Good Luck" inside, she wrote that she would always remember me. After that, she had drawn a peace sign and a heart and had signed her full name, including the *E* on the end of Browne I never even considered might be there.

She stooped next to me, and I gave her as much of a hug as I could, pushing my face into her apricot-smelling hair and wishing I could ask to be her pen pal, so I might at least have the mail to look forward to and the hope that in it there might be a cheery yellow envelope with my name marked on it in her wispy penmanship, news of her workday and of her dumb parents and of her car troubles and of Sandy and Gina filling the notecard inside. But I was unable to speak any of the words that I wanted to attempt, and my father wasted no time in wheeling me out of the room, away from Betty, away from the waving Maureen Browne, down the hall past where Dr. Young, his back to us, was intently writing something as he held the phone receiver between his left shoulder and ear and didn't even see me passing and grabbing my perhaps final bit of information about him, that, don't you worry, he was headed straight for the train station the minute he got out of here, and, oh, baby, were you and he going to make the most of the next twenty-four hours.

After nearly three weeks indoors, it felt strange but so wonderful and so new to be outside, under a bright sun, crows screaming in a tree and the snow melting from the entrance overhang racing down in fast drops that hit the ground sounding like applause. The air was fresh and delicious, and I would have been content just to sit in that entryway and breathe in and out for the rest of the day. But my father had shifted his lunch hour because of the 1 P.M. release time, and he had to get back, so there would be no dallying. He had pulled the car up to the hospital's front stairs, and he and my mother helped me up, out of the chair, then shakingly down, one, two, three, four steps, then across the wide walk and into the backseat, handing me my plastic bag of water pitcher, cup, bedpan, and throw-up tray, souvenirs given by the hospital as if they were things I would want to have for all time.

My parents didn't say anything as we rolled away, down the street, past the housing for the elderly, where a man in a big blue jacket smiled as he scraped the last bits of snow from a far corner of the driveway that nobody but him would have cared was clear, past the farm, where somebody had made a horse from snow in the front yard and had put a pile of hay in front of it in case it got hungry, across the thin concrete bridge, right over a squashed and furry dead thing in the road that caused a slight bump-bump sound as our wheels made it flatter.

Finally we came up to our house, which I had seen the last time on my television screen, the night that I learned exactly what the situation was, the night when they showed a Milton Bradley truck parked outside and two delivery men waving a Chutes and Ladders game and an Uncle Wiggly doll at the camera. But here was no commotion today, no people at all. At the garage, the doors were pulled down, and I didn't have to wonder what was behind them.

Babci was standing behind the storm door, waving at me as I sat there waiting for somebody to open my side of the car, which my mother did, and then my father was there, helping me onto the driveway.

He held me strongly and steadily, even whispered "careful" once, but that's about all he said to me before he brought me slowly up the steps and onto a chair in the kitchen, then grabbed a slice of bread for himself from the box in the pantry and went to drive back to work, saying nothing as he went out the door.

Babci kissed me about ten times before saying what I knew would be next:

"May God bring little Betty home now, too," she prayed into her folded hands.

I didn't want to hear it right now, and I stood up and headed for the other room.

"Rest, rest," my mother told me, guiding me back into the chair.

I shook my head and moved my hand to point around the house. I was nervous, feeling antsy, though this was the place you would think I would be most comfortable. But it was nothing like the home I remembered. The dining room and living room looked like we'd won the lottery. That was the only way you could have explained how we would end up with so many brand-new things in our house, stacked and leaning against the next thing, all the stuff, the folded clothes, the boxes of games, the little child-sized roll-top desk and chair, the laundry baskets full of envelopes and packages, the shiny red go-cart and, what was that? A saddle? Betty was getting a horse? Now I really needed to sit down.

My mother, who had followed me, moved a dining room chair behind me and pushed me into it. She crouched next to me, and I realized for the first time that day that she looked terrible, all tired and worn out, though she smelled really good, as she always did. My father often joked, though it was more true than it was farfetched, that even if she were going to the mailbox, my mother first applied perfume.

"They're for Betty," she said plainly, not making it sound like the riches were something they were not. Not coloring it in any way.

"They're from people we don't even know. Far away, strange people. It got in the newspaper—about what happened. Everybody heard about her, and they said it made them want to do something. Some of the people came to the door, some of them just left things on the sidewalk, on the porch. It's just because she's not from here, you understand. They do feel sorry for you, too—nobody likes to see anybody get hurt. But Betty, well, she's been so underprivileged, and for what she did . . ."

She faded off, then quickly stuttered, "But . . . but it's too much. It's all too much." She waved her hands at the things that cluttered the room, like they were birds that could frighten and fly off and they would be gone from there.

I pointed to the saddle, but my mother couldn't tell what I was aiming at, it being perched between the Easy-Bake Oven that came packaged with a pizza mix and the Lite Brite someone had taken out of the box and written "Betty" on with multicolored pegs, and it being ridden by a Chatty Cathy doll who was dressed in a blue stewardess outfit and who, according to the tag that hung from the golden pair of wings pinned to her uniform, could speak French when you filled her with batteries and jammed the proper record into the slit in her side.

"Yes," my mother said, guessing being all she could do with me. "Isn't it amazing?"

You wouldn't think so, but just riding those two miles home and climbing the stairs up to my room tired me out so much that I slept the rest of the afternoon, back in my own bed, which, after the hard hospital bed, felt like a cloud. And I floated on it without a dream that I can remember, until Babci woke me for supper and helped me back down the stairs.

"I was going to bring you a tray, but you need exercise," she whispered. I held her boney hand, wondering what help she would be if I slipped down the stairs. I realized I'd probably end up taking her with me, and breaking her in half in the process, so I took smaller steps as we descended into the forest of gifts.

We all had soup that night, and, except for our bowls and spoons and napkins, the tureen it filled was the only thing on the table. There was not even a piece of parsley to garnish, or even to give us clear thinking for the rest of the evening. No basket of bread dotted with wisdom-bearing poppy seeds, no butter carved into a fish shape so we might be reminded of the apostles' original jobs. It was just soup—a salty chicken broth—then, when we were done, a very runny butterscotch pudding for dessert. Everything the consistency to fit through a straw, nothing that required any chewing. Nobody said too much of anything. Babci is the only one I recall making any sound, talking for a short time about how she could tell it was beginning to remain lighter later each afternoon. My mother answered "yes" to that one, that Babci was right, but she gave no explanation or example, no hopeful comment about how spring is coming. Just a "yes" that hung heavily in the air.

They didn't want me to help clean up—a switch from what had been going on before all of this. My father, who looked only into his bowl during the meal, finished his share and disappeared into the cellar to do some kind of hammering, and Babci and my mother cleared the table and hurried to wash everything so my parents could get going to visit Betty, which they did for only one short hour that first night, nervous about my being back home, I'd like to think, though they didn't give an explanation.

With Babci at my side again, I slowly made it back up to my room after supper. When she left me alone, I went to the closet, where my accordion used to be kept, but found only the empty case on the closet floor, open, the way I'd left it when I'd sneaked out that afternoon. The orange velvet that lined the box was matted and marked where for so long it had bumped up against the thing that now was gone and destroyed and thrown away who knew where.

I got ready for bed and shut off the light before anybody had the chance to come and say good night, though my mother did come to the doorway and stop, I saw through eyes faking sleep, and she stood there for a while before tiptoeing in and straightening my covers, then leaving on my nightstand a glass of water with a straw in it. After she left, I watched through the grate as my parents put on their coats to leave. Then, I don't know how long later, I woke to the sound of the television and looked down to see them, back home by then, sitting surrounded by Betty's presents and watching a crime show about counterfeiters. They did not sit as closely as they usually did,

and they did not hold a conversation. They ate small sandwiches from plates on their laps, staring at the crooks on TV,
chewing very slowly.

Don't ask me how they found out I was home, or who let
them up there, but there they were in my bedroom the next
morning, standing next to me, Carolyn sniffling into a bunch
of pink and white carnations, and Theresa leaning over me
and asking me did I see all that stuff downstairs, and would I
show her my teeth, and, boy, what kind of friend was I—why
hadn't I told them I was Bobby Smola's girl?

They looked older to me, though I knew that could not be
really true. It had only been a couple of weeks since we did
whatever it was we had last done together—polished apples at
the fruit store, tried to imagine Brother Mike in normal-
people's clothes, maybe crabbed about how the eighth-graders
over at the French school were allowed to have a Valentine's
dance. Whatever it was, I couldn't remember exactly, that
being one of the couple of faded parts of my recent past that
had yet to come back to me.

"Honest—you can't talk?" Theresa asked, wide-eyed, giggling. "Nothing? Say something! Say a word."

I shook my head. I hated what it sounded like when I had
spoken the few times to myself, so I was not lying.

"Just a word! One word. Say . . . say 'Hi.' "

I shook my head.

"Wow! Is that cool! I wouldn't mind that!"

Carolyn blubbered. "It . . . it is not cool! I'm so sorry for
you, Donna . . . We were so worried . . ."

She knelt next to the bed and cried into my quilt, first hitting
my slinged arm with her head, which made her sob louder for
fear she'd made me feel worse. I tried to touch her head with
my left hand, but couldn't reach without moving more than I
really wanted to, so I gave up and lay there, motionless.

"Come on, Carolyn . . . ," Theresa said in as soothing a
manner as she could get together. "Donna feels bad enough."
Then she looked at me, "I mean you must. Right? Everybody
knowing what you were up to."

Even they believed the worst about me. The whole world

had gone crazy since I'd last been in it. I turned my head toward the wall.

"We thought you were gonna diiiieeee . . ." I peeked over to see Carolyn at Theresa's waist, hugging her, and even Theresa looked like she had tears in her eyes. It was uncomfortable for me to watch, but I was also feeling that it was about high time that somebody got upset about me.

"She's right. We really did. We thought you were, you know, gone," Theresa said slowly, wincing. "We even had a special mass for you—they said yours and Betty's name up at the altar, like they usually do only for dead people. All the nuns told us is that even though Betty went to save you, you still ended up getting hit anyway. But they say it could have been lots worse if she hadn't done anything. You know that people say she's a real celebrity—that there might even be a parade for her? You know how much money everybody says your parents are getting from insurance 'cause of this?"

Carolyn pushed at Theresa. "Shut up! Donna's sick. Think about her!" Then Carolyn quickly turned and looked at me and said seriously and quickly: "They say you were doing things with Bobby in the woods. Tookie and Mark saw you and told everybody . . . they were down there, at the river—did you know that?" Then she added cheerfully, like it made sense to attach this right there, "We got you a get-well present! Nobody was allowed to go see you—they said you were too sick—so we had to wait till now."

Something inside me lifted a little. So that's why there hadn't been any visitors! People probably got as far as the main desk, then were told how grave the situation was and got turned away. Bobby—whom I could imagine praying for me at that mass, kneeling and mashing his face into his folded hands, begging God to bring me back to him—I'm sure he had to have been inside the hospital building more than a couple of times, maybe trying night after night, hoping to be let upstairs. Maybe he looked for a stairwell he could sneak up, or maybe, like I had seen one day on "Love of Life," he found a linen closet and put on a doctor's outfit and had tried to locate my room, only to get caught and struggle so much to get free that it took two muscle-man orderlies, one on each side, lifting him in the air, to throw him out of the hospital. I didn't know any of that for sure, but I did know at least that people had been kept out for a good reason—not because they never wanted to see me again. And that made me feel a little bit better.

Carolyn and Theresa moved to the foot of my bed and argued over something, then both pulled a faded black case over and onto the bed, setting it next to my knees.

Then Carolyn spoke, placing the words carefully, like this was a speech she had been practicing for a long time: "We thought this was something you would need, so we put our money together. It's not the best—because a good one was too expensive for us—but at least you will have one . . . for when you're ready."

I knew what it was before that moment, as I'm sure anyone would who knows this story up to this point. I had lost a couple of things in the collision, but only one was something you could actually put your hands on and do something with. Except for that photograph of a portion of it I'd seen on the TV show, I knew nothing about exactly what had happened to my own accordion. But I figured out from what I was getting here that the damage had been such that I needed a replacement, and that I was getting one, this small, old, dingy white one that Carolyn was making stand up in its case so I could see its faded keys and the rust on the metal at the edge of the bellows and the crack on the trade name that ran the length of the front in slanted, delicate letters: *Spero.* It was not a Frabotta, like my real one had been, the graceful silver *F* so elaborate and looking more like a jeweled decoration than just a plain old letter, its right foot extending delicately to underline the rest of the word, and the large, glinting rhinestones set into the spaces in the *E, O,* and *A.* No, this dirty old accordion was named after a dinky little bird, one that was drab and plain and so ordinary you could see anywhere, any time of day, that you wouldn't miss at all if you never saw one again in your life.

But they were so excited to be giving it to me, you would have thought it was made of gold. Theresa was enthusiastic and tripping over her words: "It was at a flea market on Depot Street! Mrs. Dranka wanted you to have one of hers, but I told her we could take care of you just fine ourselves. That *we* were your friends, and it was our job. We even had enough money for it. What'ya think?"

I couldn't tell them, so I just nodded my head. I waved the box closed, and so they set it on its back and put the case on the floor.

"You like it, don't you?" Carolyn told me and asked at the same time.

I tried to smile. Then—and I don't know why—I looked to Betty's side of the room, and I thought about her for the first time that day. I wondered if they would give my hospital bed to someone else. How that, if they did, Betty would be sleeping in her cage across from a total stranger.

When I looked back to where the girls had been standing, they were gone. But in the hall I could hear Carolyn telling Theresa, her voice getting farther away as she spoke, "She really liked it, didn't she?" and Theresa saying, "Geez! She looks terrible!"

Their leaving made me very sad, and it was then, rather than when I had them with me just a minute before, that I realized how greatly I had missed my friends. But I would be seeing plenty of them: They would be bringing my homework over every night, and it would be just like how it had been in what now seemed like years ago, all of us working away on problems and compositions and multiple choices. The nuns said I could graduate from eighth grade without showing up for class the rest of the school year as long as I completed all the assignments the girls delivered to me. Sister Superior had summoned my parents to the convent to tell them this, and they returned home with a fat typed-out reading list for me and a handmade three-foot-tall rhinestone-bejeweled Infant of Prague doll for Betty.

It was something to me how easy it was not to have to speak. Mainly what struck me was how relaxing it was, if you didn't bother yourself with wanting to put your two cents into whatever conversations were going on around you. I was silent, and I could have been a piece of furniture—a stick or a box or a cement mixer—not engaging in anything, not contributing, not giving my opinion. Then again, no one in my house really wanted much of anything from me anymore. To be fair, I should say that if they did, they never asked. After my return home, my mother and Babci were protective and cautious with me, but it still was nothing like the last time that there were only four people in our house. My father, well, forget it. He hardly acknowledged I was there, and maybe it was my imagination, but he spoke very loudly when, upon returning from his and my mother's nightly trip to the hospital, he would telephone the nurse's desk one final time, just to say, "I only call to ask how my daughter is." Not niece. Not the little girl. Not Betty. Not the little one, even. But his *daughter*. I wanted to yell, "I'm your daughter. And I'm right here! And I'm not doing so great!" But I just watched him wait for Nurse Durkin to take her time and stroll three doors down the hall, poke her bouffant in the doorway, see that Betty was as still as a corpse, then return to pick up the phone and say, "No change," and he would answer, "Well, thenk you," then hang up and kiss the feet of the crucified Lord that hung over the phone stand eavesdropping on every conversation you held.

As for me, I mainly sat on my end of the couch and read and sucked things through a straw and watched the clock turn to the position at which the girls would knock at the kitchen door and Babci would keep them in that room, before we started our homework, to eat a plate of Chips Ahoy and Fig Newtons out of my sight (being who she was, Babci refrained from doing any fragrant baking in the time I was unable to chew).

As for me, there was the awful prescriptioned protein drink every morning, to make sure any bones that hadn't fully formed yet would get enough nourishment and I wouldn't end up a cripple. But for the rest of the meals, Babci came through, fascinating me every day by translating all kinds of things into smooth liquid.

It was Holy Thursday night and I was drinking something that, and I know it sounds impossible, tasted like her saltine-cracker-covered schrod, when they got the call. My father answered, then dropped to his knees, the phone slipping from his hands and bouncing down on the rug.

"She's awake!" he shouted, shaking and blessing himself

and bowing low like the catechism film we once were shown of worshippers in the Middle East.

"She's awake, *mój Boże!*" he whispered to the rug. "She's awake. She's AWAKE! She's calling for her family!"

I nearly dropped my glass of fish. My heart was pounding so fast I thought maybe I'd need a once-over by Dr. Young. Finally! Now they would all know, now she could tell them! Betty was the one who had been in the wrong! Yes, I had skipped out, but she wasn't supposed to follow me! And, boy, was everybody going to feel rotten when she explained everything! I was ecstatic.

My parents and Babci bumped into each other as they fumbled into their coats and went and called Mrs. Zak from down the street to come over and sit in the wing chair between the aquarium kit and the official Junior Olympic bobsled. I was not allowed to be alone because of the fact that if I threw up I would choke to death. The oral surgeon, Dr. Pressman, had interrupted his annoying whistling long enough during his final visit with me in the hospital to give me a tiny pair of scissors with which I was to cut my rubber bands if I was about to heave. If I didn't clip them at that point, I could choke, and, as he put it sternly, "the consequences could be fatal." I carried them in a suede pouch I'd made in day camp the year before, with slits in the back to thread your belt through. One of the few times I felt like talking was when someone asked me what was in that bag. Though the details were disgusting, I found it somewhat thrilling that at any moment I could be at death's door.

The second my parents left, Mrs. Zak turned toward me and hissed, "I'm missing the Holy Thursday service, you know. I'm only here because your father shovels me out. I don't happen to like your kind of girl." Then she picked up her crochet hook and her orange-and-brown granny square and said nothing more.

Fine, because I felt the same about her, a lady so cheap that for Trick or Treat she gave out buttered slices of rye bread that stuck to the side of your bag and left big greasy circles behind when you pulled them off. I sat as quietly as she did, the Etch-

A-Sketch in my lap. I should say I had Betty's Etch-A-Sketch, which I had stolen from the trunk of the pedal-powered Cadillac that the Ludlow Boys and Girls Club had stuffed with toys and wrapped in a huge white ribbon and then called the newspaper so it could make a photograph of the donation, which was purchased with the allowance money of forty-three club members who signed the get-well card that awaited Betty in her glove compartment.

My goal was to erase the entire screen so I could view the mechanism that allowed you to etch your sketch. But because I wasn't supposed to have the thing, really, I could only work on it so much before somebody came by. Then I'd have to shove it under the afghan or into the couch, and that would be enough movement to ruin any progress I'd made. One day I got as far as to where I could see part of a gear and a metal arm inside, but then my mother came running through the room to answer the bell rung by the mailman, who, like most days, had too many things to fit them all into the box.

Mrs. Zak pushed herself off the chair and walked over to snap on the TV, then turned the channel until she found the Waltons sitting in their church, listening to a sermon. I loved Jim-Bob Walton, his quiet ways, his spending all that time in the barn repairing engines, so young yet he knew his life's goal: to be an aviator. I was jealous of the little Catholic girl who was his first love, until—and you could see this coming even if you were Betty flat on her back with your eyes closed and your brain out of service for a couple of weeks—she decided to enter the convent. But there Jim-Bob was on the screen in front of me, intent on the reverend's words. I should have been pleased, but, sadly, little Elizabeth's red hair reminded me of Maureen Browne, and the church reminded me that's where I was supposed to be—not in the Walton's one but in my own, for the Holy Thursday service at which the priest would read the story of the Last Supper, and then, to illustrate how awful the world would be without Jesus for the three days to come, would clear the altar of linens and candlesticks and flowers and crucifixes. They would be returned to their proper places in time for the sunrise service on Sunday, though this year, Father Kulpa would probably just pack all that precious stuff in a box and ship it on over to Betty, since that seemed to be the thing everybody around here was doing.

Though I was so excited that Betty soon would be clearing up this whole mess, I was restless and sad that night, knowing I was missing the procession. It would have been the final year I would wear my uniform and communion veil and carry a pot of Easter lilies around the church three times before leaving it at the papier-mâché grave in which a plaster crucified Jesus the next day would be laid to rest—the same grave to which Bobby, in his freshly pressed uniform, would be looking strong as he joined the other older boys in carrying one of the Styrofoam boulders that would seal the crypt on Good Friday. Instead, I was a mile away, in my pajamas, Mrs. Zak sucking so loudly on her diabetic hard candy that she was drowning out John Boy's admissions interview at Boatwright College.

"You're going to bed after this is over," she snarled, but I shook my head stubbornly, not caring if I was being difficult—she already disliked me. I sat in my place and had a good fifth of the screen etched away when I heard the car doors. Then the kitchen door. Then they all came in, the happiest they'd looked in ages. My mother ran in and hugged me, her coat chilly.

"She said hello! She knew each of us! They want to test her, but they think she will be home in a day or two. Isn't that perfect? By Easter morning!"

It was perfect! Finally, everybody would know I wasn't the awful person who dragged a kid out of the house without her hat and mittens, that I wasn't somebody who would take a small child out to a dangerous place and not think of her, all because of a boy! Finally, people wouldn't be mad at me! I was certain my parents would call up some of the reporters who kept tucking their business cards under the door, writing on them things like, "Please call when Betty comes to" and "Would like to spend 24 hours with the family for special feature," even "Interested in Sunday Roto story on the elder Mrs. Milewski's cooking. . . ." My parents would tell them all to come over and write the most unbelievable story—how I had to endure weeks and weeks of alienation and ill feelings, all the while being the one in the right. I would say I was sorry about leaving the house without full permission, but that this should be a lesson to children everywhere, that they should mind their elders, including elder children in the family. And I would point at Betty and would say, "Or this could be you," and Betty would be told to nod solemnly, then she would give me a hug and thank me for trying to save her life, for flinging her up onto that bush, up and out of the way of getting clipped by the truck worse than she had been, and maybe she would start to cry when she saw how much it had cost me, in so many ways, to have done that. There would be photos, this time mine the biggest one, a freshly shot portrait, after I'd recovered fully, of course, with my collar straightened the way it ought to be, and there I would be on the film and radio reports that they would run over and over after starting out, "An incredible story tonight, one of misunderstanding and explanation, and a look at a true hero . . ."

I got up to go to my room. And that's when I heard the phone call. To Worcester. The one that informed me I was not going to be so lucky as to have Betty put it all in order. Whereas I could only remember bits and pieces of that last hour before the accident, it turned out Betty could only recall up to Christmas—the day after she got to this country. My mother spoke into the phone: "It's sad, but it's so sweet—she keeps talking about yesterday as being the big tree and all the food and the songs and the presents. That's all she remembers."

The alphabet, what she'd caught of it, had gone out the window. She knew little more than she had known when she'd arrived here. "But at least she is alive," my mother kept saying. "She's young—how bad is missing a couple of months out of her life at this age?"

"How wonderful it is," my father yelled into the phone while my mother still held it, "that my little girl will be returning home!" With her bandages and her flowers and her many pills, and with no idea that she'd disobeyed. With no idea what it all had done to me.

I went up to my room, to get as far away as I could from them, and their chatter, and their laughter, and their celebration, and the hurt and the reality that this was how it was going to be from now on. Forever.

On Holy Saturday morning, my father and Johnny Frydryk carried Betty's twin bed downstairs and set it up in the living room. The kid was unable to walk, never mind climb a whole flight of stairs, and this would be her bedroom until she got better. Humming the whole time, even though to keep the solemn mood of the weekend we weren't supposed to play any music until sunset on that day, they hauled down the mattress and the box spring, then headboard and footboard, the sideboards and the slats, the sheets and the pillows and the quilt with the two little girls who never should have left the shelter of that mushroom. Then they assembled everything in the middle of the room, so Betty could have a perfect view of the television set.

"You know I lit two candles every Sunday for the girls—the big kind, that last seven days," Johnny told my father. "I bet that's what did it."

Under the bed with his screwdriver, my father just said, "Thenk you."

They no sooner had completed their work, even fitted the mattress with its linens and lined up a few of Betty's stuffed animals, when the front bell rang, and I hid in the kitchen and watched from behind the door as my father, looking stunned, allowed three huge men to carry in pieces of the same kind of bed I'd had at the hospital. Huge, dull metal. With a quiet electric motor that, once they put everything together, they quickly demonstrated would move the top half of the bed up and down. The men turned the couch on its end and leaned it in a corner from which they'd cleared the four big boxes containing the recent delivery from members of the Kosciuszko Hall in Enfield: a portable television, a phonograph, an eight-track player, a reel-to-reel tape recorder, a set of speakers, and the pieces of a cabinet into which they all would fit once you put it together. The men set to work tearing down the little twin bed and insisted my father show them where they should return it. Representative Conway would want it that way, the men said. So touched had he been by Betty's act of bravery and selflessness that this donation was the least he could do for such a fine child.

I mistakenly had thought all this type of thing was winding down. The presents and letters had dwindled to ten or a dozen a day, though they had not decreased in their power to make you scratch your head. Postmarks were from all over the place—Kansas and Bermuda, Michigan, Alaska even, and Lake Tahoe. Canada, too, and one from somebody in Paris who had a relative in New York who had clipped out some story that ran there. Betty had received her fifth toy wagon, this one filled entirely with individual boxes of breakfast cereal. And now there was a bed that took up a good half of our front room, and my father standing next to it, arms folded across his chest, with no expression that I could read, so I made up a thought for him: "What did I get myself into with this Betty?" I imagined this, though I was almost positive such a thing had no way of entering his mind.

When they all left to pick her up from the hospital, they again left me alone with Mrs. Zak, who had just had her hair done for Easter and smelled of dye. She absentmindedly kept poking her fingers into the pieces of hair curled and lacquered at the edge of her neck while she walked around the house and commented how very lovely were the signs my mother and Babci had drawn and hung above the Frigidaire and from the buffet and over the hospital bed: "Welcome home, Betty!" "We missed you!" "Get well!" and all the other messages of love and encouragement nobody had bothered to sit down and spell out in poster paint when they were told I was getting out.

When she was done with her snooping (she thought I couldn't see her, but I know she went into the pantry for quite some time and that she stopped to read the personal appointments and notations written on the calendar on the back of the back door), Mrs. Zak peered out the window.

"Will you get a load of this . . . ," she said, stunned, but I wasn't interested, so I didn't. I was depressed, sitting at the dining room table picking through Betty's letters just to make myself feel worse. "Good luck," they said cheerily. "The Lord will help you persevere." "You make us proud!" "We don't know you, but we love you so much!" One was signed by a dog, somebody having put its paw in ink and pressed it inside a card.

Mrs. Zak was at the window, giggling and waving. I figured Betty had to have gotten here, so I went to hide upstairs. It was then I saw the commotion outside the window. Cars everywhere in the street. And trucks, one with the local TV station's name painted on the side. People from up and down the street suddenly there: Mrs. Chrusciel holding her cat. Mrs. Marcinkiewicz, who sang lead in the choir and had a big scarf wrapped around her important neck to keep it warm lest she catch something with the sunrise service only hours away. The plumber Eddie Swist, speaking and gesturing to a reporter who wrote down a lot of his words. Bibi Zbylot had her baby boy in a stroller and was showing him off to Carolyn's mother, who offered him a banana from the huge fruit basket she was holding. There were men with shoulderbags full of camera equipment standing and looking bored, smoking, once in a while cracking up over some joke. One woman I didn't know came over to them, and she must have thought she would make a good picture because she held out to their cameras her sign, in blue cut-out letters, with a yellow sun over the words "Welcome home, Betty!"

I wanted to yell, "She doesn't know anything you're saying! She doesn't know anything! She won't be able to tell anybody what really happened! I didn't do anything! Don't hate me!" But I didn't. I just watched and ran my tongue around the inside of my mouth as the crowd of people on the driveway parted, and my father, looking nervous, drove slowly into the driveway through the crowd. I spotted Betty in the backseat just as she looked up and spotted me in the house.

"*Siostra!*" I saw her scream as she bounced happily, and my mother, sitting next to her, reached over to make her still so she wouldn't have some kind of relapse.

"Donna!"

Chapter

*S*o we had our Easter complete with Betty risen from the dead.

Even with all they had to do with celebrating four elaborate Easter Sunday Masses in a row, Father Kulpa and Brother Mike found the time to come by the house for a few minutes that morning to do a special ceremony of thanksgiving next to Betty's fancy new bed. Father blessed her and her bandaged head and her one crunched-up foot, using a long, nasal Latin-sounding incantation that only Brother Mike knew the response to. Father gave communion to my parents and Babci and my Worcester grandparents, who needed a modern-day resurrection as a reason to stop their work for the day and come on out. Then Father walked over to me and set a hand on my head for a slow couple of seconds without saying a word. That right there was just about how everybody dealt with me. It's like there was something more wrong with me than the things you could see bandaged or sewn up, and nobody knew quite what to do with it.

Nobody, I have to say, except for Betty. She wanted me near

her at all times. And on the other side of the coin, I wanted nothing to do with her. Look at it my way: How had everything been before she came? Perfect, that's how. How about after she got here? One awful mess. I hated her for being here, and I hated my father, who was the one responsible.

Understand that except for Communism and the Devil, I had never, ever hated anything. Certainly no people. There had been no reason to. And it was a new experience, like tasting a food you'd heard a lot about but never tried yourself. And as it is with some new foods, it was a lousy taste—metallic, bitter, and even sickening at first. But I have to say I found I certainly could get used to it, the flavor of this intense, trembling disdain of two people. And I found I could even crave it. So hate was what I took in more and more of every day, steeling my eyes at my father and Betty, cursing them from behind my metal and elastics, loathing them for how they'd wrecked my world. My life. How they'd taken the perfect place that had been my home. How they'd taken my family. How they'd taken my music. How they'd run everything over and crushed it up, then swept it into a heap and disposed of it where I'd never be able to find it and put it back together. How they'd made it so I wouldn't even be interested in fixing everything if I had the chance.

Dragging around all that hate, I moped around the house not caring about anything, and looking it. My mother had to yell at me to get me to change my clothes, or brush my hair. I stopped marking off the days on my calendar until Dr. Pressman would free my mouth. Because I didn't care anymore. Why should I want to talk when I wasn't going to try to explain?

I went to bed early and hoped for long dreams about Aniela teaching me how to ride that horse fast past everything I hated. We'd hop on—I even had my very own drab, aproned, farm-girl dress on during these visits—and we'd go flying past the blurs that were my father and Betty and their big phonics book, past the crowd of people lining up with their desserts and checks and newspaper clippings, past the reporters with their notebooks and the photographers with their cameras, the men with their film footage and the women with their radio microphones. Aniela and I would end up in that field, picking flowers for our mothers and our Babcis, watching the Polish boys dancing on a rock in the middle of the river, calling to us in words that both of us could understand. I felt she waited for me in my head every night, and I was disappointed on the mornings when I woke to find I never had met up with her, or remembering nothing if I had. Every morning I slept as late as I wanted to, which was very, very late for me—well into "Truth or Consequences" some days, once in a while catching only Bob Barker's cheerful farewell before the noontime news began. When I'd finally come down the stairs and pass through the living room on the way to my sixteen-ounce glass of breakfast, Betty would wave a stack of books for me to read to her—like that was something I actually could do. I'd walk right by without looking, and she'd whimper, and finally my mother would beg me to pay her attention.

"Donna, please," she would ask. "Do it for me—so I can get some work done?"

So, for my mother only—not for Betty and not for all the friends of Mrs. Conway who suddenly thought there was nothing better in the world than a homemade shift—I'd sit next to the hospital bed and would simply turn the pages in front of Betty's face, my eyes on the television, letting the kid figure out the rest.

"Pretty," she'd say, pointing to the pictures in front of her, then looking to me for praise, I guess, that she had used the correct word. I didn't acknowledge her. I felt defeated. Persecuted. The last thing I wanted to do was entertain the person whose fault it was that I was like this, that we were like this, that everything was so awful. Besides, she had plenty to amuse herself with. We were tripping over the stuff, booting aside the Tressy doll with the crank in its back that made her hair longer or shorter, the Thumbelina infant that you wound up to make it circle its head ever so slightly, like it was alive. We knocked into the wooden blocks meant to teach her the alphabet, the children's encyclopedia set that would fit into the oak bookcase that my father had yet to assemble. Along with the two baskets the Easter bunny had left on the porch for Betty and me, seven other baskets, each with her name written on it in a different hand, were waiting out there, a few on the front porch, a few on the side porch, one out on the curb, balanced on a snowbank, all fluorescent pink against the frozen gray mush. Still, Betty wanted none of that stuff. She wanted only me.

"Donna!" "Donna!" "Donna!"

When I ignored her, I knew there would be my mother, with a look that I imagined was saying, "You did this, now go and try to give her some happiness," even though her voice was saying only, "Please? For five more minutes? I have to get these buttons sewn on today."

So I went along with it and we played Mouse Trap and Easy Money and Operation, baked rubber scorpions in her Thingmaker, assembled a Yellow Submarine mobile, its little paper Johns, Pauls, Georges, and Ringos dangling from black threads. We put film in her new camera and plants in her terrarium, milk and ice and salt into her ice-cream maker and cranked it for hours. One whole afternoon was spent dressing Betty's rubber leg in the dozens of tiny socks a home economics class at a high school up near Bangor had knitted after hearing about her beloved toy in a news report.

We worked on the potholder loom, on the bead-stringing kit. We made pipe-cleaner people, we braided a doll's rug and stenciled sheets of stationery. We flew Colorform bees into her Colorform flowers, played Yertle the Turtle about a thousand times, and one stupid ring-toss game even more than that. In the game of Life, I cheated so as not to land on a space that would make me take a peg as a husband, or a pair of them as twins or any other kind of relatives. My pink peg and my pink peg alone sat in my little blue sedan as I spun the big dial and slid through the perils and obligations and thrills of modern, adult existence. I found I liked it that way. I liked it very much all by myself.

Then there was the overflowing basket of mail my mother finally wanted to deal with, and she suggested I be the one to take care of it, as I had all the time in the world, though in her defense she didn't put it that way. I couldn't read it to Betty, and she wouldn't have understood it anyway, so I just slit the envelopes and drew out card after card, showing her the pictures on the fronts, so many clowns and sad puppies and wishing wells wishing her well, then the writing and messages on the inside. Different colors of ink, some crayons, felt tips, several in pencil, all relaying the messages of so many people who were so sorry to hear about her accident, and were praying for her, and were thinking of her, and were wondering what they could do for her. Some said that in Polish writing, but, strangely to me, none of those were from her real family. No telegram assuring Betty her mother and father would be there soon, no inspirational prayer handwritten by Kasia, no drawing of her favorite tree from Olisia. Nothing. But Betty didn't seem to be concerned. She only smiled and clapped at the slitting of each envelope—especially once the money started falling out. Ones. Fives, tens. I went and got my mother when we hit the first twenty-dollar bill.

My parents took over the mail job after that, and after an argument over returning the cards (my father thought it was not proper to accept money from strangers, and my mother pointed around the room and told him then they should return all these gifts, too, and he answered didn't she remember he had wanted to do that in the first place, and she said that no, she didn't remember that, because she certainly would have agreed with him), they made a long list of who sent what so they could return a proper thank-you. Half the dining room table was taken over by the pile of greeting cards, the notepaper, and the stacks and stacks of more money than I'd ever seen.

One lady wrote how she had come from Poland, too, though it was long ago, and that a cardboard box had fallen on her head while she had been walking past the Square Lunch in downtown Springfield her second week here.

"Thought it was empty, the corner of it was what hit me, and that pointy part caused enough damage to require stitches and three days' pay missed from my job at the American Bosch," the lady, Jennie Szeliga, wrote in neat printing. "So even though I cannot afford it, I am sending a money order for

$25 because I know some of what trials Betty is going through."

One couple from Hatfield wrote that they had been trying to adopt a baby for a long time, and that Betty had inspired them to take in an older child. They sent a prayer card and promised they would mail her a photo of the little girl or boy that would have a home all because Betty had given them the idea. "The story of your pain will save one more life," they wrote, and I had to get some fresh air after that one.

Another card was handmade, by a kid, with a sailboat drawn in pencil on the outside, and one line on the inside, written in beginner's cursive: "I have a jerk for a sister, too."

For me, there were few pieces of mail except those from my godparents, my grandparents, Walter, Mrs. Dranka—people you'd expect to receive something from even if you went and murdered an entire town. I should add Maureen Browne to that list. Once a week I'd get a goofy card with a drawing of one of the Peanuts characters or a photograph of a zoo animal with some slogan like "Hang in There," or "Keep the Faith," or "Keep on Truckin.'" She'd usually write a few lines, like how they were considering moving her to the second floor, where she told me all the crazy people were kept, then would add her closure: Fondly, Maureen Browne. No one ever had written that word on anything meant for me. In my life I had received "love" endings, whether or not that was how the sender truly felt, along with enough "sincerely yourses" and "yours trulies," but no one had ever written the word "fond." It was like something you could climb into and curl up in, and it made me homesick for her, the only friend I had known in all that boring, lonesome, confusing hospital time. I wondered how she was, what she was doing. I made up scenarios like Maureen Browne was a fashion doll you have to invent a life for. I had her going into work and being surprised by a promotion that would make her the head nurse over all, with her own office. I had Dr. Young bursting into that office, which would be new and on the top floor, to present her with her own large box of maple sugar candy and to confess his love for her. Then I realized I had made myself jealous so I turned the interested man into someone else—the drug salesman who had given her the fancy nail file. Maureen Browne never told me what he looked like, but I made him into a toothy, boyish Bobby Kennedy type, with shirtsleeves rolled and striped tie tucked between the buttons of his expensive dress shirt as he leaned over the dead engine of his expensive company car just as Maureen was leaving the hospital, and she pulled over and asked if she could be of any assistance.

Sleeping, dreaming, drinking, trying out another or three or four of Betty's new things, this was the bulk of my day, every day. I most looked forward to the girls coming up to my room with my homework, a routine that had turned into their spreading their books out on the floor doing my tests and papers and projects and my staring out the window across the park and the hills and the sky as they told me what I was missing. Like how the gerbil Timmy Lech brought in for the science fair got loose in the corridor and how Pan, the maintenance man who just got here from Gdansk, thought it was a mouse rather than somebody's pet and chased it into the coal cellar with a broom. That Kathy Jurczyk's little sister used a black pen rather than a No. 2 pencil on her Iowa test, and how Sister Superior called all the classes onto the corridor and announced (though nobody but the little kids really believed it) that the entire school's results might be in jeopardy because of her not following specific directions. How Barbara Sloat, who always was getting yelled at for staring out the window, was doing that on Friday and saw a brush fire eating its way across the field behind the school. How the volunteer firemen raced to the school, still wearing their bar cloths and mechanics' coveralls and bank suits and butcher's aprons, and put it out before it got anywhere near the building. How Barbara was praised by the nuns, who said they would give her extra credit if she wrote a composition on what it was like to save a whole building full of the leaders of tomorrow.

The girls never once mentioned Bobby. And, not wanting to think about him or any of that anymore, I never asked.

"Your desk looks so funny with nobody sitting in it," Carolyn said sadly one afternoon, as she and Theresa completed my English assignment—the composition I was supposed to be dictating to them about how the Virgin Mary had intervened in my life. It was homework, but it also would be reviewed by the committee of nuns that would decide who would get to be this year's May Queen, the lucky, lucky eighth-grade girl who would wear a dress almost like a bride's and, in the culmination of a long evening ceremony of prayer and singing, would climb a special satin-covered staircase up to the statue of Mary, and would get to place a rhinestone crown right on the head of the Mother of God. I had about as much of a chance of being selected May Queen as I did Sister of the Year, but that wasn't mentioned by my ghostwriters, who hunched over sheets of scrap paper, scribbling and giggling. I'd never seen Theresa take such joy in an assignment.

"It's a lot more fun to make things up than it is to actually write what is true," she observed. "How about this:

" 'I thought it was a car headlight coming into my window the other night, but, no, it was St. Mary. She told me not to tell anybody, but I cannot keep it to myself anymore . . .' "

Carolyn snatched the paper from her and looked at the words. "You can't write that! Who's gonna believe it?"

"It'll get her to be May Queen—how many people do you think will have an essay like this? They're all going to be writing about how they prayed to her to pass a math test, and it worked."

"But this is such a lie," Carolyn said, then she looked at me. "Isn't it?"

I rolled my eyes.

"Everybody lies on these things," Theresa argued. "Last year? When Linda Bish won? She wrote how she talked her parents into naming their new baby Mary? Saying all that stuff about how it would start her life out on the right foot, and what an honor it would be for the baby? That was a bunch of baloney! Her parents were the ones who wanted Mary. Linda was dying for them to call her Brittany Twilight."

I remembered last May, watching Linda Bish walk gingerly up those slippery steps in an actual wedding gown given her by an aunt who ended up having only boys, so who was she going to hand it down to? Her arms shook as she raised the crown high, then lowered it onto Mary's head, then, how rather than begin the first few words to *"O Maryo Życie Moje"*— "O Mary, My Life"—she just looked out at the parishioners and broke down in tears, and everyone in the church did the same, the moment being such a touching one. But, I now realized, Linda probably had just been hit at that very moment by the fact that she was up there because of a lie, and she was headed straight to hell.

"Let's not goof around—we'll just get caught," Carolyn said, reading my mind. "Just put how Donna likes St. Mary because she wears blue."

"Oh, that's real interesting . . ."

Except when they had their music lessons on Tuesdays, the girls stayed each afternoon for a long time, filling in my history workbook and using my protractor to measure the angles on my test sheet, all in all getting me very good marks. The first afternoon, they stayed for supper, then into the night, and we all fell asleep on the floor as, one of them on either side of me, they talked back and forth about the guidance counselor with the floppy ears that the high school had sent over to speak to the eighth-graders about the courses they might want to take come September, and the careers they might want to steer toward in the next four years.

"But, you know," they'd always end up, "none of this is any good without you there, Donna." And in the dark I would smile to hear such a thing, that a place could be that much worse just for its lack of me.

Seven weeks and three days after the accident, Dr. Pressman took his own little pair of scissors and snipped the elastics from my teeth. My jaw dropped open and stayed that way. I needed a hand to close it, and it fell open again. Dr. Pressman took that opportunity to reach inside and pry the metal fittings from my teeth with several quick yanks that probably would have hurt if I hadn't been so preoccupied thinking about being finally freed.

Then he instructed me, "Say something," and he began to whistle, softly, like background music to some important scene in a movie.

"Hey," I said back, quietly, blandly. I was aware of how I sounded round and funny.

"Oh, doctor, this is wonderful!" my mother told him happily from behind me. I heard her clap her hands.

"Yes," he said. "The muscles have atrophied. But she'll be all right once she starts using them regularly. You'll be begging for her to shut up!"

Dr. Pressman laughed heartily. My mother laughed nervously. As for me, I just thought how that was nothing she was going to have to worry about. Let those muscles atrophy some more—whatever atrophying was—for all I cared. I had been thin to begin with—"Stringy" was the only nickname I was ever given by the kids in school—but I had dropped twenty-four pounds from living out of a glass. Often I heard several of my mother's customers say something about my being "model thin" now, and I thought that was great. If anything good could come out of this, maybe it could be a career for me in London or Paris. Stringy: the next Twiggy. Wearing go-go boots and minis and false eyelashes and dating famous people. Living by herself. Far, far, far away from home.

"How can we ever thank you, doctor?" my mother asked, clasping his fat, antiseptic hand.

"Just stay out of trouble," he scolded, pointing his finger at me, good-naturedly, I have to say, but it still hurt.

I didn't speak all the way back from Dr. Pressman's, but my mother made up for that, talking nonstop for most of the twenty-two miles back to home.

"I am so happy for you!" she said.

"It is just fantastic how well you are recovering!"

"This is such a wonderful day!"

I nodded, gripping the armrest, waiting for what she must have been dying to ask. But there was nothing, no questions, no "So what really happened that afternoon?" It was odd, considering there had to be one or two things she might have wondered in all the time that I hadn't been able to reply properly. But there was no interrogation. She must have been waiting for a confession. I turned to look out the window and to hide how I was testing the jaw, moving it up and down every once in a while, trying out the weird, rubbery sensation of its new ability to move, and I remember we were passing the Arby's roast beef place on Boston Road when I decided to see where talking might get me.

"I told her to stay home," I said. The words were soft and had big spaces between them, and my mother had to ask me, "What?"

"I said . . . ," I stopped here for a few seconds. "I told her to stay home. Betty. I told her to stay in the kitchen that day. She didn't listen."

My mother was looking at me and back at the road, back at me, then at the road. I could see another accident in the making. But, luckily for some other innocent person in this world, she decided to put on her blinker, and she drove into the parking lot of Friendly's ice cream home office and stopped the car next to a big yellow bus belonging to the Quaboag Valley YMCA.

"Tell me," my mother said. So I did. I told her every detail of what I knew of that afternoon, about Bobby on the phone, about Betty in the kitchen, about Betty suddenly in the forest, then suddenly in the road, grabbing for my paper, then me, trying to pitch her out of the way. I told her everything while dozens of kids who'd just taken a tour of the plant stood around our car finishing their free cones before riding home and while a man in a white lab coat and white plastic helmet with a maroon *F* on its front ushered another eager group through the door marked "TOURS ONLY." And when I was done telling her, my mother slid over and held me tightly and for so long that the kids outside started to point at us and laugh, though I didn't care. Eventually, she started the car and got us home, without saying anything else.

In the kitchen, I said "hi" to Babci, who hugged me delicately. "Noodles tonight!" she exclaimed like they were some kind of delicacy only rich people ever got to eat. I passed right by Betty, who called fruitlessly for me to operate the Ken

doll so Skipper and he could dance, and I climbed the stairs up
to my room and put on the radio loudly and spoke to myself
behind the three o'clock news and its report on a woman in
Ludlow who had a frozen pizza stolen from the spare freezer
she keeps on her back porch, and I said aloud what I had
wanted to hear from somebody for so long:

"Everything will be okay."

I repeated that several times, but it ended up making me
uneasy, talking to myself like that, saying such things to no
one, as if I were a crazy person. But I went and said it one more
time, just to make sure that I had heard it.

Just for me, the noodles had been boiled to the consistency
of glue, but I ate them anyway, along with the mushrooms
sliced so thin and the onions chopped into neat, soft, miniscule
cubes. My father knew I'd had my appointment, but he made
no mention of anything when he came in the door, or when he
came to the dinner table. My mother, usually good for a few
bits about something that had happened during the day, was
as quiet as she'd been after I talked to her. Only Babci and
Betty spoke—well, Babci, mostly, with Betty throwing in a few
words when she detected they were the right ones to say—and
they told us how Johnny Frydryk's house was getting mea-
sured for aluminum siding.

After supper, I saw my mother follow my father when he
disappeared down into the cellar, and as I helped carry a few
things to the kitchen I noticed I heard none of his usual work
sounds coming up through the floor. There was just silence.

"I'll throw this out," I told Babci, taking the small dish of
onion wrappings and heading outside, but I first went to the
cellar window, and I crouched next to the screen, and I
watched my father leaning against his workbench, his arms
folded across his chest, listening as my mother spoke to him.
She gestured with a hand occasionally, but most of the time
she stood still and told him very slowly the things I had said to
her. "A thousand times I've begged you to give her a break,"
my mother said. "Now you see you must."

A thousand times? She had been pulling for me in stray

moments that I never knew about! Even before I'd told her all the truth. I don't think I ever loved her more than I did at that moment.

As she spoke, my father did not nod back at her, he did not disagree. He simply looked at my mother with the same unreadable expression I remembered his wearing when the car salesman was trying to tack a list of what he called options onto the basic auto we'd picked out.

My father did not buy the bucket seats, he did not buy the vinyl roof, he did not buy the air conditioning. And he did not buy what I had told my mother on the way home.

"So this is Betty's fault?" he asked her quietly, still in his place next to the vise.

"Well, not her *fault*, I'd say," my mother answered carefully, "she was just acting like a child. They both were—they're kids, after all. Weren't you ever a kid, Adam? Didn't you ever do anything stupid?"

At that moment, ten storms blew across my father's face, each one of them wilder and more devastating than the last. He stood up straight, and he took a step toward my mother, and he spoke with a sternness I'd never heard him use on her or on anybody else.

"Donna must realize responsibility," he said slowly. "She didn't that day, but she must now. That girl is a cripple, it is Donna's fault, and both of them must live with that. I'll hear no more of her lies. We're not talking about this again. Ever."

Then my father walked away, over to the table saw and plugged it in. He frowned as he guided a long thin piece of wood into the teeth of the blade, and the machine screamed and rang as it made two halves of what once had been a whole. My mother stayed where she'd been standing, but now she had her hands flat against her ears, and she was shaking her head slowly. Outside, I collapsed against the foundation, resolving then and there for the final time to let people think of me what they wanted to think. I would never again try to tell them, and I meant it this time. A small wind, probably left over from what had just blown through the basement, rolled across the driveway and caught the biggest onion skin in my bowl of garbage and sent it flying helpless past the back porch, past the garage, into the black darkness where you never know what is waiting for you.

Later that night I was moving Aniela's photo to the page containing the prayer for the conversion of Russia when my mother came into my room and brought the vanity stool over to my side of the bed and told me of what she called their conversation.

I didn't even pretend it was news to me. I just listened, and I nodded my head at the right times to show that I was hearing what she was saying—how she had tried to tell him what I had spilled out to her on the way home, how he would not even take it into consideration, how she had tried to defend me, how he was such a good man but there are just some things he has not one ounce of patience or understanding for and she wished she could explain why but she hadn't a clue.

"I don't get it," she said. "I tried to tell him, Donna. I tried. I've tried to talk to him so many times about you—ever since all this happened. He won't hear anything. I just don't get it." She sniffled, and wiped her eyes with the tails of her bathrobe belt. Then she took my hand. "He is a good man, though—you know that. He does love you. Some people are just different, that's all."

I felt there was nothing I could do but tell her that I understood, even though I didn't. I just wanted to make her feel a little better, and I just wanted to put an end to our talk. "It's late," she said, and she slid me into her freshly Oil of Olayed neck and held onto me tightly, then stood up, flipped off my light and left the room.

I turned the lamp back on and I prayed for Russia. I flipped the pages and Aniela and I read whatever I came across: the Prayer for Heathens, the Prayer for the Unborn, the Prayer for Vocations. Finally, I said the Prayer for a Quick and Painless Death, and I shut out the light.

The nuns allowed me to graduate from eighth grade that first Sunday in June, but only on the condition that I showed up for the ceremony. I did, and it was one of the most awful days of my life. I had to stand on stage, with everybody staring at me, and I not once even attempted to look over at Bobby, though I knew he was there somewhere in the group of kids on the boys' side of the stage.

Due to my height, I was assigned to stand between Terri Ann Wojtowicz and Debbie Dymek on the highest step of the risers at the back of the stage, and from there I stared the whole two and a half hours way over the heads in the audience, over Babci and my mother (try as he might have—though I wonder how hard he actually had tried—my father told me quickly one night he could not get out of his Sunday cleaning job that day), out the front door to the huge green bushes down by the roadside, and I did so all the way through the national anthem, through "Moon River," through the speech by Barney Korzec in which we were reminded that today was the first day of the rest of our lives and several women in the audience looked at one another with wide eyes, like they believed he had gone and thought that up himself. I stared out the door through the rendition of "I'd Like to Teach the World to Sing" by the grade three and four girls and through "Joy to the World" by the sixth-grade boys' chorus. And I stared out the door through the "Zorba the Greek" dance by the first-grade boys and the cancan by the fifth-grade girls. Then, finally, came the time for the presentation of diplomas by, as he was described in the program, our beloved pastor.

Sister Superior stood at the side of the stage and called the graduates' names, boys first, and when they walked over to Father Kulpa, she read aloud the description that was printed next to their photos in the programs that most people in the audience were fanning themselves with by that point.

I awaited the S's, my chance finally to see Bobby, to make eye contact, maybe to have a word—I *would* speak to him— after this was over and to tell him, finally, that before the snowballs, those few minutes at the river had been the most perfect piece of time I had ever known. There were sixteen boys, and he was near the end alphabetically, between, I knew, Richie Smist ("Richie is a whiz at math. Already he has paved his path. A good job may he earn. Let this good man get his turn.") and Phil Ugrodnik ("With his great personality and charm, Phil could not be harmed. He will in the future be great. Everyone who knows Phil, could not hate."). But there went Richie, and next came Phil, in between them only the announcement by Sister that though he was listed in the programs, which had been written months ago to take advantage of a savings offer at the printer, former class member Robert Smola since has moved away with his family.

No Bobby across the stage, no Bobby anywhere around here. I didn't even have a state or a country to place him in. I only knew he was gone, and gone for a while now. I was stunned. Ill. Shaking. Nothing like the description of me in the program, which had been written back before Christmas, back when what Sister read was true:

> Donna is short and funny, and always as sweet as honey.
> She has plenty of musical brains, and is sure to reach what she aims.

Near tears, which the audience probably translated as great embarrassment for my past evil deeds rather than fresh heartbreak, I grabbed from Father Pastor the rolled-up piece of paper that was my diploma for the Class of 1973 and that was, as Barney Korzec had called it in his lengthy monologue, my key to the future.

The most important thing, I had to keep telling myself, was that I was moving on. Out of that school and into summer. On to high school, to graduate from there and be on my own for good, each moment that passed being one more kick toward shore, away from the things I wanted to forget or get away from. I was moving on all right—I just didn't know I would be moving for real.

None of us knew it, actually. There was just a knock on the side door that Saturday morning in the middle of June, while my mother sprayed on Windex to shine the slats of Betty's bed, where the kid and I had the cartoons on and the Play-Doh out.

I had both my arms to use by then, and was generally feeling pretty good, though I got tired a lot, mainly from just being lazy and not going outside and not eating as much as I always had. But I must have looked somewhat like my old self because one day my mother came to me with a request.

"How about playing a little music?" she asked me gently as I listlessly flipped the pages of Volume N in the *Little Folks Encyclopedia*. Betty was pointing and laughing at the drawing of the nene, a goose that the book said lives in the Hawaiian Islands, where it eats berries and vegetation as it whiles away its days on the endangered species list.

Music. I looked around the room—did she mean the record player, the 8-track, the reel-to-reel? Which of Betty's toys did she want me to turn on for her now?

"On your accordion?" my mother added gently. "To amuse Betty?"

Like she needed some other diversion. Five months after she had been stupid enough to run out in front of the truck, Betty continued to get mail and packages and attention, including a monthly photo feature in the *Penny Saver* showing her progress—one less bandage, one more step across the living room. Though my parents drove down to the office and asked the paper not to, they kept on running the pictures, and they kept on including our address in the little story that ran beneath each photograph, and then it would start all over again—more cards and boxes and pies and candies. Betty had enough to distract her from the fact that she couldn't run and jump like other kids right then, something I have to say didn't really seem to bother her.

"No," I said to my mother with a sharp shake of my head and the grim face to match, refusing her for what had to be the first time in my life. The person I had played for when I did play was now somebody who was as close to me as Mars and about as visible, working double shifts as he was and now largely as black and silent as his records, their tales of joyful feet and happy farmers and sunny fields buried under supplies for the sickroom and cartons of thank-you cards waiting to be addressed by my mother and signed with a shaky B by the Betty herself. It would take a whole lot more than a slow day for the little one to get me to start all that again.

"No," I mouthed, turning away, wondering if the nene knew how few were its numbers, and whether it just looked around at all the extra food and space and figured "more for me!"

Carolyn and Theresa were still interested in their music, and I would sometimes sit and listen to their duets, feeling even worse when I heard the places where I might have joined in, where I would have added a chord or even broken away into my own solo and made them mad by drowning them out. If I closed my eyes, I could see the three of us up on some stage, wearing identical costumes, making somebody's wedding day that much more special because they were able to book my all-girl polka band when everyone else had told them there was no way that we would even return the telephone call—we were on the road too much or in the recording studio too often to deal directly with our fans. An answering service would collect our calls, and I would need both sides of a piece of paper to write on each time I phoned it to retrieve the messages.

Even though the girls, too, urged me to play, asking me to remember what fun we had, I said no.

"My arm doesn't work that way anymore," I told them, and I would add something about how I felt really bad about that. Next to Babci and my mother, it hurt the most to lie to those two. You see, physically, I was perfect. I could chew Tootsie Rolls with not even the slightest pain, and, when I was sure that nobody was looking, I swung like Tarzan on the rope that hung from the walnut tree next to the railroad tracks.

Betty was much improved as well, but she didn't hide it from anybody. And the reporters made sure that the entire world knew how great she was doing, returning every so often to do a follow-up piece on how Betty could walk without crutches or how her hair was growing long again, all of them ending their stories with comments about Betty now being "just like any other child." The *Daily News* marked her return to school that fall with a special four-page pullout on her "heart-wrenching, heartwarming journey back to life," and the editor, a Fu-Manchued guy whom my father years later stood with for a photograph because of his resemblance to Lech Walesa, drove out to the house to present Betty with a scrapbook containing each and every story and photo run on her—which was a lot. The cover was of fake red leather and had been stamped in gold paint with the words "You have touched our hearts." My parents cried when they saw it, pointing at the shiny letters reverently like God himself had put them there.

When the doorbell rang that Saturday, my mother looked up from shining Betty's bars and asked me, "Who's that?" like I was supposed to know. I didn't say anything and continued to squish different colors of Play-Doh together, blending them forever into a whole new shade.

My mother gave a huff and shook her head at me. I was being difficult and knew it, but I didn't care—though it sometimes made me sad to do this to her. I knew from the heating grate that she hadn't been keen on the Betty idea from the start. So, secretly, she was on my side. She just didn't know that I knew she had shared some of my reservations about Betty from the beginning.

"Hello," called a voice through the screen door. "Mr. Milewski? Mrs. Milewski?"

I saw my mother step back from the door, then look down at herself, at her apron and sneakers, at the dust rag in her hand. "Representative Conway! Mrs. Conway!" she breathed. "Oh, please, pardon my appearance." She stopped, and none of them spoke. Then she hurried, "Won't you come in?"

My mother nervously told the Conways that she was afraid the house was a mess, though that truly was not the case. She alone saw dust and spots and dirt that nobody else did, and Saturday morning was the time she worked to get rid of what she'd been glaring at all week, scrubbing and wiping and sweeping to the beat of Andy Chubryla's show blasting crystal clear from Betty's new stereo.

"I'm not here to inspect," Representative Conway said with a chuckle. "I'm not staying—and neither are you."

Mrs. Conway beamed, and her husband twirled his straw hat around his right hand and smiled at my mother as if he were giving her time to figure out what he was talking about.

She had no clue. "I'm sorry? What do you mean?"

"Get everybody together. We're going for a ride." He looked into the living room. "Come, children!" he called. I smirked.

Did he expect Betty could just hop up and run out the door? And did he expect me to want to go anywhere with him, this phoney?

Mrs. Conway had been to our house more times than a calculator could total. Mr. Conway—Representative Conway, as my parents and Babci called him since his big victory the first week of May, when he won the job in the special election made necessary by the resignation of a representative who was offered a big-time job in what the Conways called the private sector, wherever that was—had been here once before, the first week Betty was home from the hospital. He had carried into the house a cage containing four live and tiny chicks that peeped and shuddered and that now, grown the size of pigeons, lived in a coop my father attached to the garage and carved a wooden sign for: "Betty's Barn," with a neat row of eggs scratched across the bottom. Representative Conway shook all our hands that day—even mine—with an enthusiastic grip, and gave Betty's bed a try, laughing and stretching out next to her as she proudly worked the controls that made it move. He said the gift of the bed was the least he could do for such a fine family that had helped him win the chance to reach out and assist his fellow human beings.

He appeared to be on one of those missions that Saturday, arriving in a spacious van that would allow Betty to ride in comfort without being scrunched up. My mother ordered me to change into something presentable, as she put it, and I lingered upstairs until I saw she was done primping Betty, something I detested being any part of.

"Hurry, please?" she asked me, and I sighed and slowly cooperated.

"Hurry!" Betty echoed, clapping.

My mother's back turned, I shot the kid a dirty look, and she stared at me, frowning in puzzlement, as my mother carried her from the room. Babci was called from next door, and required not only ten repetitions of the story of how the Conways had appeared at our door, but she also needed extra time to change from the housedress in which she had been cleaning her own spots and dust since way before the sun had come up. Finally, we piled into the van, Representative Conway carrying Betty to the front seat, where he belted her in, and he drove us in the direction of Blue Ribbon.

So he wanted us to see how *kielbasa* was made. Big deal, and something I'd witnessed a thousand times. Only I had news for him: The plant was closed for cleaning on weekends. I knew that because that's why he didn't see my father anywhere at our house, where, like any normal father, he should have been, cutting the grass, then using an old putty knife to scrape the thick layer of chopped-up clippings from underneath the mower. Instead, my father was inside Blue Ribbon, scraping God knows what from inside the machines that all worked together to turn out the sausages that scented the neighborhood—and the town on a good windy day—with garlic and hickory. But no, look, there was my father, not crawling around inside some sausage-making gizmo, but outside the plant, in his regular clothes, standing on the front walk, smoking next to the trademark plastic pig and steer that wore plastic blue ribbons fresh with new coats of cerulean paint. He ground his cigarette into the gutter when we pulled up, and he climbed inside wordlessly, giving my mother a confused look, then shaking Representative Conway's hand and nodding at Mrs. Conway, who sat up front, next to Betty, in a daisy-print halter dress and jacket, the scraps from which my mother had made into a shoulder bag for me that I feebly had pretended to like but that I wouldn't have been caught dead using in public.

"Find their station, dear," Representative Conway directed his wife, pointing at the van's radio. She turned it on and then turned around to us.

"What number is it?" she wanted to know. "You know. Your polkas." My father consulted his watch to see which program was on at that hour, and he quietly informed Mrs. Conway, sort of self-consciously using its slogan: "WARE–AM1250— Where the polkas play!"

Mrs. Conway spun the dial, and we heard blips and pieces of talking, then preaching, then drumming, then singing, and the chilling tone that was a test of the Emergency Broadcast System. Then some static, then Mrs. Conway landed right on

"J.D.'s Polish Variety Program," where J.D. weekly reminded us that variety truly was the name of the game. And he also reminded us that Ray Henry would be appearing at the park tomorrow, to kick off the new season of picnics.

"Pulaski Park is one of my favorite places in the district," Representative Conway broke in as if he were answering a question, leaning toward the backseat and looking at us in the rearview mirror. "Such wonderful people! And that food!"

He was driving us up Baptist Hill now, farther and farther away from town, past the water tanks and the orchard that allows you to "pick your own pears," a phrase my father never got used to seeing, saying that to him it sounded like we should all stay home. I knew that if we kept on driving, we'd soon be on Boston Road. And heading left on that for a few hours, we could be in Boston itself. Going right for the same amount of time, we'd land in New York. Maybe this would be kind of interesting after all.

But nobody said anything. None of us asked where we were going. It was like we were used to having somebody come to our house and to our work in the middle of the day and yank us away in a strange car, with sort of strange people, bound for a destination unknown. We all just silently watched all the trees go by and listened to the music. At one break in the woods there was a field, where Chrissy Zombak led four kids on a pony ride. The mule she rode looked old and had sad eyes.

J.D.'s theme for the day was bird tunes, so we heard *"Miała Baba Koguta,"* about some old lady who kept a rooster in her shoe. Then *"Przepioreczka"*—"My Little Quail"—about a hen who escaped its cage and ran into the wheat field, and the guy telling the story was singing how he sped after it with his feet bare. I had a suspicion that it was one of those songs that sounded like it was about a bird, but really was about a girl.

My father tapped his hand on my mother's. Babci gave little bounces of her head to the beat of the music. Representative Conway was humming along to the music, though he didn't really know the melody. He looked very happy, and once in a while Mrs. Conway would turn and smile at all of us. We would smile right back, until she turned away.

"I hope I didn't leave my oven on," Babci worried, as she always did every time she was anywhere farther than ten feet from her door, even though she routinely unplugged every lamp and radio, absolutely everything short of the stove and the refrigerator, and then made sure everything was in the "off" position each time she left the house.

"You checked, I saw you," my mother assured her, as somebody always had to.

"Well, I had a *ciastka* in there this morning, I would hate to think that I left it on. The frosting's ready . . ."

"Here we are," Mrs. Conway said happily.

Representative Conway slowed down the van and took a right at a tree marked by a bunch of red and white balloons. They looked so out of place, being out in the middle of nowhere, not even a street sign to mark the dirt road. We drove for another minute, then suddenly, "Here we are," Mrs. Conway said again, and we turned into the driveway of a long, low, blindingly white modernish house with a big red-and-white bow attached to its front door.

So the Conways had bought themselves a home in the country and wanted us to see it. Just so they could show us how much better off they were than we were. I decided I'd stay in the van, in protest against their disgusting pride. Besides, they wouldn't miss me. Enough other people apparently had made the trip all the way out to the woods to gawk at the tidy front yard, at the rosebushes blooming red and white beneath the wide front bay window, at the wrought-iron bench on the flagstone landing, at the neat two-car garage filled with shiny new lawn equipment that had been pushed aside to make room for a line of long, decorated tables holding party food.

"We're here!" Representative Conway called. "Everyone—please—step outside!"

Like I said, I remained in my place, against the window, even after Betty had been unbuckled and unloaded into the tiny wheelchair the hospital had loaned us for trips to mass and the doctor. I stayed in my seat even after they had helped Babci make her way out the side door.

"Come on," my mother ordered seriously, but I only shook my head, then turned away, looking into the thick trees, finding a woodpecker hopping up the side of one, banging its red head and making a loud noise that sounded like it would hurt.

"She's tired," I heard my mother tell Mrs. Conway, who clucked sadly in my direction and, using baby talk, whispered "The poor thing."

I sank down and watched my family add to the growing number of people now crowded onto the grass, including some of the same photographers and TV people I recognized from Betty's stories. Not only were the Conways showing this off to us, they wanted to tell the world how they could afford two houses, their lives being such a chore that they just needed a place to get away to and relax. It was pathetic, Representative Conway beaming and taking his place behind a little podium that somebody wheeled out from the garage. He clapped into the air: "Everyone, everyone, it's time to begin!"

The news people shuffled up closely, craning their necks to get the best view, the best shot. I hated them all for the part they had played in making me the guilty one. Not a single one of them ever had come up and asked me my side of things, never did any of them show any interest in me and my story. They just wanted to know about Betty, whose face they described as "button-nosed," her hair "angel-like," her new parents and her new grandmother "devoted," "spiritual," and "loving," her plight "unfair," "undeserved."

Except for the time one of them had taken our photograph from the hospital room door, I had never been so close to the news people without the wall of my home between us. Here was their perfect chance if they wanted to write the truth about me. But none of them even glanced into the van. They just mashed into a semicircle and called "Betty—over here! Smile!" and dozens of flashes went off.

Several men in hot-looking business suits lined up behind Representative Conway, and I watched Mrs. Conway herd my family up next to them, settling Betty in front, where she could better see the people who were yelling to her. Representative Conway clapped again and removed some cards from inside the white blazer that a sweaty young man had run over with. The guy even had people to get him his clothes.

Representative Conway began to speak. He said what a wonderful day this was, and wasn't it something how even the weather had cooperated. He thanked everyone for coming and said they would not leave disappointed. "No, no," he stressed, his face serious. "Not in the least!" He promised there would be tours of the house later, and that there was plenty of food and drink for everyone in the garage. Then he turned and winked back at Babci, saying, "And for once, you didn't have to cook!" She either didn't hear or didn't get his comment, for she displayed no reaction.

Then Representative Conway explained. "Because, after all, this is *your* party. This is *your* celebration." And then he swept his hand widely around, like the models did on "Let's Make a Deal," and he said. "This, all this, is *your new home!*"

The people in the audience clapped and cheered and whistled. More flashbulbs went off, and the TV people jockeyed their cameras in closely as my parents looked at one another, confused.

"I said," Representative Conway repeated, "this is your new home!" Now he was positioning his glasses onto his face and was reading from a paper: "All courtesy of the wonderful Carpentry Department at Pathfinder Regional Vocational Technical High School, the generous students of which chose as this year's home-building project the complete and total renovation of this once-delapidated, deserted home into the state-of-the-art showcase it now is—and into the new home for you that it now is!"

More cheering, more applause, more pictures taken, more blank looks from my mother, my father, my Babci. I watched all this from my seat, through the van's gaping side door, like this was happening to somebody else, to somebody else's family. Betty knew nothing of what was going on, her attention focused on my mother's handbag as she snapped and unsnapped and snapped the catch.

"And this dear little girl," Representative Conway went on, pointing at Betty, "is the reason."

Betty didn't look up, now busy pulling my mother's rain bonnet from its little vinyl sleeve.

"Touched beyond words by her misfortune earlier this year,

the students were brokenhearted to learn that our little Betty was confined to the first floor of her home because of her indefinite inability to climb stairs," Representative Conway boomed. "When this one-floor building became town property through a tax problem, Carpentry Department Chairman Louis Krolik approached selectmen and asked that this project be approved."

Here the guy who had to be Louis Krolik stepped forward slightly from the line of people in suits and nodded his head to acknowledge the cheers for his thoughtfulness. Then he brought out his own speech card and headed to the podium. When he got there, he turned to look at my parents, managing to speak into the microphone at the same time.

"You were not informed ahead of time because we have learned you are a proud family who might not want to accept such a gift," he read to them stiffly. "But we also have learned that you do so many things for others, and it is only right that something is done for you. So it is on behalf of your school district, of your town, of your Pathfinder Regional Vocational Technical High School, that I present you—specifically that I present Elżbieta "Betty" Milewski—with the key to your new home."

He looked relieved to have the talking part over as he crouched to hand Betty her prize for being a stupid kid who would run into the street in front of an out-of-control truck. The photographers lunged at her, clicking in unison, little fireworks of light exploding brightly even though they were under a strong sun. She grabbed the keys from the man, threw them into my mother's purse, and slammed it shut with a giggle. Everybody laughed and laughed and laughed.

"Speech!" someone in the crowd called, and others shouted the same thing. I was sweating now, both from the baking van, and from the reality of the whole thing—how people could just take your life and do something with it, without even asking. Then I thought, my parents wouldn't take this, a whole huge house. Toys and some cakes were one thing. Even the money, well, it came a little bit at a time, and they spoke about it to no one. A house was another thing. Especially when we already had one, the one that was our home, that had been our home for so long. I realized I had nothing to worry about. My father would tell them thenks but no thenks, and I saw he was whispering something—probably that—to my mother, then was making his way over to the podium to give them the bad news that he could never in a million years accept such a gift.

At first he said nothing, just looked out at the dozens of faces. That had to be the largest crowd my father ever had to say one word in front of, and to be put on the spot in such a way only had to make it that much more frightening. I felt bad for him, but I couldn't wait for him to put Representative Conway in his place. Do it! I yelled inside my head. What do they think we are? Poor people?

My father licked at his lips, and I saw his hands shaking. He curled them around the front edge of the podium, to steady himself. Then he spoke.

"I came to this country twenty-one years ago. I was pushed to come here, really," he said, head down, talking more to the ground than the people, and that seemed to make it easier for him. "So I went, but I was not happy. And I can be a stubborn man. But I will say aloud today what has crossed my mind so many times in those twenty-one years: My parents were right about this being a wonderful country. I hesitate, but, on the condition that I pay back every single cent spent on it, and on behalf of my injured daughter, for whom I want the best, I accept this beautiful, beautiful, beautiful home."

My heart had moved up between my ears, so I only saw, rather than heard, all the people clap one more time, all the photographers call Betty's name as they snapped their final pictures, Mrs. Conway gather my parents and Babci and Betty on the flagstone landing at the front door and yell "Three! Two! One!" as Betty turned the key in the lock, and the door opened, and, one by one, each of them disappeared inside.

Chapter

9

$\mathcal{W}$e moved up the hill on July Fourth.

My father had the day off, as did the rest of the plant, and most of the rest of the dozens of Blue Ribbon workers postponed or missed their barbecues and horse shoe tournaments and parades and family reunions and instead pitched in and helped us, emptying our house carload by carload, filling the backs of their pickups and their station wagons and one smelly Blue Ribbon delivery truck with our furniture, our clothes, our knickknacks, our canned goods, driving everything four and three-tenths of a mile away, to 1 Conway Street, where the wives and elder daughters of the workers wore red-white-and-blue bandanas and clamdiggers and sang "God Bless America" and "Yankee Doodle Dandy" as they fit everything into new drawers and closets and cabinets and rooms and then stood back, hands planted on their hips, and exclaimed aloud how good it felt to be doing something for someone else for a change.

"We don't realize how lucky we are," an older lady named Mrs. Boczar, who was wearing a paper bag over her hair to protect it from any dust, told everybody as she stood on a stepstool and filled a kitchen shelf with the contents of a wicker basket of canned goods sent with best wishes from Tenczar's Superette.

A woman who had bad pollen allergies but no name that she ever disclosed answered, "Amen to that!" and informed us all that, from now on, she would spend every major holiday in service to others.

The lady at the window over the sink, arranging a long row of tiny potted herbs that the Pathfinder kids had grown from seed, turned and shook her head slowly.

"That is *such* a beautiful idea," she said slowly. "Plus, you thought of it because you're here, and you're here all because of one little girl. See how one person—even an innocent little girl—can change other people's lives?"

I was working in the living room with Carolyn and Theresa, supposedly shelving books in the new cases built into the low wall between that and the kitchen, but mostly we just sat and eavesdropped on the meat people.

"She's changing lives all right," Theresa snorted. Neither she nor Carolyn was happy about my moving. I, of course, was devastated, and I suspected the same of Babci.

We loved not only our real home, but the neighborhood, too, and were connected to it in so many ways. The two of us had always walked where we wanted to go, she to her stores and church and friends, me to school and the Melody Academy and to Theresa's and Carolyn's. The house on Conway Street was nearly a mile from any other people, and about four times that from the rock candy and headcheese and flesh-toned stockings, from Theresa's fields and from Carolyn's front steps, from the polka park and from the river.

The girls had helped me pack, and we sobbed the entire time, angrily stuffing my underwear and paperbacks and old toys and bottles of Earth Born shampoo into boxes donated by some big insurance company from Springfield that had printed that self-serving fact in big letters on the side of each carton, anticipating that the move would make the news.

I refused to enter the new house before I had to. I did not go in that first day, sitting in the van for nearly five hours, despite starving and sweating and needing to use the bathroom, and despite being told firmly by my mother that my father wanted me inside NOW.

"NO!" I shouted right back, the first time I ever had raised my voice to her, and one of the few times I said much of anything to anyone that summer. "I'm not going in there!" And I added what, at that point in my life, had come to be true: "I don't care what he wants."

No, he couldn't make me do anything anymore. And, as I saw it, that was all his fault.

So I did not go in that first day, and I did not go along the three other times my parents and Betty and Babci traveled up there to measure for curtains and plan what would go where and then probably stood on the front lawn and hugged each other and tried to get it into their heads that this big, solid, dreamlike place was real and was really all theirs.

But on July Fourth, I had no choice. My bed was gone, as were my socks, my radio, my little shamrock from Maureen Browne, my one tiny picture of Bobby cut from the graduation program he never saw and set under the base of my statue of Saint Jude, as I'd watched Babci do under her own statue with the petitions she'd write in Polish on small squares of paper. No, I did not really need photographs or a headboard, but I needed a place to live. And my parents had politely refused the invitations from the Lyszkos and from Mr. Zych to have me stay at their places until all the commotion from the move was over. So up the hill I was going, but not before Babci and I stood hanging on to each other in the middle of my living room, our sniffles bouncing off the bare floors and the walls that had been stripped of their pictures and crucifixes, leaving behind bright shapes of themselves against the walls that prior to that day never had appeared dingy.

That first night, after Carolyn and Theresa had checked out every one of the many conveniences in the new place (the trash compactor was their favorite) and were picked up by Mr. Zych, and I sadly watched their taillights get smaller and smaller and disappear into the black woods, I climbed up into the tree house the Pathfinder kids had built with leftover wood and had even made a window box for and put a shingled roof on, and I stayed up there until the fireworks began exploding over the polka park. I knew exactly the kind of splashes of color they were throwing across what had been my bedroom, and, imagining how the sharp lights were flashing now across nothing but a dusty shag rug and a dead silence, I began to cry again, and I did so for such a long time that I honestly thought soon there would have been nothing left of me.

In my dream that night, I was back in the old room, looking through the grate one final time.

"This is Dorota," my father was saying. "She loves to work in the field. She will be a great help in the yard."

My mother took the photo from him and scanned the face of the unsmiling child with the big, sad eyes. "Dorota. I like that!" she chirped. "She will be good."

"And this, this is Genia," my father went on. "How she can cook, they tell me! And with all the ingredients we have in this great country, she would not want to leave the kitchen!"

"A cook. How handy!" my mother said enthusiastically. "Perfect! Just what we need!"

"And Kasia. This is Kasia," my father continued, handing her a First Communion picture of a girl whose dress reached to the ground. "She probably will go to the convent in several years, so she will not be that much of a burden."

"We can provide in the meantime," my mother said gently.

"And Olisia," my father said. "Look—you can see her intelligence. A teacher she might be. Or a fine leader, like Representative Conway. You never know. She could go to the best school here."

"Knowledge is power," my mother chimed happily.

"This is Aniela," my father said. "The eldest. She just loves to make the pictures."

My mother took the photo of Aniela, the eldest, the photo of her looking exactly like me, wearing my long watermelon head and my square shoulders and my dark braids and my U-shaped smile.

"She looks like Donna," my mother observed.

"Yes, but this one, she is good," my father told her reassuringly.

"Then we'll take her," my mother said. "We'll take them all!"

On the day we moved in, Mrs. Conway consulted her clipboard and took me by the arm and directed me to move into the bedroom at the very end of the corridor.

"This is especially for you, dear," she said. "W-a-a-a-a-y down here. We know a teenager needs her privacy, so this will be made to order!"

I'd never stayed in a hotel, but I imagined this is how it had to be—one long hallway with door after door, a different person behind each, insulated from each other, protected from the stranger next to them. This new place was not a home but simply a house, even though so many people came and told us how wonderful it was, with its huge kitchen and its built-in refrigerator, its dishwasher, microwave oven, its laundry room, dining room, TV room, formal living front room, and that long hallway, with the first door leading to the room of my parents and having its own bathroom with a built-in tub in the avocado shade of the kitchen appliances. And, look, off that: a separate room for the mother's sewing, with an ironing board that swung down from a cabinet in the wall and counters and shelves and mirrors everywhere, with a hundred little wooden pegs stuck into the wall and just waiting for you to organize your thread by color and shade. The next room, across the hall, was for Betty, its walls covered with lavender Dumbos flying across a pale yellow sky and over the desk and bookcases the students had built around the window that opened to the front yard. Next to hers, Babci's room, with, just for her, an extra length of the electric baseboards that now would heat us, replacing the radiators that had so nicely warmed towels and dried caps and mittens and, in warmer months, so conveniently held potted plants and magazines.

Across from Babci's, at the right-hand end of the hall, past the sewing room, was my place. White ceiling, white walls, white rug, my half of the white bedroom set disappearing into the blankness. If I hadn't felt so defeated, I would have fought for a space in the basement, even farther away from the center of everything, down in the house's warm, neat gut, with its

147

red-and-blue shuffleboard court linoleumed right into the floor and a real pool table waiting under a green glass light fixture that looked like a Chinaman's hat. Or I would have asked for the entire attic, which could be reached by a set of stairs that unfolded automatically when you pulled on a string that hung from the ceiling. Up there, the students had installed cedar storage cabinets for your woolens, and empty shelves that would accommodate all the extra out-of-season things you wanted to store. Still, there was plenty of other space for a single mattress and a box of clothes and my prayer book, which was all I would have needed wherever I was put.

But I didn't ask for anything at all. I kept the room my mother and Babci had come in to check out with hopeful smiles, and I kept my mouth shut. I had no control over anything anymore, not even over the hope that my father would realize what a commitment this house was and would change his mind so we could all move back to River Street. But—wouldn't you know it, everything else being so perfect—it turned out my father would not have to pay a dime on the place. Everything in it, on it, under it, around it, had been donated by businesses and private people who were more than happy to write off as tax deductions their wall coverings, cement footings, asphalt shingles, electrical wires, flower bulbs, masonry, doorknobs, cesspool and built-in toaster. When they began to decorate, my parents placed into a frame a formal campaign photo of Representative and Mrs. Conway, and they displayed it on the top of the television, next to the photos of the rest of us who used to be in an entirely separate family that did not contain these two outsiders.

The second night in the house, I began my plan. I saw the new house as the county jail they were talking about building over in Ludlow, and I saw my sentence as being the four years up to my high school graduation day, when I would take my bag of things and my Babci and we would go move in with Maureen Browne, if she would have us, and I would begin the kind of life I wanted, which in my head held no more details than having some say about what happened to me.

In the garage, I found a huge piece of cardboard that once

had been wrapped around sections of vinyl siding. It took some work, but I tore it in half, and I took it into my room, and I drew row after row of small circles on it, counting now and then and tallying the totals until I reached exactly 1,460—the number of days you roughly would have to endure to make it four years down the line. Before I pushed the cardboard under my bed, I took a red Magic Marker, and I filled in the first dot, neatly and perfectly, marking the end of Day One.

Chapter

10

Sean Riley first noticed it in the parking lot of the Big Y, as we sat in his car, parked and steaming up the windows while it sprinkled outside and while, next to us, one of the ladies who I knew worked at the Town Hall fished around under her car on her hands and knees and in a dress and stockings for the can of Hawaiian Punch that had fallen from a rip in her soggy grocery bag.

Our new house was so far from everything that for the first time I needed a bus to get to and from high school, and I often missed it at the end of the day, being used to taking my time as I did back in the days when I could walk to get everywhere I needed to go. Sean, a year older, with a license and a jacked-up Dodge Dart to use it in, pulled over and offered me a ride one rainy afternoon the second week after classes began.

He'd been a public school kid, which in my world meant he might as well have been from another country, exotic in his foreignness, though he probably had grown up only at the other end of Main Street, in the small Irish neighborhood for which they'd long ago built tiny little St. Mary's, the people for whom Tenczar's offered a short row of corned beefs in the meat case every March, lining its borders with bright green crepe paper, stabbing the reserved cuts with tags bearing the families' sunny, perky surnames—Kerry and Kelly and Christy, and some others that began with an *O*, then had an apostrophe interrupting the rest, like it was a contraction rather than somebody's last name.

I met Sean in Introductory Physical Science, while working with a bead balance and sitting in the pairs Mr. Nahabedian had made by announcing our last names, randomly, in sets of two. While in their respective classes, Theresa had been stuck with a girl with two first names who combed her long hair continuously and gazed out the window the entire time at the football players circling the track during gym class, and Carolyn got a boy who happened to have one of the gizmos at home and who raced ahead of the instructions and excitedly completed each experiment without allowing her to do one single thing, I got the best-looking boy in the room, and I was more than happy to do all the work, to allow him to continue the elaborate battle drawings he was making in his binder.

After only ten minutes of being so close to him that I could count the eight freckles scattered across his right cheek and the fourteen others thrown over his left, sitting so near that I could marvel at how wavy his shining copper hair was without his having to sleep on curlers all night, my mind raced ahead, as it can do, and I was imagining how he and I would someday be living in an artist's attic like the one Dick Van Dyke had in the movie in which he played a struggling artist who pretended to be dead so his paintings would sell. Like Dick's, our place had piles of canvases everywhere, kooky neighbors who barged in at all hours, and a perfect view of the Eiffel Tower. But in our case, Sean didn't need to fake his death to be successful. Everybody loved his drawings, and when they told him so, he would reply:

"I owe everything to Donna, because back when I was just starting out in my art, in high school, she would take over the work in Introductory Physical Science to allow me extra time to practice."

And I would laugh and wave him away and tell them that it

had been no big sacrifice simply to do all the experiments on the bead balance, weighing pencils and pocket change against the strings of the metal beads that were kept in neat little drawers in its blue plastic base. Aside from the kiddie microscope Betty had received from Nurse Durkin her second Christmas with us, it was the first piece of high technology I had ever been allowed to play with, and I was fascinated by it, using the pair of tweezers to move the beads precisely from the drawer onto the scale. Even the invisible sweats and oils of our fingers, Mr. Nahabedian had cautioned, could add weight to the thing. I couldn't get that off my mind, how something you couldn't see could upset the balance of something. I opened my notebook and flipped to a blank page and wrote that fact down, so I never would forget it.

Sean was supposed to be keeping the data, was supposed to be the one in our pair who made the laboratory notes on how much his Bic weighed, but all he had on his page so far was a drawing of two fighter planes headed on a collision course and blasting away at one another with the huge weapons mounted on their roofs. As he leaned close to draw the bullets, he made little shooting noises that dotted his paper with saliva. It made sense suddenly that he was having to take this course for the second year in a row.

"This pen weighs seven beads," I told him, and he looked up at me for longer than you'd think was necessary, then wrote seven on his sheet, right between the two jets, which then shot at it until you could read the number no more.

Sean was the first boy since Bobby Smola to try to come anywhere near me. There had been a stretch of about ten months in between those two events, and the first one hadn't ended well at all—though I spent a great deal of time daydreaming about how beautiful the river had looked that afternoon, and even more time recalling Bobby edging closer and closer to me. But that was the last time I had seen him. And if I allowed Sean Riley very near to me, I believed he might disappear, too. Since I liked him, I looked out for his best interest.

"You have Florida on your head," he told me that day in the car.

I was struggling with my practical algebra. In public school, X's and Y's suddenly were numbers. It was craziness, and I was lost. "What?" I asked him, not paying attention.

"Your forehead. That thing, that mark—that's the exact shape of Florida. I went there twice, to see my grandmother. She lives in Hollywood—not the real one, the movie one, but there's one in Florida. It's right on this part, here on the right." And he moved to point to what he saw as the southeastern coast, but I jumped back, out of his reach.

"I wasn't going to do anything—just show you's all," he said defensively.

I moved forward so I could look at my head in the rearview mirror. I saw the familiar scar—a reddish pink shape that grew scarlet and obvious if you exposed it to too much sun. But I did not see a state, at least one that I could make out. Then again, I was looking at it backward, plus I wasn't that good in geography—maybe he was right after all. I turned to Sean, and he pointed at Ft. Lauderdale, where his family's plane had landed at an airport in which, if you put a quarter in his jar, a rabbit in a cage would jump on a treadmill that would turn a crank that after a while would make you a glass of fresh orange juice. Then Sean moved his finger a tiny bit down to where his grandmother lived and where, every morning before it got too hot, she drove a battery-powered cart through her housing complex for the elderly to exercise the fat little Chihuahua she tied to her fender.

"We went to Miami for Sunday dinner, I remember," he continued, "but is that down or up from there? I'm confused . . ." He was staring at me—at the map—at the scar— like he was going to see some words, a highway sign, that might help him. He moved closer and closer. Then he suddenly leaned and slowly kissed the entire state, and I realized he wasn't confused at all.

I missed the bus a lot that first year, using Sean's car as my new living room, one that was parked in the far corner near the idling Sweet Life Food trucks, where we sat doing my homework, doing Sean's homework, playing his "American Pie" 8-track and getting him to tell more stories about his grandmother just so he'd have to go looking for her town. School let out at 2:10 P.M., and I could get in a good two and a half hours with Sean before having to go home, arriving just in time to eat, with my assignments all completed. I told my parents I was studying with the girls after school, and after her suffering through my long, hot, mopey, and silent summer, my mother was so happy to see me happy and saying more than a few words at a time that she didn't care I was going to someone else's home before I went to my own.

She also was pleased that I had gone back to the old neighborhood after refusing to do so for so long. But that was just another lie. I still really couldn't go anywhere near the old house—the old street even—it saddened me so not to be there from day to day. Especially since I might see the people who now lived in my house—that "lovely" family that Mrs. Balicki the realtor had so conveniently produced out of thin air and had telephoned us about the night we finally came back from our joy ride with the Conways. I had run off to Theresa's and worked in the barn with her the entire day that included the one hour they were supposed to come and tour the house. What if I now went by and saw those people reading their newspapers on my front porch or playing hopscotch on my driveway or planting zinnias in Babci's garden? What if I saw a girl up in my window, leaning on the sill and just looking out at all the things I used to take in? I couldn't imagine it, not that I wanted even to try.

That whole summer had been just a dud. For the first time in my life, I did not attend a single one of the polka picnics, which used to be—excuse me, God, but I'm just being honest—the highlight of my Sunday and my week. My father worked weekends all the time now, so he couldn't go down there to help out at the bar as he used to—not that he would have invited me to come along anyway—and, somehow, I just wasn't that interested in being there, not caring to be sitting with the kids down near the brook, lying in the sun in our halters and cutoffs, braiding lilies of the valley, and waiting for some boy from out of town to wander down the hill and

maybe ask for a waltz, finally giving up and pooling change
and ordering a Polish plate to split between six people, and it
would be only after we had *kielbasa* breath that somebody like
Gail Luzi's halfway-decent-looking cousin down from Cheek-
towaga would be noticed staring at the bunch of us, and we
would frantically pass around the bottle of Binaca that Sharon
Romanski carried in her back pocket for such emergencies and
pronounced "Bianca," telling us each time she brought it out
how this stuff was named after Mick Jagger's wife.

Things like that probably went on without me every Sunday
that summer—okay, I know they did, but I don't like to think
about not being part of them. Carolyn and Theresa reported
that I wasn't missing much, though. They were among a group
of girls that had been asked to help out in the main kitchen that
summer, and they could eat all they wanted, plus were given
$14.50 for an afternoon—along with any tips people bothered
to place into the beer cup that stood next to the condiment tray.
They were doing it for the money, they said, and because of
the fact that I wasn't around there anymore. It just wasn't the
same without me, the girls said, and I would lower my head
when they would tell me such things, and I hoped that at that
angle they couldn't see how they were making me smile.

But I guess I would have liked to have been there to see them
in the kitchen, dishing up the slimy *pierogi* that can act like live
fish, flipping and slipping onto the paper plates. It would have
been fun to see the Lejman sisters pull Brother Mike onto the
dance floor to do the dance that starts out with everyone
throwing a shoe into the center of the floor, then having to pair
up with the owner of the shoe they grab out of the pile. It must
have been something when they ran out of *gołąbki* at the parish
picnic and Alice Pilch had to drive around town and bang on
the doors of people who had bought the ones she makes year-
round in her kitchen, offering to buy them back at more than
the people had paid for them. And I would have given money
to see how nervous Theresa was when she had to take an order
from hunky Paweł, of Paweł and the Polka Playboys, who wore
the tightest pair of red-and-white-striped jeans you ever saw
and who always would have his white peasant blouse unlaced
low so that everyone could admire his muscles and could see

close up when they passed the bandstand the tangle of thick gold chains that hung from his neck and dangled into his chest hairs a ruby-and-diamond Polish flag, a gold Liberty Bell, a pair of folded, praying hands, also golden, and a silver rhinestone-encrusted P the size of a hood ornament.

I missed it all because I wasn't there. But the music had tried to find me, valiantly climbing up the hill, yet arriving weak and muffled, like a radio playing from inside a neighbor's house. So, except for the trip down to church, and the stop at the drugstore afterward for papers and milk, Sunday had become just like any other day, one more to circle to fill in, while around me, as they did every other day, the rest of the family settled in, finding new favorite places to sit, calling to each other when finding a special view from a different room, my mother needing a jar opened, my father (once home from work) taking requests for the next number he'd spin, Babci turning up her TV so loudly that the "60 Minutes" stopwatch ticked right through the walls, Betty counting to her animals, though still not in any order you'd recognize.

She would be going back to school the next September, though on crutches and with a big metal-and-leather brace that had something to do with making sure her leg would grow correctly and straight in future years. Her hair was starting to grow back in from where they had to cut much of it off, so filled with blood and pieces of skin had it been from the whack she'd received. Whoever had charge of the scissors in the emergency room had not been thinking of her appearance that afternoon, so, by the time they removed the bandages from her head, Betty's hair was growing back around the damage in ragged lengths that my mother tried to even out, but then she gave up and sewed seven kerchiefs, each embroidered with a different day of the week, for Betty to put on if she ever got self-conscious, which she didn't, instead going bareheaded so we could all be further reminded of what I had done to her, how her head now looked like a baseball, with tufts of yellow fuzz edging the seams that held her scalp together, all that mess above a face that never, ever stopped smiling.

I stayed in my own room a lot of the time, lying on the bed, concocting vivid daydreams about what Aniela was doing right at that very minute and coveting her peaceful, uncomplicated life. I imagined she lived very much like Shirley Temple did in the *Heidi* movie, sleeping in a billowy, fragrant hay pile, leading cows past scenery right out of one of the *National Geographic*s in Dr. Anton's waiting room, stopping in a hayfield for a lunch of that rough rye bread while bluebirds perched and harmonized all around her, climbing on the back of that big white horse and riding through town, where she was revered by not only her parents and her sisters, but by everyone who lived there. Wise Aniela, they called her, when they were not calling her beautiful.

Nobody called me for much of anything, other than meals. They didn't have to look far—I was either in my room or in the tree house, which had been made for Betty, but there was no way she could get up there, and I claimed it as my own. It was my favorite part about the new place, and I brought blankets and pillows up there and sneaked out to sleep in it every chance I could. In the daytime, I sat up high and stared down into the valley, at the crown of the tall white water tower and at the copper steeple of our church, and at the low clouds of green that were the trees that hid the rest of the land. But I knew by heart what was down there: the stores and the homes and the sidewalks I once had seen every day, the smell of their interiors and the weight of their doors, the height of their steps, the width of the streets, and me, up here on the hill, on a still, dirt road, now so far away that I might as well have been somebody looking down from a passing airplane.

The tree house was the only place I decorated, bringing up a poster of Gerry Cheevers in his stitch-covered goalie mask and a little plant stand on which I placed a doily and my portable radio. I made it my new home, even lugging up a spare cooler into which I would dump ice trays and cans of Tab. Then one day that fall, some obnoxiously benevolent Pathfinder kids with nothing better to do on a gorgeous Indian summer Saturday drove up in a pickup truck filled with tools and ropes and pulleys and pieces of lumber, and they assembled a sturdy little box in which Betty could be hauled up to the door of the tree house so that she, too, might enjoy it. A TV crew came to film her first ascent, and on cue she laughed and pointed to the house as she neared it, the students, their shirts off in the humidity, hoisting her with great strong pulls on the rope and then one of them scrambling up the ladder and drawing her contraption inside.

"Look!" she yelled down to my mother and Babci, who stood in the shade of the house and waved to her.

"Look!" she yelled, spotting me in my bedroom window.

I looked, at my sanctuary, another thing gone.

That's why Sean Riley was such a godsend. He and his car provided a place away from the new house, and away from the old neighborhood—somewhere safe and quiet, with few questions and no history. He seemed not to be aware of the thing with me and Betty, or didn't care that much if he did. I never asked him what he knew about me, though I had plenty of opportunities to, the way he was always right in my face, staring at my forehead, and then came the afternoon that he moved his fingers up the coast, into my bangs, all the way to Daytona, and he traced how it was somewhere in that town that the Allman Brothers had grown up—and wasn't it so cool that that's exactly where his father was being transferred?

So Sean Riley went away, too, was gone in a fast three weeks, his family's every possession loaded into a green-and-yellow Mayflower moving van with a little ship painted on the side of it, sailing to a new land far away. I quickly hid in my room the couple of postcards he sent me the first month after he left, each of them showing cars racing down a wide, flat, hot-looking beach, each one of them, in his wirey hand, telling me little more than what a "happenin' place" he lived in now, and how no one could believe what a "hick town" he had come from. And then I heard nothing more. But I remember Sean Riley well, mostly for his being the first in a long and pretty forgettable string of boys and men who have seen something in my head. And I can trace my high school years, my life, really, by remembering the person, and his interpretation, whether he was the one who saw a leg and who told me

his dziadziu had magical powers and would interpret that
symbol for me, or the one for whom it resembled a cloud he
had seen just the day before while smoking something at the
Quabbin Reservoir, or the one whose beagle had the same
shape on his back (only in black fur), or the one who had
hopes of working as a cartographer and who thought it looked
like the country of Liechtenstein, which I checked on in Betty's
encyclopedia when I got home after hearing that, and I never
saw such a small country. But I suddenly felt a connection to it
and from then on would always root for Liechtenstein athletes
and their sixty-two square miles of land whenever the Olympic
games rolled around.

Whoever it had been, whatever they thought they saw, they
each would want to show me their own gashes and slashes and
gouges left from knuckles slammed in car doors, from bare feet
that found the one rusty nail in all the boardwalk, from dogs
that didn't know that somebody was just playing, from a glass
dropped into a swimming pool, an entire thumbprint erased
by a barbecue that looked cold, and, fortunately only once, a
cyst at the nape of a neck that had taken nearly three years to
heal. Some of these victims should have received stitches, only
there was nobody to take them to the doctor, and their wounds
had closed gaping and wide, the Zarod boy ending up with a
depression so deep even now you could sink half a dime into
it. Others were worked on by doctors who were overly
enthusiastic and who used many more stitches than you'd
think were needed, or who were so skilled that you could
hardly locate the scar, but it was there, the guy would promise,
if you'd only look closer and closer and closer.

You could fill up a whole night with just relating how you
came to be hurt, and what somebody did to try to stop you
from feeling that way. For my contribution to the conversation,
if I knew that the person didn't know anything about me, and
if I had a hunch they were pretty gullible, I would tell how I
fell off the mast of a sailboat or that it happened during
skydiving. I got one guy, an exchange student named Luis
Orozco, to believe I had been attacked by a bear up on the hill,
and after that story, he never again came around after dark.

If it sounds like I had lots of dates, well, that was the case. I found that having a social life had two benefits: It got me out of the house for another day or night, and it greatly riled my father—which had become my goal in this new life. No, things did not improve in my high school years, which even under normal circumstances never are a good space of time for such things as meaningful parent/child relationships to thrive. I think his accepting a whole new house and uprooting us all, just for Betty's sake, really was the second to the last straw as far as we were concerned. As for his side of things, my father was making few steps toward getting us back to where we once had been, if only in our heads. He spent most of his free time with Betty, coaching her in her studies so intensely that she really began to catch on, and she took off like a shot once she got the language down. Her favorite thing was hobbling to the end of Conway Street every Wednesday afternoon and waiting for the bookmobile to pull up. The ladies inside would lift her up the stairs and then would stand back and marvel at how Betty always would reach for books written for those far beyond her grade level—some even with no pictures—and asked them to recommend titles in the topics she loved: science, mathematics and art.

The boring newspaper features continued, chronicling not only the progression of her health but her intellectual accomplishments. There was second-grade Betty limping back from the corner with a tote bag filled with junior-high schoolbooks; waving the test papers she passed with flying colors, the nuns applauding in the background; my father constructing extra bookcases in her room for all the volumes she began receiving in the mail once people learned how much she loved to read; my mother laughing and framing the note from a publishing company in Boston that offered Betty the chance to write her autobiography.

Unlike my father, my mother and Babci eventually got back to some kind of normal with me. Mostly, I should note, that was most evident when my father wasn't home. Before that time of day, my mother would ask me to try on something— heightwise, I was getting to be the size of some of the ladies she sewed for, though with my still-sparse diet I came nowhere near filling in all their darts and pleats—and she would make me spin, and then she would stand back and clasp her hands together and would tell me, "You know"—then she would stop, and it was a nice effect—"you look 'lovely.'" It was like "fond," a word soft and kind. I looked lovely to her. I would hug her the times when she said things like that, and I enjoyed how she hung on to me with a desperation I felt clearly, like we had extrasensory powers and she was trying to send me a message she could not bring herself to verbalize. And I pretended to be receiving it, leaning there in her arms, feeling the words pulse into my waiting brain:

"I am sorry about all this. You are good."

I would leave the room content.

When my father was not home, Babci would ask me into the kitchen to lick the beaters when she made a cake, or to fetch her a medication from the top drawer in her room, where, in both this house and our real one, she also stashed Hershey's Kisses for me to take when I did her such a favor. I'd return and pull up one of the fancy little wooden stools we were supposed to sit on when we ate at what Mrs. Conway told us was called a "breakfast bar," and Babci would slam bread dough onto a hardly scarred butcher block and would tell me stories about the olden days back in Poland, about growing up the eldest of nine children in a family so poor they had no dinnerware, only shallow dents carved in their table into which her mother would pile *ziemniak* after *ziemniak*, potato after potato, for breakfast, lunch, and dinner, and for a snack, cold, if anybody was still hungry and could stomach the thought of eating yet another one. Once in a while, when her mind was back to the time when, as the eldest girl, she was the second mother in the house, with eight younger ones to look after for as long as she could remember, she would tell me I really couldn't understand that part of her life because I had never been there.

"Well, I would like to go," I told her, toying with the notion of walking down a dirt road to find Aniela sitting in the shade, looking so pleased to see me, but not surprised, because she knew we would meet. I wondered if Babci would ever send me back there—I knew she had the money, stacked thick by denomination and tied with twine and lined up in row after row between her mattress and her box spring—maybe if I hinted enough. But the conversations never got that far, usually spiraling into something else, like asking me to get her a couple of jars of *kiszenie ogórki,* her best pickles, from the cellar (in this house, called a "basement"), and hurry now, I'm waiting.

When my father came home from work, things would change. But it was not like the old days, when we'd jump around him and celebrate how wonderful it was that this man simply had walked through the back door. In the new years, Betty was the one who got excited, swinging her messed-up leg as fast as she could to catch up with the other one that wanted to race to her *Tatuś,* as she called him, as she had once called her father back in the life that had to seem like someone else's memory by now.

"Tatuś! Tatuś!" She would bang with her meaty little fists on the bay window when she heard his car, then she'd get herself over to the door in the laundry room that led to the garage, and she would be there, waiting, hands wringing behind her back, when he came in the house and picked her up and yelled, *"Do góra!"*—then, translating it, still on his all-English kick—"To the mountain!" and he would swing her high above his head, and they would go on like that for quite some time before he even took off his coat and came into the real part of the house.

It reminded me of how he and I used to be, but all this I could take okay. I'd seen so much of it between the two of them in a brief span of time, and I guess I resigned myself that things between me and my father weren't ever going to get any better. He had no forgiveness for me, for the things he thought I had done, and he had no interest in hearing what I had to say—not that I would have bothered to give my side at that point. It was more sad than anything, that there was so much lost between us that there could be no way back.

I mentioned the second-to-the-last straw. The very last one? Let me just say this: Mrs. Dranka had another sale, she put another ad in the paper, she held another open house, and my parents took Betty to it, and guess what instrument she picked? And guess what she did every night after supper? Guess where she set up her chair and her music stand, guess whom she played for. And guess, just guess, how he loved it so very, very much.

So there you have some idea. Betty's upward flight, my sideways skittering. Most of what my father would say to me, when he would say anything at all, was something he'd repeated again and again since the day I began first grade— only he no longer said it with a laugh and a pull on my ear: that I'd better study or I'd end up spending my life working the line at Safe-Tam. Or, as he pronounced it, Sef-Tom.

That usually would send me down the hall, past my mother's sewing room, where she would be putting together yet another outfit for yet another of Mrs. Conway's acquaintances, and I would run into my own room and would slam the door and flop facedown on the bed, and through the walls soon would sneak in the sound of Betty's accordion, playing "The Blue Skirt Waltz," "You, You, You Are the One," the mermaid's "Syrena Polka." She played *"Czarny Las,"* about the Black Forest," she asked "Where is My Youth" in *"Kde Jsi Me Mlada?"*

She flew through *"Zelena se Zelena"* ("Green Is Green"), *"Na Jamarku"* ("At the Market"), "Purple Cow," and "Eskimo Kiss." Once in a while I would find my fingers moving, without any help from me, tapping invisible keys and buttons, following along with Betty, who, I have to admit, really was getting to be quite good, adding her gay little trills to connect notes, jumping an octave on the second refrain. And I would pick up my head and watch my fingers in front of me like they were somebody else's, how they knew where to go next and how odd they looked playing the bedspread. And I would make them stop, pushing them under the pillow and squashing them into the mattress so they wouldn't be able to move. Then I would listen to her music, and I would wonder how we had gotten here to this point, and I would marvel, almost, at how weird life can get, especially when it is your own that has gone so crazy.

Boys were good for taking my mind off such troubles, but more for connecting me with Theresa and Carolyn, who, in the big new high school, I didn't see half as much as I wanted to, though we talked on the phone at night as often as we could get away with, I from my house, of course, and they at the Lyszkos'—Theresa on the upstairs phone and Carolyn on the fruit store extension, sitting on a wooden chair beneath the scenic calendar sent at Christmas from the So-Good Grapes company and, though she wasn't supposed to, not being able to resist pushing her fingers through the end of the big, wide roll of clear plastic wrap that was used for covering gift baskets.

I had Theresa in my Spanish I class, but we sat nowhere near each other. Carolyn was in my homeroom, which contained *L* through *S*, but that was only for the five minutes it took to listen to the names being summoned to the vice-principal's office, then to pledge allegiance, and then to observe a "moment of silence," something the nuns back at the old school sadly had told us once had been the time for a real prayer before a bunch of atheists complained to the president. Now it was a few seconds of quiet into which, even if you tried—and I honestly did every day—you couldn't even jam the first half of a Hail Mary.

The girls and I even were on separate lunches, and, on my schedule, I would enter the cafeteria for my mealtime to see them already finishing their pudding, sitting side by side, laughing about something I wasn't in on and probably wouldn't ever be told, not out of any meanness, but simply because, you know, you had to be there, and I knew that to be true. The list of the things I wasn't there for was growing fast: Where I'd abandoned music, Theresa and Carolyn charged ahead with theirs, joining the stage band and playing not only the polkas Mrs. Dranka had assigned week after week but the national anthem, and songs you'd hear sung on soft-rock radio, by Gordon Lightfoot and John Denver and Carole King. They were loaned double-breasted blazers in the school colors of blue and gold and were given busy schedules of rehearsals and performances and competitions they were not to miss, and they soon were telling me about other student bands that travel to compete in places like Austria. Hearing such things gave me a sick and jealous feeling way down in my stomach. I

often panicked, thinking they would not have time for me—
that I would lose them and all they meant. So I gave them the
only thing I knew they couldn't resist: a change of scenery—
not Austria, but who really cared if it got you out and about?

I would pick a boy and make him drive me to meet the girls
somewhere other than the old neighborhood, and I would
make the boy buy us all ice cream or french fries or fat party-
size bags of State Line potato chips, and I would make him
wait in the car while I visited with my friends, then I would
make him take me home. I took advantage of most of the boys
in that way, but I didn't care. They didn't seem to care, either,
as I picked ones that no one else would be interested in going
anywhere near. Except for Sean Riley, who actually selected
me rather than the other way around, they were nothing to
make note of lookswise, or personalitywise or anything else-
wise. My requirement was that they have a car, and that they
would be so grateful to have a girl's interest that they wouldn't
care what boring things they were asked to do for her.

One slow Saturday afternoon I got freaky little Stanley
Barnek, known to only the pathetic people who have nothing
better to do than watch TV on Saturday evening as our town's
"As Scholars Match Wits" team captain, to drive the three of
us to Hampton Beach, a good two hours away, and he played
with his Rubik's Cube keychain in the parking lot for the
whole seven hours we hung out in the casino and got guys
with tough Boston accents and polyester dress shirts with
chopped-off sleeves to buy us snow cones and rounds on the
pinball machines. I talked Joey Schlatter, who lived on the
riverbank in a scary, junky house with a roof of homemade
solar panels, into taking us up to Shelburne Falls, so we all
could watch the slim, daring local boys in their battered cutoffs
dive fearlessly into the mysterious glacial potholes. We made it
to the Mystic Seaport in Connecticut, to the Mayflower in
Plymouth, to Vermont and to Boston, even, and almost were
successful in persuading this kid who was picked on because
he had ears like Mr. Spock to take us to Canada one Sunday,
but he was too worried about what kind of laws they might
have up there in a foreign country, and he was quite sure he

might break one without knowing it and end up in jail, and his family would disown him, and ruining his future was just too great a risk, he said, even, to please me.

When it worked, which was quite often, all this was a pretty good deal. The only thing I had to do was kiss the guy once or twice when we finally got back to my house. It was the least I could do for all that gasoline, and it was dark by that point, so I could easily pretend they were the well-built Tim Bobskill, embracing me joyously after scoring yet another touchdown, or the silent but obviously deep-thinking Donny Bondoon, wanting to celebrate after finishing another one of those cardboard skyscrapers he constructed on the drawing tables in Mr. Garstka's class, or, when I dared, the wondrous Ray Lyszko Jr., telling me what I wanted to hear—how he had his eye on me ever since he could remember, and how all those years he had been unable to rest whenever his sister had a sleepover, knowing I was in a bed just a few thin boards away. Then I would open my eyes to find my reality—the pudgy, rashy "Cookie" Lemier, chocolate chips on his breath, or the skeletal Lee Jarvis, embossing my face with the dental retainer he apologized for having to pull across his face each evening at exactly at 6.

The real payment for all the fun came due once I went inside the house, where my parents sat in the living room with all the lights on, ready to pounce on me when I walked through the door either an hour or so past my 10 P.M. curfew or having neglected to tell them in the first place that I was going anywhere at all.

My mother was always the one to start, with "Thank God you're all right . . . ," then she would bless herself in two quick windmill swipes and would look at me with sad eyes that made me feel guilty I ever had to involve her in anything unpleasant. She would say nothing else, leaving the floor to my father, who would begin shouting his questions: Who did I think I was? Someone who could come and go as I pleased? Who did I think he was? A fool who didn't know what I was up to? Did I want to get in trouble? (And don't tell me you don't know what I'm talking about.) Didn't I care about my reputation? What was left of it, that is?

The truth was, I really wasn't doing anything that bad. I smoked cigarettes—but not many—starting in my freshman year, when James Ennis, a junior who had a large glass right eye that didn't move and who straightened the shelves three afternoons a week at Charkoudian Drug, stole me a carton of Virginia Slims as a sign of affection and kept it under his front seat as a guarantee I'd come back for another ride. And it was only once in a while that I could find a guy who would be willing to try to buy us liquor, and he'd usually pick out something he thought was adult-looking, but was only something disgusting, like Cherry Driver—sort of a screwdriver but with cherry juice—and you could only drink so much of that without getting sick, which I never had enjoyed doing, especially on purpose. Mostly, I just liked to stay away from home, getting someone to help me collect the girls and sit on the sand hills behind the Metro Drive-In and make up the dialogue to the movies being shown. In my life there was no heroin, no orgies, no crime. Yet my behavior worried my parents to near illness ("What, do you want us to get sick over you?" was a question I forgot to list). Once, after getting shy little Tony Bouchard to drive us to a Red Sox game that ran seventeen innings, I came home at 2:30 A.M. to find my mother and Babci busy frosting the tall marble layer cakes for the reception the family would hold after my funeral.

I got grounded regularly, and though I didn't like the yelling that went along with it, the punishment never really made any difference to me. The days I was forced to stay home were just that many more circles to fill in, that much more of the calendar marked off, inching toward the day I would be able to start my own life, where I would feel no guilt over my mother and Babci, no hate toward my father and Betty. It would just be me. Like Aniela on her horse. Headed somewhere. Confident. Alone, and happy about it.

I turned sixteen with little fanfare, with none of the pink-and-white Sweet Sixteen-imprinted paper banners that they strung across Carolyn's living room for the party to which she got to invite any boy she wanted, and she asked the guy who played the cymbals in the stage band and who had the name of Paul Wright, and Carolyn's mother, so thrilled that he really seemed like a nice person, went so far as to giggle to relatives, within the boy's earshot yet, that it appeared her daughter had found Mr. Wright.

My sixteenth birthday arrived and departed with no touching dedication from my father like the one Mr. Zych had sent Theresa on "Freddie Brozek's Polka Explosion," where the "My Girl" polka was spun after Freddie remarked in Polish how there is nothing in this world like a father's love for his only daughter, who, he added, clearing his throat to read the rest of what was before him, "I am proud to be the one to announce will be honored by her father with the renaming of Zych's Dairy Farm as 'Theresa's Acres' from now on. That'll be printed on the bottles and everything. You'll see it on your porch tomorrow morning, folks. It's supposed to look real nice—from what I hear at least."

The Conways, who still were trying to win me over, and who for two consecutive years had marked Betty's birthday by paying for a free afternoon at Mountain Park, granting her all the rides and concessions and games she wanted for herself and as many little friends as she cared to invite, got the idea to celebrate my big day with an entire afternoon at the new mall in Springfield, where forty-eight stores and their contents lay waiting in climate-controlled comfort, and where, the Conways proposed, I could, courtesy of them, select an entire outfit complete with jewelry, shoes, any cosmetics I would be allowed to wear, and a haircut and blow-dry. It was greatly tempting: I knew exactly the pair of mustard-colored suede Earth Shoes I wanted at Thom McAn's—the real, genuine Earth Shoes that came in an Earth Shoes box inserted into a burlap sack bearing the Earth Shoes name; and the few times I'd bought clothes for myself there had been a great excitement about going into a store and picking something right off the rack to wear, rather than seeing the blouse or skirt from its fetal days back when it was still part of a bolt of cloth on a shelf up so high at Osgood's Fabrics that you had to ask one of the muscled Puerto Rican clerks to climb up on a ladder and bring it down for you. But even with such an offer, the Conways would never get to me. I was not one that could be bought.

"No, thank you," I told them when they stopped by with the plan one night when I happened to be stuck home after getting in big trouble for hanging up on the bishop's secretary when she called to ask if Betty wanted to be the featured reader during a special televised mass for the handicapped of the diocese (My hand slipped, I swear). I told the Conways: "I don't need to go to a store. My mother makes all my clothes, and she is a wonderful designer." I used that word because I had heard Mrs. Conway praise her in that manner—that she was not just a seamstress, but a "designer."

Mrs. Conway's eyes widened, and her mouth fell open, and she swung her hand to her face and exclaimed: "Of course, what was I thinking! I've insulted your mother. Oh dear! Of course you wouldn't want anything from a regular store, with all she can do for you. I just thought, well, a young girl, you probably had your eyes on some dungarees or whatever. You know, a 'brand name.' Oh, I am sorry."

It was fun to see her squirm, but it didn't last long. My mother rushed over and patted Mrs. Conway on the shoulder and assured her that no one had been insulted, and that it had been a wonderful idea, Mrs. . . . I mean Patricia, er, Pattie. (My parents had been asked to go ahead and call Mrs. Conway by her first name—not just that, but by the nickname of her first name. Though he requested the same treatment, they all still called Representative Conway Representative Conway, not William, and certainly not, though he wanted it and signed all his boring correspondences to us in that way, Willie.)

"You're always too generous," my father reinforced after my mother returned to him from comforting Mrs. Conway. "You have done enough." And, he added, as if I weren't there and as if I were a million years old or something, "Anyway, she's getting too old for birthdays."

What I got for my birthday was a regular "Happy Birthday to Our Daughter" card that only my mother had signed with love from both of them, and a box containing a large piggy bank made of amber-colored glass. It was one of those gifts that had a great hope attached to it, like the way you might buy someone clothing two sizes too small to encourage them to lose weight, or a calendar and pen because they never remember to show up for anything, or a book of prayers because you think that is what they should be doing more of, if they do any of that sort of thing at all. With the pig, my parents were saying, without saying, that I should become more responsible and more adult, thinking of the future that already was getting so close I could smell it, and that I should realize that whatever it held, that future would require a job, and money. The pig had no cork or secret door. To get to anything you might drop into it, you would have to smash it. Once you retrieved what you'd saved, you no longer had someplace to continue saving. It was pretty black and white.

When they handed it to me in a wrapped box after Babci had made an entirely Italian meal just for me and my occasion, a whole long table containing lasagna after ravioli after miniature pizza and not even one forkful holding any kind of fable or cure, each of my parents gave me a kiss. It was the first I had received from my father in several years, and it was more of a brush, but he came close enough that I smelled on him the warm Old Spice that I once in a while still sadly inhaled from its bottle as I leaned against the closed door of their bathroom.

Babci, not one to make Hallmark any richer, that day folded a cut-out magazine photo of flowers around a $20 bill and slipped it under my door. Betty had no money to give, only a piece of white posterboard to which she'd neatly glued tiny, smooth stones that made up the lumpy bodies of two girls standing on a hill next to a long white house. The rocks that were their faces bore red paint smiles, and their matching green eyes were looking right at you. They lovingly held fat rock hands.

Then the kid led me into the kitchen, where there was a chair set up under the kitchen light that we lit by pressing a flat space-age button on the wall. Next to the table sat her accordion, shining black, a Giulietta as dramatically beautiful as its name. She limped over to it, drew it on, and sat down. Then, without error, and repeating it one time in a different key, she played and sang "Heppy Bersday," smiling at me all the while, with nothing, I have to be honest and admit, but a look of love. I did not join in the applause, only said I'd see everybody later, as Paul Korvak pulled into the driveway and sounded his horn with the carved piece of wood that was his right hand.

It took me two years to fill the pig, which I stuffed every Thursday with most of my earnings from my after-school job at the Food Basket grocery store that was across the park from the high school. Paper money or coins, it didn't matter. Everything but what I kept aside to treat myself occasionally or to buy essentials that nobody else would get for me was dropped in there the minute I got home on payday. The day after my birthday, I had obtained a work permit from the school superintendent's office, and I had signed up for driving lessons, then I walked over to the grocery store and filled out an application, marking under "Experience" that I often helped out at Lyszko and Son, which wasn't a lie because if Mrs. Lyszko asks me to hand her something or to hold the door for her when I'm in there, I do exactly that. The next night, after firing both a girl from the bakery and a stockboy from the breakfast cereals/baking needs aisle for necking by the incinerator while sparks flew into the storeroom through the door they'd forgotten to shut, the manager phoned me to ask if I could come in after school the next day.

Mr. Lenker told me I had a choice of a still-warm position in the bakery, or one in the meat department. I had managed to keep my skinny, wired-mouth physique over the couple of years since I risked my life to save Betty, so I selected the meat department, where there would be fewer things I would be able to just pop into my mouth. I was given a white smock, a starter envelope of hairnets (I would have to supply my own after those were stretched out), and the job of standing behind the counter and wrapping the various meat products the butchers sliced and set on the stainless steel trays and rolled down a conveyor belt through a hole in the wall that separated the public from the sight of bloody carcasses hanging on hooks.

It was not only blobs of hamburger and matching pairs of steaks that I wrapped, but fish and pork, too, and lots of chicken breasts after they got cracked and deboned out back by a tall black man who asked that everybody call him Sticks, who smoked cigarettes while he worked, though he was not supposed to, and who slipped me a dollar a day out of his own pocket just so I'd promise to alert him if anyone identifying himself as being from the town's Board of Health wanted to be let behind the cases.

The job sometimes was an odd one. I wrapped things you couldn't imagine anyone making a meal of, though I guess it proved to me the truth of what Babci said about if you're hungry enough you'll eat anything. I had seen pig's knuckles all my life, on our refrigerator door, in a long, thin jar into which four of them fit perfectly, pointing to the sky, looking almost delicate and in a pinkish color that matched my flesh. But I learned there were people out there who dined on worse stuff. On tongues longer than half your forearm. On goat brains. On ox tails. On livers and kidneys. Even on hearts.

When these kinds of things came rolling down to me, I looked away from them as I worked, and I pretended I was packaging them for a fitting burial, drawing the thin, clear plastic over them, tucking it beneath their little cardboard trays, then sealing it all closed with a quick touch to a heated pad.

I worked quickly, efficiently, timing my repetitious movements to the Muzak versions of old television theme songs that floated from the speaker over my head: "Family Affair," "Gidget," "My Three Sons," "Petticoat Junction," "Bewitched." Hefty tenderloins, long picnic packs of twenty-four drumsticks, expensive center-cut pork chops, and the occasional fluke-threaded flounder blurred past me as I sang along in my head and would flash back to wonderful Saturday nights of staying up with Babci back in the old days in the old house, when my parents would go dancing each weekend at the Polish Home in Chicopee, and I would gorge on the sitcoms and on the snacks Babci would bring to my TV tray at the end of each half hour. I wanted to be back watching the happy sisters in their gingham bathing suits swimming in the railroad water tank next to the Shady Rest, and I wanted to be back arguing with Babci that Katie and Robbie's triplets really weren't theirs from real life. If I did enough of this daydreaming, I would look up and there would be no more trays to wrap, and Sticks would have his head poked through the opening, exhaling smoke as he asked me good-naturedly, "Slow down, will you? I can't keep up!"

Mr. Lenker, who every couple of days had me wrap clumps of suet for his yard birds, overheard Sticks cracking something like that one Monday afternoon, and then, I noticed, he made several slow trips past the cases over the next couple of hours. The following day, he said he had been observing what a good worker I was, and he asked me if I would be interested in putting in some extra time at the grinder counter that separated my station from the delicatessen and its busy group of laughing clerks—on my shift, usually Dottie, Evelyn, and Sue—who decorated the lapels of their smocks with fake flowers and buttons with funny sayings and with pins heralding the arrival of a new type of German potato salad or specials on deviled ham. They always seemed to be having such a good time over there, howling at each other's jokes, shouting who's nexts and hellos to favorite customers, spinning so effortlessly from case to slicer to scale to wrapping area, completing each request with a bright "What else can I getcha?" I would be one of them now—at least when somebody came to the grinder counter and pulled on the wooden-handled bell.

"Are you kidding?" I asked him. "That would be great!"

More fun, more money, more hours. I couldn't believe this was happening to me! I left the store thrilled, and with a free Italian I was allowed to put together myself, mushy with lots of extra salad oil, just like I liked it. I thought of my parents: Would they love to hear this news—a promotion after only one month on the job! A few points for me, I was sure. A daughter whom somebody trusted enough to allow her to make food that people were going to take home and eat. That alone had to say something about me.

But when my shift was over, my mother, who picked me up each night at 6:30, was not in the rainy parking lot to tell this to in the cool, oh-yeah-by-the-way manner I had planned. And she was not there a half hour later, and when I used the pay phone to call home, the line was busy, busy, busy. When the store closed at eight, I was still waiting for her, had tossed my leaking grinder into the trash, and was reading for the fourth time the flyer for our next week's specials, taking note that the featured sandwich would be made of Lebanon bologna. Mr. Lenker was leaving and volunteered to drive me home, and so I went with him in his pointy white sportscar that was so small it had no backseat.

"Christ, you live in the woods," he told me as we climbed the hill, managing to hit each of the many potholes on the way up, and I said that was true, that I did live in the woods.

"But I guess when you get a house for free," he added, "you can't be picky about location. Right?" I said that was true, too, you can't.

"Take a right. Here." I pointed into the dark.

"There? There's a road? Oh, yeah." His lights hit the sign. "Conway Street . . ."

Mr. Lenker's car made a little purring sound as it slowed, then crawled onto the bumpy road. He speeded up the windshield wipers to clear the view, of nothing, then of nothing again, then of the lone white house on the left, its porch lights on, fifteen or so vehicles packing its driveway and edging its lawn. Even in the dark, I knew them from their silhouettes: the TV station's remote van, with its little platform on the roof to set up a camera there and get a better view if there is a big crowd in your way; the radio station's truck with its cluster of antennae growing from the roof; the four-wheel-drives of the newspaper photographers; and the messy little compacts of the newspaper reporters. At the head of all of them, what was that doing here, too—the nuns' station wagon?

"A party?" Mr. Lenker asked.

"Probably," I said flatly. I hadn't even opened the door, but this smelled of Betty and another page in her scrapbook.

"You want me to walk you to the door?"

I said no.

"You at least want an umbrella?"

I said no.

I thanked him for the ride and pulled my book bag from the space behind the seat, where he'd jammed green plastic rain gear and bird-watching books and one of those tiny folding canvas stools I used to see people bring to the polka park.

Mr. Lenker didn't move his car until I was up to the front of

the house and was waving back at him, assuring him that
nobody out here in the woods had grabbed me before I
reached my door. When he steered to turn around, I ran to the
backyard and climbed the wet slats up to the tree house. I
hadn't been up there in more than a year, and I wouldn't have
recognized where I was if I'd been brought up there blind-
folded. My posters had been covered by maps of the world,
and by a blackboard filled with Betty's first attempts at Palmer-
method penmanship. A coffee can of crayons, a tin of watercol-
ors next to a tiny easel and chair, one of her sweatshirts, neatly
folded, on its seat. My radio, its orange dial moved to where I
knew they played music like I heard at work, and worse, stuff
like you hear the choir trying to do at High Mass. Books
curling in the dampness: three Bobbsey Twins volumes, including the one in which I could remember their going down
the river in a houseboat; an encyclopedia volume open to a
full-page drawing of the human skeleton; "Raising Chickens
for Fun and Profit," the thick pamphlet she'd proudly bought
at the feed store with her own quarter; the hardcover French-
English English-French dictionary one of the reporters had
brought her long ago so Betty could hold a conversation with
Chatty Cathy.

The reporters. I remembered why I was up there, freezing, in
the first place, and I peered down into the house. The kitchen
was lit blindingly by the TV people and their silver lamps on
long legs, and it looked so warm in there I only then
remembered I should be shivering out in the cold. I wrapped
the damp little sweatshirt around my shoulders and watched
the people down there holding cameras and notepads and
microphones, blocking some of the view, circling around the
great kitchen table, pointing to what it held in one large pile, a
heap that looked to me like all the reports and paintings and
sculptures and booklets, even the stupid little pieces of sheet
music, that ever came from Betty's hands, and, seated at the
head of the table, Betty, Sister Superior to one side of her, my
parents on the other, posing with some laminated honor she'd
just found out she'd won.

Renaissance Child, I was to learn they called it—and now
called Betty—in the national competition the nuns secretly

had entered her in, though at only eight she was half the eligible age. She won it anyway, along with a $5,000 savings bond, shocking my parents so much they forgot to come and get Renaissance Child's sister, who had been stupid enough to think they would have gotten excited about my being given the new responsibility of packing greasy meatballs into a bun.

By the end of my junior year, I was working at the Food Basket twenty-nine-and-a-half hours a week, forced to limit it at that amount because it was half an hour less than the point at which they would have to give me health benefits and a brief paid vacation. I missed Theresa and Carolyn, whom I usually saw only a couple of times at school, then a few times a week afterward, when they came in to get grinders for their band friends. While I split the rolls and lined them up for assembly, they chattered about people I didn't know or only had seen listed on the programs of the concerts I more and more often wasn't showing up for. I asked them did they want American or Swiss, and they said "whatever" and told me I just HAD to make it to the pops concert—they were in a quartet that would be "interpreting," as they called it, a Barry Manilow medley. But "Mandy" was so beautiful it made Carolyn weep, and she said she was not sure she could get through it dry-eyed. I asked if they wanted oil or mayo. Mayo for Kathy and Michael, but not on Joe's or Johnny's. Oil on those, and nothing on Patrick's. Or Mary's. Like I was supposed to know who was getting what. Pickles? Just on the side, Theresa ordered, and she slapped the counter and said how it was the funniest thing, I should have been there—when they all had that picnic at the Quabbin, she has the image in her mind so clearly, of all of their little group flipping pickle chips from the tops of their sandwiches, to eat as dessert, and can you imagine having a whole carload of people who would find they had that same strange habit? I shook my head, and, my back still turned, added an extra 10 cents onto the price of each sandwich, though I had done nothing special to any of them.

With these strange people and the music and the talk of college, even, the girls were slipping away from me just as my real family had, and the pain, when I paid attention to it, was dull and familiar. Other than them, I missed Babci, who I saw only in the morning, returning too late at night to expect her to be awake for me. But she'd make it clear she was thinking of me, straightening my room even though she'd often remind me I shouldn't get used to such treatment, leaving a plate of cookies on my nightstand, leaving a prayer card from some long-dead person's funeral under my covers so that when I pulled them back, I would spot the loving face of God staring back at me, reminding me he had a plan. I felt sad about being so busy that this was the extent of my contact with Babci, but my schedule also gave me reason to miss the increasing number of Betty dates that kept the family running: scholastic practices, competitions, playoffs, award ceremonies, and the kitchen table press conferences that, I knew from the paper, she always ended eloquently by acknowledging the help from my parents, Babci, the Conways, and "my loving sister, Donna, who unfortunately could not be with us to-night."

I had no time to stick around and watch Betty accept yet another plaque or envelope full of cash. I had work to do, finishing my homework in the last-period study hall I was able to arrange for, then running over to the Food Basket for another race with Sticks, who liked to have as many trays as possible full and waiting for me when I arrived. There even was no time for boys, except for the few stock workers who stopped to flirt every so often, begging for a brain to toss around in the break room and gross out the cashiers who were trying to eat their cups of yogurt two feet away. The boys I liked, I'd make huge grinders for, but they didn't seem to take it as a compliment. One told me his whole family had sandwiches for an entire week after taking apart a 99-cent cold cut special that I'd packed with only him in mind.

But most of the time I was alone at my post in front of the enlarged photographs showing cuts of red meat wearing little paper decorations and lying on beds of parsley, angled just so, to show off their perfect marbling. Except for Sticks's occasional comments, or a shopper requesting a particular cut of something or some free bones for the dog, but who was probably going to go home and make soup of them, and except for some commotion when a shopper dropped a bottle of something slimy near the cases and the boys scrambled to mop it up before somebody fell and there would be a lawsuit, I was by myself. Once in a while, though, probably once every couple of weeks, I'd get the odd feeling you do when you are certain somebody is watching you. But I'd spin around, and no one would be there. One time it was a dog who apparently had been passing the store and must have walked across the pad that opened the door and entered that way. I knew something was there, and I turned to see him peeing on a stack of paper tablecloths that made up a corner of the Fourth of July display. Then he walked around the other side of the merchandise and let himself back outside.

Then, one night about a year later, I was slathering mayonnaise on the roast beef grinder ordered by some tall professional-looking woman in a bouclé business suit who said she loved the stuff even though her doctor said it was going to clog her arteries and probably kill her in the end, and I got that creepy feeling that somebody other than the lady was watching me. I turned around to see my father standing in front of a big cardboard heart that held a Valentine candy display. We just looked at one another for a few seconds, and then he walked away.

High school graduation was held at 6 P.M. on the football field. I attended only because I otherwise would not receive my diploma, and that had been the point of the previous four years of life. Theresa and Carolyn and I had gone shoe shopping together to purchase the correct heels that would make us all the same height, so we would have a better chance to be lined up together, and that's exactly how we ended up, though the spikes that Carolyn, the shortest of the three of us, had to purchase for the plan sunk into the grass as we walked to the staging, and she muttered under her breath with every halting "Pomp and Circumstance" step.

I thought I would go home to fill in silently but joyously that last red circle on my calendar, and then spend ten or fifteen minutes at the special supper that would include Worcester Babci and Dziadziu and that whole crew, who had managed not only to put aside their work for the day and come out for my graduation, but planned to continue on the next day for an unheard-of short vacation in the Berkshires, ending up, it turned out, at the Waverly Fabric mill ends store there. After seeing what I'd have to see of them, I thought, I'd beg for the car keys and drive down to the Lyszkos' house where there was going to be a big barbecue out back, and then Carolyn and I would go over to Theresa's, where her father was to be holding a party in the barn.

But you can never plan anything, even something as simple as gobbling a couple of *pierogi*, then saying see ya later and heading out to have your own fun with the people you really want to be with. The future I had longed for arrived unexpectedly that very night, wrapped inside the cut-out picture of a mountain scene that Babci delivered to my room and placed into my hand.

Though it embarrassed me to admit it to myself, I had dreamed of something big from her—a plane ticket to Aniela. Instead, I was given a key.

"Oh, my God—a car? Oh, Babci!" I jumped and jumped and hugged her, all so fast I almost knocked her over, and she laughed and shouted, "No, no. No car."

I stopped jumping. "A truck?"

"No truck." She looked into my eyes. I looked back, and I had the kind of a moment when you wonder about something that has nothing to do with what is going on at the time: I thought about all the things and people and time those eyes must have seen over the years, and how once they captured the same image that everyone else was getting, the rest of Babci went to work putting her blessing on it. Tugging my hand, she brought me back to the here and now, to where I was, there in my bedroom, the calendar I'd begun filling in kicked back under the bed when she had knocked.

"A house," she said, and her eyes went underwater.

I didn't get it, and she could tell.

"The old house. From your Babci, who never really sold it, was just renting for these years." The words were coming very slowly now. "To save for you. The thing you wanted the most. You need to be happy, I don't know what else would make you happy. You are an adult now. Go where you want to be. You don't think I know, but I know. I understand."

In the doorway, my mother, whom I hadn't noticed before, was wiping her eyes. All this didn't seem to be the surprise to her that it was to me. I looked at her, back at Babci. "You don't want to live there, too? You loved it there. You have to come."

"I'm too old," she said, telling me what I guess I expected would be her answer, but that I still hoped she wouldn't say. "Too many stairs. Too much up and down. I got used to modern. Who wouldn't?"

"But the neighborhood. You could walk to the store again!" She cut me off. "I'm too old. Too old to do any walking."

What do you say? I wasn't sure of that, but I knew what not to say. I did not say "Why did you do this" or "I can't accept this" or "I don't want this." So I said "Thank you," and the rest is something I remember like I was watching it from above, as they say you do in a near-death experience, looking down at the person you were, at the place you've always known, but feeling a mysterious, holy pull to where you're headed—wherever that is.

For me, I remember hearing the party noise that came from down the hall as I got out my backpack and set the pig bank in the bottom, wrapped in a sweatsuit. I pushed underwear and socks and a pair of jeans around it, and took my nightshirt from under my pillow, which I squished up and shoved into the top of the pack, pushing my prayer book into that wad, then buckling the whole thing closed. I took some necessities from the bathroom, with Babci and my mother trailing me in and out, handing me a towel, a face cloth, a shower cap, like I had ever used one in my life. I remember seeing myself in the bathroom mirror, still wearing the white silk graduation dress my mother had made—a clingy, grown-up wrapped thing made from a genuine $5 Vogue pattern designed by Diane von Furstenburg—pushing my tube of Winter-Fresh Close-Up toothpaste into a side pocket of the backpack, my mother and Babci behind me, their faces solemn.

I took my denim jacket from the hook on the back of my door, and then I went into the kitchen.

"Going out?" Worcester Dziadziu asked.

"Yes." Those who didn't know would find out soon enough. I didn't want to get into it right then.

"Those young people and their parties . . . ," Worcester Babci started, hugging. "You go on now. You're only young once!"

My father sat at the head of the table, smoking. He didn't look at me.

"Donna's going, dear," my mother said.

"I know," he replied, not looking up from his ashtray.

"She's going," Babci repeated for my mother.

"I said I know." He turned to me, and only I could hear this, low and absolute: "Leave, and there's no coming back. Ever. That's it. The end."

Betty all of a sudden got a strange look on her face, shot off Worcester Babci's lap and shrieked, "She's going!" and ran her lopsided way over to me as fast as she could, landing against me, pulling at my fine dress. "Don't go, Donna!"

"She's only going to a party," Cioci Urszula consoled, trying to remove Betty from me with no luck.

"She's go-o-o-oing!" Betty cried.

My father got up from the table and picked up Betty and brought her back to his chair, where she sniffled and looked at me sadly. "She's going, *Tatuś*," Betty bawled again.

"Hush," he told her stiffly, looking out the window, the dark shooting back to him only the reflection of the scene he had turned away from.

That's when I took my diploma from the table, where, in its blue-and-gold folder, it had been stood up next to the square cake Babci had put a blue upholstery tassel on to make it look like a mortarboard, and I turned, and without saying good-bye to any of them, I walked out the front door. On the porch, my mother choked out, did I want to go to counseling, a word I never would have imagined her using, and it made me feel a little sick to hear her say that. Maybe, she said, I could sort things out and be happy here, like she wanted me to be.

"Stay," she pleaded. "We can work on all this. We are your family. Here."

She was wrong. The family that I knew lived at 74 River Street, and that's where I was headed.

I would have liked to tell my mother and Babci that I loved them, but that was not what we did. So I hugged them both, individually, but not nearly as long as they wanted me to, and then I was gone, walking down Conway Street, the heavy coins shifting with each of my steps, the stones crunching under my feet as I put one foot in front of the other then again and again until I was away from the light of the house, and I looked back at the porch, where my mother and Babci still stood, their hands clasped like there was nothing else they could do now but pray. Behind the two of them, the curtain moved, and I saw my father's face looking out, but I knew he could not see me way out here in the dark. The front door pushed open, and Betty flew out onto the front lawn, running as best as she could down to the very edge of the road and stopping quickly, like there was an electric fence there that had caught her.

"Donna!" she screamed into the woods. "Donnaaaaaaa!!!"

I turned onto the street and headed down the hill, feeling each of those filled-in dots on my calendar as another step taken, as another foot closer to my new start. I walked down the center of the road, knowing well that nobody would be coming either way. Every so often, I stood there and closed my eyes and just listened. Crickets, nothing else. Then a sound. One that to me that was both sad and joyous at the same time. I went in its direction.

In a while, I passed the orchard, then picked up speed as the downhill got steeper and led me into the soft light of town, onto the common, past the gazebo, under the neon sign that blinked the words *Safe-Tam* over a deserted Main Street, closer and closer to what I heard, which was getting louder and clearer all the time. Halfway across the bridge, I stopped again and leaned over the railing and looked into the nothing that I knew was the water, way down there in the darkness, passing by so fast that it roared. I wondered how many times I had crossed that bridge, and I couldn't even try to guess where, right now, was the water that had been passing under it the first time I had gone over the river, and that had to be as a baby brought home from the hospital, wrapped and safe and not having one single idea of what the rest of my life would be like, which is the same way I was feeling right then.

I knew that water long ago had met the Chicopee and then the Connecticut, and then had flowed into Long Island Sound, and then got mixed up in the Atlantic, and I imagined it had gone on from there maybe around the world. And I was still crossing the same bridge I'd passed over that first time.

At the Lyszkos' were parked the cars of Carolyn's aunts and uncles and cousins, and of the fruit wholesaler who brought us girls free pomegranates, and of the newspaper's ad man who always left behind pens and rulers and notepads imprinted with the paper's masthead. Music and voices, singing and laughter swelled from the backyard, rising and spreading out over the street as did the smoke from the barbecue Mr. Lyszko and Ray Jr. had built years ago out near the stone wall.

For me, the store marked the beginning of the neighborhood, and it had been just one of the many places on these streets that I hadn't allowed myself near in almost four years. The building seemed both familiar and strange. There was the door I'd gone in and out of how many thousands of times, pushing the long, metal, orange-and-blue loaf-shaped Dreikorn's Bread ad that stretched across the screening. And there against the front of the building was the same wooden shelving I remembered Ray Jr. putting together all by himself way back in grade school, when even then he showed great abilities for construction. I watched him sweat and got a big thrill each time we touched fingers while I handed him nails that May Saturday that was so hot that Carolyn went inside and made us cantaloupe halves with vanilla ice cream scooped into the hole where the seeds had been. Now, in the cool dark, I set my pack down on the lowest shelf, the one that in the day, before they brought them in to keep them from animals and crooks, held sacks of potatoes and onions. In the darkened store window, I saw the round little tiger-striped watermelons stacked like cannon balls into a neat pyramid. The season's first, probably from Georgia, I knew. Grown so far from here, now look at them. Something about that made me pull on my load again and get on my way. As I passed the alley between the garage and the house, I could see a bonfire now blazing in the backyard, and, in the skinny space between the buildings, a silhouetted couple leaning against a stack of fruit crates, kissing like the world was about to end.

Up the street, a string of blue and gold balloons thumped against the mailbox of Theresa's Acres Dairy Farm, to which somebody had taped a sign that read "Party" in Mr. Zych's handwriting. A noisy car went by me, then passed the mailbox, then rammed into reverse, then jerked forward and headed up to the farm, its occupants whooping.

A little more length of woods, and there it was. The entrance to the park. The little blackboard wired to the chain-link fence was chalked with the words "LENNY GOMULKA AND CHICAGO PUSH," whose music was the sound I had followed all the way down the hillside.

As you'd expect, cars were parked all the way back to the fence. People who either didn't like being in the crowded pavilion or who were sneaking their own food and drink from their trunks sat in folding chairs, a citronella candle here and there to break up the dark.

"I have a honey, she is a dear," sang Lenny. *"All that she likes is ice cubes and beer."*

I knew that song, back when I lived in the house I was walking up to the front of, the one I had not seen in such a long time that I had to stop and make sure it was real. The dark, the long walk, the mere fact that I had left them all behind in the space of a few minutes all made this more dreamlike, and everything about it was larger, even though there was little light, and everything was much more vivid than my mind had ever replayed it in those hundreds of worn-out memories. But there it was, exactly as I had remembered it, not an inch of it changed in the four years, as much as I could see in the dim streetlight. Babci's parlor lights even were on, which gave me a welcoming feeling, even though I knew they now had to belong to strangers.

I saw this from above as if in a dream, how I walk up the stairs of the side porch and fit the key into the lock. How the door clicks open and I go inside. How, over my head, the cross, still hanging from the braided string, glows in the dark. How I am home.

Chapter

11

$\mathcal{I}$t happened on the day the Super Plus tampon was launched, and it is one of those crazy things about life how you look forward to a particular date for a year or so, thinking only how you are going to be getting from the company a free T-shirt and all the pizza you want, not that you will get from your sister a knock on your door during your bowl of Rice-A-Roni and the news that your father is dead.

But how could you know such a thing ahead of time? And, certainly, if you could know it, wouldn't you have started acting a whole lot differently a long time before you finally got around to it?

I can only guess that.

I worked on the Super Plus line for two whole years before it was introduced to the public. It was the first time in all my sixteen years at Safe-Tam that I went to work so excited each day. I had always liked my job all right—it was a clean place, the work was not strenuous, the women with whom I worked were the kind that were always collecting money to help somebody through a broken bone or some other hardship, and

186

most of the men were the kind that apologized when they used any really serious swears—but work is work, and unless you're an inventor or something, I can't imagine any kind of a career being so fascinating day in and day out that it would be the best part of your life. But the Super Plus project was something else—a secret within the industry that Safe-Tam had founded, an industry that now, half a century later, was packed with brash, fast-moving competitors who broke new ground by creating television commercials that showed women verbalizing their menstrual woes in great detail as easily as the ladies on TV had once discussed ring around the collar.

Safe-Tam had built its empire on the hope that mothers would pass down to their daughters the same products they had used, and its scant few advertisements, scattered in the foggy last dozen or so pages of a couple of women's magazines, showed those mothers and daughters chatting as they brushed their hair in the same mirror.

"Another thing you can share with her," read the copy.

There were no words like "fluids" or "bloating" or "leakage" in Safe-Tam's ads, and certainly no anatomical diagrams like those that took up half of the ad space for Ladyfairs, an up-and-comer that boasted also how they were designed by a woman, as opposed to, it would add, "what your mother used, which was created by a MAN."

The new Super Plus was to "reposition" Safe-Tam, the plant newsletter, *Tam Times*, said. ("Ouch!" was the big joke on the floor.) Not only would this groundbreaking product be the most efficient tampon ever on the market, its packaging would be of recycled and recyclable materials, and one percent of all profits would be donated to a variety of not-too-controversial women's groups. It all was to be heralded by the company's first television campaign, starring real-life females who over the years had written fan letters to Safe-Tam, never imagining at the time they sat down at their typewriters or their flowery note cards that their words someday would be beamed by satellite from one end of the continent to the other. Many months of discussions between the public relations people and Safe-Tam executives preceded the choices, which ended up including a teacher up in Alaska who flew her plane from one tiny village to the next to teach kids who otherwise would not be in school, and a veterinarian in New Mexico who spent most of her free time driving a car full of friendly dogs to visit lonely old people whom nobody else ever went to see. In a bow to the company's hometown, they also picked Mrs. Strzemienski, who ran a dairy farm, served on the Board of Selectmen, founded a recycling center run by Boy Scouts, and twice a week baked macaroons that were sold next to the cash register at the town's only convenience store, their proceeds benefitting our library's new literacy program. The campaign featured a dozen women in all, and each was described as someone who was much too busy and didn't have the time to waste worrying about her choice of feminine protection—like the rest of us who weren't out saving the world did.

It was a big undertaking, and we had been there at the start, seated at a special station, just me and my friend Stella Muniec, checking the sample batches for defects.

The Super Plusses were created, as the label said, to provide "the ultimate protection you deserve," and, in order to do that, were sized as its name suggested: Super Plus, and Super Plus enough to have Safe-Tam's engineers produce a series of special new Super Plus-scale machines, including the mammoth shiny contraption that spit out the special huge Super Plus-sized applicators—the ones that Stella informed me more than a few times were the size of the tubes that her tin foil came rolled around.

What landed on our inspection table were the assembled and wrapped Super Plusses that had fallen from their long conveyor belt ride that began way across the factory, over at the stuffing machine, and ended at our end of the building, at the nearby machine that would have inserted thirty-eight of them—plus a bonus two in a daisy-printed plastic purse container—into the world-famous Safe-Tam cartons, the ones with a revamped version of the famous soft-focus photograph of a woman skipping through a meadow toward the slogan, "Freedom 365 days a year," that billowed above the horizon.

But instead of being on their way to the medicine cabinets and pocketbooks and glove compartments of women in Providence and Duluth and Yakima, their next stop after falling for some reason into the special troughs edging the conveyor belts was a rolling crate that, when filled, was wheeled over to Stella and me, who sat at a table beneath a sign that, for the benefit of the tour groups who regularly passed through, explained that we were "Safe-Tam Quality Control, Special Project."

Stella and her pincurls and bifocals had been stationed under a regular Safe-Tam Quality Control sign for ages—since way before the higher-ups even got the bright idea to name the workstation that. Since 1950, when her kids entered school and Safe-Tam advertised its need for part-timers, there she has been, raking through the products, searching for problems, making sure that those that had fallen were good enough to return to the line. The rest, with their ripped wrappers or wrinkles or bends or smudges, were tossed into a trash can (in later years, into a blue plastic bin labeled RECYCLING). The work was a most important part of the process: Safe-Tams were, after all, sanitary protection.

Stella had twenty-seven years experience at the plant and thirty years experience at life over me and enjoyed never letting me forget it, through such comments as "When you've been doing this as long as I have, you can tell me how to do it" were made good-naturedly and with the full knowledge that I could spot a flawed wrapper from across the building.

I was kind in return. After all, it was due to Stella that I got this job when I needed it, when I moved out a whole lot quicker than I would have thought. Mr. Lenker loved my work in the meat department, but he sadly informed me there was nothing available full-time, which was the type of job I had determined I would need if I were to survive on my own. But on the same day he told me that, Stella came by my cases for the essentials she would turn into marrow balls for her niece's daughter's neighbor's baby shower, and as I handed her a fresh package that had just been scraped from a barrel of beef bones, she leaned over the row of gizzards and whispered, "They're hiring at Safe-Tam."

It was not just any job. Getting hired at the tampon factory was both a way to make money and a big way, from miles away, to step on my father's heart one more time.

Not having given a thought to a career other than living on

my own, and not too sure I wanted to study more than I already had, I hadn't bothered to send out any college applications. So, like my father with Winkie Papuga picking him up every morning, I had Stella Muniec coming by the house at 6:45 A.M. and tapping her wedding band on my kitchen door window and walking with me down the street and over the bridge and up the loading dock steps into the warm, humming, brightly lit factory. When you came right down to it, it was not a much different situation than my father's ending up working at Blue Ribbon. It was a good and a regular paycheck, and we were both stuffing things that, while not necessary for existence, were such that, had they not been made by somebody, sorely would be missed in daily life.

Stella—and she liked to put it this way with a wink—had "pulled a few strings" to get my application to the top of the pile in the personnel office, and within half a year of starting my new life back in the old house, I was holding a paycheck that by itself was enough to get me half of the five-piece Naugahyde living room set I had seen displayed in the window of Topor Furniture: a sofa, a recliner, an end table, a coffee table, and a lamp covered with ancient maps that showed serpents floating in the oceans. And besides the good money, the rest of what Stella had whispered to me that day in the Food Basket also had turned out to be the truth: Safe-Tam did not require weekend hours, was within walking distance of my home, had a polite management, and offered a modest profit-sharing program, separate cafeterias for smokers and non-smokers, and a free box a month.

You could get used to things like that, and I did. I made for myself a nice little life that consisted of working from 7 A.M. to 3 P.M., then coming home to do what needed to be done there. Mainly, I was on my own, and though it could be a lot of work with household chores and such, I was by myself, with nobody around to disappoint me but me. And that had been the point of all this. I wasn't bothered much by my next-door neighbors, the people who lived where Babci had, Mr. and Mrs. Kulis—Henryk and Ann—a retired couple who for something like thirty years had driven the little over two hours from their home in Vermont just to polka dance across the street. Four summers ago they thought they were hallucinating when they saw the realtor's sign in front of my house, and they decided this would be their retirement home—or at least half of it. For the winter, they drove to a golf resort in Florida that they got interested in when they saw Ted Williams talking about it on a television commercial. They didn't golf, but they loved baseball, and they thought maybe Ted would be living there and might be available at all hours to talk about his many great accomplishments and pose for photographs. He'd yet to show up, but they continued to hope.

Henryk and Ann told me that when they moved in during what was my family's first summer on the hill, there had been a young couple with two little boys living on my side of the house, and that they stayed only for about a year. The wife had been a gymnast at Springfield College, which couldn't have been too long ago from the young and flexible appearance of her, they said, and when her kids were napping, she'd put on a pink leotard and white tights and would leap around the backyard, jumping through plastic hoops that she held for herself in midair, and whirling dramatically while she held long ribbons that spun the way she did.

"She also could roll a beach ball-sized ball down her arms, and kick it up to balance it on her toes while doing a handstand," Mrs. Kulis told me, moving her arms and a leg at the appropriate times in the story. "She told us that it would be only a matter of time before the Olympics people accepted her type of sport, and she wanted to be ready. My husband and me, we're not judges, but you know she certainly appeared to be good enough."

They told the gymnast they would watch for her on TV, which they did every Saturday afternoon, tuning in to "ABC's Wide World of Sports," hoping to see her in some preliminary competition even long after the woman and her husband and the two little boys packed their car and left without saying not only where they were going but that they were going at all.

The next tenants were the Fosters, a forty-ish no-nonsense couple who stayed for another short time—only eight months or so after they had sold their home in Enfield and before the old house they had bought out near Warren was renovated, from top to bottom, into an inn. They were home only to sleep, the rest of the time at their jobs as real-estate agents in Springfield, or driving all over creation selecting bathroom fixtures, or helping the workmen tear down plaster, or driving to printers to design brochures and business cards. The Kulises called them "high-powered" people who never ate at home, and by the time they moved out, they hardly had unpacked any of the dozens of boxes that had been unloaded from a rental truck. When the work was done and they moved their things over to Warren, the Fosters gave the Kulises an envelope containing a gift certificate for one free night at the Riverview Bed and Breakfast, where innkeepers Gloria and Trip Foster would offer them historic accommodations, a free continental breakfast and the use of folding chairs and binoculars and insect repellent if they wished to go and sit near the water.

"We really want to go and stay there some day," Ann told me, "and I don't know why we haven't yet. This has nothing to do with it, but do you know that Trip's name had been Phil on all the mail I collected for them the couple of times they'd asked me to?"

My side of the house had been empty for more than a year by the time I let myself in on graduation night, set down my stuff, and roamed the two floors, trying to walk softly so as not to alarm the people next door, but trying to inspect as much as I could in the light of the few bulbs that had been left behind. The place was as empty as we'd left it, but the walls had been stripped of any wallpaper, and all of them, even the ones that had been light blue or soft yellow, had been painted a creamy white, and in that way the space was like one big canvas I could throw my future unknown life against. I was awake most of that night, just stretched out on a rectangle made of the clothes I'd brought, afraid to actually sleep and maybe wake to find out I'd been dreaming all this.

At one point, I tried to call Theresa and Carolyn, knowing they would leave their parties in an instant if they knew where I was, and we would all be here, the three of us, celebrating together. But the phone had no sound on any of the twenty times I checked it, and I eventually gave up. I would call them in the morning. I would say come on over, come over to my house.

After I moved out, I saw my family only at mass, in their usual pew on the side of the church that had the St. Joseph's statue, one row before the second pillar from the rear, in back of the Swiderskis and in front of Mr. Ziemba and the son who came home from his job down in Farmington to visit every weekend except those on which we were having a blizzard. In their usual order, from the middle of the pew out, sat my mother, Betty, Babci, then my father. I wondered how the back of my head and shoulders used to look tucked in between Babci and my father, then I wondered if it had looked any different for the couple of months after Betty arrived and nothing really bad had happened yet and she had been given my space—for translation purposes, they had said—and I had been relocated between my mother and Babci and their rosaries that revolved with the swiftness of a bicycle chain. But when I went off on my own, for the first time I took a seat separate from them, a folding chair and a portable kneeler under the choir loft, one row away from the confessional, where nobody ever sat during confession time because it's so close there is no way you can help but hear someone's entire guts being spilled.

The organ and choir boomed and vibrated above me as I knelt on the wiggling kneeler and asked God for guidance and more people like Mrs. Walters to happen across my path and help me with things I knew nothing about, as she had with the opening of a checking account and the explanation of how I could get in big trouble not only if I didn't make out enough checks to the people who sent me bills, but also if I didn't deposit enough money to make those pieces of paper worth something. I would pray for such things, then I would skip communion, sneaking out the door for fear of bumping into most of them when church let out, and would get a head start on my walk home.

I didn't know what I expected from my family when I first left, but I really didn't care. There was a headiness about being away from them, and it rolled over most of any homesickness that might have found me. After all, how could I get homesick when I was truly home? Back where there were neighbors, and activity, and a sidewalk I could take at night and walk up one street and across the next, passing houses lit by dim lamps or television screens, laugh tracks rolling out front screen doors, someone coming onto the porch in a housecoat to water a geranium or to hand someone another beer, unseen dogs barking at me, then, when I passed their territory, they'd stop, and there'd be nothing but silence—the kind that was on the hill, but it was different in a way—because it was not strange. I can truly say I was never afraid to be alone, and that I most certainly never rolled over in anger when my sleep would be cut by the train at night, barreling down the tracks laid six feet from my bedroom wall, bound for somewhere that you would not know about unless you were that engineer.

Theresa was at the clothesline when I rounded the bend in her long driveway late the next morning. Fat stuffed garbage bags dotted the lawn, overflowing with beer cans and stained paper plates and all the other remnants of the night's party. I picked up a paper napkin that had blown into my path and threw it into one of the sacks.

"Oh, *now* you come over," Theresa said crabbily, not turning from her work, which, now that I was closer, I could tell was hanging out to dry all the rags she'd used in cleaning the mess I had missed helping to make the night before.

"I'm sorry," I said, handing her a clothespin, which she grabbed without looking at me.

"Just 'cause the Lyszkos were having steak," Theresa said with disgust. "Big deal. So we have hamburgers. You could at least have come by for a minute."

"I didn't go there."

"Right."

"I didn't."

Theresa stopped her work. "So," she said, finally turning to me, her eyes, which probably had shut for two hours before Mr. Zych came along and told her to get up and start cleaning up the place, bloodshot and sinking into her head. "Where'd you go?"

My smile started small, then, without any help from me, spread wide like somebody was pulling the sides of my face apart.

I said to Theresa: "I went home."

That night, the three of us had our own party, with more leftover steaks and hamburgers and cans of beer than thirty-three people would have needed. The girls walked through the house like they'd never been in it before, looking around corners, then looking back at me, and saying things like "All this is yours?" Theresa was rather speechless for the first time I knew of, and Carolyn spun around and waved her hands like she was going to make things appear out of thin air.

"Here," she said, pointing to nothing, "you put your big stuffed chair. Here, you put your television set. Here, you get a hook and hang one of those ferns that never needs water."

"And where's she gonna get all that stuff?" Theresa asked.

Carolyn thought about it. "From that guy, over there," she said, pleased with herself, pointing at another empty space, at something else she had invented. "He's going to pay for everything!"

"And where's she gonna get him?"

Carolyn took another second. "How should I know?" she asked. "But when she finds him, everything's gonna be perfect!"

I had to stop this. "That might be fine for you, but I'm paying for my own things, thank you very much," I said. "So tell whatever-his-name is to go back where he came from."

Carolyn waved her hands in the direction of the front door. "Beat it," she said. "Donna is an adult in her very own house who doesn't need anybody—even you." Then she waited a few seconds and turned to me. "He's gone," she said.

"Good," I said. Then I looked into the empty room. "What'd he look like, anyway?"

I was there for just short of two weeks when Babci appeared at the door, on the second Thursday night, with bags full of all the fresh bread and cleanser and utensils and blankets and pillows I could use, and with knickknacks I really didn't want, but that I accepted with fake enthusiasm for fear of hurting her feelings, Babci looking so nervous and all to come into what was her own house. She smiled and nodded at how clean I kept the place and stood still and admired any attempts I made at decoration—even how I might arrange on the pantry counter the single celery-colored drinking glass and plate I had picked up for an even dollar at Zebo's dusty little secondhand store.

"It is none of my business," she said, running her finger along the edge of the counter, but do you know that peelings kept under the sink for too long will attract ants?"

"I know."

"You know that the storm windows will have to be pulled down once the furnace starts turning on in the fall?"

"Okay."

"If you get a welcome mat, you will be tracking that much less dirt into the house."

"Good idea."

"And you shouldn't open the door to just anybody. You know that, don't you?"

I said I did. Those were the easy things. What I needed tips on were the things enclosed in the file of house papers she handed to me—the numbers for oil delivery and chimney cleaner, the schedule of rental payments for the tenants, the receipt for that year's tax payment—all the stuff I found out had been the business of Johnny Frydryk in the years we were gone, and she told me that Johnny had said to just go next door and knock if I needed anything and to keep in mind he would be willing still to do the mowing and shoveling if I wanted him to, free of charge, as it would get him up off his duff and out of the house that much more, something he would appreciate.

I made us some iced tea, and Babci and I sat on the back steps—the only chairs I had at the time—and she talked to me about the hot weather and the blueberries she was planning to pick and the presser foot that had broken on my mother's machine and the deer that had run through the yard early that morning. But she never said one word about my father and Betty. Then my mother drove up and honked, and Babci kissed me and got her handbag and walked to the car and they were gone.

My mother did not get out of the car because, I eventually

found out from Babci, who felt I deserved an explanation, my father had told her she mustn't go down to the house—that if I was going to live like an adult, I had to be treated like one, and that meant not running to me to help. So what she did was to say, once he came home with the car, that she was going to the new Stop & Shop on Boston Road, and that Babci was coming along. And, as she would do the first and third Thursday night a month, my mother would drop Babci at my door while she went off to the grocery, and then she would pick her up on the way back, motioning for her to come quickly, and telling me, "Sorry, I can't stay—everything okay?" and throwing me a tank top or a wraparound skirt or a tea cozy or a set of four napkins in a maroon paisley I could imagine might have been used for someone's coatdress. Because she was nervous about what she was doing—she had never before lied to him, Babci told me (though I knew that as well as I knew about the ants and the storm windows)—there was no time to talk. It was as if my mother was doing what she could, throwing me this lifeline of warmth and homemade food and housekeeping tips every couple of weeks, and then sailing past to reel it back in until next time.

Babci, church, the polkas I enjoyed from my porch every Sunday afternoon, those were my constants. And I treasured such connections to my old circle, which by the fall quickly was becoming more of a tiny dot. I was seeing Theresa and Carolyn less and less frequently as time went by, though we kept a standing phone date at 7 P.M. every Monday, me on my end, the two of them bumping heads as they shared the pay phone in the stairwell at the end of their floor. Mr. Edgewood, the high school bandleader, had talked them into applying for music scholarships at UMass, and I was at their houses to hear them scream when they opened the envelopes that told them they'd been given enough money not only to go there for half the price but even to live on campus in huge brick dormitories where boys and girls used the same toilets.

Carolyn enrolled because she decided she would like to become a music teacher. Theresa went along because they let her in, and because the actor Richard Gere had attended the school, and she had this idea that he might come back often, just to walk around, and, as the Kulises had thought with Ted Williams, she might get the opportunity to run into him. The university was only about half an hour away from town, yet it was frighteningly simple to fall out of touch. Early on, I went often to see the two of them, eagerly hitching a ride with Ray Jr. when he mentioned he had the time to head out there. The traveling part of the few trips we made was fun, bouncing down the back roads in Ray Jr.'s truck, closing my eyes and listening to his sad Jackson Browne cassettes, and pretending his sister Marilyn wasn't sitting between us jiggling her leg. But once we arrived, it was like the high school music department all over again—Carolyn and Theresa glad to see me but thick among all kinds of lively, dramatic people I didn't know and didn't care to get to know, packing into strange cars to drive to Poor Richard's and dance wildly in big, out-of-control groups that laughed hysterically over things I knew nothing about. It wasn't too long before I found myself not going out of my way to visit, even if it meant losing a chance to see Ray Jr.

I began to make my own friends, reconnecting with a few old neighbors—the Frydryks, of course, and, in the next house down, Blind Tekla and her dog, and, across the tracks, the Mazurs and the Sobons and Zbylots—none of whom had hated me too much after the accident and actually were excited to see at least one member of my family back in the home, which they saw as the way things ought to be. At work, I met lots of new people, including new boys—men, actually, I guess you could call them here in the adult world.

Stella had warned me not to get involved with anyone at work, but early on I couldn't help myself. I was still a teenager when I began there, with my own place and without any parents that you could see, and with not a whole lot of sense about a whole lot of things. And it took a while for me to wise up. But not before I checked out what was available in production, maintenance, shipping and packing, and in the night watchmen's break room.

Such behavior was not what I had been taught, but it became the main goal of my social life—to piss off my father. I use that word because not only was that what my choices did, but that very word, used by me in front of him, also would have accomplished the same thing.

As I once had chosen my boyfriends for what rides or free meals with the girls I could get out of them, I went on to select them for how much mileage they could get me in infuriating my father. If I could remember his ever saying one word or expression against a particular family, I searched that entire tree for an eligible male to go around town with. This wasn't easy, as my father usually didn't have many bad words to say about anyone, other than those he held in his head about me. But I raked my memory, and if my father ten years ago had said the Wtoreks were ignorant or if he had been laughed at by a Bitalski or gypped by a Malonek or a Rys, I went and asked one of them out.

The sad thing—okay, one of the sad things—was that I had really no idea if my father ever would find out about any of this. All the machinations, the energy put into running around, the many hours spent with people I couldn't have cared less about or for, all that work put into getting back at someone, all that energy used in my first attempts at revenge, were, like my early tastes of hate, enough to make you lose your appetite.

But I found myself coming back for more. The choice of a date, a partner, was so important to my father; he had often mentioned, usually at holidays or on his wedding anniversary, when there was the silence that happens as you are about to propose a toast, that the person you chose to be with said so much about you. Easy for my father to say, with his pick running right into him as she had, and she being the exact perfect one for him. But I had never fallen in love at first sight. Except with him.

So I overlooked or ignored the people who had no negative connotations. Little George Manyak was funny and smiled at me when I was in the cafeteria at work, but my father liked his parents even though they attended the kind of Polish church that didn't recognize the Pope. I remember my father even had delivered them a carton of eggs once Betty's hens began laying.

Peter Dolat had wanted me to go to Bermuda with him— even would have paid for the plane and everything—but when he was about twelve he had helped Babci home with her cart in a rainstorm, and I remember my father saying he would never forget that kindness.

Arthur Krowka brought me flowers from his garden, but my father always had commented on the neatness of his family's yard each time we passed it, and that eliminated him, and any possibility that my father would get excited about maybe eventually having a son-in-law who could work magic with bearded irises.

It was different with Greg Neboski. He not only had a dump for a front lawn (the mailman eventually just started tossing his mail onto the ripped-up front seat of the rusty old truck that blocked the porch, rather than climb over it to get to the letter slot in the door), but he had been kicked out of the St. Stan's Club for making an extra key to the bar and helping himself after hours.

It was different with Dickie Patla, who got his picture in the *Penny Saver*, right over Betty's. But while she was digging a hole in which to plant a tree she bought with her own savings in honor of Sister Superior's fiftieth year in the convent, he was shown digging post holes along Route 181 as part of a community service sentence he had been handed—later claiming he didn't mean nobody no grief—after he drove his car down the same road while his friend hung out the window and whacked every mailbox with a baseball bat.

It was different with Leo Stolba, whose father, everybody knew, was a business partner in an adult video store in Wilbraham.

And it was different with Carl Gosse, who could be seen on Main Street every Sunday morning, shaking hands next to his father, who was the minister of the only Protestant church in town.

I took a regular spot next to the dazed-looking guy who hung out on the bridge. I swam at Forest Lake with the shady little man who ran the package store on the way to Ware and had fathered at least two kids without ever getting married. I danced slow with the art teacher who wore an earring and, some said, did not wear underwear.

Each of them another stone I wanted to pile on my father,

another shot right back at him. It might seem different to you, but it all made perfect, perfect sense to me.

Maybe there was some kind of a curse in all this, but few of these people were someone you'd want to have anything to do with more than once or twice. As I had in high school, I surrounded myself with people I really didn't want to be around. But as it is with these kinds of ruts, I was so deep into it that it was all I saw around me, and I knew little else than another blip on my radar when I saw a loser slouching his way toward me.

Barney Lembo was a pretty typical beau. Somebody whose family's roofing business long ago had nailed inferior shingles onto our house and had denied all responsibility when they began curling in the sun a couple of months later. And somebody whose idea of a date was crashing a wedding reception.

A lot of preparation went into this—a lot for somebody like Barney Lembo, that is. It meant forking over a couple of dimes for a *Daily News* on Saturday morning and studying the wedding announcements and figuring out which ones were taking place that day, then calling me up and telling me to get all dressed up, like I did with much anticipation that first time, then driving past halls and pavilions and matching the names written in shaving cream on the backs of the wedding get-away car to the ones he'd seen on the social page.

The first time, I didn't know what he was up to. I just figured he had been invited, and I was excited, never before having attended a wedding.

"Where's your gift?" I asked him as he parked his car on a side street, exactly in the circle of a shade tree. I knew that much, that you had to bring something.

That's when Barney Lembo opened his glove compartment and took a long white envelope from a whole box of them. He found a pen inside his jacket and wrote on the outside the names I'd seen shaving-creamed onto the car.

"It's right here," he said with a smile, and he licked it closed, without putting a thing inside.

It both fascinated me and made me nervous how easily he

walked into that crowd and pulled me by the hand over to a small wishing well frothy with white tulle, and how he confidently tucked his envelope inside and patted it for good luck. An old lady sitting next to the well nodded at him, and he shook her hand and told her it was wonderful to see her again.

Then Barney Lembo added, "This is my girlfriend—I don't believe you've met her before," and there I was, shaking the old lady's weightless little hand, telling her how good she looked and how nice it was to be here.

There were drinks. Music. Long tables of the kind of food they put out for you when you've already eaten a big sit-down meal earlier on: macaroni salad, cold cut platters, little bread boats jammed with tuna or chicken salad, large pans of Jell-O with pieces of canned fruit hanging suspended. We feasted and talked only with drunk people who could not be expected to place us, and if they did, others would only chuckle at their attempts. You were at her school? No. From the Boy Scouts? No. From when his family lived above the auto parts store? No. From that first job, that one summer at Lake Bomoseen?

When you thought about it, Barney Lembo really had come up with a great idea. The parties were all wonderful and free. We got to dress up and see other people who also were in their finery. Plus, aside from all the matches and napkins you could carry away, there sometimes were real prizes—small, handy souvenirs imprinted with the couple's names and date: change purses, rain bonnets, shoe-shine kits, flashlights the size of a pen, drinking cups that expanded from a tight circle of plastic and included a container for your pills in the lid. I kept these things on my dresser, and lining them up I could trace a whole summer of parties. June 20, Danuta and Marek. June 27, Yvette and Bruce. July 19, Roma and Fred. August 1, Julianne and Michael. The Polish American Citizens Club. The Gremio Lusitano Club. Chez Celeste. The Villa Rose. Pilch's Plantation. A whole bunch of VFWs.

Sometimes I liked how it was, that we were anonymous, and that we were forced in a way to stay by ourselves, lest someone ask too many questions. Other times I craved being part of it all, more than I was by simply being there. In the ladies' room,

I'd accept the cigarette from the maid of honor and, as she reblended her eyeshadow, would listen to how she never liked the groom, how she knew this was all a mistake, but what could she do? Mark her words, though, Claudia would live to regret this. I wanted to shout—let's go and free her—let's save her while we can—while she can still get this annulled— while the presents are still unopened and everyone who brought them is still here to take them back—while it's still easy! But somewhere in that whole process of rescuing Claudia, I would become so involved that someone surely would ask me what did I care—and, most importantly, who was I anyhow? And then what would I do? So I stayed silent and just shook my head, exhaled smoke with a disgusted puff and said "I have to get back outside, to my man," as I called Barney Lembo that one time, never before in my life remembering having used such a term.

"Yeah, my man's out there somewhere, too," hacked the maid of honor, now pulling an eyelid down to line the inside of it with a thick blue pencil.

"But he can rot waiting for me."

At one of the weddings, Barney Lembo had a beautiful, darkly tanned bridesmaid trailing him all day, and I found myself standing by him often and protectively. Even though I told him I really wouldn't have cared much if he ended up going off with her, I found that I liked having something somebody else wanted, even if he wasn't that much at all to begin with. At another reception, the bride and groom spent the afternoon drinking tall bottles of beer in separate corners of the hall, and as they were being led away by their parents at the end of the night, the groom—a guy I'd never seen before that day and couldn't have because, I learned in the conga line, he flew in the night before from somewhere in Alabama— lunged at me, and they had to pull him off me as he whispered hotly into my ear that he was so glad I had finally shown up, that I was the one he always truly wanted to marry.

I shrugged off such things—they happened more often than you might at first think, with all the emotions and whiskey that flow at such parties. I found I became hooked on the meals and the festive atmosphere and the music (Barney Lembo wasn't even a bad dancer), on the traditions, the speeches and toasts. We got to live for a late afternoon and an evening in a fantasy world where most everybody was the happiest they were ever going to be. And, best of all, it didn't cost us one red cent.

Each of our outings was such a Garden of Eden experience—until the reception for a Gene Petruszka and a Mary Los, whose name, I didn't find out until it was way too late, really was Mary Loszcz. She had changed it for professional reasons (even though she didn't have a job), so there's no way I could have known that we would crash a party attended by the entire Loszcz family, including Sleepy Loszcz, who was not only the bride's father but the guy my father had picked out of a snowdrift one night outside St. Stan's, where he'd passed out long enough for a stiff coating of sleet to form over him, and where, his family shrieked when my father brought him to the door with his head still a cap of ice, he certainly would have died if it weren't for Adam Milewski, who didn't see what the big deal was because, though he didn't tell them this, Sleepy Loszcz regularly collapsed onto the snow, only usually not when it was sleeting out. While his children chipped away at their father in the front hall, my father was given a cup of coffee and a slice of warm *babka* and was assured he never would be forgotten by a single one of them.

So that explains why the Loszczs always sent a Christmas card (usually a photo of their kids, Sleepy Jr., Marysia, and Phyllis, who usually were wearing their pajamas and looking stiff and self-conscious as they peered up the fake chimney of the Loszcz's fake fireplace), why they delivered Betty a different knitted garment (Mrs. Loszcz was a fiend with the needles) every month for the entire first year after the accident, why they were always bringing over surplus zucchini, and why, at the reception for a Gene Petruszka and a Mary Los, when, fueled by shots of the label-less vodka the bartender informed us came from the potatoes grown on the groom's ancestral land near Bialystok, Barney Lembo and I, whirling past the band, eyes shut, whooping and shouting through the chorus of

"Who Stole the Kiszka?," slammed right straight into my parents.

They both looked shocked, probably as shocked as I did. First nobody moved, then my mother leaned forward, hugged me quickly, then stepped back. I awaited my father's reaction to my being out with such a cheat. Instead, he heartily shook Barney Lembo's hand and said how he remembered so clearly that when little Betty was in the hospital, Mr. Lembo had come to the door one night, crying and saying he was going to be mending his ways, and how he would put a new roof on not only the house but the garage, too, both free of charge, the next single, snowless day.

The party was over, I told Barney Lembo five minutes later, on the way home.

The same year Betty became a doctor, I was named a Safe-Tam Safe Employee and got my photograph hung next to the Coke machine for 30 days.

Other than Babci once every couple of weeks, and my mother's pale face in the dome light when she dropped her off and hurriedly collected her, I saw my family only in church. I never went up to the house. Ever. That's it. The end. My mother and Babci were extra generous with the food around the holidays, to make sure I had at least one dishful of all the stuff they were turning out at the house, which could be mine in endless quantities if I wanted to come up. But I didn't, as much as a part of me wanted to be there from day to day, if only to see my mother and Babci so often that their getting older—that their graying hair and their getting shorter and softer and rounder and wrinklier and wearier—wouldn't be as unsettling to me as it was when I did see them.

And except for what I saw of him in church, I really didn't know what my father looked like, and I really didn't care. As for updates on Betty, there was always the paper's cloying "Betty's Progress" feature, which, long, long, long after you'd think it would be of interest to anyone, reported on how "our Betty" was doing. It ran far less frequently as the years went on, but if you were a regular reader, you would have seen something about her every month or so for the first couple of years after I left. Then for a couple of times a year, first mostly at the holidays, then on just about any other occasion—or non-occasion—the paper came up with.

On Valentine's Day, a photo captioned "Love from Many" showed an eleven-year-old Betty, tongue between her teeth, working hard at slitting a pile of envelopes sent by people who still treasured her and probably always would.

Or Betty, a couple of months later, coloring Easter eggs, etching her initials into the shells of eggs she'd dyed with onion skins just like she would have back in her homeland. Later that year, on the first day of school, waiting on the corner of Conway Street. She had walked there all by herself, with just one thin cane, for the first time.

Betty, at thirteen, a mascot. Bursting through a huge January calendar page, wearing a party hat and tooting a paper horn that read "Happy New Year!" On Groundhog Day, Betty peering into a hole, waiting for the animal to come waddling out and see its shadow. At Halloween, her hand to her chin and her head tilted as she deliberated over which pumpkin she should select from the hill of them that appeared in front of Olson's farm every fall.

Betty, at fourteen, a parakeet on her shoulder, a bandaged cat in her arms, at the high school's career day. "Now healed, she helps others," read the caption that disclosed how the girl was thinking she might want to become a veterinarian. Then as a candy striper, a photo run to remind everyone of National Volunteer Appreciation Week, Betty being the perfect subject, as twice a week she not only delivered books and mail to patients at Our Lady of Hope Hospital, "where she once lingered near death," but she also gave up her Sunday mornings to teach Confraternity of Christian Doctrine classes to first-graders at her parish (the only student ever to teach), found time one evening a week to tutor new Polish immigrants in the library's English as a Second Language program, and organized monthly pickups of roadside trash, inviting every-one up the hill, when they were through, for refreshments and brochures on ecology guidelines.

Betty, at fifteen, winning the Western Massachusetts region-al accordion championship, posing with a trophy that had to be half a foot taller than she was. The caption noted that she won the final round, against her last competitor out of fifty-three, by playing a graceful and awe-inspiring version of "How Great Thou Art" set to a danceable beat she'd heard while attending Dick Pillar's Polkabration in New London.

Betty, at sixteen, posing before going off to her junior prom, two orchids tied with ribbon to the one cane she still used, the flowers being admired by her date, Mickey Stallings, the boy who mopped the floor of the operating room after school and who'd met Betty when they got stuck in the service elevator.

Betty, the same year, waving her college entrance exams, a finger pointing to the perfect score of 1600, which would just about guarantee her admission to the school of her choice. And six months later, Betty, sifting through her letters of early acceptance from big-deal places like Stamford and Tufts and Harvard and Dartmouth. (There were others listed, but to tell you the truth I had to put the paper down halfway through reading them all.)

Betty, at twenty, receiving her pre-med diploma from Dartmouth, which she'd chosen because, even at four and a half hours away, she still considered it close enough to allow her to come home every weekend. In the photo, my mother and father, standing on either side of her billowing black graduation gown, even after all these years of photos looked uncomfortable to be in the spotlight, yet so proud it would have touched you even if you weren't acquainted with the people in the picture.

Betty, at twenty-three, graduating early from the university's medical center and weeping, her face caught, I was amused to see, in one of the terrible expressions you can have when you're in such a state. She might have looked inconsolable there, but, the caption noted, "soon she'll be drying her eyes, off for an internship at world-famous Boston Children's Hospital."

Betty, still at twenty-three, on her first day of work in the special orthopedic department there, reviewing the chart of a tiny child who had three of her four limbs crushed when her neighbor accidentally felled a tree on her while cleaning up the yard after an electrical storm.

Betty, at twenty-four, spending her short vacation break operating on kids in some part of Central America where they didn't have doctors for miles, hugging a smiling girl who, thanks to *"la curandera"*—the village's name for her (meaning "the healer," the caption interpreted)—would be able to use both her arms for the first time in her life.

Betty, at twenty-five, sorting cartons in her new office at her new job at Baystate Medical Center in Springfield, as large a hospital as she could work at and still live at home, which the caption said she had longed to do ever since the day she had gone off to college. Betty, a couple of months later, encircled by the arms of Craig Weldon, a nurse who had proposed on New Year's Day of 1993 in a tiny clinic in Appalachia, after working together in a fourteen-hour operation that pieced back together the arm of a teenaged boy who rode his bike too close to the side of a Trailways bus going seventy miles an hour. Craig Weldon was not only so handsome you had to keep going back to the photo to make sure you had seen him right the first time, but he was also artistic, having designed the engagement ring that appeared in a separate photo, a flat band with a raised *B* and a *C* cradling either side of the setting of a large, round diamond that the paper assured you had been photographed at actual size.

Betty, that next March, at a surprise shower thrown for her at St. Casimir's Hall, caught at the actual moment she came in the door (she had been told it was going to be a testimonial for Father Kulpa), her mouth dropped open, her hands flung upward like she was getting arrested, and on either side of the doorway, piles and piles of more gift packages than I think they showed when Lady Diana was getting married.

Then Betty, on her wedding day, the star of the *Penny Saver's* special six-page section that illustrated in black and white my long-ago nightmare come true. Not only did Father Kulpa, Brother Mike, and the diocese's auxiliary bishop officiate, but the wedding party included Betty's real-life Poland family, flown over as one huge surprise by her husband-to-be, who, though nobody asked him, thought it was high time the family reunite after all these years, and who, I guessed, had to come from money, judging from the size of that ring and the price of regular airplane tickets never mind trans-Atlantic ones.

So that's how not only my mother, but Stryjanka Józefa, too, came to be the last ones escorted into the church before the ceremony began. That's how Betty came to be walked down the aisle not needing her cane because she had my sad-faced father on one side of her and big, beaming Uncle Czesław on the other. That's how her eight bridesmaids came to include, in gowns hastily sewn together by my mother, the limping little Dorota, mother of five, though she looked like she should still have a career baby-sitting after school; the beefy Genia, forearms like lamb legs and a great smiling pie of a face; and the tall and elegant Olisia, an esteemed physics professor at the Jagiellonian University in Krakow. A reading was done in Polish by Kasia, who indeed had ended up being a nun, and the kind of nun that dressed as one, all in black, from head to toe, with a pair of huge wooden rosary beads for a belt.

But though I searched for her in the words and in the out-of-focus faces that made up the backgrounds of the photos showing happy couples dancing, there was no Aniela still wearing my long watermelon head and my square shoulders and my dark braids I had cut off with two big chops of Mrs. Kulis's craft scissors my first month back in my old house. No Aniela in the wedding party. No Aniela in my town. No Aniela in this country, as far as I knew. She probably had her own fine life by now, though after all these years of making one up for her I was very curious just what that had turned out to be. Whatever it was, she definitely had to have better things to do than drag herself halfway around the world just to be another color-coordinated accessory. Who wouldn't?

In the photos that made up the special supplement, Father Kulpa held an icon of Our Lady of Częstochowa over the heads of the wedding couple. He placed their hands one over the other and then bound them with a holy stole. He gripped the sides of the pulpit as he tearfully recalled so long ago giving the last rights to a smashed little Betty, the same Betty who, though still just a young, young woman, already had saved or repaired so many lives herself, and had selected as her life's partner a man who shares her sanctity for human existence. He blessed and used for Holy Communion the bread Stryjanka Jozefa had made that morning at 4 A.M., the same dark and rough and crusty kind that I knew—well at least it certainly looked it from the picture—that Betty had pulled from her pack in the airport parking lot to feed us with that first hour she landed in our lives.

Betty and Craig Weldon exchanged wedding bands, they took flames from two separate candles and used them to light the wick on a single one, they walked to the end of each pew and shared the sign of peace with as many people as they could touch, signaling, the story said, to those they could not reach. They stood outside the church and greeted a long line of well-wishers that stretched back into the parking lot as if they were going to be receiving free samples of something. Among what the paper noted was "an endless stretch of proud and loving people" I spotted Uncle Abie and Uncle Joe, puffing on cigars and wearing their good suits. Others in the crush, the captions said, were from the Weldon side of the family, all the way from some huge ranch in Idaho, and others were simply local people who had followed Betty's life so closely that when they learned of her engagement, they began telephoning the rectory at all hours to learn the date of the ceremony. Some of those people held signs and waved as the limousines left for the reception. "Good luck Betty and Craig!" "You deserve happiness!"

The rest of the day I didn't have to read about or see in pictures. I heard it, plain as day, from right across the street, where the wedding reception was held.

"Private Party Today," read the blackboard at the gate, white ribbons waving from the corners of its newly painted frame.

I had seen Eddie Forman's equipment van pull into the park earlier, then soon came his bus, the one with the large head of Pope John Paul II painted on the back, waving his pope wave and blessing tailgaters.

I had seen the refrigerated Millie's Pierogi truck drive up to the shelter and unload at least ten cases of the things. I had seen a minivan park next to the bandstand, and soon huge bunches of gold and white balloons were being tied to each of the shelter's posts. I had seen Mr. Skrowronek crank open the window to the bar and shout *"Wesele!"*—"Wedding!" And all the people unfolding linens over the beat-up picnic tables and fanning out the white flowers in golden vases and rolling the ugly, rusting oil-drum trash cans into hiding behind the smokey chicken pit, where men had been gathered since before breakfast, yelled back, "Yaaaaaaaayyy!"

"Gonna be some party over there," Harry said, sipping his coffee loudly behind his screen door. "I never seen so much preparation. Usually don't they just boil a few *golumbies* and play music?"

"That's *gołąbki*, and that's going to be a wedding. Don't come out here. I'm painting the porch."

"No problem," said Harry cheerfully. "Hang loose!"

Then he turned and went away, probably to bring a cup of what he called "java" up to Jessie, the woman with whom he lived in sin on the other side of my house.

When I first rented to them, Johnny Frydryk would only frown when he came over to do the lawn, ducking his head extra low under the rows of Jessie's skimpy cutoff blue jeans and polyester leopard-print teddies and bright red string bikini pants so as to not touch any of them when he cut the area beneath the clothesline. Though the couple was from way out near Fall River and had no friends or relatives in town, and had no co-workers because Jessie stayed home and made art while Harry sat alone in a trailer at the Quabbin all day and watched computers that monitored the type of air we were breathing in this part of the state, Johnny had gotten the lowdown on them anyway—at least enough to know that they were not married. They were probably the first couple in the history of our street to be living and breathing and doing everything else under the same roof for more than a single night without having the same last name. I hadn't been out to make such history when I rented to them. I only knew that if Johnny Frydryk found out—and I was certain he eventually would—then my father would find out. So when they introduced themselves, and I found nothing when I checked for wedding bands, I put two and two together and nearly tripped when I ran next door to get my receipt book.

Harry and Jessie turned out to be wonderful people, so laid-back and low-key you almost had to slap yourself back to consciousness after spending more than a few minutes with them. Even the most aggravating household crises—a busted water heater, a raccoon stuck in the chimney—were answered with a grin and a "no problem." Everything was cool and groovy and far out. They called one another "Babe" and when in the same room always were touching, leaning on one another, even when involved in separate conversations. I never heard them raise their voices or say an angry word to each other or anyone else. The psychic from Pelham who brought the lovely pear bread to their first potluck supper explained to me that Harry and Jessie had been each other's parents in various previous lives, and that had given them the opportunity to teach each other what was important. Now, in this life, together, they were getting to live what they had learned. That idea, probably the weirdest thing I'd ever heard said in Babci's front room, struck me as beautiful. It also made me envious. Why couldn't I have come into this life equipped with what I needed to know? Why did I have to scramble to collect it along the way? After a few cupfuls of the stuff Jessie had mixed up and poured into a punchbowl marked with a decorated sign that read "Potent," I tracked down the psychic in the bathroom line and I asked her those questions. She rummaged inside her brocade vest, searching, I hoped, for a rock or a gem or something I could hold on to and gain such wisdom from. Instead she produced a card listing her address and hours of business. "Thursday afternoons are open right now," she said. "First reading's 10 percent off."

"Man will you look at all that!"

Jessie was in the front doorway now, wearing nothing but one of Harry's sleeveless T-shirts, one with armholes that went down nearly to her waist. She had nothing on underneath, and that was how she sometimes ran out to the compost pile, in broad daylight.

"Great job, Donna! Porch is gonna look dy-no-mite!"

"Thanks," I said. "You'll remember not to come out, right?"

"Lockin' the door right now, Donz." (That's what they called me.) "You ever see such a fuss made over there?"

"Never," I said, without looking up.

"Must be some celebrity."

"Why'd you say that?" I asked this because, as far as I knew, Harry and Jessie knew nothing about me and Betty.

" 'Cause look at the TV trucks. When we were living in Providence, they had the same things parked outside the Claus von Bulow trial."

I followed the point of her hand, its silver thumb ring white against the tan she got while concocting her handmade paper all summer on the old window screens she spread across the backyard grass. Sure enough, there were the TV trucks. And the photographers' wagons and the radio vans. Again. Only this time they were not over here but across the street, aiming their lenses, being herded to the far side of the parking lot so that, I guessed, the decorated shelter could be admired clearly as the wedding party and the guests drove into the park.

The day was sunny, with only a few cartoonish clouds riding by now and again just for effect. I know Babci and my mother must have had something to do with it, hanging their rosaries in the window the night before, in the hopes of good weather for the day. They didn't know it, but they also had done me a favor—we'd had a week of on and off rain in between my scraping the porch and getting a chance to paint it. Slowly, the new, fresh dark green finally was taking over the old faded color. I liked the work, and it felt good to be busy, to have something I had to do that day.

Like bees swarming closer and closer, the noise of car horns could be heard coming up the street, and suddenly through the gates to the park rolled a line of black limousines, white banners waving from their aerials.

Behind them came car after car after car—so many that old Tad Kropka had to put down his early Budweiser and use both his hands to direct them to park in tight, neat rows so that all of them would be able to fit. The limos pulled up to the shelter, and the band kicked into "Here Comes the Bride" as the doors opened, and out stepped so many men in gray tuxedos and so many women in blue gowns and picture hats, and one bride in what even from way across the field and the street looked like the kind of gown you dream about all your life, if you are the type to hold such aspirations.

I can't be too detailed here, because I really was quite far away, but it looked like the kind of party you mention to the couple even when you run into them ten years down the line. You would tell them you still remember how the lobster claws wore fancy metal wedding bands etched with the date. How you had never seen a cut of meat so thick as that prime rib (but you'll leave out how you asked for a second, then later a piece of tin foil, and brought it home to enjoy the next night). How the bride's family from Poland assembled at the bandstand and sang self-consciously but so beautifully that even those who couldn't understand them were visibly moved by the senti- ments being expressed. How the groom walked up and down each row of tables until he had located every aunt and uncle and cousin and close friend of his new wife to thank them personally for their part, no matter how small, in making her the person she had turned out to be. How the cake had been made under the direction of Babci, who instructed that the first slice be set aside while the music stopped and everyone bowed their heads to acknowledge those family and friends who could not be there for this beautiful day. How you never saw such a gorgeous bride, certainly never have seen one so loved by her parents—especially by her father. How thinking about his toast brings tears to the eyes even now. . . .

To be fair, I should make it clear that I had been invited to the event.

"Donna and Guest" had been written neatly on the inner envelope that held the elegant white cards that were un- touched by ink, just embossed with the words that told me Elżbieta Milewski, the daughter of Mr. and Mrs. Adam Milewski (which was a lie), and Craig Weldon, the son of Mr. and Mrs. Pierce Weldon (which was one of those names, it struck me, that would sound okay even flipped around), requested the honor of my presence as they became joined in the bonds of Holy Matrimony. You had to look very closely, but the corners of the paper held not only embossed bunches of flowers, but the tiniest of embossed stethoscopes intertwining them like vines. Behind the invitation, separated by a sheet of tissue paper, was a small reply card, then another piece of tissue and a neatly hand-drawn map that illustrated the route from the turnpike exit to the church, then to the polka park. Behind that, another piece of tissue, then a small envelope bearing my name, in Betty's trim writing. She said:

Dear Donna:
> You never are home when I come by!
> You must be very busy!
> But I hope you won't be too busy to attend my wedding!
> I want you to meet your brother-in-law-to-be!
> You will love him!
> Call me!

> Love from your sister,
> Betty

Over the years, Betty had made many sincere attempts to get in touch with me. Somehow, shortly after I moved out, she got ahold of my phone number and started calling all the time.

"Donnaaa . . . when are you coming baaack?" she'd wail into the phone, and I'd hang up on her. The bum leg prevented her from riding a bicycle and from walking any great distance, so I didn't have to worry about her showing up at my door out of nowhere. But she wrote to me constantly for several years, her crayon drawings and her penmanship and her vocabulary improving steadily, and if I were anyone else I would have been marveling at her ability to rhyme so many phrases, and to draw from long-ago memory the front of my house complete with the raised bricks decorating the top of the chimney and the curlicues on the end of the wrought-iron front railings and the number of cracks in the concrete of the front walk and the correct lineup of panes in each window (eight over eight on the first-floor ones, six over six on the second).

She drew herself, always with a cane, and me, always with a smile and a long arm wrapped around her shoulders. We were close in her pictures, always happy, always in matching dresses, though in real life we only had that one pair for that first Christmas—green velvet jumpers over white blouses with puffy sleeves and Peter Pan collars that my mother had embroidered with a holly pattern complete with little red berries. Always in the same side-by-side pose, she drew us smiling in fields of flowers each spring, under huge and bloodied crosses at Easter, next to a giant Uncle Sam on Independence Day, with rakes in our hands come autumn, and on donkeys headed toward the manger in Bethlehem when the end of the year rolled around. "I miss you! Love from your sister, Betty." was written on the bottom of each thing she sent.

When she was in the sixth grade, Betty made a friend who lived on Norbell Street, a short road that contained only two homes and that jutted off River Street past Chick Wlodyka's woodpile. I always thought the relationship was started only so she could worm her way into my neighborhood and go for walks with her past my house, which she did, and more than a few times I would hear little voices and would peer out to see Betty standing on the front sidewalk with the pudgy brown-haired girl from Norbell Street, the one from whom I'd once bought a jar of blueberry preserves the time she was pulling them door-to-door in a wagon. Betty would be waving her cane in the direction of the bedroom window that had been ours, or at the back door, saying that's how she used to get inside.

"My sister lives here now—all by herself—like a *grown-up*," Betty would say with a hint of boasting in her voice. Then she'd come up to the door and would bang and bang on it until her friend complained how she was bored and was going to walk back home.

When Betty began to date, she picked, on purpose, I knew, one of the Skrowronek boys from up the street. For fun they'd ride his little brown horse around the neighborhood, and of course it would need to eat grass somewhere right around my house, and there would be Betty, waving to Johnny Frydryk, yelling, "Have you seen my sister lately?" and he'd yell back, "She's home right now," and I'd have to run in the bathroom and close the door and stay in there until she got tired of knocking and I could hear the horse hooves clopping farther and farther down the street.

When Betty learned to drive, there came the startling sight of my father's car rolling into the driveway. After that first time, I knew it was her, and when I heard its whirring engine slow into the yard, I would dive to the floor like somebody was shooting bullets into the house. I'd crawl and flatten myself beneath the windowsills, so if you looked in you would see right over me and only the stillness that was the rest of the house. You would have to be pretty dumb to believe no one was in there some of the time, like when I had the stereo on full blast or all the lamps lit. She'd rap on the back door for a time, then would leave only after writing me a note and wadding it into the keyhole.

For three visits in a row the last winter, she had written, "Donna—I want to talk to you about something important! Call me—I'm home for the weekend!" But I never did call, just like I never did return the phone messages she left on the machine I kept on steadily since the day I bought it—and that was the very day I learned from Sylvia in purchasing that such things were available to the general public—just to screen Betty from my life. Then came the letter, all perfect from a word processor that she spent the first paragraph apologizing for having to use to write such a personal message, but she was so pressed for time she just had to take advantage of such a convenience—even if she had to use it to ask her sister to be her maid of honor at her wedding that summer.

"You are the only person I would want," she wrote with a pen before signing her name, with love from your sister. But when I never called her, even after she made three more visits with no luck of seeing me, there turned out to be someone else she wanted after all—an oncologist with whom she had "clicked" as med students back at Dartmouth, according to the caption under the photo of Betty and the woman who had once been a girl shoved by her parents into the hull of a leaky sailboat that sailed for Miami in the middle of the night.

"Please come to the wedding—please do it for me," Babci pleaded one night after my mother left her at the house and drove to Party World in West Springfield to buy chocolates that were shaped like champagne bottles, and about a thousand other useless things that Betty probably had written on a list labeled "Details—If We Have Time . . ."

"I don't ask you anything," Babci added, then she corrected herself. "I mean I don't ask you for anything."

She was right on both counts.

She asked me if I was eating enough, which wasn't hard to do with all the Blue Bonnet margarine containers she packed with her gooey lasagnas with the long strips of green and red peppers, with her shepherd's pies and their tanned mashed-potato roofs, with her circular hand-cut french fries, with her tiny daisy hams, with her buttered baby peas, with her hamburgers, and with her spicy breaded frozen fish sticks all stacked in my freezer each visit as if I had subscribed to one of those special delivered meal plans that I have read in *People* is how some celebrities exist.

Regularly, she asked me if I was saving my money, which wasn't hard to do with my good salary and only the utilities and taxes to pay—and the tenants taking care of that bill with a couple of months' rent.

Regularly, she asked me if I was saying my prayers, and I would tell her I was, because I was, but—mainly because it was not her fault—I did not go into how very few of them seemed to be answered.

There were no other prying questions, just easy ones— where did I get those slippers, did I see how they cut down that big tree by the French church, had I seen John Iwanicki's photograph under "Promotions" in the business section, and won't all his big family be proud? She did not volunteer information and never ever tucked my father or Betty into any general story, like some people might have done just to break the ice. Babci knew better. Our visits were pleasant times, and the topics were general and present tense. Nice day. Good sale. Wrong number. On the way over I saw a gray fox run into the woods or Mr. Horgan riding his bicycle from the drugstore. She didn't ask me about my social life. If she had spotted him there in the dark, she didn't bother to ask who was that man I was hiding in the other room when she was left on the driveway one Wednesday instead of a Thursday and, expecting no one, I was in the middle of drawing a huge and very real-looking (if I do say so myself) laundry marker tattoo of a dragon on the back of Dennis Carter, whom I was trying to cheer after his abrupt firing from Blue Ribbon that afternoon for totaling the company's new Kielbasa Kar—a promotional van wrapped in a giant fiberglass link pinned with a giant fiberglass blue ribbon—on a bet that it couldn't go over one hundred miles an hour on the turnpike. If she had seen that photo on the refrigerator door—and how could she have missed it since she went straight to the refrigerator right after she came in the house—the Halloween photo of Babes Lussier dressed as a priest and me done up as a nun. To me, Babci was the way people should be. You live your life, I live mine, you know where to find me if you need me. And, if your decisions aren't what I would like, well, that's life.

So that's why, though it was tough only because I didn't want to disappoint her, that's why I told her I would not go to the wedding.

"I can't," I said. "I hope you understand."

She didn't. She shook her head.

"People are not around forever," she told me.

I took that to mean her, eighty-one at that point, though you'd think her fifteen years younger than that, and I hugged her and said, "But I see you all the time," though that was not really true when you think how that only happened every couple of weeks.

"I am not the only one in the family," Babci said.

I did not reply. I did not reply to the invitation, either. I did not fill out the response card, with its matching stethoscope flowers and its lengthy line for filling in the number of people who would be attending, as if the figure for one family would be more than one digit. I did not check whether I wanted Maine lobster, prime rib, or something called the vegetarian platter. I did not mail it back to 1 Conway Street, back to Mr. and Mrs. Adam Milewski. I did not go.

Instead, I worked on the porch, made a trip to the dump, came back and heated up a frozen pizza, went over to Kmart to pick up some fabric softener, came back and did the laundry

and hung it on the line, took a bath and even threw in one of
the lilac-scented oil beads I got in a Christmas grab bag at
work, went to 5:30 mass and saw the altar dressed in the
armloads of white roses and golden bows left over from the
wedding, tried to pray for good things, came back and got
Jessie's message that if I wanted to go up to the Sportsmen's
Club later I should call them, touched a finger to the floor of
the porch and found it was still tacky, took a bottle of wine and
a glass and a lawn chair and went out under the tree near the
railroad tracks and watched the sun slip behind the hill and
mark the close of what, for me and many in this world, had
been the most ordinary of days.

But once it got real dark, I spent a whole lot more time than I
care to admit sitting on the floor of my bedroom, looking out
the window. Across the street, the long strings of yellow bug
lights glowed along the edge of the polka pavilion like an
electric rosary, one big enough, I was still certain, to fit the
hands of God. They had been plugged in back when it started
to get dark, back when you still could count the rows of cars
stretching from the street and across the ballfield to the
bandstand, back when you still could make out the couples
bobbing on the dance floor, and lining up for the supper buffet,
and walking quickly to their cars to get the presents they'd
almost forgotten they'd put in the trunk. In the dark, the
details were reduced to the music and the lights and the buzz
of the crowd, and, very, very late, the couple announcing the
start of the Grand March, in which everyone would dance as
they waited in a line for their last opportunity to wish the
couple well and to collect a piece of napkin-wrapped cake, a
shot of whiskey and one of those newfangled forehead ther-
mometers imprinted with the words "Health and Happiness
from Nurse Weldon and Dr. Milewski-Weldon."

"Thank you all," I heard Betty sniffle into the microphone.
"Good night to everyone." Then there was a pause, like she
wanted to say something else, but she just said, "Good-night
from both of us."

Several months later, the paper carried a photo of Betty and
Craig Weldon on their honeymoon, which had been spent

taking ferries from one little Maine island to the next, sightseeing, and, of course, as the photo sent to our paper by some paper up there showed, tending to any of the ills of the little Maine island kids who rarely see anybody, much less a physician.

For a while there was a break. The corner of page 3 that usually held Betty instead was filled with ads for bicycle repairs, wallpaper, cabbage, a locksmith, motor oil, pet grooming, and trusses.

Then. Craig and Betty, sweating but elated as they watched cement pour from a big striped truck into the foundation of what would be their dream home. Located at 3 Conway Street. Right next to 1 Conway Street.

Then. Betty at twenty-six, a few months after I threw out the little invitation that had a stork printed on the envelope and her oncologist friend's name on the return address. My father at her side. Smiles so wide you could practically count all their back teeth. They were holding a baby.

A new baby. Betty and Craig Weldon's baby. A baby named Adam Milewski Weldon.

Since that bad one with the upturned collar so long ago, there had been no other photos of me in the *Penny Saver*. But if the paper had been interested in chronicling my every move, you would have seen me, in that first year, on my first night back at the house, lying there on my pile of clothes, still and calm for the first time since I walked out of the house on Conway Street, still, yes, but whirling, feeling like you do when you get off one of those spinning rides at the Belchertown Fair.

Then watching from the back door of the bank building, as the manager, Anna Baldyga, in her dressy suit and heels, covered my pig in a paper bag and smashed it with a rock from the riverbank.

Shopping, my first time at the grocery all for myself, filling my handbasket with the single-serving jars of peanut butter and cans of peas that, before, I'd only seen old people buy (that was before I figured out the large sizes were cheaper, and that I could polish off most of that size in one sitting anyhow).

Balancing my checkbook, working with a solar-powered calculator that kept quitting until I had to bring a light over to the table to keep it running, and wasn't saving energy the whole idea in the first place?

Banging on Johnny Frydryk's door after finding that the entire pipe under the kitchen sink had rotted out and was allowing water to just pour all over the place, only Johnny was betting at Hinsdale, and so, in a panic, I picked the first plumber listed in the Yellow Pages, and it cost me $145 for the guy to bring in a new piece of elbow-shaped pipe and bang it into place so easily, not even using any wrenches or blow-torches, which I could have figured out if only I had one of those Time-Life series of household solution books.

Celebrating my first birthday alone, though not really alone—no family you could match with blood type, certainly, but with Carolyn and Theresa there instead, just as good, to mix me a Duncan-Hines German chocolate cake and give me wrapped presents—a thick *Householder's Bible* they'd pitched in for after hearing me complain about the plumber, and a small wind chime they said would remind me of them whenever I heard it. I would need such a thing because they were going away. A few weeks after my birthday, we were saying our awful, choking good-byes, and I stood watching the little caravan of the Lyszko and Son fruit truck and the Theresa's Acres Dairy pickup and its horse trailer full of cartons roll up River Street, headed for UMass. I walked home, depressed and weepy, called directory assistance, asked for the number of Maureen Browne, and found there was no such listing anywhere in Western Massachusetts.

The next day I marked my first holiday alone. Labor Day might not mean much to you, but my father had been thrilled to be a working man bringing home a more-than-decent paycheck, and he'd always used the day to reflect on his good fortune and to take us to Lake Congamond for one of the last swims of the year. We'd eat huge sandwiches of Blue Ribbon meats and Countryside Bakery bread, then my father would find the ballgame on his transistor radio, and Babci would crochet the bandages she'd read in the paper that a local woman was collecting to send to lepers, and my mother and I would draw the scenery with colored pencils while we waited the hour it would take for the food we'd eaten to move its way through us far enough that it would not kill us once we went back into the water.

I did not go to Lake Congamond that day. I stayed home with the telethon, watching Jerry Lewis get hoarser and tireder and sweatier as the hours wore on and the numbers added up, and though it was not in the budget that the bank ladies had helped me map, I called and pledged $5 so someone might cure these people, some of whom, the short films set to sad music informed us viewers, could move nothing but their eyeballs.

If the paper had been interested, you would have seen me buying a rusting little wagon at a tag sale and using it to make four trips home with a pair of wooden kitchen chairs, a beige vinyl hassock, an oval mirror with just enough black paint flaking off its frame to make it look antique, a wooden ice bucket I really didn't want but for a dollar it came filled with all the kitchen utensils you would ever need, a portable radio with an extra-long power cord that someone handy had attached themselves, a flashlight, a laundry basket, and a gauzy long dress I couldn't imagine ever leaving the house in, but it only cost a quarter.

But nobody cared if I went car shopping by myself. Nobody cared if I joined the candlepin bowling team. Nobody cared if I had a real dinner party, making broccoli quiche for three girls from work who didn't mind if I asked them to bring their own plates and utensils. Nobody cared if I replanted a respectable garden where it nearly had been reclaimed by grass. Nobody cared that I liked to end my summer weekends by sitting on the front porch after dusk, listening to the music from across the street and letting my fingers move to the notes that they went right to as if they were long-lost friends, following along with Ray Henry on "Blonde Bombshell" as if it were something I had written myself.

Nobody at all cared that at one time in my life I was truly in love with a man other than my father. And nobody cared if it turned out to be just another instance where I gave up something good just to get back at him.

Eric was a Safe-Tam executive. There is no other way to describe him accurately, jobwise, because his exact work changed every few months as higher-ups scrambled to find something else for Jan Skarzynski's godson to do. So, through his parents' careful selecting as a godparent the guy whose father happened to have invented a tampon, Eric did not have to work on the noisy manufacturing floor but in one of the hushed, carpeted offices that took up one whole side of the building and included a lunchroom with a wall of windows that overlooked the Swift River.

Studying *Gentlemen's Quarterly*, Eric Bigos wore what he saw on its many fashion spreads. The textured suits and interesting ties designed to benefit some illness or animal group, loafers with tassels that flopped with his loping walk, and suspenders (or bracers, as the magazine called them). He purchased the body-sculpting multi-station workout machine advertised on the health pages. He used the cuff links worn by the dressed-up rock star. He had his hair cut into what he hoped was an intriguing young executive look he'd snipped from a fashion spread and brought in to his barber. But not many people got a chance to admire all this, as Eric Bigos worked mostly as the daytime supervisor of 1-800-SAFETAM, the company's first telephone line offering assistance to puzzled customers. He sat all day in a small inner room and collected data from two registered nurses who balanced their checkbooks and wrote out their greeting cards between the few phone calls received, about one-third of which came from teenage boys asking dirty questions.

I had other matters to think about that day, so I didn't know until later that what we had got its start at the 1993 company picnic. Eric on that occasion was with some very pretty redhead who, everyone was saying, had been the runner-up choice to be the woman on the Safe-Tam carton. I was with Tony Kempesty, on my third try at having a last date with somebody I never should have started seeing in the first place.

He was Tony of TonyJoe Auto, where I had my car repaired the
odd times it went on the fritz. Camille, over in maintenance,
was married to the Joe part of the name, the guy who owned
30 percent of the company to Tony's 70, and she was always
after me to date Joe's boss.

"Come on, Donna, the guy is lonely," Camille would whine
whenever her job tickets brought her near my station. "All he
does in his spare time is drink beer."

"That's great," I would say. "Sounds wonderful."

"By himself. Alone. In the garage. He's got no friends."

"Maybe there's a reason for that."

"He just works too much. Maybe if you wanted to go out
with him, he'd make the time to do something fun."

"What's this got to do with you?"

I remember Camille hunching her shoulders, and I knew she
wasn't lying when she said, "I just feel sorry for the guy."

Her answer got to me, and once I thought about it, he wasn't
that much different from anyone else I'd been seeing, so that's
why there was supper at Silvano's, an Italian restaurant in
Springfield at which Tony Kempesty ordered five consecutive
Michelobs to wash a side of squid and a plate of lasagna down
his long neck and into his volleyball of a belly before inviting
me back to his apartment to enjoy a few more.

Then, just to show them I really had given it a try, there was
St. Mary's seventy-fifth anniversary picnic—a public event
where Joey and Camille and anyone else who wanted to could
see that I was on a date with Tony Kempesty, and could see
him, as I did, drinking six huge cups of beer during the
Ziemienski Brothers' first set alone, then could see him leaving
me in line at the *gołąbki* booth for about half an hour while he
ran off to the bar with one of the trays meant for food.

"You're beautiful," he said gratefully when he returned with
a neat arrangement of eight brimming cups, and I was
standing there waiting for him, with our orders all bought and
paid for with my own money.

I knew Safe-Tam's company picnic would have beer, but it
would also have lots of people I knew, people I could escape to
once I let Tony know it was over.

"Look, Tony, I'm gonna go home, and I think you should

too," I said once he came back and plowed through everything from his third trip to the barbecue pit, which was conveniently located next to a small tent holding a row of silver kegs marked with signs reading "Help Yourself."

Tony's glassy gray eyes brightened, and he ran a hand through his dark crew cut. "We're going to your place?"

"No. No. I go to my place, you go to yours. I don't think we should see each other again. Not on a date, I mean. Okay?"

His head shifted from side to side—he could make his neck crack when he did that—then he began to pick at the shreds of meat that clung to the rack of ribs he earlier had said he'd finished eating. His silence made me nervous.

"Okay?" I asked. "You understand? No hard feelings? I just don't think we have much in common."

Tony wore an injured look and he answered, "It's . . . it's my clothes, ain't it?"

I made a quick inventory of the day's outfit: tight and short unbelted chinos, white ankle-high tennis socks, black steel-toed work shoes, and a T-shirt that demanded "Gimme a Heine(ken)." I said, "Well . . ." and Tony rubbed hard at his face, then finished off the cup on the table in front of him, which only had about a quarter of it gone before that point.

"Well," he slurred mockingly, standing up. "Like me any better this way?"

Off he pulled the shirt and threw it on top of the half a barbecued chicken I hadn't had the chance to touch yet. His hands reached around the bottom of his gut and found the hook at the top of his fly. I said, "Tony," calmly, but he did not stop to ask what I wanted. He just pulled down his trousers and stood tugging one pantleg over one white sock and black shoe, then the other. I didn't know what to do and found my eyes landing at the food line, where the men in chef's hats had stopped carving and the people waiting with their empty plates had turned to follow their gaping, and those at the nearby tables enjoying their steamers and lobster tails pressed their hands to their plastic bibs in horror.

It took one checkered tablecloth and two uniformed Safe-Tam security guards to take care of Tony, who, as he was being led off to the police car, yelled only did I want to go somewhere next weekend.

"He's a guy—whaddaya want?" Cindy Sanchez asked me consolingly as I tried to stop shaking from embarrassment and disgust.

When I finally looked up from my lap, I caught sight of Eric Bigos, seeming oblivious to any commotion, sitting close to the model, delicately feeding her the last bits of his lobster, brushing back her hair with his other hand. Joey Purda had been good for about four words a day and barely could wait for me to get both feet inside the car before he started it moving. Dennis Bowlier had been a nice guy, but chewed with his mouth open. Stan Czan had suggested we try out his new waterbed even though his grandfather was snoring in the rocker next to it. And once you got real close, Art Walsh just plain smelled.

"Something like that. I want something like that," I answered Cindy, and at the same moment, my answer, Eric Bigos, took the woman's hand and kissed it slowly, so delicately and tenderly, as if it were made of sugar crystals.

"Wow," whispered Cindy.

"Yeah," I sighed.

"I hear you want the idiot."

Stella said this without looking up from her work, which was a lot of work, that being a Monday and the machines having the same kinds of problems and mistakes humans have on that particular day of the week.

"What did you say?"

"The idiot."

"What idiot?"

"You know what idiot. Young Bigos."

I straightened. "What about him?"

"You want him."

"For what?"

"Don't give me that. Everybody knows . . ."

The line was down, and Andre LaFlamme was next to us, testing the tension on a belt that powered a conveyor on which tampon components were supposed to ride in an orderly fashion. He was going to be retiring in a month, after thirty-two years, and was telling everybody how he planned to make birdhouses to sell from his front porch.

"It's extra income, all tax-free—if the government don't catch me," he would say with a laugh and a wink.

I took advantage of the stoppage and hopped off my stool to head over to Cindy Sanchez, who was applying a new coat of coral lipstick in the mirror of a little round case the tube fit into when not being used.

"Why is Stella asking me about Eric Bigos?" I asked, startling her.

"How should I know?"

"Because you're the only person I mentioned him to."

Cindy took a short breath. "Well, you said you wanted him."

I felt like screaming. "I said I wanted something *like* him. *Like* that, I think I said. Something like that. Something like how he was nice, and kind-looking, all those romantic things he was doing. I don't know anything about him—except that he's related to somebody, and they can't really find anything for him to do. Stella even calls him the idiot."

"So maybe he's nice," Cindy offered. "A nice idiot."

And that's when I heard my name being paged. Twice.

Eric Bigos hung his coat each morning in more of what you would call a pod than an office. Its walls were covered by denim-shaded fabric and went only to chin height, to give a sense of privacy but still a feeling of openness. There was a row of six or seven of these little enclosures lined up along the windows that looked out over the river. Eric Bigos's was the fourth office I counted, and it was identified by a black plastic plaque engraved with his name and set into a holder from which, I noticed, it could be removed if he were to be transferred or fired. I knocked on the wall, though it was like knocking on the living room carpet, all insulating fiber that deadened the sounds in the room: the click of a keyboard, the repetitive whine of a printer, a snapping stapler, someone whispering into a telephone that yes, you most certainly did mean it, but this is neither the time nor the place to talk about it.

I knocked a second time, but on the hard surface of the nameplate. Eric appeared in his entryway, wearing a shiny blue suit with larger lapels that you'd usually see worn by men in this country.

"Eric Bigos," he said, and we shook hands. "Please come in." Then he called around a corner: "Coffee, Sharon. For two?"

An older business-suited woman who was busy filing things and looking like she had a whole lot more to do than fetch refreshments, said yes without turning, dragging her answer out like she was annoyed.

"You drink coffee, don't you?" He pointed to a chair upholstered to match the walls. I told him I did drink coffee, but that he didn't have to go to any trouble.

"This is no trouble," he said, emphasizing the "this." "Believe me."

I told him he had a nice office, though it was mostly the view outside that made it so. Eric had decorated his limited wall space with the kind of art you find in salad bar restaurants— pastel-toned prints of watercolor seashells with the exact word *seashells* written in script below in case you needed help figuring out what the picture was of. Outside, the river scene didn't need an explanation. It was just there, roaring past, and on the opposite bank, tanned muscleman Ray Jr., wearing only workboots and high white tube socks and what I knew were his red bathing trunks, was clearing some brush near his back porch.

"I love it here," Eric Bigos said. "Yes, I do."

Then nothing else was said. So I figured I'd ask: "Am I in trouble?" Though I knew that if that were the case, I would have been paged by Mr. Newbury's office. Plus, everybody knew Eric Bigos had no power, other than, apparently, being able to order coffee.

"No, no," he answered soothingly, and I flashed back to him with the model, and thought how he probably used that tone when they were out on the town and she said she was going to ask if the gourmet restaurant's kitchen had any low-calorie selections.

"No, no," I imagined him cutting in with that same soft tone. "I will ask that question for you."

"No, no," Eric Bigos told me. "Of course you aren't!" He stopped to accept from Sharon a tray with two coffee mugs, a small creamer and sugar bowl, and a white oval plate holding some vanilla wafers she'd taken the trouble to arrange in a daisy pattern.

"Thank you, Sharon. That'll be all." You could tell he loved saying that, and you could tell how she hated hearing it from him.

"Right," she answered and left, probably to catch some trans-Atlantic flight so she could go finalize some big international deal. Safe-Tams in yet another foreign land. (There already was a case in the entryway displaying cartons that had all the same woman-in-the-meadow design, but with words printed in German, French, Spanish, Hebrew, and even Japanese.)

"Donna—I may call you that?" Eric Bigos was asking.

I said yes, and he commented how it was a fine name, something I'd never before given any thought to.

"Donna, I called you here because I was concerned for you," Eric Bigos said. "I was otherwise occupied at the time, but I understand you had a personal problem while at the picnic, and, well, we here at Safe-Tam take an interest in our employees."

He sounded like one of the pamphlets that once a year— usually around Christmas—were enclosed with our paychecks when the company, in the interest of us employees, wanted to remind us of the Safe-Tam Employee Assistance Program that would connect anyone who needed it with a psychiatrist or whatever kind of professional it was that could help them get better. It was all confidential, of course, and after the initial visit, you should realize that the bills will be your responsibility.

I felt ill, physically, thinking back to Tony's display, you could call it, at the picnic. And how someone like him had been connected to me.

"Thank you, but it really was nothing big," I said, meaning just that, and both ashamed of then mad at Tony for causing this to happen. Being called off the factory floor was one thing. Having to return and, because they would nag me until I did, having to explain to everybody down there that it was because of stupid Tony, would be humiliating.

"I'm sorry, I don't mean to pry. I only was concerned." Eric looked like he genuinely was, then he looked down, at his polished shoes. A shag of his bangs fell onto his forehead, and he looked suddenly extra handsome. I thought of his touches to the model, and I looked at his hands. They were large and strong looking, and he wore a signet ring on his pinky. *EB*, it said. His initials. No wonder Matilda, the cafeteria cashier, when she had some story to tell concerning Eric Bigos and his lack of get up and go called him Eb. I thought it had been another one of her put-downs. A hillbilly name. One of the neighbors from "Green Acres." But she must have seen his ring, the one he played with during our talk, twisting it around everyone once in a while, rubbing a fingertip over the letters like it was a message written in Braille.

"He wasn't important to me at all—he's just a troubled guy, and I'm sorry for the scene he caused," I said, then, and I don't know why, I quickly added more than I wanted to: "I only went out with him in the first place as a favor. For a friend." I stopped, because something occurred to me, and I said it aloud, but quietly, and without thinking: "That'll teach me."

Eric looked into my eyes. I looked back. From behind the wall, the woman on the phone asked how many times did she have to tell you not to call her at work.

"A favor," Eric Bigos said softly, testing out the word, leaning forward.

"Then would you do such a favor, for me?"

For four and a half months, Eric Bigos and I were a true item. I did him the favor of going out with him that first Friday night, then every single night after that, except when he had to travel on business.

This was no video-and-a-six-pack guy, not one to slump in a chair and roll his eyes and mumble, "I thought *you* were gonna think of somethin' to do." Eric Bigos was never at a loss for activities to suggest. First off, he had a fascination with small-town life and loved going to all those events so many of the rest of us always see listed under "News and Notes" in the paper, but never bother to attend unless we have a niece in the horn section or know the person in need for whom the money is being raised. We didn't directly know a soul involved, but there we were at community band concerts, all-you-can-eat ham and bean suppers, talks on local history, weather lore and button collections. Gardening seminars. Birdhouse-building workshops. Cub Scout bake sales. Walkathons. Hoe-downs. Dog shows. Horse shows. Boat shows. Craft shows. Grange fairs. Health expos. Drives collecting refundable cans and re-cyclable newspapers and blood. Eric Bigos always came away with a Baggie full of hermits, or folders with hot-line numbers, or pages of notes written in his boxy architect-style handwriting, and always, he told me, he left those events carrying the general good feeling that he was part of a community.

But many of the other things he took me to, showed me, fed to me, said to me, I never knew we had on this planet. Okay, maybe they'd been here all along, but I must have missed them.

I'd never eaten—hey I'd never even pronounced—hummus, or mahi-mahi, or osso buco, mole sauce, star fruit, or free-range chicken. I'd never heard rock-a-billy, or jazz fusion. For all that driving around in high school, I'd never seen the wondrous things practically in my backyard: the pounding and narrow Chesterfield Gorge; deserted Dana Center and its overgrown triangle of a town common; a cave—an actual cave—far down a path at the end of a turnoff just before you hit Belchertown, cool and dark and silent, with a big rock at either side of the entrance like chairs neatly arranged on a front porch; the tiny monastery at which all the smiling, sandal-footed monks—Eric told me after we sat silently in their hushed, candle-lit chapel and then backed his car down their steep dirt driveway—had been in prison at one time or another and had sworn off their former lives to start anew, and even from one monk to the next, no one knew what their pasts had been.

We also went to weddings. But these were of people that he actually knew. The third and most memorable one celebrated the union of Todd and Cecile, a couple he'd gone to the University of Rhode Island with, and he had been there the exact moment they met at the salad bar in the dining commons, when Todd handed Cecile the tongs that were missing from the crock of chickpeas.

Waves crashed their applause as the wedding couple stood next to a sea wall at Eric's godfather's massive dollhouse of a summer home on Nantucket, and, on cue from the female minister, exchanged the vows they'd composed during a long weekend in New Hampshire, where they'd holed up in a small inn just to have the privacy and quiet to take care of that chore. It was a large crowd there that day—maybe two hundred people—but each of us had a handwritten message written on parchment and left on our plate from the couple, expressing their inexpressible gratitude that we were there on this most important occasion. Every note seemed to be different, as far as the dozen people at our huge circular table could tell, and each contained a personalized touch. The guy across from me, Nick something, was told they'd be waiting for him to lead the Greek dance he promised he'd start. The guy next to him was told they'd chosen the cous-cous in the third course because they knew how much he always talked about it in the letters he'd sent from abroad. His date, a sullen woman named Joy, was informed that the wedding couple had once visited her home state of Wyoming and had many fond memories of its natural beauty. Mine said they were happy that Eric was happy with me, and that they held Safe-Tam stock. Eric's note said they hoped he noticed the single meaning-filled chickpea placed in each salad, and that they looked forward to his knowing the wonder of finding someone to share his life with. I noticed that he looked at the message for a long time before folding it and tucking it away inside his suit-coat.

There were other touches—family members who took to the bandstand and played the instruments they'd brought; bowls of fresh rose petals and stacks of real towels in the bathrooms; souvenir ceramic candlesticks that bore, instead of the regular name and date, a creamy purple glaze Cecile and Todd themselves had mixed at the potter's studio by combining the powders that made up his favorite color, red, and hers, milky blue. At dusk, a plane circled overhead, trailing a lit-up banner that proclaimed "CECILE IS MY LIFE. T."

With Barney Lembo, I had been to more than a dozen weddings—two in one day, even. And except for that feeling of wanting to be part of something, I never had come away too much affected. But that day's ceremony and reception, the little fussed-over details, all made me yearn for this: a garden of a cake covered in edible flowers, a honeymoon stretching over months and planned by my groom alone so that every turn in the road would be a surprise to me, napkins folded in the shape of my new surname, and, as Cecile had done, the foregoing of an engagement ring—she had requested a bracelet instead because the circle of her and Todd's love, she told us when she visited our table the first of five times, was much too large to be contained in such a tiny thing as a ring.

It both frightened and excited me how much I wanted what I saw, and how I wanted it more intensely with each hour, and how, with each glass of the brand-name champagne that appeared magically when the flute you were drinking was anywhere less than half full, I wanted in the worst way to tell Eric Bigos that I loved him and that I wanted to marry him, just exactly like this.

He was over at the sea wall, magazine-posed with his back to the crowd, one foot up on the bricks, his coat over his left shoulder, held in place with the crook of a finger. The wind was blowing his hair back, and the setting sun was making him squint handsomely. Here was my moment, and I surprised myself by not only what I was about to do, but how easy it was going to be and the stunning confidence I had that he would want what I wanted. I extracted myself from a conversation that Joy and I had only been nodding to as a childhood friend of the bride's complained how hard it is to find a wedding gift that is so unique that the couple will think of you each and every time they see it and how (and here she invited you to call her stupid if you wanted to) that is for some reason of extreme importance to her. I didn't stick around to learn what she had ended up selecting, and I didn't start worrying that Todd and Cecile might not exclaim "Eric and Donna!" every time they hopped under the antique quilt we found for them at the Brimfield Flea Market. (Actually, I would kind of hope they wouldn't.) I got up from the table, and I walked over to Eric and stood next to him and asked him what he was thinking, because he did look like he was lost in something. He put his arm around me, and I leaned into the deltoids being restructured by that new office chair he'd ordered from his magazine a few weeks back, one that looked like a regular high-back executive's chair, but held concealed and weighted arms that allowed busy people like Eric to get a few lifts in between appointments. He gazed happily out at the water some more, then turned to me.

"Funny you should ask that," he said perfectly as if you'd written it down for him. "Because I'm thinking I'm in love."

I once wanted Johnny West's cow town so badly I thought I would die without it. It was a string of plastic wild-West storefronts just the right size for jointed plastic cowboy doll Johnny West and his sidekicks to live in and tie up their horses in front of. I owned Johnny West and Jane West and the rest of the gang, plus all their horses, but I just didn't own the cow town. Well I prayed, and I was good, and I did extra chores, and I got the cow town from my parents for my tenth birthday. And I remember unwrapping it and looking at the long, heavy cardboard box, with its picture of Jane on the boardwalk, talking with Johnny, who'd just ridden up on Lightning, and I couldn't believe it was mine. Forever. That I had gotten what I wanted was almost too unbelievable. The minute I had it in my hands, the fact that I once had been without it seemed incomprehensible.

Eric Bigos and his love were the ultimate cow town. One second into knowing he loved me, too, I could not imagine ever having been without that. It completely knocked the wind out of me, and I let myself be folded against the firmed pectorals that five days a week, in three easy-to-schedule sets of twenty reps per day, pulled forward thirty-five pounds.

We kissed, turning into the couple in Carolyn's alleyway, a huge bonfire of passion burning behind us, the end of the world here and what did we care? How often in life does someone feel the exact way you do, and it is not that they, too, need to go to the grocery store, or that they, too, are a little bored by the movie. Here, Eric Bigos, too, was in love with me, and I was in love with him. You could have knocked us over that wall and into the ocean, and we wouldn't have noticed.

A little later—all right, I'm not sure at all, so it could have been five hours after, or maybe even the next night—someone was at the microphone, stopping the band and asking for everyone's attention. It was Cecile's father—little, bald Mr. Prine—who, I'd noticed, had cried more that day than anyone else in the place, male or female. He was at it again, wiping his eyes even as he unfolded the paper holding what I hoped would be a short speech.

"If I ever had to point to one thing to prove the existence of God, it would be my Cecile," he said, louder than was necessary, considering all the loudspeakers.

"Having to grow up in a busy household, often without the attentions of a mother, and to act many times as a mother to her sickly younger sister—continuing that role as much as possible despite her studies and her career—and to do so selflessly with not a single complaint uttered, Cecile is the finest person I know."

Then Mr. Prine looked at Todd, who was one of about five men extending their pocket squares to a weeping Cecile, and said, "She is starting a new family with you, but I want you to remember this: The relationship between a father and a daughter never ends, no matter what the circumstances."

With that, he walked over to Cecile and took her hand, and the band played something slow and with no words, probably because none were needed.

I could tell you that I don't know why I did it, but I would be lying. What I did was pull out of the hold of Eric and run through the dim Christmas-bulb-lit backyard and into the ladies' room, where I snatched a real cloth towel from the uniformed attendant, ran into a stall, and bawled my eyes out into the monogrammed initials *T&C*, enclosed forever in a heart.

At some point in each workday, I'd catch Eric sneaking a

look at me through a little second-floor window from which Paolo Gomes, the safety officer, was supposed to scan the floor every hour, though Paolo did so only about once a day, usually with his back turned, while he traded jokes with the executives who were on their way to the fancy washrooms we heard they had up there. Because I never knew when Eric would be watching, I practiced wearing a pleasant look at all times, just so he would think that was the real me.

"It killed me today to get up and come into this godforsaken hell hole—you're looking entirely too happy for somebody who's stuck here all day," Carol Wilcox would razz as she rolled her cart of tools past me, on her way to solving some newfound problem with somebody's machine.

"Must be all those executive privileges," Dolly Wostena would yell, and a whole bunch of people would snicker.

I got some such comments from folks on the line, but they didn't bother me, since, other than the Super Plus project and the time Tommy Pytka scratched a $250 lottery ticket he'd bought during a walk at lunch, my going out with Eric Bigos was the most noteworthy thing that had happened to anybody on the Safe-Tam floor in a long time. And people at least were getting to know him and to see that, yeah, he didn't do too much work around the plant, but you certainly couldn't find a much nicer person.

My neighbors loved him instantly, first for how, though he parked his golden BMW in the driveway, he always went around to the front door to collect me, rather than to the side entrance, which, Blind Tekla explained to me once she heard of his practice, showed respect and acknowledged that this young man did not want to "presume the level of familiarity that coming straight into one's kitchen implied." That hadn't occurred to me, especially in such grand speech, but she was right. Eric Bigos was very well-mannered and prided himself on the little gestures like holding doors and standing up when a woman approached and regularly using ma'ams and sirs and misses. He told me he had been sent to a school to learn such things and had to give up Little League for a whole season in fifth grade just to spend his Saturdays practicing the box step and how to correctly hold glasses and cups. He wasn't crazy about it at the time, but now he didn't regret it, Eric Bigos said, because it had helped make him the man he was.

I didn't have any complaints, either. It was fun to be pampered and considered morning, noon, and night—even when I wasn't around him. Eric traveled for business regularly and never failed to buy me wonderful souvenirs, samplings of what the people ate there, wore there, made there—and lots of it. Cases of barbecue sauce, wheels of cheese, pounds of frozen sourdough, the same handknit mohair gloves in six different colors, and not just a single piece of turquoise, but a necklace, bracelet, earrings, and ring made up with the stone. Eric gave me boots from Spain, 18-karat-gold earrings from Greece, a hand-carved cuckoo clock from Germany, a pair of fish paintings from Japan, a tiny white lamp from Denmark that could fold into itself when not in use. But my favorite gift cost nothing. It was a small, clear plastic film canister filled with water from the Dead Sea, which Eric had visited while at a health conference in Israel that ended up being so boring that he skipped the last day and just floated in the famous water that had so many minerals in it, no matter how you tried, you could not sink. Eric couldn't stop talking about it, this feeling he'd never experienced before, how no matter what he did, even if he stopped paddling or stopped concentrating, there was no way he was going to sink. He would be fine. "You would love it," he'd tell me, and I'd look at the water and wish he'd brought me a room full of it.

All this, and then it was over. When my parents found out I was dating a tampon heir, they nearly went out of their minds. It was not Babci's fault—I knew she'd said nothing to them, even though she clearly was so happy with this young man who had the kind of manners you pay for and the kind of clothes you never could afford. When she visited, he spoke to her in the Polish he'd learned as a child, and had brushed up on with audiocassettes when he was chosen to man the Safe-Tam International booth at a women's health conference in Wrocław.

"*Młoda kobieta*"—young lady—he would call to her when he saw her, and she would giggle and pull on my sleeve. "*Ładny chłopiec,*" she would whisper, and I'd tell her that I agreed—if there ever was a nice boy, Eric Bigos was it.

No, it was not Babci who ratted. It was Mrs. Harrington, who is best known for the tag sale she runs under big tarps stretched across her front lawn every day of the year. My mother called, all excited, to confirm the rumor she'd heard while in the personal care aisle at Tenczar's, when Mrs. Harrington had stopped her cart at the feminine hygiene shelf and remarked aloud how Donna now was set for life, in more ways than one.

"Is it true?" my mother asked me. "The Bigos boy?"

"What about him?" I dragged it out, puzzled by her call, something that was so rare I couldn't tell you when the last one had been. For some reason, I found myself annoyed that the other sort of nice guys I had seen over the years didn't count, hadn't merited a call. She hadn't phoned when I was seeing Doug Hapcook, who was helping his sister raise the three kids she had out of wedlock. Not when I had my few dates with Ronnie Westerman, who had divorced out of boredom the eldest Konicki girl seven months after her parents spent most of their savings on a wedding reception that sent all 247 guests and the entire fourteen-piece Jan Lewan Orchestra down the Connecticut River on a genuine steamboat. She hadn't phoned to see how I was getting along with the bearded Chip Dziel, or the ponytailed Al Everett, or the scarred Billy Boyce. She didn't dial me back in the days of boozing Tony Kempesty, who, if there was nothing else good you could have said about him, could have repaired all our transmissions until we were too old to drive.

"Are you dating him?"

I smiled, though she couldn't see me. "I guess. I guess we're 'dating.'"

I didn't tell her about how I was seeing him every night he was in town, certainly not about the full drawer of clothes I had over at his condo on Mt. Dumplin, how, while playing his celestial New Age albums, he touched me as dramatically as the passionate soap opera actors who were the reason she'd abandoned watching her serials. "Your mother says they now are nothing but filth," Babci had explained to me. She paused a moment before adding matter-of-factly, "But, you know, I still think they are pretty good!"

Just to get her goat, I wanted to say to my mother, yes, I'm dating him, you know—like Desiree is dating Wade on your two o'clock show? And her mind would have flashed to the way the camera pans every visible inch of skin when the two are embracing, which is often, and she would have hung up the phone screaming. But it wasn't my mother I wanted to be mean to. I knew she was only a conduit in all this.

"Dating Eric Bigos!" she exclaimed. "Isn't that just wonderful!"

Then she asked me to wait just a second, and she covered the receiver, and there was a voice, muffled, but I knew whose it was—my father's—then my mother back to him, then my father again, for a longer time. Then my mother with a few words, then a clear line again.

"Listen, Donna. How would you and that Mr. Bigos like to come for supper?"

Always with a "that" when it came to any male I'd ever hung around with. That boy. That kid. That Mr. Bigos. I was shaking my head over that weird habit of hers when the lightbulb switched on, and I saw how that Eric Bigos might be looking like some kind of redemption. Yes, I was spending my life working at the place I'd been cautioned against, but at least I was making up for that decision with a surprisingly good choice of a man. Someone who dressed up. Who had a revered position. Who someday would be real rich. Not like Jim Rozzen and Lyle Healy and Rickie Crago, who didn't even have bank accounts or checkbooks. There it was—something dark and sad and familiar crawling over me—and I knew what I had to do.

That night Eric Bigos came home from a yoga colony in the Berkshires, where he'd attended an intensive two-day seminar on the healing properties of herbs. I'd come to learn that he had a whole lot of stuff going on in his head regarding work—a standing file on the desk in his home workroom held folder after folder of clippings and documents on natural healing, one of his favorite subjects. He had confided in me that one of his big ideas was to formulate for Safe-Tam a mass-market 100-percent-herbal remedy for what he politely termed "women's discomforts." He even had a name all picked out: "Safe-Releaf," which, wanting to be encouraging, I didn't have the heart to tell him sounded to me like something you would use on your garden. Attending this seminar was his first real step toward that project, after a whole lot of reading and a whole lot of filing of the things that he'd read. Eric was proud of himself and in a good mood, and he brought me back a whole big carton of things from the gift shop there, run by yoga students who ate in silence while staring at framed photos of their yogi in the way Eric Bigos told me as a kid he used to read the side of his cereal box each morning.

On my coffee table, he lined up fat sticks of incense with labels bearing hopeful words like *Abundance* and *Growth* and *Prosperity*, and a little ceramic holder on which to burn them. He unwrapped a dozen hand-dipped candles made from wax formed by bees who pollinated the colony's organic garden, a hand-carved wooden wind chime from nonendangered trees that clacked soothingly when he waved his hand at it, and a rope of chilly sky-blue glass beads made of sand from some sacred site in India that he had a magazine story about in his files and would get me a copy of as soon as possible. Once he had lit two candles and one stick of the smell labeled *Destiny*, he gently arranged the string around my neck.

Eric Bigos pushed my hair back to get a better look at the necklace, and as he did, he told me of the lumpy futon he'd been given for the night in a long shed full of them—each occupied, many by people who grunted and shifted constantly in their sleep—and he told me of the dream he'd had there. The dream in which a long line of people were walking peacefully, carrying armloads of flowers. He was near the end of their line. When he asked where they were going, they only would smile at him. He moved up in the line, passing people, walking the crooked and turning route with them, but getting no help in finding out what this procession was all about. He moved ahead, farther and farther, and, in time, saw he had come almost to the front of the crowd. That was when somebody handed him an armload of white lilies, and that's when the rest of the people parted. That's when he saw me.

"Right there," he whispered, parting my hair and pointing to the top of my scar. "This was the exact shape of the long path I was taking, and there you were at the end of it. I saw us . . . I don't want you to think I'm crazy or anything, but I saw us. Fast forward–like, at the ends of our lives. And we were looking back, at how we had spent our lives together. Happy. In love. The whole time."

He slid to the floor, onto his knees. I had never seen Eric Bigos look so hopeful.

"Could you see that, too?" he asked me, taking my hand. "Us, together? For our whole lives?"

I had let him go on too long already. Those last two questions alone sparked in me one tempting, disjointed flash of what could be in my future—the beautiful wedding thank-yous we would send, each one laminated with a single petal from my bouquet, as a lasting reminder of the day—and I wanted to lunge for it. But I shouldn't even have answered the door. I shot off the couch and flipped on the ceiling light, then I blew out the candles as fast as I could and gave a few desperate blasts to the incense, which only made it burn more.

"No. I can't." The voice was harsh. Fast. Mine, though it wasn't. "You have to leave. Sorry."

"What?" he looked pathetic crouched on the floor under the harsh lightbulb. "What's wrong?"

"Nothing." I gathered the candles, still smoking, back into their box. I pulled to find the catch on the necklace and fumbled with it until it came open. I put everything into one of the bags he'd brought in, and I held it out to him. "I'll send you the rest this week."

"Donna? What'd I say? I don't get it." His eyes were big and confused and were getting wet. Some part of me wanted to stop what I was doing, but I knew I couldn't. At that point, I also knew that if I ever needed another job, after this, I could go down to the dog pound and easily fill in for the guy who has to do whatever he must do to kill the innocent animals that are brought in there.

This is how I put Eric Bigos to death, as far as having him in my life went: I said to his face, "Go on! Get outa here! Your last name means stew! Who'd want that?"

I saw him next at the door, with his mountain of presents, looking at me almost with a fear.

"I don't get it," he kept saying. "What did I do? I love you!"

"Go away. Thanks for everything, but don't bother me again."

I pushed him out the door, onto the porch, and I turned the lock and shut off the light. All around me, Destiny hung in the air, wrapping around nobody but me, left all alone, like I thought I wanted it. I went to the window and looked out to where I knew the hill was. I thought about the moment he— and all of them up there—would find out what I'd done, and I was pleased. Then, the next second, headlights came on beneath the window, and the whole dream of a life with Eric Bigos pulled out of the driveway and never came anywhere near me again.

I called in sick that week, and left the house only to get boxes from the package store, and to go back out, to the post office, to mail them less than a mile to Eric's condo. It was only after I had pulled every last bit of his souvenirs from every room in the house that I first realized what I had done. The place was hollow, stripped of all the life that he had been brought into it, of all the bits of color and scent and texture and memory he had slowly added to what surrounded me. The empty spaces that once held his presents, the tablecloths and vases and pillows and kilts and flavored vinegars, only under-lined what I had done, that Eric Bigos truly was gone from my life.

I was so mad I can't tell you. But to show you, I'll explain how I focused my anger not only on my father, but on Eric, who had to go and have nothing wrong with him at all. So to stick it real bad to both of them, I went off the following weekend with somebody they both couldn't stand—Rene Cournoyer, who sold gasoline at the Citgo and who would cheat you if you didn't watch the numbers on the pump. He was always greasy-smooth pleasant to me, and more than a few times had told me about his grandfather's place way up in

Maine, and, hey, the offer's good anytime if you want to get away. I knew he didn't mean by myself.

I drove straight to the gas station right after my last load was dropped off at the post office.

"What'll it be," Rene asked, sticking his head a lot farther into the window than he needed to.

I didn't recoil this time. I just asked him, "When do we head north?"

I was eating my supper and frowning over my Christmas card design when she called.

I hesitated a moment before I picked up the receiver, hoping that standing up would give a new perspective on what at that point in my life was my greatest problem: whether I should go with a one-humped camel or a two. One-humped camels fit better on the vertical format I wanted and would be simpler to cut out. But they looked harder for wise men to ride. Maybe that would force me to skip having the wise men at all, something I'd been considering in order to make the whole thing easier. Just make three camels, a dune, a shining star beaming its hope from above. Three colors: brown camel, golden dune, white light—all cut out and stuck on dark blue paper. Message inside: He Is Born, in white ink. Already I could hear Walter in Worcester, in some future phone call, telling me how when he got my card, he cried.

I'd been making my own Christmas cards since the fifth grade, when we learned how to make potato prints at 4-H. The first year it was a dove with the word *PEACE* written in my first attempt at Old English calligraphy, shaky serifs making the word look like it was underwater. The second year, I cut an eraser into a Christmas tree shape and dipped it in poster paints to print a forest, a star above only one of the trees. The next year, I used a small silk-screen kit meant for decorating the corners of cloth napkins and cut a stencil for an elaborate manger scene that I hand-colored in pencil. In eighth grade, the year Betty came but just before she arrived, I returned to the dove motif, but that time it appeared inside, and with the help of carefully positioned and glued paper strips, the bird slowly flapped its wings when the card was opened.

The nuns were in awe of my work. "You should go into the card-making business," Sister Superior advised me more than once, and in seventh grade she helped me package up a few samples of my designs with a letter she had typed and sent to Kansas City, telling Hallmark that I had the free time after my studies and music each night to supply them regularly with card ideas. Hallmark wrote back, and my mother even framed the letter, more of a memo, really, that told me under a shiny crown trademark that I showed extraordinary talent for such a young girl, but that they could not consider me for any work until I held at least a high school diploma.

Though the company had rejected me, I was the star of the family when that letter came, as I was every day back then, back before you know who.

Betty would not be getting one of these cards from me, though she was very generous with the mail she sent my way. She freely wrote me just-thinking-of-you notes from her home four and a half miles away, and postcards from business trips to the many conferences at which she lectured on how important a positive mental state is in the physical healing process. Frequently, not just on a birthday or at a holiday, she picked up and packaged and sent things: a blue enameled trivet in the shape of a lighthouse, a calendar that offered a new geographical fact each day, a fake stone with a trap door in its base so you could hide your key in it and leave it in your garden right out there where you could find it easily if you got locked out, a small radio that ran on solar energy, a paperweight with a dandelion bloom trapped in it. All of them came with notes that said, "I saw this and I was reminded of you!" And I would look at the things, and I would wonder exactly what she thought of me that she might come across one of these items in a gift shop and find my image popping up in her mind.

Some of the gifts I kept. Some I brought to the Goodwill. Many I put neatly back in their boxes and wrapped and gave to other people as presents, and they never failed to please and to bring to my mailbox sweet little thank-you notes from people who praised my generosity and good taste.

When Betty called me that night, all I could think of was she was checking to see if I enjoyed the jar of caramel sauce she'd had a candy store send me all the way from California, where, the enclosed note told me, the site of the physicians' conference she was out there for turned out to be a "clothing optional" health spa. She put many exclamation points after that bit of information, like I really wanted to think of her and Craig Weldon jotting medical notes while naked. I left the jar of "Carmel Caramel" in the poor people's food basket at church, the image disgusted me so.

"Donna . . ." Her voice was breathless, desperate, had some automatically scary quality to it. And not just because it was hers.

"What? I'm busy." I knew I never should have picked up the phone. I had my four camel drawing finalists positioned around my bowl of Spanish-flavor Rice-A-Roni, to which I'd added a can of mushroom stems and pieces, which are less costly, though less attractive, than the sliced variety, but once you put them in with other ingredients, you really don't notice that they're not perfect. I looked at my drawings. In each of them, I realized at that moment, the camels were looking way too much like cows.

"Donna . . ." Then she said nothing.

"Spit it out! I don't have time."

"You're—you're home."

"No, this is a recording. Leave a message." I went to hang up, and as I did I heard a little voice saying, "I'm coming over."

There was something really strange about how she sounded, and I thought the best—I mean worst. Maybe she and Craig Weldon were breaking up. Maybe he'd finally gotten so sick of her constant fascination with all of life and her stupid love of everything and everyone she came across that he decided to move all his stuff to a little apartment out near the Medical Center, which was such a huge place he never ran into her even in the days before this big painful split-up they had to be going through right now. Maybe he was even taking their dumb little kid with him, away from her. I was almost gleeful, imagining it all.

But I was also nervous. We'd been in the same church and parish center and grocery and polka park, but we hadn't been face-to-face for the seventeen years years since I'd walked away from the new house—and that's a whole lifetime for some unfortunate people. Sure, I'd seen her from afar, and in the stupid newspaper more times than you could imagine, but here she would be inches from me, and in some kind of distraught state. I thought of leaving, or at least hiding, but she was at the door before I knew it, looking far more terrible than I could have predicted. Under her eyes she had sick gray circles that went halfway down to her mouth, though I know that doesn't sound possible. Her hair was flat against her head as if she'd washed it, then hadn't bothered to comb it while it had dried on its own. She had on none of the cosmetics that even in the black-and-white photographs you could tell she usually applied to bring some life to her movie screen of a face. She hadn't bothered to button her stylish coat, had just wrapped it one side over the other behind her folded arms as she stood shivering on the porch. This was one miserable person. But what did she think I was able to do for her?

"Didn't you see my note?" She pointed to the glass on the door, where one of those small yellow stick-on things read, "Call home. Urgent." The words were underlined, and the writing had been done quickly. I didn't want to get into how this place here was home, for me at least, and why did I need to call it, here, so I just said, "I've been away. I got in late. It was dark."

"Why don't you listen to your answering machine?" she asked sharply.

I didn't need this. I started to close the door, but she grabbed my arm, and I turned around. Her eyes were full of tears, and she was shaking from more than cold.

"What *is* your problem?" I asked.

All of her was shuddering now, and she held herself tighter. "Ta . . . Tatuś . . ."

I don't know the rest of the sentence, only that next we were inside the house, slumped on the couch, and that Betty was crumpled in my lap crying her eyes out and telling me how he'd been fine all that day, that he had been down at St. Stan's going over the bands for next season, was toasting the feat of nabbing the Zabek Boys before the Polish Home of Enfield did, like they had last year. Then he stood up suddenly, put on his coat, handed his car keys to Mitch Kupiec, and asked him matter-of-factly to drive him to the hospital.

Then Betty said something about how my mother had gotten a call that just said there'd been an "emergency," they termed it, and could someone come quickly. How she ran next door and got Betty, and they drove so fast they knew they were going to get a ticket, but it turned out they didn't. How he was there on a bed, with only a sheet for the curtain separating him from the crowd of doctors that were yelling for instruments and help as they tried to put back together the hand of some screaming guy from Hardwick who went to unclog his snow-blower without first turning the thing off. How my father was flat and gray and still against a bed that had light blue sheets. How he had looked at my mother in a pleading way, but how he didn't say anything. How, still silent, he'd looked at Betty with an expression she couldn't interpret. How, next, he'd said his one and only word—not a word really, but the start of my name. At least that's what it sounded like to her.

Maybe if I got hypnotized I could go back and see and then tell you the exact things I felt right at the moment that Betty told me my father was gone from this world. But all I remember are things I shouldn't have been noticing at the time: the television, playing a commercial for a facial cream made with crushed pearls from the Far East. And how the lady who was telling you how it made her so beautiful pronounced the word "puhhhl." How just then Johnny Frydryk was knocking icicles from his roof with a bamboo rake he'd made real long by duct-taping a broom onto it. He had to keep jumping aside when he swatted a really big one, to save himself from getting speared in the head. And in those same few seconds I spotted the little silver rose-shaped earring I'd long ago given up looking for, and now it was winking at me from behind the leg of the stereo cabinet, one of the many places I know I looked for it about ten times, after losing it when Eric chased me around the house with a spoonful from the can of snails he'd brought back from some trip to France.

Eric. Would he come to the wake? Would he send a floral arrangement or perhaps a donation made to some benevolent cause, attaching a simple note that I would scan over and over for clues as to his feelings for me now? Would he maybe drive over to console me, his car trunk full of everything I'd sent back to him, asking me where should we begin putting all this back? Would this be the thing that would give us a new start?

You are thinking the same thing that I was right then: What is the matter with me? I have just been told that my father is dead, and all I can think of is whether or not it will be an excuse for one more bit of attention from a guy I just kicked out of my life for really no good reason at all except to disappoint a person I told myself doesn't mean anything to me anymore. How pathetic can you get?

But all I can say is that, for me, that is what happened. I did not think of exactly what I had just lost here. My mind bounced off that and over to the last time I saw him—and I am talking about my father here, not Eric. It was three Sundays ago in church, the Sunday of the weekend that Eric was at the yoga place for his seminar, using his free periods to collect all those things he probably thought we'd still be burning and inhaling on our silver wedding anniversary. Baby Adam was fussing as, in the choir above me, Mary Besko was singing a solo with the kind of pronunciation you'd use if you'd been born in Poland, her voice climbing as it told us of the Black Madonna. As I listened, I was looking at my father and thinking how he had never lost one strand of hair on the back of his head, and he was fifty-six years old. I came to take notice of such things because of Ross Peel, a nervous guy who guarded the town landfill and who lived there in a twelve-foot Shasta trailer someone had driven in there and never drove back out, who dated me for the the last month before he got in big trouble for allowing big tractor-trailer trucks filled with dangerous hospital waste onto the landfill grounds in the middle of the night. Anyhow, Ross Peel carried with him a small round mirror so constantly that the left back pocket of all of his pants were worn with an impression of the shape of it.

And whenever he had a spare few minutes, he would bring it out and find another thing to reflect it off, and would examine the bald spot he said he was getting but that none of the rest of us could see. He checked other guys' heads, too, swinging around on a street to see if one man's crown was doing as badly as his receding hairline was, whispering how that particular hairstyle only pointed out that the man there was trying to hide something. In movie theaters, Ross Peel held my hand, but looked elsewhere, tsk-tsking at the rows full of bald spots that stretched way down to the screen, and saying how that would be him soon, like next week maybe.

That's why I was looking at my father's head that Sunday. I'd never thought about such things before knowing Ross Peel, but since knowing him, it had become a regular thing, like the way I always checked out a person's clothes or jewelry. And as I was looking at my father, he turned around to look up at the choir. But first his eyes fell to the back of the church, and he saw me there. We looked at each other without blinking, and the next thing I knew the song was over, and we were rising to our feet as the priest continued on with the mass.

"I know he was asking for you," Betty was sobbing into my sweatshirt. "He just couldn't get the words out . . ."

My father had been waked at Wazocha's the previous Wednesday and Thursday and had been buried at the parish cemetery that Friday, all this back when Rene Cournoyer and I were nine and a half hours north, getting lost every day for a week trying to find our way back to his uncle's plumbing-less shack of a cabin after a long day of freezing and fighting in his car as we sat parked at the edge of a dead farmer's land trying to sell Christmas trees that weren't ours to the rich tourists he swore would be driving past any minute. On that trip I had a lot of time to think, mostly about how much I, too, really hated Rene Cournoyer, but one of my thoughts, which lasted about a minute before I went on to something else, was whether or not what I was doing was worth it, just to get somebody's goat. Now I had my answer.

My father would never know that I had gone off with Rene

Cournoyer. He would never know anything else that I would do, bad or good.

Was I happy now?

Betty explained they'd had no choice but to do everything without me, not knowing anything about where I was, and, not to get graphic, she added, but you can only display a body for so long. She had called Safe-Tam, where they said I was out sick, and then consulted Stella, who whispered I probably was off skiing. Betty had even asked to be transferred to Eric Bigos, but had been told he was out of town, indefinitely.

"We didn't know you skiied," Betty choked, rolling a few more lengths from the spare toilet paper roll I'd brought her to cry into. "We love to ski! Baby Adam had his first lesson last week at Mt. Tom. Tatuś drove up to watch. He was so proud . . ."

She went right on to another question: Could they have a reception here—at my house?

"The first memorial mass will be next Sunday. Mother wants to know, can we have the meal down here, in this house, where he grew up? Where he lived for so long? Where everybody used to see him day after day? Mostly, you know— the older people worry about going up the hill in the winter, even if there's no snow?" Her eyes were big, red and big, awaiting my answer.

Mother, she always called her. "Mom . . . ," I said to the floor, embarrassed to be thinking of her now only for the first time in all of what I had learned. Then—oh my God—Babci. Her baby, gone.

I looked at Betty. "Is Babci all right?"

Betty winced. "Now . . ."

Now, I knew she would add, now that we've found you, everyone will be feeling a whole lot better.

"Now," said Betty, "now that Mrs. Conway has come to stay for a while, she's really doing wonders for Mother and Babci both, talking with them, doing things for them. And we're right next door, and Baby Adam brings them such delight. It'll be tough, but they'll get through this." She put her arm around my shoulders. "We all will."

Betty was as close to me as she could have been. My sister, most people would say, but she might as well have been a kitten or a gerbil or something else that was nothing like me, not even of my species or even from the same planet. The hand that grasped mine might as well have been the paw of a dog that no one wanted, or that of a space alien that had nothing in common with me, but here she was, edging up to me, not knowing what was going to happen next, and none of us being able to find the right words to ask the question.

I looked down at her stubby thumb, still half the size of my own, its nail buffed and clipped short as you would expect on someone who regularly goes probing around in people's insides. I looked at her engagement ring, the raised *B* and *C* reminding me again of *EB*. There was the wide wedding band I'd seen Craig Weldon slipping onto her hand in the newspaper. After nearly a year and a half, the gold bore only one or two scratches, which I was sure she could have polished out, as Stella did with her mother's set. I could tell Betty that. I could even give her, as Stella did for me, the name of the new guy who's running Village Jewelers, who'll do small things like change a watchband or clean a crystal for no charge at all. Could I start there, I wondered, with something small like that, and then add on household tips from my big fat book of them, and child-rearing hints I had seen on TV, and soon would I be showing her and telling her all that she needed to know? Soon would I be as important to Betty as all those grown-ups once had thought I was going to be? Like right at that moment, when I picked her car keys from the space between the couch cushions so they wouldn't get lost and we'd be here all day looking for them.

It was too much to think about right now. I turned my attention to Johnny Frydryk, now shoveling the fallen hunks of icicles into a wheelbarrow, picking up the bits of what he'd smashed and what had crashed to the ground and what would be dumped out of sight in the backyard. I realized that his good friend was gone. I checked to see if I could tell that by his face, but his back was turned.

Betty straightened herself and squished a wad of toilet paper, then turned to me. "Of course, you know, they really want to see you," Betty said. "Would you go up the hill? Please?"

So that's why I went back up there for the first time in seventeen years, Betty driving me down my street, over the bridge, past Safe-Tam and the common and the gazebo and up steep Baptist Hill, climbing farther and farther away from town, past the water tanks and past the orchard offering cider and fruit for your holiday pies. Taking the right onto Conway Street, seeing the two long, white identical houses lined one next to the other on the left-hand side, parking in the driveway and going inside, straight to Babci, who crushed herself to me, then quickly shooed me to my mother, and I fell down next to her sitting in my father's old TV-watching chair and got the kind of hug you know a loving mother would give. I stayed there with her for most of that night as she told me stories of the olden days down on River Street, back before the house on the hill, back before Betty, back before me, even, back when it was just my mother and my father on their side of the house, telling me of the mouse that ran over their bed one morning and the strange man who walked in the back door offering to defrost their freezer for a quarter (what were you going to do— we let him and were pleased with the job), and the way they would dance across the street every time they played the song that sounded like "Hoopi Shoopi Donna," the picnics they'd have under the walnut tree next to the railroad track, and how when trains were stalled there, she and my father would bring coffee to the men on board, and how there are some pictures, though she doesn't know where they are anymore, but if you want to look for them someday you can, of her and my father at the controls of the huge engine, bound for somewhere, pulling on the horn, telling everybody get out of their way. Things like that. Scenes and stories and comments and memories, pieces and colors and smells of so many of the things that were two people's memories, and that, now, only one person knew.

There was nothing I could do but to say I would be honored to have the reception down at the house, and to add that I would take care of it all myself.

So that's why I had the Busy Bees come through my house and go over it from top to bottom at a price of $15 a room, and that's why I had Pride Cleaning Contractors take up the rugs, and that's why I had Johnny Frydryk come over with a stack of the old wooden folding chairs he'd taken from St. Stan's when they bought the new aluminum ones, and that's why I had Bebe Galaszowski's cousin who cooks at the Publick House make up all the food. Not just his favorite headcheese and *pierogi*, but the things that Babci used to make when she really got going. Some dill pickle soup. *Naleśniki* with fillings of mushrooms, sausage, potato, and brains. Mushroom cutlets. A roulade of eel, a carp stuffed with anchovies. Tripe and vegetables. Duck with red cabbage. A leg of venison. Butter horns. Half a dozen *babki* with raisins. Honey cookies. Berry compote. *Krupnik*. Lots and lots of *krupnik*.

And that's why I sat in church with my family for the first time in seventeen years, my mother working out our bench so that I was on one side of her and Betty was on the other, and during the parts of the mass that your hands are not folded, she would reach for one of each of ours and would hold them with her own cold, cold ones.

And that's why, after mass, Winkie Papuga came to my house and opened his mouth and said what he did.

And that's why I got the idea to do this with my life.

That is how it started.

Chapter

12

$\mathcal{T}$he night of the day that I gave Mr. Newbury my letter of resignation, I baked myself an entire family-size Encore Salisbury steak dinner, washed the pan it had come in, along with my plate, glass, fork, and knife, put everything away so neatly you would have thought I was expecting somebody, and at 6:30 I dragged an armless chair from the table to the center of the kitchen, unfolded my metal music stand under the plastic glow-in-the-dark cross braided to the string of the ceiling light, then went up to the closet in my bedroom.

I lugged the heavy, faded black case down the stairs, gently cleaned it off with a damp dishrag, and slowly opened it on the kitchen floor. I had not seen the thing since Theresa and Carolyn brought it to my house that first day home from the hospital, and the accordion hadn't gotten any better-looking in all those years. It was still small, still old, still dingy white, even had become yellow now, or hadn't I noticed that before? Its keys were dulled with a flat finish, and rust had eaten more of the metal on the rounded corners of the bellows. Plus, a crack had widened through the length of the trade name that ran across the front: *Spero.*

I sat on the floor for the longest time, smelling the richness of the old leather and the mustiness of the case, touching the long keys, just looking at the thing, something that appeared more ready for the dump than for the start of my mission. I had figured there would be roadblocks in all this, but I didn't think they'd happen as soon as five minutes into my plan. But the accordion looked about as bad as I'd come to feel, and I took that as a sign that this was a place to start. So I sat down. I pulled it on. I unsnapped the bellows, and they fell open with a sound that shouldn't have been there, the moan of a stuck key or button, though I could see nothing that looked pressed down. I put my hand to the keyboard and lightly touched the C, the D. The E, the F. The notes were rich and steady, but when I stopped pressing the keys, their tones continued. Something was wrong, but I felt it probably could be repaired. I played one chord, then another. Then, as if I had just practiced it an hour before, the entire American national anthem, with only my left hand. I laughed out loud. Then, trying both hands, on to "Happy Birthday," though it was no one's that I knew of, just a simple song that didn't require sharps or flats or great skill. It didn't sound too bad. I moved on to "The Alley Cat," bucking the sadness that came, before I knew what hit me, from the flashed memory of Babci and my mother stopping whatever work they were doing at the time to line up and do the steps to the dance, adding a little "Hey!" and a clap before they jumped and turned to face a new direction as the tune sped up.

It was like coming back to the old house for the first time, and knowing the way from one room to the next, though I hadn't been there for years. The keys were still in the same places, and "Fascination," "Spanish Eyes," "Come Back to Sorrento" and "The Song of the Volga Boatmen" were as easy to find as the pantry in the middle of the night. I sat up straighter in my kitchen chair, proud of what was happening. I played without any sheet music, without any of the Palmer-Hughes books and their line drawings illustrating each title: "You Tell Me Your Dream (I'll Tell You Mine)," "The Skater's Waltz," "The Battle Hymn of the Republic," "Drink to Me

Only with Thine Eyes" and "Chiapanecas," which I learned
was the real name of the Mexican Hat Dance. Mrs. Dranka had
allowed me to color in the drawings that went with the
numbers that earned me gold stars. I had ended up doing a lot
of coloring.

In all the years that I hadn't gone anywhere near playing
music, I would find myself now and then feeling some level of
jealousy when I saw somebody who really knew what they
were doing with a piano or a pair of spoons even. One of the
worst times I remember its really hitting me was at the
Eastfield Mall, where a band competition was taking place on
the same night that I went there to buy the Swiss Army knife
the seven-to-three shift had collected money for to present to
Hector Silva upon his retirement to a fishing cottage he'd
purchased over in Otis. The knife store was near the main
courtyard in which a band of old men in mismatched
dandruff-powdered dark suits was playing "Yesterday" on a
variety of wind instruments. The one who sat on the folding
chair closest to the knife store looked like the guy on the
Quaker Oats box, with a ruddy, smiling face and with nearly
shoulder-length white hair that waved and curled at the ends.
But that was not what I noticed first. What took my attention
from the window display of the huge and mechanized knife,
its spoon and corkscrew and nail file and toothpick gracefully
moving in and out of their slots like they should have been set
to the music that was in the background, was the man's flute
solo, which he offered so beautifully, his hair cascading as he
swayed his head into the sound, his whole self moving to the
music as it came from not only his flute but somewhere in his
soul.

I had to leave. I never bought the knife. If I had, I would have
had to kill the man with it for the good time he was having
with the gift he had been given, and then I would have had to
turn it on myself, out of shame for how I was wasting the one
that had been granted me.

That night in the kitchen, I became the oatmeal man without
even trying, finding myself helpless against the need to put

myself into what I was doing, to move into the sounds I was creating, to make it mean something other than a familiar tune played for the billionth time. I floated on the music, reveling in the sounds being made and in the fact that they were all there because of what I knew how to do. You could have paid me, and I wouldn't have had a better night.

And I don't know exactly when it happened, but polkas began to sneak into the regular numbers my Babci had called "Americanski music." I looked down to find my hands bringing out *"Mój Złoty Koralu"*—"My Golden Necklace." "The Red Handkerchief." Even *"Wędrówka"*—the wanderer—about a girl who leaves home.

By the second refrain of "Apples, Peaches, Pumpkin Pie," I was unstoppable. Until, that is, I stretched the bellows out wide, and a slip of white paper fell to the floor.

I stopped and picked it up—loose-leaf, folded and flattened from years of being tucked inside the accordion. I opened it, some of the creases splitting as I separated them, and there, inside, like a time capsule I had unearthed complete with background music, was the fat high school handwriting of Theresa, who'd put "Hope you feel better soon! Let us help!" three lines tall, with a circle under the exclamation point, and a heart, then her name, then Carolyn had added hers, with a long line of X's and O's following it.

The house was still. I laid my cheek on the top of the accordion. It was smooth and cold, but it warmed the longer I laid my head on it. And I left it there a long time, long after my eyes closed.

The first person I told my plan to was the guy in the bright yellow vest behind the counter at Falcetti's, a huge music store in Holyoke that boasted in the Yellow Pages that, other than offering personalized lessons and renting practice space, it could repair any kind of instrument you could bring in. Falcetti's ad even contained a drawing of a saxophone wearing a sling, with a G-clef pushing it in a wheelchair. I took that to mean they fixed even the instruments that were in really bad shape, so that's where I brought the accordion.

"This for your kid?" the man asked as he took a pencil out of his top pocket, licked the end of it, and then wrote up my claim ticket all in huge capital letters that you could have read from across the street if you needed to.

"It's for me," I answered. Then I added: "I am going to form (that word came out of nowhere, surprising me, and at once I enjoyed using it) an all-girl polka band."

"Ha!" the man laughed once, but I didn't take it too personally because I could tell he was not really paying attention to the answer. "Call me in three weeks. Something in this bad shape we might end up having to send out. I can't tell."

"I'm starting a band," I repeated. "I'm forming an all-girl polka band."

"Well, good luck then."

Mrs. Dranka, the second person I told, made up for the music store guy's lack of enthusiasm. In fact, she got so excited she began to weep when I telephoned her to ask if she still gave lessons. Her nephew Victor—I remembered him, didn't I?—had taken over most of the work at the Melody Academy, but Mrs. Dranka said she would love nothing more than to get me back on track. Could I come over that night—she couldn't wait to get started.

I remembered Victor Filipiak well. He had arrived in town when I was in first grade, two days after his college graduation, to collect on the promise with which his aunt had ended every birthday card for the sixteen years since he first placed beneath his chin a tiny fiddle: "Keep up your practicing, and one day you will work alongside me." I remember Babci telling my mother the story and saying it was a good lesson that you should not say something if you do not mean it.

And that was why Mrs. Dranka expanded her staff, that is why she called the ad man to have something put in the *Penny Saver*, and that is why she called a sign painter to add on her door, under the line "Sophie Dranka, instructor," one long stretch of gold-leafed letters that would read "Victor A. Filipiak, graduate of the New England Conservatory of Music."

I looked at those words before I opened the door the afternoon of my first adult-life session. Some of them were nicked, but the glass was as shiny as it ever had been and the same bell that was there thirty-one years ago clanged my arrival as I swung open the door.

My experiences playing in a band were brief and bittersweet. The first was on May 26, 1964, nine months after our first lesson at the Melody Academy, when Theresa, Carolyn, and I performed at our school's Ninety-Ninth Name Day celebration for Pastor Krótki, who dozed in his special thronelike chair carried over from the rectory next door to the school hall by four of the strongest altar boys.

Slumped hand to fist, he had snored through the entire shaky "Who Do You Love? It's My Daddy-O." Through Carolyn's squeaky trill on the clarinet, through Theresa's overpowering notes, through my more-shouted-than-sang "He's got apples and peaches for you. Hey!" He finally and slowly lifted one eyelid at the applause and whistles and foot stomping that followed the end of the number—noise that was so great that Sister Tobia, standing backstage to work the curtain and keep performers from running off in fright, made rolling motions with her hands, signaling us to do another song because the crowd wanted it that badly. And because Mrs. Dranka had taught us only one other song at that point, there were no difficult decisions to make.

"*Sto lat, sto lat, niechaj żyje żyje nam . . . ,*" I began, a *capella* until my shaking hands could locate the C and the G on an accordion with keys and buttons that suddenly seemed to be melting right down to the floor. Though confused, the rest of the girls began to follow along, and just about the entire audience took to its feet and began singing that traditional toast wishing good health, good cheer, a life of a hundred years. In the front row, the one who was being wished all this had gone back to sleep. But next to him and behind him and all the way back to the water bubbler and the door, people were swaying and singing. Some held hands. Others grabbed partners and danced in little circles. There was nothing but smiling faces as far as I could see. Nothing but people having a real good time. And after the first time through, the audience began to sing the words again, and we raced to catch up with them. You could get used to having the power to create such a good feeling, to know that you are the one responsible for all of what was going on in front of you. But we ended up being responsible for something else, too—the reason for our second and final gig: a hurriedly learned version of the Polish national anthem, which we played at Father Krótki's funeral three days later.

"Youngsters Know the Oldies" was the title of the four paragraphs my father wrote and submitted to the paper on the night of the funeral, barely able to contain himself after watching his own daughter be blessed by the real live bishop who had celebrated Father's mass.

> The girls have their success in the musical world guaranteed, almost, thanks to a special blessing bestowed upon them by Our Most Reverend Bishop Charles Jan DiMascola last Wednesday, after the real sad funeral service for the late Rev. Alphonse Krótki, who died right in his sleep less than one hour after being entertained by the band at his 99th Name Day Celebration.
>
> At a reception in the school hall following the funeral, the bishop came up and said to the girls, 'I'm sure your Father Pastor thought it was the angels coming down for him when you sang to him on that day.' Then Our Most Reverend Bishop blessed each on their heads and asked if that next tray of cheesecake was brought out yet.

It took only one school day of the kids chanting, "You killed Father Krótki," every time we stepped out of view of the nuns to sour any aspirations of a musical career: We could kill people.

But now, I had to believe the opposite.

I met with Mrs. Dranka as I had so long ago, every Tuesday afternoon at 3:30. I sat to her left in Classroom A, as I had so long ago, and placed my music on the same rickety wooden stand that I remembered as being taller than I was. The routine was the same, too: Play the assignment given the week before, get a critique, play it once again—this time using the suggestions Mrs. Dranka had made—then begin to work on the assignment for next week, usually the next few bars rather than an entire piece, as she didn't want to overwhelm me. The hour was over before you knew it, and I paid the fee—now increased from $1.25 but a still reasonable $5 per hour—at a new cash register, an electronic one that silently printed out my receipt, followed by a notation that read "The Melody Academy prefers American Express, but gladly also accepts Visa and MasterCard."

Except for that bit of high technology, I could have been back in grade school, learning "Born Free," "Penny Lane," "The Ballad of the Green Beret," "Winchester Cathedral," and "Tammy." Mrs. Dranka had kept her beehive, her dressy dresses, her simple gold wedding band with the one line etched around the center of it, her encouraging tone that made you want to learn the whole book in one week, and she still had the habit that no one else in my life ever had, the one of calling me "Dunnah."

She also remained greatly on my side.

"You are meant to be a musician," she would tell me at the end of each lesson, the kind of thing you wish you had somebody at home to run and repeat that to.

I used one of the academy's accordions to start with, while I awaited the prognosis for the Sperro. I spent most of my day with the borrowed one, working on the scales and the exercises Mrs. Dranka had prescribed to get my fingers reacquainted with the geography of the keys and buttons. After supper, I played the hour for myself, then sat down and planned out what I had to do next, adding more ideas and comments to a notebook full of details that would lead up to my new career as the leader of an all-girl polka band that would make a killing at weddings. Sometimes I flipped through the LPs that John Sobon had lent me when I went over with an extra banana bread for him and Stasia. It really wasn't extra—it was from a mix, so I knew exactly how many loaves I would be ending up with. It was simply a way to get invited into their house, and to do a little research there without anybody finding out what I was up to, before I wanted them to, before I was ready.

John Sobon owned nearly every polka record ever cut, and I knew that had to include those by all-girl bands. I hinted around about how I was wondering if such bands existed, and he handed me an album by the Roly-Polys, who were three men and three women, "half all-girl," as John Sobon pointed out.

"As you may have noticed, Women's Lib has invaded this Polka Band," read the copy under the band's photo. "In addition to adding good looks to the band, the girls are pretty darn talented too; and with three girls in the band, the men have got to keep on their toes . . ."

I tossed it aside, though onto a cushion so it wouldn't break in front of John, who had struck gold.

"This is more what you're asking about," he said, and there in front of me was the "Renata and Girls, Girls, Girls" collection—"Love and Inspiration," "Tickled Pink," "I Love My Music," "Heart-Felt Polkas"—the covers of which featured International Polka Association "Favorite Female Vocalist" Renata Marie Romanek, usually in a fur or a shiny tube top, sometimes with a concertina bearing the word *RENATA* on one end and *STAR* on the other. I studied the titles—traditional ones like the oberek "*Laseczku Mój Zielony*," and ones she'd written, polkas like "Shake It" and "Fool for Love." I pored over the liner notes, one of which ended with a comment about how important Renata's parents had been to the group's success. How her mother, Floss, and her father, Cubby, sold records, loaded equipment, drove vehicles, handled correspondence and booking. Who would do that for me, I wondered, with my Floss otherwise occupied up on Conway Street and my Cubby gone for good?

Worrying about such things was a vital part of the preparation and took up a good part of my spare time. I had hours and hours of solitude in which to think about these important details, as the guy I was renting to at the time never made too much noise. He worked a lot. Both at his home desk and at the newspaper. Yes, I had a reporter as a tenant.

I can blame it on the environmentally conscious and in every other way perfect Ray Jr., who, the spring before my father died, organized a benefit polka/rock dance for the Four Rivers Preservation Society, which was working to raise appreciation of the rivers that all town residents who didn't live on the hill had right next to, or within a short walk of, their homes. Ray Jr., living with the Swift River as the backyard to his cabin, was a very active member, and he gave up many of his weekends to lead informational canoe trips that had remarkable attendance from the young women in the area.

Ray Jr. got Happy Louie and Julcia to play for nothing, since the river ran a stone's throw from the garage where they parked their bus between gigs. And, appropriately for the day, he also got a rock group named Forest, which consisted of some friends of Ray Jr.'s who worked in a big office in Springfield and who spent too much of their days composing song lyrics on their word processors when they should have been writing insurance policies. He needed a lot of other volunteers, and of course I jumped when he called and asked me to assist, and I ended up sitting at a card table, selling raffle tickets and stacking people's dollar bills into a Tiparillo box when I wasn't admiring Ray Jr., as he dashed between the kitchen and the bandstand and the various booths, carrying, fixing, lifting, paying, peacemaking, doing all the dirty work that nobody notices but that organizers must do in order for an event to run without a hitch.

The items you could win on my table were pretty good, and all were tied to a theme of the environment or to healthy living. You put your stub into the recyclable paper cup that stood in front of the thing you wanted to win, and you hoped someone pulled your name when the time came. There was a prize of fruit, of course, from Lyszko's store—not just a single basket, but a different assortment each week for a month, and you got to pick the month you wanted. There was a gift certificate for a summer's worth of "earth-friendly" lawn care, which used things like hungry natural bacteria to attack the bugs in your lawn. An herbal "wrap" that, according to the stack of pamphlets, would have some woman in Amherst mushing boiled leaves onto your skin, then binding you up like a mummy while all the beneficial qualities seeped into your pores. You could win a bicycle helmet, or a weeping willow, a box of gadgets that would make your faucets dole out water more efficiently, or a special brick that would conserve many gallons each time you flushed your toilet. There was a little pump full of a soothing oil that you were supposed to carry with you and apply to the center of your sternum whenever you were experiencing tension. And a gift certificate for a free consultation for something called Rolfing. (There were very few stubs in that cup.)

The event was a mix of polka regulars in matching red and white and lots of tanned, fit young people in hiking shorts and clunky boots, multipurpose knives snapped onto their canvas belts. The dance floor was crowded with *babcis* in cotton-candyish bouffants, teens with stringy ponytails, smooth waltzers, hopping first-timers, T-shirts inviting you to "Kiss Me—I'm Polish," and others suggest you "Save Water— Shower with a Friend."

And popping up next to the kitchen, behind the bar, over at the picnic grove, at the edge of the dance floor, and, finally, right in front of me, was a thin, dark-featured young man in a tan, baggy, polyester suit, looking overheated and serious and professional as he made page after page of scribbles in a long notepad and habitually swung out of the way the 35-millimeter camera that hung from his shoulder.

He looked at me and stuck out his hand, a hot, inky palm that he clamped on to mine and shook sideways, right to left and back, like you might shake a jar of something to get the dregs to mix with the liquid.

"Joseph Angelo. Photojournalist. *Penny Saver.*" He said all this with more than the necessary space after the periods.

"Donna Milewski," I said, and watched to see if he would write either of those words down. Like the rest of the reporters I'd ever seen, he didn't.

"I'm doing a piece on the benefit. May I ask you some questions?"

"No."

"I'm sorry?"

"I don't want to talk to you."

"Well, then, have a good day." He said this, then turned and went right over to the snow-cone stand, to Missy Robidoux, who screamed and clapped her hands after the guy made his introduction, and she stood next to him and pointed to how he was spelling her name, so it wouldn't come out wrong in the paper.

I looked at his story when it was printed that following Thursday. After, of course, I ran out of other things to read.

> Happy Louie and Forest played for an estimated 2,000 people on Sunday at Pulaski Park. But they also played for the earth.
>
> The two bands, along with 22 town residents, generously volunteered their talents and five hours of their time at a benefit for the Four Rivers Preservation Society. Organizer Ray Lyszko Jr. reported that $4,657 was collected for the cause from revelers. Missy Robidoux was one of those, but she wasn't there simply for a good time.
>
> "I care about the earth," the 35-year-old factory worker said. "I work inside all day. I miss the earth when I'm not on it."

I'd heard her say that. His quotes were accurate.

I didn't think of Joseph Angelo again until he showed up at Safe-Tam to do a story on Maria Joao, a tiny overdressed secretary in consumer relations who happened to be cutting through the parking lot on the way back from a lunchtime trip to the bank when she saw Honka Koprowski's empty Buick Regal slowly rolling backward toward the riverbank, and toward the row of kids who sat there fishing with their backs turned to the thing that was about to crush them. Luckily, Honka Koprowski never locks her doors—not in her house or her car or anywhere—and Maria Joao was able to jump in and slam her shiny silver high heels on the brakes just two feet shy of the guardrail, of the unknowing kids, and of the unobstructed drop to the water.

When Joseph Angelo came to the plant to immortalize her and her deed, I hid behind a stack of cartons. But I knew he saw me. And whether he recognized me or not, there was something about this guy that made it embarrassing, for the first time in my life, to have someone find out what I did for work.

But who cared? I wouldn't see him again, I thought. However, as these things go, I did—on my own front porch, no less.

I needed a tenant at that time. Badly. I had no luck keeping anybody since Mr. Kulis got hit on the head by a golf ball three winters ago, and he and Mrs. Kulis moved for good to his sister's place in South Carolina, to an apartment set next to a tennis club, where the balls were a lot softer. Then Jessie and Harry had to leave when he got transferred to monitor the air quality on the North Shore after the state decided that our levels of pollution were way too boring. Then there was the hairdresser I had to kick out because she was doing her work in her living room, something she was supposed to have a Board of Health permit for and refused to get because she held no beautician's license. And I lost a month's rent when those two girls from Southbridge moved out in the middle of the night, taking with them the kitchen things and bath towels I'd let them borrow after they told me their story about having to escape from a dangerous boyfriend who had threatened the one who was his girlfriend. For four depressing months there was the sad little separated guy who slept on an air mattress like you take to the beach (I am pretty sure of this because he brought no furniture with him, and then I found an empty carton for such a thing in the trash barrel) and who cried so loudly at night you could hear him no matter what room you went into to escape him. Then for the longest time, something like a year and two months, there was nobody. Nobody was answering my ads for the "homey two-bedroom apartment with yard and garage and free musical entertainment in season," nobody slamming on their brakes at the sight of the orange-and-black APARTMENT FOR RENT sign I'd bought at Chudy's and staple-gunned to an old tomato stake and shoved into the front lawn. Nobody.

Nobody, that is, until Joseph Angelo.

I was fighting on the phone with Allen Gooch when he knocked on the door, and I used that as a good reason to end the conversation. Allen Gooch's noisy drag racing down Woodmont Street had made him somebody I once wanted to spend time with, but he was calling me from jail now, and he wouldn't tell me why—though he would tell me that he needed $250 for bail. I laughed before I hung up.

I opened the door, and there was Joseph Angelo, both of us surprised that the other one was standing where he and she was.

"Joseph Angelo, apartment seeker," he said with a little bit of a smile, and, side to side, a lot drier this time, I noticed, we shook hands.

I asked him to come in and sit down, and in about two minutes Joseph Angelo was telling me how lucky I was to have grown up in such a quiet little place. He had been raised in Camden, New Jersey, he told me, and from his bathroom window he could see the *p* and the *b* and a silver of the *e* of the neon sign that told passersby that this factory was where all the Campbell's soup they'd been slurping down all their lives came from. It was a good-sized Italian neighborhood, Joseph Angelo said, but his parents, who had been born in this country, weren't ones for keeping with the old ways.

"Other than food, I don't know a single word in Italian," he told me, and I felt strangely sad for him, figuring that, as it was with my family, at the very least there had to be all kinds of songs and expressions he was missing out on, not to mention the connection that went way back to people who lived in a totally different country, especially those who made that unimaginable decision to get up and go to this unknown one and in that way brought him here even before he was born.

"Not a word?" I asked.

"Not a word," he said.

It was hard to believe. But Joseph Angelo told me he figured he would have been good with language if they'd given it to him in his childhood, as he had been a bright kid. His smarts even earned him the 1973 Campbell's "Use Your Noodle" scholarship that paid for two whole years at Yale, where he began working toward a history degree, which he got, then taught high school, until one unremarkable day last January when it came to him that he was no longer interested in telling people what had gone on years ago—he wanted to tell them what was going on now. He liked to write and figured being a reporter would allow him to do both those things; so he left his job, researched and made a list of small New England papers that might be of a size not to care whether you had any talent or experience, and sent to those in the most rural areas an impassioned letter about his change of viewpoint, including the fact that his hobby was photography and that he had his own black-and-white darkroom equipment and an uncle in the business who would supply him with all the film he needed.

Elsie Bigelow took in one intern every summer at the *Penny Saver*, paying him or her some of what she would have paid her only full-timer, Tom Pochalski, if he worked the summer rather than spending it, as he had for seventeen years without pay from her, as a volunteer for the National Parks Service. So to temporarily replace the employee who was headed for three months of recording data in a fire tower somewhere so far into Vermont that the roads weren't even printed on any map and so remote that he got his mail from some guy who rode by on a donkey occasionally, she decided, after reviewing Joseph Angelo's letter, to give him a try.

Joseph Angelo liked the prospect of having some time to sample the job and to decide whether or not this was for him, and he wrote back, yes, Mrs. Bigelow, I will be there.

He had arrived in late March, which means he was brandnew to the job when he'd covered Ray Jr.'s benefit and had been sleeping for the five weeks since on the orange vinyl love seat next to the coffeemaker in the newspaper's supply room. He needed a place to live. I needed a tenant, though after having my life dented by way too many of his kind for so long, I wasn't that crazy about having under my roof someone who did for a living what Joseph Angelo did.

"I need a reference before I can tell you anything," I said, businesslike.

Joseph Angelo said he understood.

He gave me the name and number of Mrs. Bigelow, whose name I first noticed years back, when Betty started appearing in the paper, and I started disliking the people who were glorifying her. But to her credit, Mrs. Bigelow didn't say anything about knowing who I was. She only went on and on about her new reporter, how fortunate she was to be working with such a fine person, and how she would take him in herself in an instant if she had the room.

Mrs. Bigelow said she quickly realized that Joey, as she called him, though she noted that he signed "Joseph Angelo" on all his notes and phone messages, was nothing like her usual summer interns, only a few of whom knew how to type and most of whom were housewives or retired men who wanted the job solely for the press card they could use to get to the head of the line at the movies or to the front of the mob at any disaster they might happen upon.

"He not only wants to write, but he actually has some talent!" she exclaimed, her voice underlining how this was something she was not used to. And, Mrs. Bigelow added, he used that talent in fresh ways that never had occurred to anybody who either wrote for or read the *Penny Saver*.

On Flag Day, for instance, she said Angelo drove through town and stopped at some of the houses that did not have flags displayed and knocked on the door to ask why not. On Father's Day, he visited several bars and talked to any fathers he found there about why they were there and not at home opening ties and slippers and aftershave. He even got permission to photograph one of the men as he held his wallet open to a baby picture of a scrawny, howling, diapered infant he'd only seen once, twenty years ago. In a series that carried the general theme of what it's like to be different from everybody else, he found and interviewed the two Jewish families in town, and did the same with the one black family and with the woman up near Soltys' farm who schools all her five children at their kitchen table and raises most of her own food, hardly having many reasons at all to come down the road to mix in with the rest of us.

People loved it, and they loved the new reporter. Mrs. Bigelow told me that every day the mail included a few envelopes bearing suggestions for the next piece, or neatly clipped-out copies of one of his stories, with words of praise written across the copy in red marker. Singlehandedly, Joseph Angelo was transforming the *Penny Saver* into something you might actually look forward to, a far cry from its days just a few weeks before, when people read it only for its extensive classifieds, skipping the front page entirely, which was usually filled with stories like how the Sewer Commission was getting a new filing cabinet free of charge because one had been abandoned at the side of Sibley Street. Mrs. Bigelow even went so far as to snicker that she wished Tom Pochalski would take a wrong step out of his tower.

"Imagine what this boy could do full-time!" she hooted. Then she confided: "I'm going to keep him on as long as I can—you'll have yourself a tenant for at least a year. Really— I'd take him in if I were able to."

What could I do at that point? I had the room—hey, I had a whole half of the house. So I let him have it, but for $35 more a month than I'd planned on renting it. I told him the increase was due to some insulation I'd just put in, though I'd done no such thing and held no such plans.

The night of the day I called Joseph Angelo to tell him he could have the apartment, I watched from my bedroom window as he unloaded his car and carried everything in through the front door.

He seemed to own very few things—a suitcase that I assumed held his clothes, a couple of boxes probably packed with the same necessities, a goose-neck lamp, an ugly painting of a cowboy riding through a boring desert, and a couple of new-looking boxes—two squarish ones, with the word FRAG-ILE and big rainbow-colored apples painted on the side. And two long, flat ones that read: "Home Office Center. Assembly Required."

For most of that night, there were some thumps and hammering noises. Then it was quiet for a time, then I heard an "All right!" shouted, and nothing more.

Most times I didn't want to hear anything at all from next door, but when I really was wondering about somebody or what they were up to, it was best to go in the pantry and listen near the old passageway door that Babci had pushed so many huge meals through all those years ago. It was just a hinged board that my father had placed over the hole he'd cut into the wall, and because no one ever latched it back then—it was used too much in those days to bother ever to really close it all the way—the door was warped and bowed at the sides, and if I put my face real close to it, I could see a good-sized vertical slice of the room in which Babci had spent so many thousands of hours of her life.

One time I had watched the Kulises dancing on a Sunday morning, when the smell of their bacon and toast and frying potatoes and onions drew me into the pantry. I looked in to see them moving slowly to a waltz that Freddie Brozek's "Polka Explosion" played from their kitchen counter radio, and every few turns, Mrs. Kulis would reach for her spatula and would flip a bacon strip or an egg or move something around in her frying pan, but none of her movements interrupted their dance. It was so beautiful and second nature and enviable that I finally had to force myself to stop watching them come in and out of my slice of a view.

I had watched one couple named the Tutweillers scream at each other once, and it was disturbing to me to see such behavior in a place that for me had always held love. They stood where Babci had stood to push sticks of softened butter and plates mounded with sifted flour into her cake mixer, and they called each other names that I would be embarrassed to repeat here. It was not hard to leave them alone.

I had watched the little separated guy sweat and pace in and out of the kitchen with the cordless phone, over which he softly pleaded for one more meeting to try to make things right. I, of course, had to stay until I learned whether or not he'd get it (he didn't).

It was a bad habit, I knew, and I wouldn't have wanted it done to me, and I most certainly wouldn't have wanted to be caught, but I was drawn to it. I had collected some of the most important information of my life by snooping, and all I can say is, once it pays off, I guess you're hooked—for no other reason than the chance that you might hit it big again.

The night Joseph Angelo moved all that stuff into the house, I tiptoed into the pantry to see what I could see. A shiny red kettle had appeared on the stove, and there were a couple of cheap mugs with slogans I couldn't read on the counter next to it. A little ceramic milk jug held an assortment of wooden spoons so new they still had little slivers sticking up from where they'd been sawed into their shapes. He had threaded a still-ironed-from-the-store dishtowel through the handle of the refrigerator and had placed a blue hand-shaped potholder on the shelf above the stove. Beyond that, I could only see a piece of the dining room, but I could make out a long, dark brown table in front of the windows, and the edge of a piece of boxy putty-colored electronic equipment that had to be a computer. If I got myself up onto the pantry counter and pushed my face all the way up to the wall, I could see a right arm, wearing a short sleeved white T-shirt, clacking away at the keyboard. The sounds were even and steady, like Joseph Angelo was copying page after page from a very long book. But, according to what Mrs. Bigelow had told me, he was probably just taking down all the incredible stories that were flowing out of his very, very rare brain.

Most times that he was home, when I did bother to get over into the right position and take a look, Joseph Angelo was sitting at his computer, tapping his words onto his screen. Once in a while, he would pause and shift his right leg (I could see that, too), stretch his arm out, reach for the cup of something he had fixed for himself, then, like somebody had rung a doorbell in his head announcing that the information he needed had arrived, he would fling his hands back to the keys and start up again.

Joseph Angelo lived next to me for the last seven months before I quit Safe-Tam, and once I did and was around from morning until night, I found myself surprisingly in tune to his

daily schedule. I had never done this before with another
tenant—and I had had men alone there before, not just the
little separated guy, but the quiet UMass professor who stayed
for the year he needed to finish up some degree in economics,
which I thought meant he was going to be sewing aprons and
rolling piecrusts, like we had done in high school home ec. But
he set me straight after I told him how lucky he was to have an
apartment that actually had a flour bin, and after learning
what a genius he was, I was too intimidated to hold much of a
conversation with him.

I would be hard-pressed to come up with what time any of
these other people ate or washed their dishes or put on their
favorite shows, but I could easily tell you that Joseph Angelo
woke at 8:30 or so, which I thought was pretty good considering he often was awake way past midnight. And that soon after
I heard his first steps around the house, he would head out the
front door, stretch his legs on the steps, and then take one very
fast run up the street, not returning for another fifty minutes or
so. And that when he did get back, he would crank his radio
up loudly, to the all-sports channel that any time of day has
people giving their opinions on how athletes make way too
much money, and then I would hear the shower running. I
didn't mind any of the noises he made. They were predictable,
and once I left my job it became kind of nice to have something
you knew was going to happen in your own home, especially
when you didn't know what was going to happen in your own
life.

After the shower, Joseph Angelo would go into his kitchen
and pour himself a bowl of cereal. He must have passed
Lyszko's at the end of his run, because he always came back
with some kind of fresh fruit to slice on top of his breakfast.
Bananas, of course, or strawberries, blueberries, kiwis, and
when he was out of that, he'd throw on a handful of raisins,
even if what he'd poured into his bowl was Raisin Bran.

He stood wearing only his underwear when he did this—
baggy, funny boxer shorts with drawings on them, of palm
trees or black dogs or dollar bills or sailboats. He was neither
thin nor fat; actually he was pretty boring, physiquewise,
considering all that running he did, but all in all, I thought, he

was in pretty good shape for somebody who sat at a desk so much, and the first time I happened to look in and see him there like that, I remember I turned away. I had seen guys in their underwear before, but this was not Sandy Fertado sleeping one off on my couch. This was someone I didn't know, and I was spying. Like I said, I turned my face away. But then I slowly moved it back.

It's not like he was doing anything private, anyhow. He was pouring out some Rice Krispies or Apple Jacks, some whole milk, slicing a canteloupe, then he would go and sit at the little kitchen table and would unfold his *Daily News* and would eat his cereal with a big soup spoon.

After breakfast, he would go off to put on some more clothes, then he would return to the computer and get to work on whatever it was he was working on. Some days there would be thick files next to his machine, and he would take things out and study them, then make some more entries onto his screen. But mostly, he just wrote. I couldn't see what he was looking at as he did, but something was powering him, inspiring him, and he got a whole lot of work done in one sitting, it seemed to me, though I really can't say that I know what would be considered a good day in that kind of occupation.

At noon he would turn on the local TV news, and then he would flip at 12:30 to "The Young and the Restless" while eating his lunch, which was always a bottle of seltzer water and two cans of the kind of pasta meant for kids—noodles in the shape of dinosaurs or letters, or spaceships, flags, cartoon figures. And he would bring his glass and his bowl and spoon into the other room and would talk to the TV as I previously had only heard women do, yelling his opinion of the characters' lives, yelling at the melodrama. I hadn't been interested in soaps since the days when Babci used to blast them through the wall, back when a woman named Jo Tate searched for tomorrow. I knew that Jo and her long, painful multiple-husbanded hunt were TV history now, but it wasn't too hard to get hooked on some new characters, and soon I found myself tuning to the same station at the same time, one wall away, watching what Joseph Angelo was watching, and taking note of his muffled reactions, of what confrontations he cheered, of which women he applauded, of which parts were so boring that he chose them to return to the kitchen for more of something.

Around 1:30 or so, Joseph Angelo left for the newspaper. Always wearing one of the two beige suits he owned—one a little darker than the other and with side vents on the jacket—he'd exit out his back door and would place his black cloth briefcase onto the passenger's side of his car, then he would drive off.

Joseph Angelo and I talked, but never went too much out of our way to do so. It was more that we just happened to meet in the driveway, or out at the clothesline, or when he brought his rent check to my door. We discussed the weather, or a salesman that had come by, and did you hear that loud noise last night—what was that? Once in a while, he stood so close that I could smell the soap he used, and I would find myself distracted for the remainder of my day.

When I held the reception after my father's memorial mass, Joseph Angelo must have put two and two together, with all those people in their dark suits, all that food, and not much laughter, certainly no music, and being at a newspaper he must know at least a little bit of what is happening in town, and after all that, whenever we'd run into each other, he'd say "How ya doing?" with a genuine sincerity in his voice, like he really was concerned. I would say I was fine, and how about you? I never asked him what he was up to, and he never asked me, though he must have heard my playing, as I heard what I heard of him. I don't know what I would have told him had he asked. What I was up to was not anyone's business yet. Plus, I knew there were just some people who wouldn't get it, that this was what I wanted for myself, that there were no men or kids or dreams making me want anything else. And I decided that's what I would tell Joseph Angelo, if he ever did ask why I never left for work, why I never left for much of anywhere, why I played my music so often and for so long, like there was something I was practicing for.

Babci was the third person I told my plan to, and I did so with the warning that it was our secret.

"This is not for them to know," I said, motioning toward the hill, where I hadn't been since Christmas Eve, when out of the goodness of my heart I accepted the invitation Betty left on my machine to come up for the *Wigilia* that I knew sadly would include an empty seat at the table not only for Baby Jesus, should he come knocking, but for my father as well. It took a lot for me to go up there, but I put on a dress and good shoes, and I drove up the hill just before the first star, thinking only of my mother, that I might fill in a little of the great new emptiness in the house. But there was hardly enough room for me. Worcester Babci and Dziadziu and Uncle Joe and Cioci Urszula and Uncle Abie had driven out, unfortunately leaving Walter somewhere else, Craig Weldon's parents and a godfather and an aunt had flown in, and the oncologist girl and her radiologist fiancé were there, too, along with the Conways and even Mrs. Conway's sister and her husband, all staying up for the Shepherd's Mass, all staying over at one or the other of the two houses through New Year's Eve.

A genuinely delighted-sounding "Donna" and a tired embrace were all my mother was able to greet me with before someone called to her, seeking diet soda. I didn't stay much past dessert.

I awaited Babci's reply that she would keep this between us, but there wasn't one. She just smiled, then grabbed the pair of tongs and set two more steaming, guinea pig-sized *gołąbki* onto my already loaded plate.

"Eat," she commanded, waving a hand at the steaming fare. "And everything will be all right."

Chapter

13

$\mathscr{I}$t only made sense that I ask them first. After all, the note they'd left in the Sperro said they wanted to help, and I needed help, even if it wasn't the kind they had been thinking of at the time they wrote twenty-two years ago. So I decided to ask Theresa and Carolyn to be in my band.

Right off, there was one big problem: They no longer lived down the street, they no longer had nothing else to do.

Theresa married right after college, and I mean right after, like the day after graduation. So strong, supposedly, was the love between Theresa and this kid Benny Farr that there wasn't even time to include Mr. Zych or Carolyn or me—or anyone else they knew, for that matter—in the ceremony, and so their only witnesses were a bunch of clerks who ate from insulated tote bags while they witnessed the marriage ceremony performed at lunchtime at City Hall in Northampton. Then came plenty of time for what Babci would call repenting in leisure— actually it took place behind the wheel of a car, while Theresa drove Benny Farr around New England so he could sell packets of nutritional powders to health food stores and gymnasiums, and at expositions where they offered passersby Dixie cups of thick, green seaweed-based breakfast drinks.

"It's not really that bad," Theresa wrote unconvincingly in the rare letters she'd send us, underlining *that* and always enclosing sample envelopes of strong-smelling dusts we were supposed to mix with cider or hand-squeezed orange juice or raw duck eggs. Carolyn and I disliked Benny Farr for more than the yucky stuff he wanted us to purchase subscriptions for, an arrangement that would guarantee a steady supply of Vita-Verve and Bone Builder throughout the calendar year. Benny Farr was the one who, in the interest of raising capital for his own line of powders ("Health by Farr," just about the only clever thing I ever heard come out of his mouth), talked his wife into talking her father into selling the family's farmland to a developer, a high-powered man from the city who five years ago bulldozed with sickening speed a tight grid of streets running through pastures and forests, christened them with names like Country Lane and Rural Road, and lined them with brand-new high-tech but very antique-looking homes that young professionals paid incredible amounts of money for and planted sad weeping cherry trees in front of. Teddy and Winston grabbed their shares of the money and headed for Cape Cod. The only scraps of the old days that the contract retained were the farmhouse, for Mr. Zych, and the name of the former dairy as the name of this new section of town.

It turned out that Carolyn left just as Theresa had, only it took her a few months longer, and six months after her college graduation, we all got to go to a fine formal New Year's Eve wedding. One day she was teaching music at Tantasqua Regional and saying her career was going to be her life, and the next day she'd fallen in love with Morris Kennedy, who drove for Valley Tomato and who dreamed of being part of the new age of agriculture. They moved to a test farm in Central Florida, where they raised two children in a mobile home and all kinds of vegetables in water. No soil or dirt or sand, just water—if you can imagine such a thing. Hydroponics, Carolyn called it, when she had the chance to send me a postcard. Her father told me that was just a fancy name for a technique that is so experimental it would never make them enough money ever to fly home for a visit.

"You're what?!?" Theresa cackled into the phone when I finally was able to reach her and tell her my plan. "Whattayou? Nuts?"

"I think it'll be fun," I said. "Is there any way you would want to . . . to be part of it?" There was no answer. "I mean, would you want to be in the band?"

She just laughed and laughed and laughed, a little longer than I thought she really had to once she got started.

I broke in. "Remember how great we used to sound, the three of us?"

"Like I have time," she said sarcastically. "We're only here to do laundry and pay bills, and then we head out for another week or two. When am I supposed to do all this music with you? On my day off?"

I didn't have an answer.

"Donna, really," Theresa said in a softer tone, "we're into New York now, and New Jersey, too. Didn't you get my letter?"

"Oh, that is just such a nice thing—you know, when I think of a town where you could do something as old-fashioned as that, I just get so homesick," Carolyn mewed before breaking into tears, before apologizing and explaining why she just couldn't. The children, she reminded me. Their schooling. Her job at the shoe outlet, where everything is $10, but, as a cashier there, she can get things for $8, and I should remember to trace my feet and send her the shape so she can get me a discounted pair in the exact, correct size. And then there was Morris, always busy. Too busy. You wouldn't believe how busy.

She just cried and cried and cried.

Fine. I was mad for a couple of days, it was a disappointment, but what could I do? I had to get moving. So in late February, I placed an ad in the *Penny Saver*, looking for women who wanted to be in an all-female polka band.

"Are you female?" it asked. "Do you play an instrument well? Do you want to be in a polka band? Members needed. Please call."

I added my number, and the warning that only serious callers would receive a reply. Then I waited for the response.

The only call I got in the first month came from Falcetti's, saying that my accordion was ready and could be picked up whenever I was in town. Though I was far from that town and had no other business to conduct there that day, I rushed right out the door.

The work on the reeds and the new set of bellows came to a little more than one whole month's rent from Joseph Angelo. But the cost was worth it, just as the man in the yellow vest had promised.

"You won't be sorry you did this—believe me," he said as he counted each of the many pieces of paper money I handed him.

And I wasn't. Not only had the accordion been given a grand new voice—strong and unwavering and proud—it also had been cleaned and shined and repaired, its name glued back together, and only if you knew where it had been would you be able to look closely and find the hairline that once had been that wide crack.

"Spero," I said to it.

It said nothing back.

There was nothing to stop me now. The loaner from Mrs. Dranka had been nice while waiting, but with my own accordion, I felt I truly was on the way. The sun was beginning to rise earlier each and every day. I met it, put on some clothes, brought the case into the kitchen, and played under the light string until the next thing I knew it was noon. I'd make some lunch, would turn on my program, then afterward would sit down again, to open another music book and go right through it a few times before darkness came and I had to pull on the light.

I don't know what you'd call it, but what I was doing, what I was finally doing, was giving me a feeling I'd never had in my own body. I was creating something, out of nothing. I was going along on my own track. And I was making progress. It was so exciting I could hardly keep still about it, and it was the first time in all the years on my own that I so strongly yearned for someone to share things with, to confide in. To tell the details that would be of no interest to most people—exactly how many hours I played, how well I did on *"Jak Sie Masz,"* how I was starting to imagine the sound of the other instruments joining me, at just what points they would begin their harmonizing. But there was no one who was that close. Before I knew it, I began to wish there was. And before I knew it, I began to wish that the person was Joseph Angelo.

Spring was coming, and they say that people feel like this in the spring—that they have to have somebody. I had always had a string of somebodies, yet I never really took notice of how I felt from one particular time of year to the next. But I had not dated at all since I heard Winkie Papuga's words that night and I started all this. My time was devoted to my music, and it showed in how well I was progressing; like the old days, Mrs. Dranka was marking my accomplishments with stars, and she ran out in the first month. There had been no one in the six months since Rene Cournoyer, since my father, since Eric Bigos. And I missed having the company of guys in my life, even if they had been the losers I'd almost always chosen.

Joseph Angelo and I had shared one encounter, if you want to call it that. He had knocked on my door one night, holding a red Saran-Wrapped platter covered with heart-shaped sugar cookies. It was a few weeks before Valentine's Day, and he told me how he had scanned the telephone directory and had come up with a family by the last name of Valentine and was doing a story on how they decorate year-round with heart themes. In the front of their red clapboard house with its red shingles bearing hearts and arrows, there grew a heart-shaped garden filled with the red rose bushes that he'd have to imagine in full bloom though they now were only stumps covered by hay and bushel baskets and snow. There was a heart-shaped door knocker below a heart-shaped window cut into their front door that led to an interior of red furniture, cupid vases, and bookends. Red glass hearts were leaded into the clear panels of the French doors that opened to a dining room table—set with heart-shaped dinnerware being straightened just so by the husband, who was cooking a beef heart in the kitchen. He could go on and on, Joseph Angelo told me, but it was freezing out and he just wanted to know—did I want these cookies, because he wasn't allowed to take anything for free on the job on account of how unethical that would be—which was something new as far as the *Penny Saver* went, because when Tom Pochalski was the writer, if you wanted a story on the front page, you just had to bring him a bottle of peppermint schnapps. Joseph Angelo apparently didn't go for such practices—he wouldn't even take a cookie. But these people wouldn't allow him to leave their home if he didn't accept their gift, and he'd seen enough, so he took what they wanted him to have. Ordinarily, Joseph Angelo told me, he would have swung by the nursing home or the hospital to leave them there, but the roads were getting so slippery, and he had wanted to go straight home. Would I please take them? I said why not, and he brought them into my house.

I made tea and presented it to him dark black like I knew he liked it. But I brought out the sugar and offered him milk just so he wouldn't get suspicious.

"No, this is perfect the way it is—exactly," he said, waving away the additions, and I smiled.

I had been going through a box of old music books Mrs. Dranka had offered me, trying to get some new-but-old ideas for what my band might play. They were all over the living room, so I kept Joseph Angelo away from those private things and suggested we sit at the kitchen table, and I offered him the seat next to me, where we could look straight out the window and see what kind of a mess we were safe from.

"So these Valentine people—where do they live?" I asked.

Joseph Angelo snapped a heart in two. "Out on Route 67," he said. "On a farm, on the right just before you enter Warren. You never heard of them?"

"I don't know anybody way out that way," I said, though of course the first thing I thought of when I heard of that road was Noga's Turkey Farm—which is right on it—and how the Nogas had driven four turkeys, already roasted, even, up to the new house the weekend we moved in, helping to feed the workers as their contribution in making that new home for Betty. I could amaze myself how, twenty-one years after all that, I still could call up such tiny details, like how each of the birds wore paper Uncle Sam hats over the stubs where their claws once had been, and how, once the workers had been assembled for the grand lunch, my father slowly passed Representative Conway the carving knife, and he stood at the end of the long dinner table in his creased, borrowed coveralls and rambled some long made-up prayer that he ended with Ah-men, rather than A-men.

"I don't know anybody out there at all," I said to Joseph Angelo. "Want some more hot water?"

He said he didn't, that it was time he got home, next door. I said of course it was. Yet neither of us got up from the table. The snow was becoming icy, and it beat against the window glass in little taps that sounded like somebody was throwing sand at the house. The furnace had kicked on, and the radiator underneath the windows hissed gently. The one light on the counter that was lit when he'd knocked was no longer enough, but at the same time it was just right, dim and golden behind us. Across the driveway, Johnny Frydryk turned on his bathroom light and pulled down the shade. A car passed the house, most of its sound muffled by the snow on the road. Above us, the cross on the string glowed steadily. It was the kind of calm at the end of the day that you rightfully should share with someone, and we were doing that, though I am positive that neither of us had expected to ten minutes before. At the same time, it was so natural that it felt like this was what we did at the end of each and every day of our lives. And before I knew what I was doing, I was lighting the candles I'd kept on the kitchen table ever since Eric Bigos, and that I had not used since him. We talked about the town and the neighborhood and the street and the house, and he told me that his favorite part of his place was the windowseat in the bedroom, a feature he pointed out that you don't see people bothering to add in the houses they make today. Some of the time we were just quiet and still, and it didn't feel awkward, considering I really didn't know this guy. It just felt nice.

I can't say how long we were there talking and not talking like that because I don't know. It wasn't all night, it wasn't even past the eleven o'clock news, because I switched the TV on after Joseph Angelo left, and there was Buzz Muraska proudly waving a photo of his red-faced newborn twins before predicting that, with tomorrow's rising temperatures, we would not see a speck of this snow by noon the next day. However long Joseph Angelo and I were at that table, it was long enough to fall into some kind of trance, and for a lot of that time I felt Joseph Angelo's eyes on me, when mine weren't on him.

Then he pushed his chair from the table and stood up. "The music you play—it's very nice," he said hurriedly before he put on his coat and went around the back of the house and let himself in. I went to the pantry and watched him hang his coat on a chair, then shut the light off and sit at the kitchen table and look out his own window, at the black and white that was the world.

I dreamed of Joseph Angelo a lot after that, beginning with that very night. He had written a great book—don't ask me what it was about, all I know is that, even though it had no pictures, it went over big with the critics and the reading public and it was as thick as a dictionary—and that on the first page there were the words: "To My Love, Donna." All across the country, if people wanted to know who the author and photojournalist Joseph Angelo loved, all they had to do was go to their local bookstore or library and flip to the page between the title and the start of the story, and they would find out. That it was me.

I had other dreams, too, in which I would open the little door in the pantry and slide into his kitchen like I was a platter of Babci's roast pork. Joseph Angelo would be at his kitchen table, in his shorts with the planets on them, interviewing the pope. But he would end their conversation because I had arrived.

"Can we do this another time?" he would ask the pontiff,

who graciously would leave us alone, only after bestowing the papal blessing that most people have to write to Rome to get, and snow would begin to fall in the kitchen—snow that smelled like Joseph Angelo's soap—and we fell into it and made two angels, then one, and we took off and flew up through the planets, planets that became shapes, shapes that became words, words that became sentences—sentences that Joseph Angelo told me were my story, my very own one, even though he said it began way back before I was born, that is where they all start, with things you could never know unless someone told them to you. It got confusing right there, and I usually woke up at that point, sometimes with my head and feet at the wrong ends of the bed, always feeling suddenly alone and always with a jolt to my heart that all those smells and touches and whooshing meteors were something I had made up out of nothing.

As much as a good part of me desperately wanted to see if I really could fit through that pantry door, if I really would be so enthusiastically received, if Joseph Angelo really would whisper "Stay—don't go" and would hold me that desperately when I was beginning to wake, there was no way I could ask him out. Not me. Though he'd done not one bad thing to me, I was too stubborn to separate what he did for a living from what he seemed to be doing to my heart. So I left him there, at his desk, on the other side of the house, and I decided the time had come to finally take my chance with Ray Jr.

For most of my life I'd thought about doing that, and thinking was where it had ended. That he had nothing wrong with him—no paternity suits, no lack of personal hygiene— had kept him off my list all those stupid years. But now things were different. So one night I baked up one of those bread doughs you can get in the grocery freezer, and I wrapped it in a cloth and put it in a basket like I'd cooked it up from the raw ingredients that had been listed on its plastic bag, and I walked over to see Ray Jr. Who wasn't home.

I sat on his porch swing and watched the icy river rushing past, illuminated by both the moon and a light in the Safe-Tam parking lot up on the other bank. I went from that place of peace to the torture of looking across and locating the exact window that had been Eric Bigos's before I told him to get lost and he went and did just that. The cleaning service was on duty and had all the lights on in the row of little offices, and I could see the empty blue space where his seashell print once had hung. I didn't know where it had gone, because I knew nothing about Eric Bigos anymore, though once, about a week after Christmas, when the bridge over 181 was being sand-blasted and they were detouring all the traffic over the Mt. Dumplin road, I allowed myself to glance over at his assigned parking spot at the condo and saw his alloted space taken by a maroon family van wearing a sticker that boasted how its child was the student of the month at Converse Middle School.

I stretched out on the swing and dug my hand into the center of the loaf of bread, pulling out fistfuls of warm dough. What if I lived here? Sweeping the boards of this porch every day with that broom Ray Jr. had made from branches in the yard. Hanging his red swimming trunks on that line over there—in the summer, of course—near the screenhouse he lights with votive candles like a dozen prayers are going on at once. Cooking eggs on that fat woodstove he and five friends carried out of his Babci's place when they sold it. Finding out if we could both fit at the same time in the claw-footed bathtub that slopes and rises like one big, white porcelain serving dish. Lying across the big bed he took a course at Pathfinder to learn to carve, with simple fish shapes cut into the sides of each of its four square posts. If I lived here I would love it. I knew it. But I had never even gone near expressing to Ray Jr. one word of the fascination he always had held for me. I always figured the time would come. And I decided this was it. I was up on Aniela's horse, ready to go somewhere, and I could proudly tell him what I was going to do with my life—not only that, but how I had already started. It would be like my spotting Eric Bigos's file folders, startling and impressive at the same time, to see how much was going on in this one person's life, a place where you'd never imagine much of anything else happening except for what you saw.

In all my newfound complexity, I awaited Ray Jr. But soon I was too cold to want to reveal anything at all of myself, and I took my basket and the shell of the bread and headed back up the street, disappointed but looking forward to trying again the next night. But when I got to Lyszko's, I found out where Ray Jr. had been. The store was dark but the door opened just as I was approaching, and out he came, hand in hand with Karen Cieplak, whom I had forgotten about so long ago that she might as well never have existed.

"Donna!" Ray Jr. said, his teeth glowing in the dark. "Out for a walk? Isn't the moon fantastic?"

I looked at Karen and said, "Yeah."

"Holy shit Donna Milewski how ARE you?" She squealed this so fast I had to repeat it in my head to decipher what she'd said.

I answered that I was okay, and I asked how she was, though that was obvious. She had kept her figure, and her red hair was cut to the short short length that only models dare, and I have to say that it really looked good. There was some other kind of a spirit about her, and I wished I had Jessie and Harry's mystic to decipher it for me.

"We're just going over to the house," Ray Jr. said. "Wanna come over?"

I shook my head. "I have to be somewhere," I told him, and I motioned with the nearly empty basket, like I was late for a delivery of something.

"That reminds me," Ray Jr. said quickly to Karen. "We forgot the potatoes." And he ran up the steps and went back inside, the storm door banging behind him three times before it finally shut.

Karen giggled, for no reason that I saw. I said nothing, but it was awkward. So, okay, I had to ask. "You going out with him?"

"Going out?" She asked the question like the answer was something you should have learned in a rhyme when you were three and repeated it every morning. "Are we going out?" She smiled slyly and said it like I had said to my mother when she asked about Eric Bigos. "Yeah . . . we're going out."

I thought of her getting us all in trouble back in grammar school, and tried to keep myself from imagining all that she must have learned since then—and how she now was using it to pollute the beautiful Ray Jr., who should have been leading

me out of that store, who should have been running back for
potatoes for himself and me, not for himself and her.

Karen closed her eyes as she said like a prepared speech:
"Donna, I have loved that guy for like a million years." She
stopped and let that float out into the universe, and it made it
pretty far before she continued: "I just never told him. I figured
he was long ago taken—I've been married twice myself, you
know"—I didn't—"but I read in the paper last summer, when
he had that benefit? I read how he lives by himself in that
cabin. 'By himself,' I thought. I gave him a call." She pinched
me on the arm (I guess that was supposed to be cute), and she
said, "You can't imagine how nice he is."

Because I could, and because I had spent the hour freezing
and doing just that, on the same porch swing where they had
probably done something else, over and over and over like
Sonny Corleone and some Italian girl had done all throughout
that page and a half she had marked in *The Godfather*—I said
again that I was running late.

"I'll tell Ray you said good-bye," she called as I hurried up
the hill.

I didn't answer.

In my driveway, a strange car was parked in front of Joseph
Angelo's garage door. It was white and new, with Rhode
Island license plates. As far as I knew, it was the first out-of-
town visitor that he'd had here.

Joseph Angelo's dates usually were somehow connected to
his writing. The first that I spied on was a girl from
Belchertown, whose grandfather had been the subject of one
of *Penny Saver*'s "River Valley People" features that every other
week told the stories of everyday folks you'd otherwise never
hear of, unless they happened to get arrested for something.
This girl's grandfather collected belt buckles, from vacations
all over the country and in a few foreign places where you can
speak English and they are able to understand you. He had the
walls of two whole rooms covered with his prizes, on long
custom-made wooden shelves that they fit onto perfectly. I
remember the story mostly because of the picture Joseph
Angelo had snapped of the girl's grandmother demonstrating
how, once a week, she removes the buckles from their shelves

and dusts each one lovingly, then selects the one the grandfather will wear for the next seven days, trying to get him to use each of the hundreds of buckles at least a single time before he dies.

Word of Joseph Angelo's good looks, manners, and lack of a wedding band seemed regularly to filter down to the young women in the families of such subjects as the buckle guy. Once or twice a month, there was a young woman in Babci's kitchen, watching as the frugal Joseph Angelo put together a tomato sauce from scratch, telling him how her family went all around the area and snapped up every copy of the paper they could find when the story ran about Uncle Jake and his talent for etching historical scenes on dried tree mushrooms, or about mom and the three retired greyhounds she adopted and saved from destruction at the ends of their racing careers, or about Cousin Red and his talent for removing bats from homes, or about the odd little brother who wrote poems from the information contained in strangers' obituaries, then sent them to the grieving families as anonymous tributes.

This night, though, the date wasn't anybody's relative. I could tell that much once I checked in.

They were cooking. Well, I should say Joseph Angelo was cooking. She, whoever she was, was standing there holding a glass of wine and quite often would position herself so she was in his way, somewhere you'd know better than to stand in front of when someone else was fixing a meal—in front of the refrigerator, then when you're asked to move from there, apologizing and standing in front of the stove or sink. He kept saying "sorry," "excuse me," "could you move for a moment," and she kept giggling. "I guess you're used to working alone in here, ha?" And he would say yes.

She was pretty, I guess, though she would not have been my type. She looked a little bit too much like somebody who was still trying to be twenty-five, fifteen years later. Her hair hung way past her shoulders, uniformly curly from a perm, I could tell, and she held it back at either side of her head with elaborate silver barrettes in a severe style I hadn't seen since I last flipped through my high school yearbook. She wore a shiny, white, probably silk blouse that she unbuttoned three holes down, enough to show the collar, and I have to call it that, of silver that hung from her neck, dotted with coral stones that matched the ones on the traffic jam of bracelets that clanged together and took up half the space between her wrist and her elbow. She wore two rings, one on her left thumb and one on her right middle finger. Silver again, domed and shiny as if she'd worked on them. Her miniskirt was denim, and there was nothing but about a yard of health club legs between its hem and the top of some fancy, high cowboy boots that, when she went into the living room for a second, probably to check on her horse, I saw were black with cutouts showing patches of bright red and more silver.

"Since you won't come down to see me," the woman was saying sarcastically, "I have to come see you—especially if somebody else is paying for the plane." She took a drink of her wine, her bracelets colliding. She set the glass down and studied her wrists, arranging her ornaments so that their best features—a large gem or particular design—were all lined up.

"I don't have the money to go anywhere," he told her, "never mind all the way to Texas."

"A starving writer," the woman said with a sniff, and she looked over at the computer. "Glamorous. Almost as glamorous as a starving teacher."

"It's fine with me," Joseph Angelo defended. "You're just a glorified tour guide. I wouldn't go picking on anybody else's job."

The woman came back huffily and, as if she were reading it off something proclaimed: "*I*, am an executive."

"Chamber of Commerce, tour guide, same thing," Joseph Angelo told her.

The woman took a pen from the table and threw it at him. He laughed.

"I get to meet celebrities," she boasted. "Who do you get to meet in this place? The Jolly Green Giant?"

"You said you were going to be nice if I let you come over," Joseph Angelo pointed out. He said this in the way that told me she had some history of not being very nice, and I wondered what their story was. I wished there would be somebody in the pantry filling me in, like they sometimes do at the beginning of a soap opera: "In today's episode, Joseph Angelo has an old friend for dinner, someone he met somewhere else, and they obviously know each other well . . ." That sort of thing would have been helpful. Instead, I had to fill in the blanks myself. But she was too annoying to give this much of my time. I decided to stop watching and slid off the counter. As I did, I kicked my wooden napkin dispenser from the counter and sent it clattering into the kitchen.

"What was that?" the woman wanted to know.

"Next door," I heard Joseph Angelo answer.

"Who lives there?"

This is when I decided to stick around a little longer.

"A woman. The landlord."

I'd never thought of myself with that title. It sounded like I should be in England, bossing my serfs around.

"Nice?"

"She's very nice," he said, and my heart started speeding up. "The best part is she doesn't bother me. I don't need somebody interrupting me. I have too much to do."

My heart slowed down.

"So what do you do?" the woman asked. "Other than your little job."

He picked up the pen from where it had landed on the counter and flung it back at her. She shielded herself, but it hit her on the knee.

"Other than my *little* job? Just more writing."

"About what?"

"People. Stories."

"That tells me a lot," she said, taking another sip, her words getting trapped in the glass.

"They're complicated. About how lives can go over the years, how the simplest ones can get so complicated. You wouldn't understand."

"You know," she said, stopping for a second, and doing a bad job at pretending she was angry, "right now I could be at the Newport Hilton—the governor of the entire state of Rhode Island is speaking tonight."

"Wow. All that plus convention food? What are you doing here? You must be crazy!"

I could see the woman was getting mad. "Well. The next time I get sent up here," she told him, "there is no way I am going to spend good money to rent a car and drive two hours to see your sorry ass."

This was better than any movie I'd ever seen. For the first time in my life, I understood why some people will pay such a lot of money to see a play. But this was even better—it was right here, right in front of me, and I didn't even have to leave the house.

Joseph Angelo took a paper bag from the refrigerator and started rinsing all the stuff Mrs. Lyszko had on sale that day. "How are your parents?" he asked.

"Just fine." She said this, then stopped for a while. "They still hate me after everything. Divorce is a sin, they tell me, and they can't stand it when I do this, but when they say that to me—and they say it a lot—I always ask them, 'Then show me that commandment.' Don't worry, they still love you, though. You really should call them."

"I'll call."

"No, you won't."

"I will."

"No, you won't."

"I said I will. And I will."

"I know you won't."

Joseph Angelo dropped his knife, a little louder than he really had to. "Food's ready," he said stiffly and pointed her to the table.

They stayed there and talked for a long time, their voices lowering and the conversation sounding more serious as it went on, though I couldn't hear all the words, except something, once, about how, yes, he would be lying if he said he hadn't missed her, and sometimes he just can't believe the stupid things that happened to make them now be so far apart.

"But you don't seem so bothered now," she said, kind of snottily if you ask me.

"What can you do?" Joseph Angelo asked her. "Live your days and nights kicking yourself? I forgave you, I forgave me. What choice do you have, really? If I didn't do that, how could I ever expect to have any kind of life?"

The woman didn't have an answer to any of that—or, if she did, she didn't say it out loud.

It was past the time when I should have been practicing, and so I left them to their meal, and I went and set myself up and began to play, plowing through everything in an easy binder of sheet music I had picked up for a quarter in Zebo's used book pile, moving steadily through polkas named "Evergreen" and "Favorite," "Elsa," "California," "Martha," "Unita," "Chicken," and "Springtime," numbers printed back in 1938 but still sounding pretty good to me. How they sounded to the two on the other side of the wall, I didn't find out. When I went back to the pantry, the kitchen was dark and empty, and the whole side of the house was quiet. I found my couch and slept there, trying not think about Joseph Angelo, but how could I help it?

I smelled coffee. Early. Much too early. And Joseph Angelo didn't drink coffee. I shuffled into the pantry and peered into the kitchen. There was his ex-wife, like one big morning-after cliché, wearing nothing but a big Toronto Maple Leafs T-shirt that had to be his. Her hair was evenly fluffed, and even at this hour she wore the complete level of makeup you see on the women who try to sell you the stuff at department store counters. She also had on all the jewelry I'd seen on her the night before, and her bracelets made way too much noise as she opened all Joseph Angelo's cabinets, but didn't close them, I guessed so she wouldn't make too much more noise. She swished a giant tea-bag full of coffee and stared into the mug like she was waiting for a message to appear in it, then sat at the table and wrote something on a piece of paper that she finally folded and left there.

When she went out of the kitchen, I went out of the pantry, and not long after that I heard Joseph Angelo's back door, and I sprinted to the window to watch her get into the white car, then back out of the driveway, then pull away, headed in the definitely wrong direction for somebody who was going back to Newport. I was glad she was going to get lost.

Soon I heard Joseph Angelo coming down the stairs. I ran back into the pantry and watched as he entered the kitchen quickly, with an almost hopeful look on his face. He spotted the note and unfolded it, then stood there for a long time after he read it, looking forlorn.

Joseph Angelo skipped his run that morning, for the first time that I knew of since he'd been living at the house. He went only as far as his computer, which he switched on in an instant, and then he began hammering at the keys faster than I'd ever heard anybody type.

Chapter

14

*V*ictor Filipiak wanted to be in it bad.

"Come on, Donna, you're discriminating against us men—you could get arrested for that."

He'd go on like this every time I came in, always the funny one, with the same old stale joke every time. But I never told him to shut up, because his wife, Monika, out of the goodness of her heart and on the promise that I would stick a sign reading "Costumes by Monika E. Filipiak" on the back of my music stand whenever we played, had charged me next to nothing for embroidering the outfits that were to be worn by my all-girl polka band: Donna and the Melody Girls.

I felt that since this was my idea I had every right to put my name at the beginning. The girls were not really girls—technically none of us had been anywhere near girl-age in quite some time. Corinne Platt was fifty-nine, and that alone was the reason she had answered the ad. She had a birthday, and suddenly she was eligible for 10 percent off everything every Tuesday at the Kmart, and could start cashing in her individual retirement accounts without fear of penalty, and that made her all the more intent on not acting like she was old enough to be able to do any of those Golden Years things. She had knowledge of the clarinet, but more importantly she had a closet full of good-as-new sound equipment that had been abandoned by a son who once had led a somewhat successful local rock band that went by the name of Crispus Attucks. I didn't even trouble her with an audition, only asked when we could get together and if she would mind telling me her dress size, so I could get a costume going. Leeann Pedraza was twenty-nine and knew the bass as well as I knew the accordion (I had to trust that it was her, not somebody else, playing Bobby Vinton's "My Melody of Love"—the only remotely Polish tune she knew—over the phone from Fairview). She said she wasn't trying to insult me, but she had never cared for polkas, yet she had always dreamed of playing in a band and would join whoever would take her. No one before had ever asked.

Who else answered? Well, there was a woman who called to let me know she was hoping we would be playing authentic Polish music, and she stressed the word *authentic* so strongly that I asked, do you mean like church songs, and she shot off into a big long speech about how polkas, my dear, are not Polish, that you would not hear one note of this kind of music if you went over there (You have been there, haven't you? What? You haven't? How can you call yourself Polish-American?), and how we have a rich cultural heritage with people like Ignacy Jan Paderewski to inspire us, and how polka is a big farce, and how people like me just perpetuate it with our stupid songs about sausages. She ended up so angry that she hung up, which was fine with me because what did I know about what they listened to over there? I only knew that this was the music we played here, and it happened to be sung in Polish, and sometimes told of Polish things like the mountain men called *górale* and of how they wept when they left their homeland. I wasn't trying to insult anybody, but she didn't give me a chance to tell her any of that.

There was the woman who had learned the marimba years back, just so that she could score extra points in beauty pageants by playing such an unusual instrument, but I had to be honest and tell her that I was sorry, but I didn't think I could fit that sound into a polka band. I also got a call from a high school girl who was so nervous about talking to me that her voice cracked, and we made an appointment for me to listen to her play her electric piano in its dozen different tones, but she never arrived that afternoon, and her mother sincerely apologized, when I checked to make sure she had not been in an accident on the way over, saying the girl was simply unable to come to the phone.

Blind Tekla, who had Steffia Krolik read her every single inch of the *Penny Saver* each Thursday night, notified her musically gifted niece over in Brimfield once she heard the advertisement—not even knowing it was mine—and the next week I had the woman in my living room playing "Moon River" on her trumpet, Tekla sitting deep in a nearby armchair, pounding time on the floor with her big black shoes. The niece, who introduced herself as Miss Lucille Bosman, was pretty good, but she thought she was a whole lot better than that, rattling off names of local performers that she'd shared stages with and that I'd never heard of. She'd been in three bands before, though never an all-female one, and never a polka one. But, she told me, the basics were the basics, and she'd be happy to share her great knowledge of booking and scheduling and billing and publicizing and sound and lights, that she even had a spare room in her apartment now that her daughters had gone on to school, and that we could have our headquarters there complete with that spare phone jack one of the girls had whined for their father to install. Lucille said she even had one of those van vehicles that we could use to transport everything, and a husband who would volunteer to drive if he didn't have a ball game to watch on TV that particular night. This was going to be a perfect arrangement, she told me. We just needed to widen our horizon, to include men if the musical need arose, and to perform all kinds of tunes, not just limit ourselves to the ethnic, and definitely to work on the band's name, which she had responded to with a weak smile when I told it to her. I politely informed her that I still had one more trumpeter to meet with, one who was supposed to be quite impressive, having played with five bands—five polka bands—before this, a lie that made Tekla say "oooh" but then point out I should keep in mind I would never meet anyone like her niece. I responded, no, I probably would not.

Corinne and Leeann weren't angry or nervous or intimidating. They didn't want to take over everything. They simply were happy to be included. And when I got one of them, then the other, in between all these others in the space of a month and a half, I called the paper and asked Mrs. Bigelow to stop running the ad.

That was the middle of March. We practiced three times a week at Corinne's, where all the electrical stuff was. It took the first couple of weeks to figure out what cords went into what holes, and exactly what all those dials and monitors were for. Corinne's son was not around to help, stationed over in Guam as he was, so we had to guess, and we only blew two fuses before we got all those black boxes and microphones and plugs connected and dialed up the right way, and we finally managed a timid little "Silent Night," it being a song that everyone knew without having to look at sheet music. When we sang the last "sleep in heavenly peace," and the number ended, I was almost afraid to look at the other two—we had sounded so good together, I thought, and two notes into it I was already hooked on seeing this thing through. What if I turned to Corinne and she said, "I don't think I want to do this," and what if Leeann said, "We stink. I quit." My eyes were still straight ahead, staring across the cellar into the flats of fragile vegetable seedlings that Corinne was soaking under the glow of an ultraviolet bulb, when from my left came, "Hey, we're not bad!" and from behind me came, "Let's keep going—what else do you know?"

Corinne was a cook at the high school, and she served the same kind of food in her home—gooshy sloppy joes, greasy chicken nuggets, tasteless wax beans, instant potatoes you could build retaining walls with, bland devil's food cake frosted only with a blob of generic Cool Whip. All that was missing was the individual carton of milk, a plastic tray, and the table full of popular girls looking you up and down before breaking it to you that this seat is saved.

Off duty, out of the white uniform, and with her frosted short hair free of its School Department-issued shower cap, Corinne dressed in the workout clothes her cousin embellished with garish flowers and sold at craft shows, chanting, "They're all hand-painted," whenever someone approached. Singing the whole time, Corinne usually cooked only for her mother, a lonely lady who lived next door but who, once Corinne came home, seemed to spend all her time there, talking nonstop.

"Will you look at all this stuff," she asked me when Corinne introduced me. "Just from today."

She lifted up a familiar-looking envelope. "Another one of these—'Finalist Notification. WIKTORIA DABROWA is a GUARANTEED FINALIST for the Publisher's Bonus $20 million Super Prize based on an entry from a recent contest. Another timely entry, from this contest, will activate ten extra numbers in the final round . . .'"

"That's something, Ma," Corinne said, knowing she would be hearing everything printed on that envelope if she didn't interrupt.

"And this," Mrs. Dabrowa said. " 'Summer Sale. College Coordinates.' I've never even been to college—how'd they get my name?" She flipped through a catalog showing bored-looking twenty-year-olds in oversized sweatshirts and leggings having brunch on a dock. "Pre-summer clearance up to 75 percent off regular price—OH, look at this, in the small print—'On discontinued items plus discontinued colors of ongoing items.' That's the hitch."

Corinne later told me that this is what her mother does a lot of, reading everything she sees. On a car trip to see the foliage last fall, she collected travel pamphlets at every stop and read them to Corinne one after the other. "In-ground pool. Complimentary coffee. Children's play area. Touch-tone phones. Color TV . . ." When she ran out of literature, she took what she could get, reading passing signs: "Brattleboro fifteen miles . . . Brattleboro ten miles . . . Brattleboro five miles . . . Brattleboro next right . . ." Even graffiti, all in a monotone:

"Ziggy was here . . . Megadeath . . . Jerry Garcia We Miss Ya Man . . . Frankie—Kiss My Ass . . ."

According to Corinne, the explanation was that this was how her mother learned to read English. There were no classes like they have for the lucky foreign people today, Corinne said, only your own get-up-and-go. "Stop" was her first word, learned at a stop sign. That's why now, when you're almost upon one, Mrs. Dabrowa will never fail to announce it for you.

Corinne had made the offer to cook for both me and Leeann on the nights we practiced, and I accepted. I'd never really learned to cook that well—in my house there was no need— and I was just as happy when somebody would suggest eating out, or at their place. Leeann joined us for the meal only occasionally—she usually got home late from her job, and she had a husband who liked to see her at least at supper if she was going to be gone the rest of the night. As far as husbands for Corinne, there had to have been a father for the soldier in Guam, and there had to have been a Mr. Platt to give Corinne the name that was different from the one on her mother's mailbox and to present her with that plain platinum band, but Corinne never mentioned him.

I did not snoop to find out anything about that, or anything else if you really want me to be honest. I did not ask Leeann if she wore all that same black leather clothing while she was selling books at the mall all day. Neither one of them asked me why I was doing what I was doing. We didn't get too personal, and all in all, we got along. Three times a week we shook Corinne's cellar, inching our way toward new tunes and interesting spins on them. Corinne took the longest to catch onto things. She had played clarinet in the marching band at Springfield College and would be the first to tell you that had been a long time ago. We waited for her to get the hang of something, or we modified the selections so they would be easier for her, for now. We weren't there to be famous. We were just happy to be playing in a band. To be playing "The Nancy Polka," "The Music Box Oberek," "Little White House," and "The Girl I Left Behind" to Corinne's pepper plants, which Corinne thought were responding to the music, growing taller and stronger and healthier than any she'd raised down there before we began.

I think I was doing the same. I would leave Corinne's very happy, feeling taller and stronger and healthier than maybe I ever had. I was doing what I had planned, and it felt great.

"Do you think we're good enough to have people hear us?" Leeann asked one night halfway through April. "Because I know a place we can play."

It wasn't really a paying gig, but it was a regular one, playing after dinner every Wednesday for the people who lived at the old-age home in West Brookfield, where Leeann's sister was a receptionist, one who had been promised that she'd be getting a $10 award in her next paycheck for locating yet another recreational option for the residents.

I'd never been in the place, though I'd driven past enough times on my way to get seafood platters at Howard's Drive Inn, where halves of car tires had been painted yellow and stuck into the ground, a row of huge onion rings separating the parking lot from the road. And each time I went past the home I couldn't help but glance through the big glass door at the lonely-looking people who sat in gray metal chairs and stared back out at the cars going by. Once I got inside for real, past the woman who stopped me and asked did I remember to bring the cupcakes because you know how I'd forgotten them the last time, I recognized a few of the people who lived there. I hadn't seen him in ages, but there was Charles Kwiatek, who used to help Mr. Zych with carpentry projects, now walking around haltingly in a fuzzy blue bathrobe, with a big radio held up to his ear, tuned to the Red Sox. Len Piszek's mother, whom everybody had always just called Bubbles, was in there, leaning on a walker, recovering from a broken hip, singing quietly to herself with a voice that belonged in a concert hall. From one of Joseph Angelo's photo features, I recognized the spindly-armed lady whose hobby was painting scenes of the town as she remembered it from ages ago, and there was the one that he had written about because she spent all her free time—and she had plenty of it—studying languages and was up to eight different ones besides English, and, I recalled, she hoped to hit a dozen by the year 2000, with no doubt in her mind that she would last that long.

We set up in the sunroom at five, in front of a wall decorated with children's letters thanking the home for letting them visit and sing—and especially, wrote one kid, Christopher, age eight, for letting them ride in the wheelchair. He was saving his allowance—where could he buy one, he wanted to know. While we adjusted our microphones and unfolded our music stands, the residents were finishing up in the dining hall, where round tables with colorful cloths and candles had been placed the month before to help create the restaurant feel that Leeann's sister said was one of the goals of the new director, a molish-looking man who shook each of our hands vigorously that first night and apologized that he could not stay for the performance because he had to leave for a meeting in Boston. Taking out his wallet and opening it to reveal a sea of green bills, he asked did we have a cassette of our music that he could purchase to listen to on his long drive?

By that date, Monika E. Filipiak had completed her elaborate embroidery on only two of the three black vests, had yet to tie long colored ribbons to the circles of fake flowers we were going to wear on our heads, and hadn't had the time to go anywhere near the plain red skirts and white blouses we'd purchased at Wojcik's, trying them on in the same dressing room I remember sitting in when Carolyn had modeled the wedding gown she'd finally chosen, where she told me that though the back had a long row of thirty-eight tiny buttons, they merely were sewn over a flap hiding a handy zipper that would let you get dressed ("Or undressed!" she had whispered, surprising me) in a second. Anyhow, for our first appearance, the three of us agreed we'd wear black slacks and white T-shirts, and that Corinne and Leeann would put on the vests, since once I was playing, you couldn't see much of the top of me anyway.

Before we knew it, people were coming into the room, either under their own power or in wheelchairs that some of them moved by walking their slippered feet along the floor. The nurses were directing them into a semicircle, and suddenly, there was our audience, watching, waiting for something to happen—fifteen or so of them, and at that time you really couldn't think about it because what would it do to your confidence to concentrate on how these people assembled in front of you really had nowhere else to be, and probably wouldn't be able to get there if they did.

We took our places in our practiced little triangle shape, then we just stood there.

"Well?" a lady at the end of the first row snarled. "Start!"

The first song we ever played in public was "*Matuś Moja, Matuś*"—"Mother Mine, Oh Mother"—a nice little folk song about a girl who wants to marry a guy because she loves the rings that hang from his leather belt. It held no sentimental value for us—none of us had ever known anybody who dressed like that—but it was the type of song we were looking to play: It had only one flat, and half the words were "*oj dana*," another version of the space-filling "*hupaj siupaj*." Corinne said she wouldn't mind singing if she didn't have to worry about pronouncing too many words. So we played songs like that. Half of "*Hej, Tam Pod Lasem*"—"In the Woodland"—went something like "*Ram tai raj, U ha ha!*" We played "*Czemu Ty Dziewczyno*," in which a girl stood under an oak tree waiting for her very dear one, and the entire chorus was "*Hop ciuk, ciuk, tra la la la la la*," again and again and again.

And though some in the crowd had already been there and past it, we nevertheless ended with "Sto Lat," wishing one hundred years of life, health, and good cheer to all, even to the weepy old lady by the emergency exit who looked like she'd been through all the years she wanted a long, long time ago.

We played our ten songs, without too much talk or conversation between each, just one into the next, as none of us had the nerve to make the small talk you usually hear from bandstands.

"This is a favorite of ours," is all I would offer.

Or, "We've had a request for the next one," even though that was not true.

Or, "I know you've all been waiting for this oldie, so get on your dancing shoes, folks."

And by the end, some of the audience had found our presentation enjoyable enough to get them nodding and singing along, some of them holding hands with the next person, a few of the nurses and orderlies grabbing partners and dancing in little circles. There were smiling faces, people having a real good time, right there in front of us, and when they applauded, you would have thought they were a room full of strongmen, so clear and loud was each clap, and so heartfelt that we were helpless to do anything but soak in it, the three of us grinning at one another every couple of seconds. Then Corinne had the idea to curtsy, and what could you do but follow her, to say, thank you thank you thank you for your thinking that this was such great music.

"You were fantastic!" Leeann's sister gushed, and she giggled constantly as she helped us roll up our wires and get the amplifiers and stands and instruments out to the cars. "The stuff we have here usually sucks. It's like they say, 'Go ahead, bring anything in, because they don't know what's going on anyway.' But that's not true. You know that lady in the blue running suit? She's with it like you wouldn't believe. She can talk to you in Gaelic."

Leeann's sister continued telling us that the man with half a leg used to be the town's milk inspector, that the lady who moved her mouth constantly but didn't say anything that you could hear could knit an entire man's sweater in two days if you didn't interrupt her too often. She brought up an attribute of each resident as if she needed to produce the proper résumé to get us to return the following Wednesday. The truth was, they would have had to bar the door with that big-screen TV unit in order to keep us from doing this for as long as they'd permit.

"That was—" Corinne said breathlessly once Leeann's sister got called back inside because the main phone was ringing and ringing, and after all, answering it was her job, "—that was the most fun I ever had in my life."

Leeann looked glazed as she stared into the parking lot and shook her head over and over. "I can't believe I just did that," she said slowly, and my stomach turned. She was going to quit—I just knew it. But no. She flung an arm around the two of us and announced, "We sounded damn great!"

"We are a band," Corinne said decidedly, a huge smile on her face. "A band!" She couldn't contain herself, actually jumping in place, the sequined flowers on her vest flashing under the streetlight. "Let's celebrate!"

It was all too much. I had that feeling you do when you have a cold—that everything is being said a mile away, even if the person is right there next to you, that I was under the influence of some tablet that promised it would make you feel better without causing drowsiness, except you find out during the long drive you have to make that's exactly what it did. I walked about a foot off the ground, to my car, where I slammed the door and sat in the quiet. No ceremony, no flashing lights, no nothing to signify what was happening.

I looked at myself in the rearview mirror, to see if there was any visible change. In the backseat, there was Aniela. She had seen it all, and boy, was she proud.

"Way to go!" she said to me with great enthusiasm, and I was surprised she would know such an expression. But that's what she said. And I just shook my head, the same way Leeann had, and I had to agree.

At St. Stan's, we laughed and toasted our talents with each sip of our one drink apiece.

Then: "I have to think about getting up for work tomorrow," Corinne moaned. And: "I can't wait to tell Johnny how it went," Leeann said, gulping the end of her Cape Codder.

So the party ended early, and they were out of the bar befroe I had a chance to stop these two identically dressed women, strangers who had flown out of nowhere to fit so perfectly into my plan, with no chance to say something like, "You don't know what this means to me," but not really caring that I hadn't, because, I figured—and maybe this was wrong of me, but it's how I felt—how could they understand if they weren't standing there in my shoes, in my life?

I stopped at Ramadon's on the way home and bought a bottle of the second-least-expensive champagne in the refrigerated case.

"Celebrating something?" the burly young guy in the ball cap asked as he took my money.

"I am," I said proudly.

He held back the change, obviously waiting for me to tell him what the occasion was, but I didn't. It was still between the three of us, a couple of other people and a home full of people who called each of us honey, and I enjoyed having the secret. I was beginning to ask him for the change when he cut in and asked, "Need somebody to help you party?"

"No thanks," I said. "All set there."

I had to do two separate series of knockings before Joseph Angelo pushed aside the back-door curtain and opened it to me. He looked tired, but when he saw it was me his face brightened enough to surprise me, and he asked me to come in even before knowing what I was there for.

"No thanks," I told him, "but would you like to come over?" Then I was stuck for the rest of the words. I knew I should have thought about this in the car, instead of figuring it would be easier once I got to the door. But all of a sudden it was like I had never learned one word of English, never mind Polish, never mind Italian. Then, a train whistle, and the rumble of an engine headed our way. What could I do but be honest?

"I don't know how to say this, and I don't know how it's going to sound to you, but I want to celebrate something, and it would be more fun to do that with someone," I told him. "I was thinking maybe if you didn't have anything going on? Would you be interested in coming over?"

Joseph Angelo didn't look too confused by any of that. In fact, he looked rather pleased.

"How about fifteen minutes—I have to finish up something on the computer," he said.

"You have a computer?" I tried to sound like this was news to me.

"Want to take a look at it?" He motioned me inside.

"No, that's okay. I'll be home whenever you're done with your work."

"Fine," he said. "Thanks." And he nodded and closed the door, and I stood there just facing the house, thinking how it very well could be that I'd just made all that up.

But no. Joseph Angelo was at my door about twenty minutes later, after I'd brought my accordion in from the car and had thrown some crackers on a plate and found a log of Cracker Barrel cheese that had yet to be unwrapped and given time to develop a thick fur of mold like all the other dairy products in my refrigerator had the habit of doing with amazing speed.

I let him in, and he brought from behind his back a little package, wrapped in the Sunday funnies.

"What's that for?"

Joseph Angelo looked confused. "It's your birthday, isn't it?"

No, I told him. "Just a good day, that's all."

"Promotion?"

I laughed to myself. Who was going to promote me? "No, just a good day."

He knew when to quit. "Well, open it anyway. If you don't, I'll have to keep it. I almost did, anyway, I like it so much."

I pulled back the paper. And there was the river, in winter, painted on a tiny square of board no bigger than your palm, but large enough to fit all the Alps and Pyrenees and Rockies and Himalayas, all the angles and forms and land masses, all golden in an afternoon sun. All that was missing was Bobby Smola, sitting on that old log, looking over his shoulder at me as I came down the path.

I heard Joseph Angelo saying that he didn't know if I had seen the story that he'd written about a woman who paints scenes of town as she remembers them from days gone by, and this was the one he'd picked out, and she hadn't intended to sell this one, but she figured what was she saving it for and allowed him to purchase it. But since I was from here, originally, it had to mean more to me than to him, but that's not to say, he pointed out, that he was not finding this a wonderful place to live and that it did not feel like home— actually, he said, in many ways he was coming to feel like he finally was home, if that didn't sound too corny to me.

Like before, I heard all that, but I wasn't paying attention really. His words were more like a sound track playing in the background as I took in each bit of color and line and shape, and the fact that here in my hand was the place where it had all started, and that it had landed in my hand on this very night.

Maybe—okay most likely—not too long ago I would have

looked at that picture in anger. But that night I looked at it as the beginning of the road, and here I was finally at my destination. It looked new, I felt new. Following Babci's advice, I was eating it all up, and everything was going to be okay.

"Do you like it?" Joseph Angelo was asking, and he had moved closer, I guess because I probably was concerning him, staring at it for as long as I was. "Because," he offered, he could exchange it for another one.

I finally took my eyes off it and moved them up to his face. I don't know what had happened in the few minutes since I had seen him last, but Joseph Angelo, too, was new. I did not see a reporter, I did not see someone to have a stupid grudge against even though he had never done a single thing to hurt me. I saw a fine man about whom I knew far more than he was aware, someone whom I wanted to know more about me than whatever little he did.

"I really like it," I said quietly, as if he would disappear if I scared him with a louder voice. This was the point at which I noticed the color of his eyes, which to me wasn't just regular but a rare, rich deep brown, like some endangered wood from a jungle you send money to in an attempt to save it from destruction by unscrupulous loggers. I suddenly wanted to move to whatever country that was—even if I didn't speak the language and even if there were loads of reptiles and things there that could wrap around you and be the end of you before you even knew what was happening. I didn't care. I just wanted to be there.

"I really, really like it," I said, in case he hadn't heard me. Joseph Angelo was looking right back at me, and I was wondering if he found any rarity at all in me, and what that might be. There was his soap, again, the one I'd tried in vain to find several times in the grocery store, sniffing so many of the different cakes Tenczar's had in stock that I'd ended up with a headache. I couldn't help myself with him right in front of me, something that might never happen again. I leaned in and breathed like it was my last.

"You have to forgive me," I told him, "but if everybody smelled as good as you do, there would be no wars or anything bad."

Joseph Angelo didn't move. Didn't back up, didn't push me away. He was staring at me like he had been that night we'd watched the snow, like I was the only thing in the world.

"It's handmade," he said, almost whispering, like it was some secret. He did not move his eyes from mine. "The soap. It's handmade. Somebody wants me to do some work for them, and they bribed me—with handmade soap."

I found myself whispering, too. "You gonna do it?"

"Do what?"

"The work. For the soap person."

"I don't know. We've only talked once. I've been busy with my own stuff."

We were about two inches apart.

"Then maybe I'm interrupting you?"

"Never," Joseph Angelo said, still like it was privileged information. "I never miss a celebration. Congratulations on whatever." Then he kissed me, lightly and slowly and magically, a leaf falling to the ground, the brush of a cow's eyelashes, so fantastic I should have let him live here free for a year, at least.

We ate the few things I'd put on plates, the canned black olives and the cheddar Babci got on a bus trip to Granville and the low-salt saltines from the box Lis's had in a buy-one-get-two-free offer. We drank the entire bottle of champagne that we decided was only okay even though it described itself as "perfect for any occasion that calls for the very best." And we had an entire rest of the evening all without his asking any other questions about why we were doing this. After having seen him mostly in his kitchen, or, part of him, at his desk, it was strange to see Joseph Angelo next to me, on my living room couch, like a celebrity who had stepped through the screen of my television set. The Bruins jersey and the baggy jeans he must have bought too long because he had to roll the cuffs were one of the costumes from his stage. I couldn't help but wonder which pair of shorts he was wearing.

To keep the conversation off me, I asked a million questions about the interesting people that Joseph Angelo had to run across every day, and to tell you the truth I can't remember a word of his replies, only that he had a good, long answer for everything, and that I quickly came to the conclusion that, whatever had happened, the woman from San Antonio had to be crazy ever to let him out of her sight. It was past midnight when he looked at his watch and said he had to leave.

"Safe driving," I joked as he stood up, and he laughed and said, "Funny," as he picked up a few plates and brought them into the kitchen.

"Well, let me know when it's your birthday so we can do this for real," Joseph Angelo said before he let himself out the back door.

"August," I told him. "It's in late August."

"I'll remember," he said.

Every Wednesday night, if I could see that Joseph Angelo was in when I came home from the home—and he always was—I would knock on his door and invite him over.

"Are we celebrating again?" he asked the first few times, and I said that I guessed we were, and why don't you come over when you're free? I was so energized from playing my happy little songs for those happy old people that I just couldn't help but want to extend the feeling a little longer, to be around somebody, and why not have it be him? Sure, a few of the residents at the home really didn't know that anyone else was there in the room, but most of them were so excited about us being there that they had started making lists of requests they'd wave at us from their dining room tables when we walked into the building. In handwriting that was sometimes hard to read, they dedicated numbers to the nurses, to Leeann's sister, to political figures they saw on the news, to wives they didn't remember were dead.

"I'll Never Do It Again," "You're Never Too Old" (that always went over big), *"Starość Nie Radość"* ("Old Age Is Not Fun," another hit). We played them all, and the audience never failed to plead with us to stay longer than we were supposed to, even though we got kicked out exactly one hour after we began, to allow some little tuxedoed guy who called himself The Great Gillen to set up his magic equipment and adjust his tablecloth to the correct length so nobody could see the pet rabbit that waited in a cage until the moment he was to be pulled from thin air.

I didn't buy anything fancy to eat or drink every Wednesday night, but there was always something to snack on, something to have to pour into a bowl or slice up or get out my better glasses for while Joseph Angelo sat at the kitchen table and told me about his day, or things that had happened to him in the week since we'd talked like this. How a school committee meeting went past midnight, how a special town meeting lasted only five minutes, how the police department wouldn't be expanded for another year, how the town moderator tried to get him in trouble by saying he was going to sue the paper because Joseph Angelo had quoted him as saying the word *gonna*, and he said he never, ever uses that word; only Joseph Angelo had both taken notes and recorded the town meetings, so there it was on tape, the moderator pounding his gavel and pleading with an inattentive audience, "Are we gonna have this problem with you every time?" How somebody in Gilbertville was raising llamas, how our fire chief can make a mean cheesecake, how the guy who was hit by lightning in Monson last year now claims he is able to see into the future and now is hounding Mrs. Bigelow to let him write a weekly column of local predictions.

It was all a mystery to me. "When you're writing, how do you know where to start?" I asked Joseph Angelo one night as we sat at the kitchen table.

"You choose what's the most important thing you want to say, and things usually fall into place after you decide that," he said. His eyes drifted up to my forehead, where, after all these years, you had to have real good sight to notice that something once had happened to me. "Some of the stories tell themselves for you, if you can understand that," he said. "They wander in the weirdest ways, and you just follow along and write down what you're hearing about it in your head, until you get to the end. With those it's usually worth it just to go where it takes you, since you could never imagine in the beginning you would end up where you do."

Joseph Angelo told me so much about the stories he was writing that, except for the ads, I almost didn't need to buy the paper. But I did anyway, just so I could see his name in print, in striking, bold, capital letters that floated over the stories I'd already heard about, reports that twice since we began celebrating I noted uneasily had run above photos of Betty (the feature had been relabeled "Betty's Life," the word *progress*, I guessed, long ago considered redundant when used in the same sentence as her name). Bumping up against the ending of his piece on the plans for the anniversary of the Four Corners Gas Station—"On the Hill But on the Level" for half a century—was a photograph of Craig Weldon and Mrs. Conway and Betty carrying trays of baked goods that Babci and my mother had to have made for a bake sale at the parish center, where the school kids were raising money for a computer system. And almost touching the last paragraph of Joseph Angelo's story on the town's bond rating was the picture of Betty, dewy-eyed, shaking hands with the high school's principal at the announcement of the Milewski Scholarship, which would be presented to a senior-class son or daughter of a Blue Ribbon worker and which was to be kept a big confidential secret, but the *Penny Saver* found out, and there was the photo shot by Tom Pochalski, and there was the caption that told the story and gave the address of the school, to which you could send contributions if you were the kind of person who had extra money.

Most times, though, the bottom right-hand corner of page three was just that much more space for Joseph Angelo to go on and on about his subjects, and I read every word he wrote—sometimes even more than once, just so more than once I could recall how he had worded them to me in the kitchen or in the parlor or on the porch, and how he said he hoped he wasn't boring me, and how I assured him he wasn't, and how he was silent for a while before he told me how nice it was to have whatever we were having, how he'd been cut off from a lot in life for quite a while—much of that being his own doing, he had to admit, because things had happened, and that was a big reason for the job change, to do what he really wanted, and he needed some time to get used to things.

"But my writing, my job, this house, meeting you, it's all come together, suddenly, so well," Joseph Angelo told me.

313

"It's like I've arrived at where I wanted to be—even though I never knew where I was going, or what I wanted, when I set out. But here I am."

He was at the sink when he said that, and when I didn't answer because I couldn't answer because this was a decent person saying this to me, and I could think of no reason in the world to end any of it, he started nervously washing the plate he'd had a few taco chips on, and I stood next to him, close, like I was just in from San Antonio, getting in his way when he turned to wipe his hands on the dish rag. He reached around me to get it from the hook on the side of the refrigerator, but I don't think he ever found it because his hands were still a little soapy when he placed the left one on my forehead and smoothed back my hair and traced a finger up the crooked line, then brought it down the side of my face, to lift my chin, and, he told me much later and in total seriousness, finding himself unable to resist me, Joseph Angelo kissed me over and again then and there, under the ceiling light so bright that, without parting from him, I shuffled us back into the dark pantry, under the shelf of macaroni and rice, next to the dill pickles floating among graceful dill fronds in their canning jars, and so close to the trap door that I could have peeked through it when he leaned me back on the counter, next to the bread box that held only a heel of a rye bread, and after knocking my wooden napkin holder to the floor with a clatter that I prayed he might not find too familiar, Joseph Angelo and I both held on and flew straight up through the solar system.

And every few Thursday nights, there would come Babci, with her food and her cleansers, a refrigerator magnet or a doily, and when she asked me what was new, I now could tell her I was genuinely happy.

"That's what God wants for you," she responded. "Babci, too—we all want that. It is not a sin, you know, to be happy."

"I know," I said, flipping through the coupons my mother had cut and paper-clipped together in categories she'd labeled "side dishes," "desserts," "kitchen/bath," and "misc." It was another small communication with me, though I responded only by using them on the days the grocery declared they were worth double, or even triple, their face values.

"Life is short," Babci told me.

"I know," I said, putting away the poppyseed rolls, the tin of brownies that had a perfect walnut half topping each square.

"Donna," she called so loudly that I had to look up from my work. "Whatever you have, keep it. There's no need to ruin things."

"I know," I said. "There isn't."

"Just remember," Babci said, and I gave my attention to her. "I want that new Tupperware back next time I come."

In late April, Leeann came up with another gig, as she put it—her aunt and uncle's forty-fifth anniversary. It was supposed to be a casual get-together, but wouldn't a band performance enliven things—plus make a great present from her and her Johnny? Again, no pay for us, and we would have to drive the hour to Pittsfield, but it would be an opportunity to play, to practice, to become more professional. Sure, we said, and there we were a few Saturdays later, in her aunt and uncle's backyard, playing "The Anniversary Waltz" to sixty-two members of Leeann's family.

And Leeann, rather than Auntie Hazel and Uncle Manny, was the star, all the family's videocameras and disposable instamatics trained on her as she flawlessly did her part in the "Forever" polka, "Girl from Łowicz," "Two Canaries" and about fifteen other numbers that were Greek to the people who danced in front of us, but were met with cheers just the same.

Next up, Corinne's cousin's sister-in-law Belle was retiring after eighteen years of giving motorists a hard time at the turnpike tollbooth.

"She's such a sourpuss that I doubt many people will be showing up," Corinne said as she served Mrs. Dabrowa and me potted beef one night. "But a few of her co-workers want to throw a party anyway. They even have a budget!"

We made $20 apiece—thirds of what the disc jockey they'd planned on hiring had asked for his services—and only had to drive a half hour that time. Belle, who, once I saw her, I remembered from many unsuccessful attempts to coax a "you're welcome" out of her at the Chicopee exit, sat with a scowl on her face for the entire party, but everybody else there praised us up and down, especially after I announced that our vocalist for the afternoon was a cousin of the beloved guest of honor.

Then, a birthday party for the fiancé of one of the nurses at the home. He was a big fan of Eddie Blazonczyk and the Versatones, but who could afford them? Could we play instead? We could have all we wanted to eat, and $100 on top of that.

Then, an open house at a trailer park in Enfield. "If I'm gonna pay somebody good money, I'd rather it go to the Polish, if you know what I mean," said the owner, a guy named Zenon, who had learned of us through Corinne's neighbor, Anna Salamon, who couldn't help but learn of us firsthand, her house being so close to Corinne's that she could see us through the basement window without even leaving her kitchen table.

"We're not all Polish," I told him, in case he wanted his $75 back for not getting the real thing.

He tilted his head. "Well, at least some of it will go to the Polish—we gotta stick together," Zenon said, and he elbowed me, like he was somebody I would want to claim as one of my own.

Then, a company picnic for F&D Tool, where they not only paid us $125, but gave us slices from a large gray-frosted cake shaped like a crescent wrench. Then, a Fourth of July party at the home of the owners of Millie's Pierogi, where we set up near the large swimming pool like Elvis in one of his movies.

They were not glamorous events, but we were playing, and people were happy about that. And, after each of these engagements, I knocked on Joseph Angelo's door, and he came over to visit.

"You ever going to tell me what it is that makes you so happy?" he asked the night of Felix Grochmal's family reunion up in Gill, where an older man stood in front of Corinne for most of the four hours and then bothered her for her phone number so much that she made one up and wrote it on a paper plate just to get rid of him.

"I play music," I answered.

"I know, I've heard. You're good. It's really beautiful."

I liked how he used that word, like what I did should be hanging on a wall in a frame. "Well, that's what I do," I told him.

"That's it?"

"That's it."

"That's what makes you happy?"

"Yes."

"Then it makes me very happy."

The night of screaming little Chelsea Daniella Bogobowicz-Okrasinski's christening party, which had been scheduled for the afternoon of the May crowning so there would be such beautiful flowers free of charge in the background of all the photos and videos, I wasn't in the house for ten minutes when there was a knock at the door. I knew it wouldn't be Joseph Angelo, because when he'd heard my car he'd poked his head in the back door to ask if I needed anything from the grocery, and I had cracked him up when I told him, "Baby, what I need the grocery don't have." It wasn't that funny, I didn't think, but he laughed all the way to his car, and I watched him back out, and I touched the cross hanging from the light and for the fiftieth time that day I thanked God for what my life had become.

And, as if to remind me how blessed I now was, knocking on my back door was Fuzzy Litwa, someone I shuddered to think I once had gone to the trouble of putting real perfume on for.

I heard his "Homedon?" and I got that sick feeling, remembering how all his words ran together, as did all the hair on his body.

"Iseeyacaa! Iseeyaintheya! Arncha gonna lemmein?" he asked.

"No."

"C'mon, Donna. I know—itzbenages, budi've mistya."

"Well that's nice, but I'm not interested. I'm busy."

"But I even brochasumtin! Founitinmystuff!"

And he waved in front of the screen door the unflattering photograph he'd snapped when we were hiking near Mount Monadnock, it had to be three summers ago, and he'd stolen the clothes I left on the shore when I went off to swim by myself. In the photo I was mad as anything and crouched behind a rock, but the rock was not that big, and it was easy to tell I had nothing on.

"Give me that," I yelled. I opened the door, and I grabbed for it.

"Oh, *now*yawamme!" he laughed, and he pushed his way inside. "Whaddayagoddaeat?"

I looked at Fuzzy Litwa, big bushy head inside my refrigerator, big ugly boots right in the place where Joseph Angelo's running shoes had been the night before when he took out the carton of blueberries and poured them on the kitchen table and played around with them until he spelled out I LOVE, then ran out of berries before he could finish the sentence.

I lunged for the photo, which was still in Fuzzy's left hand, but he was too quick for me.

"Izzocute!" he said, holding it out of my reach. "Loogacha!"

He held the picture away from me. I grabbed for it, he backed against the wall, then I cornered him in the pantry. He had the photo way out of my reach, up against the far wall, and before I knew it, it had disappeared into the gap in the trap door between my apartment and Joseph Angelo's.

"Zgone," Fuzzy said, shrugging sadly. "Whaddayagonnado?"

"Get out of here," I ordered. "Go home."

"Syoudonmissme?"

"Not in the least. Get out."

I had to admire him in a way—Fuzzy didn't seem too upset, as if he tried this kind of stunt daily, and daily he flopped, only to get up the next day and try it again with someone new.

"Iffyafinit, senittome," he asked as he left the pantry, then the kitchen. "Itzeonlywunigoddaya." He laughed, then slammed the door.

I hoped I could find it, but not to give Fuzzy one thing to

remember me by. I hoped I could find it before Joseph Angelo did. I had no choice but to go next door.

Though I'd seen him leave, I felt I had to call for him when I unlocked his front door with my key and listened for any sounds.

"Joseph? This is Donna—I'm here. You home?"

No answer. I went in.

I hadn't been in Babci's side of the house for the fifteen months Joseph Angelo had been living there. There had been no official reason—no electrical or plumbing complaints to have to lead a repairman to, no mysterious smells or sounds, or lack of sounds, to have to bring myself to investigate. And it turned out I hadn't been missing much—he had only a couple more possessions than the guy who slept on the air mattress.

In front of me was the desk that I'd been able to see only a fraction of through the pantry hole. It was much larger in its entirety, holding not only the computer but a printer, telephone books, a Rolodex, a basket of pens and pencils, and a phone with a long row of buttons for programming frequently called numbers. There were numbers penciled into some of the slots, but no names that I could see.

As for the rest of the room, he had one of those white plastic patio chairs set up with a matching white plastic patio table in front of it, as a footrest, and an older brass-looking floor lamp next to that. On a banged-up coffee table, there was the TV that played his soaps. It looked like he'd spent real money on that, with its built-in VCR and a huge clicker that looked more like a typewriter keyboard than something that would help you program the taping of your favorite shows. On the space of wall between the chair and the television was the cowboy painting I'd seen him unload from his car. It had to be a gift from the ex, maybe meant to spark Joseph Angelo's interest in Texas, maybe so much interest that he would want to move there, so she could regularly come to visit and be so annoying.

There was not much else in the room. A portable radio, on the floor, its plug removed from the socket. A purple sweatshirt on the back of his desk chair. A small African violet on one windowsill, flowering white and in better condition than any houseplant I'd ever seen being raised by any male person I ever knew.

I went into the kitchen and got a different view of the table there, of the two chairs, of the refrigerator, and of the hinged piece of wood that so many times had separated Joseph Angelo's world from my face. I got up real close to it and peered in through the tiny opening, but it was too dim on my side of the house to tell whether he might be doing to me the same thing I had been doing to him, though I doubted it. In front of it, facedown, was the photograph that Fuzzy had pushed through the wall. I folded it and stuffed it into my pocket, to rip up and dispose of in my own wastebasket on my own side of the house.

That safely over with, I took my time on the way out. I opened the Frigidaire. Joseph Angelo was one of those people who refrigerate their spare chocolate. There was a package of six Reese's cups and a roll of Rollos next to the butter dish. Two of the Reese's were gone, and I wondered if he'd notice that he was missing one more. I decided not to chance it and closed the door firmly. It was then that I spotted myself, looking back at me, from Joseph Angelo's desk.

At first I thought I was seeing things. Maybe a picture of someone who looked like what I once used to look like. I went closer. There, in an open manila folder, was a yellowed clipped-out newspaper photo of me, from eighth grade, the one with the crooked collar. I walked over and picked it up. Beneath it was a fat stack of more aged clippings, neatly stamped with a date and page number. The accident scene. An exterior shot of the hospital. A photo that was a new one to me, of my father and mother in church at a special mass for Betty and me, blowing their noses into big white hankies.

Beneath that, others: Babci, in her everyday coat and hat, distributing warm cookies to the pack of reporters who waited on our driveway for some word of Betty's progress. Sister Superior collecting the valentines that Betty's first-grade class-mates had made. Nurses distributing floral arrangements up and down an entire hospital corridor, handing out vases of roses and flat little dish gardens from a cart loaded with the ones that couldn't fit near Betty's bed. A Polaroid of Dr. Young, his tie loosened, his smile sly. A faded color shot of my house. A glossy of the river, all Alps and Pyrenees and Rockies and Himalayas, all angles and forms and land masses, all golden suddenly, though the picture was in black and white.

Then I heard him.

"Donna!"

Joseph Angelo, arms around a pair of grocery bags, kicking his kitchen door closed, a look on his face like he hadn't seen me in a zillion years rather than only an hour ago.

"Donna finally in my house! This is so great!"

I didn't drop the file. I didn't hide it behind my back. I didn't pretend anything. After what I'd seen, I didn't care what Joseph Angelo thought of me, or of my standing there in his home, without him around, snooping into his private work.

"What is this?" I demanded.

"What?" He genuinely couldn't tell from where he was, still in the other room. He set his bags on the kitchen table and walked into the parlor, up next to me, putting his arm around my shoulders, following my hand that shook as it pointed to the file.

"Oh—Betty's stuff . . ." He said this with such familiarity— "Betty's"—just another one of the hundreds of thousands of millions of people who felt they knew her so well they could call her by her first name.

"Yes," I snapped. "Betty's stuff. Betty's stuff and my stuff. Me. My stuff." I pointed to myself and waved the photo of me and my crooked collar. "This is me!" I was mad now. "Or hadn't you noticed? What is this, your living here—are you observing me for something? Well, it's over. Get out now! Right now. Take all your stuff and leave."

"Donna, what's . . . what's going on? What's wrong?"

I knew the answer, but I couldn't put it into words. It would call for too many, and I didn't know which one to choose to start. I found I could manage nothing but a defeated, "Why are you doing this?"

Joseph Angelo looked into the folder, then at me.

"She—Betty—Betty contacted me, oh, it had to be a year ago—soon after I got to the paper—when I was still living there," Joseph Angelo said calmly, like this was all nothing.

"She sent me a letter, telling me how so many people always had been so interested in her story, saying how inspirational and all it is, her coming to this country, getting hurt, recovering, and making it to where she has, that she thought it would be a good idea to write a book, and to donate all the proceeds to a clinic in Appalachia. Hey, she'd even had a publisher contact her when she was a kid, asking her to do a book, back before she even knew how to write, or knew English—do you remember that?"

I shook my head, even though I did, and recalled the wooden frame with the thin line of gold that was chosen at Grant's and was filled with the publisher's letter and was hung next to my Hallmark response on the wall over my mother's machine.

"She wrote to me because she said she was impressed with my work," Joseph Angelo continued, quickly, like he really wanted to get the story out. "She says she has scrapbooks of all the stories done about her over the years, and the things I'd been writing for the paper—not about Betty, but about everything I usually cover—really impressed her. So she wanted me to help her write the book." His eyes got real big. "Hey—remember? Remember the soap? She's the one who gave me the soap—as a little gesture. It's made by her family in Poland." He stopped. "I mean your family, I guess. She said that if I took the job, she was going to pay me. It seemed like a simple story, and what writer—especially somebody like me, so new to all this—would pass up the chance to do a book? I said it sounded pretty good to me, and that I wanted to learn all I could before we got started working together. But I've been so busy since I started at the newspaper, and only a couple of days ago did I finally start to read all the clippings I pulled together from Mrs. Bigelow's files after Betty called me. That's when I learned you were her sister. It's just a coincidence. I was going to mention it to you—you just haven't been around. I wasn't trying to pull anything—honest."

I looked over to the desk, where there was a big envelope marked "Weldon" on top of a folder that was stuffed with information. Joseph Angelo shook his head.

"There's more I haven't even looked at yet. God, there's a

ton of stuff—I've never seen such coverage for such a small accident. Sure, it was a sad thing, but nobody died—everybody got better eventually. Doesn't anything else ever happen around here?"

"Plenty," was all I said, though that wasn't all that true. What I meant was plenty that didn't involve Betty. But for a long time, if she wasn't involved, nobody seemed to be interested.

"You feel better—I wasn't hiding anything. You understand now?"

I did and I didn't. I felt creepy and uncomfortable.

"Maybe you can help me," Joseph Angelo suggested, probably thinking that would sound like fun. What—did he expect me to help him spread all these stories across the wood floor and decide what angle to choose—where to start, or whom to interview first?

"I'm reading all this," he said. "And it keeps hitting me that there are a few questions that don't get answered. I mean it's all supposition as to why you two were in the road in the first place. It's always, 'It appears that,' or 'one would assume that' Betty was hurt 'in a selfless act,' or some such terms. They never actually said what happened. Didn't anybody know for sure?"

As angry as I was, I couldn't believe what I was hearing, a question I'd wished somebody had asked a long time ago. I looked at Joseph Angelo. I looked for some piece of him that I could trust. "They didn't care," I said plainly. "They just went and made her a hero, and me the villain. I was just a kid, but nobody cared. That's the way it goes, I guess."

"She couldn't remember, and they didn't ask you. Right?"

He was smart. Now I knew why he did the work he did. I nodded.

"But you know, right?"

"Yeah—but, like I said, who cares? It's not important anymore."

Joseph Angelo looked at me for a long time before he said, "I care."

"Why?" I snapped back, uneasy. "For your book?"

"I'm not going to write something that's not true," he said.

"And what I see here isn't telling me everything. Like the stuff about your grandparents, wanting a kid for so long, your father's craziness about your sister, the total absence of you in all this. There are more questions there. If I can't get them answered, I don't want to do the story."

He was laying out in a neat outline the pieces of Betty's life here. I could see the giant black Roman numerals stamped above the different headings: "Chapter I: I Arrive." "Chapter II: I Am Nearly Killed." "Chapter III: I Survive and Go On to Thrive and Be Successful Beyond All Wildest Dreams."

"If you didn't get your answers," I asked, "you wouldn't write the book—even if she was going to pay you?"

"No, I wouldn't."

I looked at him, and it was at that moment that I admitted to myself I could love this person. But right now I was more disgusted than anything, feeling naked and shivering behind a rock that didn't hide quite as much of me as I would have liked.

"Write what you want," I told him. "Like you said, there's so much out there. It should be easy just to repeat it."

I closed the folder. Printed across a sticker on its front were the words: "Folder 1: Research material for 'The Luckiest Immigrant.' May 1995."

"The title's her idea," Joseph Angelo noted, obviously wanting to shake any connection to the choice. But its sheer Betty-ness hadn't hit me yet. What I was staring at was the date that was written, a month when Joseph Angelo had nothing to do with my house or my life. He had been telling me the truth.

I placed the file in his hands. I left out the front door, then turned and locked it behind me.

No, I didn't throw him out. I had taxes and utilities to pay, and not much money coming in yet from my playing. I had my savings from Safe-Tam, but I didn't want to touch more of that than I already had. I needed Joseph Angelo's contribution more than ever, so I didn't bother him further about moving out. I just avoided him as much as I could.

I put a tray up against the pantry hole. I used the washing machine only when I was sure he was not home. When he called to apologize for the misunderstanding and to plead that we talk, I let the machine pick up. When he came to my door, I did not answer, even though he knocked so steadily and so long and sounded so sad when he called my name into the side of the house that I knew Johnny Frydryk was getting an eyeful. When he slipped notes under my door, telling me, in writing that was hard to read, how he never in a million years would have hurt me intentionally, I ran my fingers over the lines of his pen, over the words *sorry, forgive me, love,* and *Joseph,* and I would have to lock my door to keep myself from running out and around the back and banging on his window to make everything the way it was. I went out and played my music, and the rest of the time I stayed in my house, alone. I got my news only from the television and the radio, and I got nothing but disapproving looks from Babci when I told her I was no longer interested in the boy next door.

I didn't see Joseph Angelo again for three whole weeks, until Piotr Klamut died of natural causes at age eighty-three while sitting in his pew at High Mass and, thinking he was meditating in prayer, everyone left him sitting there long after the mass was over. My mother had gone to the wake with the Ladies Guild that afternoon, so when she dropped Babci off that night, I drove her over to meet with the Rosary Sodality members that would be marching together into Wazocha's Funeral Home.

Babci got in line to sign her name at the guest register and to get a holy card she would add to the thick stack of them she uses as markers in her prayer book. As she reached for the pen, I read the white plastic letters stuck into the black cork above the guest book. They read "BALWINA SLOZAK." Not "PIOTR KLAMUT."

"That's Miss Slozak, Babci," I whispered, taking the pen from her.

"Ha?"

"It says Slozak."

"It's sold out?"

"It's somebody else!" I pulled at her arm and brought her to the other side of the entryway, where the correct name was displayed and where we signed our names on separate lines and folded our $5 bills into the little white envelopes on which we wrote our names again and checked off the box that designated the enclosed donation to be used at the wishes of the family. I knew that in a couple of Sundays, Father Kulpa would announce that the church had received a donation of a total of something like $85 in memory of Piotr Klamut, and there everybody's $5 bills would be, all lumped together, gathered in an impressive amount we would never hear about again and would never know whether it had been used to re-lead one of the antique stained glass windows or buy a portion of an airplane ticket for a Polish curate coming here to preach with an accent and collect money or simply for something as ordinary as a couple of cases of long white altar candles.

Babci joined the other old ladies already down on their knees, already on their second decade of the rosary, and I found an empty seat toward the back of the room, a seat that, between a neatly spaced row of heads, gave me an eerily straight-on view of Piotr Klamut's bony profile, including the eyeglasses that I wondered whether they'd leave on him for good.

I followed the long line of floral arrangements, playing my usual wake game of picking out the one that, if you brought it into someone's home, they would have no idea it had been created for a dead person. There was no such winner. All I saw were neat fans of gladioli, chrysanthemums, carnations, and ferns, each of them, even if it didn't have a ribbon that read "WITH SYMPATHY," still unmistakably spelled the word *DEAD*.

When I came to the end of the row of flowers, I saw something that was even more depressing: Joseph Angelo, sitting in a chair. Taking notes.

He didn't look at his page while he wrote. He looked at the ladies, studying every inch of their gloves and floral prints and patent leather and jowls, and when he found something he had to make note of, his hand moved to do so without his eyes leaving his subjects. He stared at them through the rest of the praying, through the ladies hefting each other up off the floor, through their forming a slow line to pass by Piotr Klamut and his one survivor—a cousin who was a nun and a nurse at a hospital over in Michigan and who smiled, cocked her head to alternating sides and softly replied "Bless you" to anything that any of the mourners said to her. Joseph Angelo sat there through the rest of us joining the line and saying our final farewell to the nun and to Piotr, who had died as unattached as the day he was born, though he had been considered a catch by some way back in the years when he would do kind acts like bringing one of his squealing piglets to our house to amuse Betty for a few moments while she was still recuperating in our living room.

"Oh, he was so good-looking in his time," Eugenia Tempska was telling Joseph Angelo on the funeral home steps when we passed. "That's E-U-G-E-N-I-A . . ."

"But what did you like about him?" Joseph Angelo wanted to know.

She looked at Joseph Angelo like he had two heads. "I just told you." And she walked away, shaking her head.

Mrs. Marchelewicz took Joseph Angelo's arm and said slowly, "He could forgive and forget. He said 'Live and let live' more than once. You don't know the things that went on in this man's life—who ever does? But always that attitude, to go on, why bother with hate?"

Joseph Angelo scribbled wildly, as Mrs. Marchelewicz went on and on, as we drove away, as a line of people waited to say what they thought about the poor dead guy and what they would remember of him.

"Your boyfriend—what's he doing?" Babci asked as my car rolled past the crowd on the front steps.

I didn't bother to correct her mistake.

"He's being nosy," I said.

"He's Bing Crosby?"

The story about Piotr Klamut came out in the next issue of the *Penny Saver*. But it was not so much about Piotr Klamut, or about his unusual place of death. It was not even a news story, as you might be used to it. It was more of an essay, one about the experience of standing outside a stranger's wake and noticing what the words are that get used over and over. In Piotr Klamut's case: Warm. Forgiving. Kind. Not easily angered, and when he was, it was over and done with and he was on with the business of living. Again it was stressed. He was forgiving. Forgiving. Forgiving.

When I finished reading the story, there were tears in my eyes. But there was no way I could tell that to Piotr Klamut, and, of course, I would never tell that to Joseph Angelo.

Chapter

15

𝒯he rest of that whole summer was one big party. You could never imagine that people had so many occasions to celebrate, to dress up for and to get together on and to slap each other on the back about and say what a great day this is. Brothers and sisters of the neighbors and relatives of friends of people who heard our music were calling more and more frequently to ask if Donna and the Melody Girls were free to play in their garden or their living room or their backyard or their picnic grove. We were just the size in just the price range (usually whatever anyone wanted to give us) to appeal to people who would hold events in smaller venues, as we call them in the business, and soon we found ourselves with at least one or two engagements a week, on top of our standing Wednesday night concert at the home.

We would play "Hosa Hosa," "Lazy Bones," "Rym Cym Cym," and "Poor Orphan" to those who revolved before us, spinning, whooping, singing along with Corinne, knowing each other so well they closed their eyes as they moved precisely, or just having met and trying to predict the length of his step, how fast she might turn, how close he might hold you. From our place two feet above everyone else, we could watch dozens of relationships take hold or break apart, or at least appear like they would have been perfect for one another, only she never got up the nerve to go over there, and now the music was over with, and we were packing up our things and heading home, exhausted, exhilarated. I would see the light in Joseph Angelo's side of the house, but I would go straight to my own door, and once inside, would try not to take notice of anything on the other side of the kitchen wall.

But at 12:30, I knew we shared "The Young and the Restless," on which, whether I liked it or not, I'd become hooked. On Sundays, we both liked to sit on the front porch and listen to the bands, but I'd fly inside, even leaving an entire lunch out there out of my reach, if I heard Joseph Angelo unclicking his lock to come out to his folding chaise lounge. And I knew he had to hear me each night when I dragged an armless chair from the table to the center of the kitchen, unfolded my metal music stand under the plastic glow-in-the-dark cross braided to the string of the ceiling light, lugged the heavy black case from my bedroom closet, pulled on the beautiful, shining instrument, unsnapped the bellows, and played over and over my father's many favorite polkas and obereks and mazureks and waltzes, "Jolly Charlie," "I'll Build You a Home," even "*Córus* Oberek," about the daughter, and "*Kłopoty Starej Panny*," about the old maid's troubles, one after the next, stopping for nothing, only to see the clock, and the time so late, and to pull the light string and head upstairs.

With timing you could have won money betting on, Babci would come over to attach newly crocheted rings to the strings on my window shades, or Stella Muniec would appear, to play double solitaire and tell me all the latest.

"They're promising me somebody," Stella would say, unconvinced, "but nobody would do the job you did. I tell them 'I trained her from day one.' I tell them that every time, you know."

"I know," I would answer, because I was sure she did.

Sometimes Camille would come along, and Vinka Kaufman, too, and they all would tell me what they knew of the improved wrappers being proposed—more of a plastic than a paper and certainly not biodegradable, which was sure to enrage women including Ray Jr.'s canoe pals, who preferred Safe-Tam out of their concern for the environment. The girls told me of the self-serve forzen yogurt machine that soon would be installed in the cafeteria. "Two flavors, different each week," Stella noted. Bogdan Chichon was being promoted to assistant supervisor of three to eleven, they said, and wasn't that nice because he could use the extra money, his teenager having smashed up not one but both of the family cars in the first month he had a license. They talked about everybody from Mr. Newbury on down, but they skipped right over Eric Bigos, and even on the hottest night, it chilled me to consider even asking about him. I couldn't help but think of him though, as I really couldn't help but think of Joseph Angelo. Not one but two decent people—who in their life is lucky enough to get even a single one?—and I had thrown them onto the roadside like they were some apple I'd bitten into and looked down to discover half a worm waving back at me.

"How's the music going, Donna?" they'd ask. And I would say I was still practicing. I didn't tell them about Corinne and Leeann, about our outfits, about our equipment and practices and about the sign Corinne had one of the art teachers at the high school letter, reading "Donna and the Melody Girls," in red script, an American flag above the words, a Polish eagle below. Sure, we were playing in front of people, but not in town yet, and in my mind, I was only halfway to my goal. We played clambakes and pig roasts and, just once, in a hallway of somebody's home in Northfield, for only two people, the background music for a dinner party set up by a man Corinne's sister knew who was trying to get back on his wife's good side and wanted all her favorite waltzes played live, but out of sight, while he carried to the table course after course from her favorite restaurant, all heated and waiting in the kitchen in little foil bags.

So under the swinging cross, sitting on my kitchen chair,

playing the "Good Old Days" oberek just like I remembered
the Chopin Group doing it on their recording, I bided my time
until my first wedding.

"Donna, I've got to talk to you," Ray Jr. said to my machine
one night. "Are you there?"

I was there, doing nothing but reading the *Polka News*, which
Stella said her businessman son told her I could deduct from
my taxes if I ever were to make a living from all this, yet I
didn't have to fake sounding out of breath when I grabbed the
phone that was only two feet away from me.

"Just came in, Ray," I practically panted. Ray Jr. was calling
me. He must have come to his senses, and Karen Cieplak had
to have been history long before the end of that sack of
potatoes they were going to share. Now I would get another
chance to woo him with a bread. I tried to calm down.

"What's going on?" I said.

"Nothing I want to talk about on the phone, Donna," Ray Jr.
said, sounding very happy. "You gonna be home? You mind
company?"

"No, no," I said. "I mean, yes, I'm home, no, I don't mind
company."

"See you in a while, then," Ray Jr. said.

I realized that my machine had recorded every word of the
conversation. Should I save the tape, I wondered, and put it in
an envelope and stick it in front of our family album, and
every time someone asked, "So how did you two finally get
together?" I would ask them to wait a minute, and I'd go and
get it and pop it into the tape deck and replay those five lines,
so plain, so boring almost, but this, I would say to those who
had asked, was the beginning of my life with Ray Jr. Long
overdue, but a least we finally got together—that doesn't
happen to everybody who wishes for such a thing.

I knew Ray wouldn't drive over—for anything under a mile
he long ago vowed to use his own power, walking or bicycling,
even in terrible weather. He lived so close that when he
chopped wood I could hear the big strong thuds he made with
his ax, and he'd be here any second. I didn't bother with little

things to serve. Babci was due this week, so I hadn't done much shopping. And, besides, the whole ritual of opening a can of peanuts and lining up crackers on a long plate reminded me too much of Joseph Angelo, who didn't bother to pound any call my name when he left his check the day before, one in which the memo line noted payment was for "RENT," not for "A GOOD TIME" like he'd written for the four months we had been a whole lot more than landlord and tenant.

The phone rang again. I grabbed it—it had to be Ray Jr., saying he couldn't remember—did I like red wine, or white, or even, did I maybe just want a beer? But, no, it was Corinne.

"I can't talk right now," I told her. "I'm expecting somebody."

"You have to talk now," she said. "You're not going to believe this."

"What?" I'd pull the phone into the kitchen, so I could watch for Ray.

"You sitting down?"

"No."

"Well, sit."

"I can't. I'm watching for somebody."

"Well, sit and watch."

I took a seat at the kitchen table. "Okay. I'm in a chair."

"Donna." She stopped there. "I got us a wedding."

My heart was back up to the racing pace it had run at while I had been talking to Ray Jr.

"Did you hear me?" Corinne asked.

I nodded, then I realized she didn't know that. "I heard you," I said slowly. "Who, When? Who did you do this?"

Once in a while, I'd noticed, Corinne could be like her mother, saying a whole lot more than anybody really needed to hear. This was one of those times.

"I had a little get-together with some of the girls from the cafeteria this afternoon," she said. "You drive each other crazy all school year, and halfway through the summer, you get to missing each other. So there we were, nearly done with dessert—it was a stained-glass cake, you know, with the different colors of Jell-O cut up and stuck into the frosting? It was so hot out that I didn't know if it was a good choice, but it held together well, and it looked so beautiful that Rosalie had us all pose with it, and she took the picture."

"Corinne, somebody's going to be coming here any minute . . ."

"Oh, sorry, well and none of us could believe it, but it wasn't until dessert—that was how long Mickey had waited before telling us her daughter is getting married! Can you believe it— wouldn't you blurt that out first thing?" She didn't give me a chance to respond, just charged ahead: "Well maybe it's because the girl's been married twice before—like she is a celebrity or something—twice, can you imagine? I figure that's why Mickey didn't go too crazy, though she is happy because I guess the boy is just a sweetheart. They're keeping it low-key, though. It'll be in a couple of weeks, just a family thing, an outdoor reception at her fiancé's place—he even owns his own home. So I said, hey, you want a deal on some live music? She looks at me and goes, 'It's polka, I hope,' and I said, 'What else?' She goes 'Sold!' A wedding, Donna. A real, live wedding!"

I'd forgotten about the window. I'd forgotten about my caller. I forgot about everything else but what Corinne had just told me. It was here. I was here. It was happening. We were going to play at a wedding.

"I don't know what to say," I told her. "I owe you a million bucks."

"Oh that reminds me. They don't have a lot of money . . ."

That's when I spotted some movement on the driveway.

"I guess he's only a clerk for his father," Corinne said.

The person out there was Ray Jr. I could tell him a mile away, and here he was, headed for my door. Mine.

"You know," Corinne said. "At that store at the end of your street?"

He was walking around my car now.

"It's the boy who works at the fruit store."

And then I could see that Ray Jr. was not alone.

It was too late to pretend I wasn't home. Too late to press myself up against the radiator under the windows, too late to run into the bathroom. I had no choice but to open the door to the future Mr. and Mrs. Ray Lyszko Jr.

"No wonder we never see you at the store that much—big band leader," Ray said, grinning, and he shoved me playfully as I let him and Karen into my kitchen.

My eyes went directly for her left hand, and there it was all right, a good-sized round diamond in a high setting that I saw only as a life sentence of snagged nylons and pulled sweaters. My knees weakened at the reality of it all, at the very least at the thought of Ray Jr. being Ray Jr. and assisting Karen with her hoisery and her knitwear for the next sixty-five years, because, after all, he was the one who'd picked out that setting, and what did he know, he would ask her when she made her millionth joke about thinking of him every time she ruined another article of clothing. He was in love, he would say in defense. At the time he had been thinking only of getting the most beautiful ring.

"Can we talk?" Ray was asking me this, what I'd hoped he'd ask when he came over. But that held a whole new meaning now that he'd come in bringing a whole other person, one who was attached to him like they'd been born together.

"Sure," I said, and I motioned to the kitchen chairs. I didn't want Karen Cieplak in my house, never mind my living room, doing her cuddling thing on my good upholstery. But I quickly realized that even the hard wooden chairs wouldn't affect her ardor. She scooted her chair so close to Ray Jr.'s that they bumped, and she kept an arm around him the entire time they were there, like they were on a speeding amusement park ride that had no seat belts.

"I don't know if you've heard," Ray Jr. began.

"We're engaged," Karen finished, and she pushed her hand out to me so quickly that I couldn't help but jump a little. The ring sparkled and looked like a catalog illustration there on her well-tended hand. She had on what Leeann, a big makeup consumer, once informed me was called a French manicure— pink polish where your nail is naturally pink, white polish where it's normally white. "So then why even bother with the paint?" I had asked Leeann, who stopped and said she had really never thought of it that way before.

I smiled as best I could. "Congratulations," I said, nodding my head, to try to make myself more believable.

They both smiled back. Karen kissed Ray on his tan cheek. "Can you believe it?" he asked. "Me? Married?" He turned to Karen. "Like I said, Donna's known me for ages. she might as well have been another sister."

"Hey—I've known Donna for ages, too," Karen told him, like he wasn't aware of our history. "We were in the same class . . ."

"Well, it was so nice of you to come over and tell me," I said, getting up, hoping to give them a hint, and lying. "It was good to see you."

"Donna, no, wait—we have to ask you something," Ray Jr. said.

I plopped back down.

They said they had no idea I was a musician now. Ray Jr. knew I was playing again in the house—he said he'd often stopped on the front lawn during his after-supper walks, and in good weather sat himself on the front porch and just enjoyed the music. He many times had wanted to tell me how great I sounded, but he hadn't wanted to disturb me. Wait a minute—he had been on my lawn? How many times? Why didn't he come in? It was too much to take. What it came down to was a request—Mrs. Cieplak had learned about Donna and the Melody Girls that very day, from a cafeteria co-worker. And coincidences of coincidences, the Donna was me.

"You're going to be at the wedding anyway, Donna," Ray Jr. told me. "Why not do the music? It's just going to be a small thing, in a couple of weeks, just the family—you'll know everyone." He was looking right at me. "It would mean so much to me."

None of it was anything I had expected, but, unless you are lying, whatever is? Karen hugged me excitedly on the way out, mooshing my face into her boy's haircut and whispering she couldn't believe how well everything was coming together, both with the wedding and her life. Ray came by next and caught me up in his long, strong, Superman arms, rocking me from side to side in a restrained version of how not fifteen minutes before I had hoped this night would end.

"A band," he said, and he laughed. "Good for you, Donna. Good for you!"

If I had been on a diet, I would have responded to the evening by going out and getting the biggest, gooiest, chocolate-mocha-dark-fudge-cream-cheese cheesecake, one that had a skull and crossbones on its box, that's how bad it was for you. But I wasn't starving myself of anything but love. So I went into the pantry, and I broke my fast, my record of eighteen days without seeing even one part of Joseph Angelo as the top of his head passed by my living room window. One tiny nudge of the tray, and there was the space again, and there I fit my eye, and there was the light on, and there I saw the right half of him, at his desk, in his purple sweatshirt, sleeves pushed up, and in the jeans that were too long, tapping away at his keyboard like it was one big long song he was playing on the piano. Quietly, I climbed up on the counter and lay there and watched him, his only extra movements being a scratch of his neck, or his hand finding his mug. His hair had grown a little longer and was spikey and uneven on the sides where he especially needed a trim. I was there, watching, for a very long time, and nothing much happened. He would hit the keys, and words would appear on the screen, one after another, filling the gray space at the end of the line, then beginning a new one and starting all over. It was not that exciting to watch, but, if you thought about it, really it was. Because this was what Joseph Angelo had wanted to do with his life, and he was doing it. To look at me, stretched out one shelf below the Fruit Loops and the Niblets and the Cream of Wheat, you would not believe the same could be said for Donna Milewski. But, whether or not I liked how it had come about, I had just been given the final bit of what I needed in order to say I was truly doing what I had made up my mind to do in the middle of the night. That I was doing the one thing that I felt could make up for my side of the problems that can come when you love somebody too much—even though to simply look at the two of you in the many recent years nobody would have guessed that—and you lose them forever in an instant right out of the clear blue sky without your getting a chance to set things straight with them, and you see how short and how unpredictable life is, and that now is the time for that change.

I remained there, on the cool Formica, watching the half of Joseph Angelo that I could see, knowing full well he was good, wondering why I did to myself what I did to myself, and when was I ever going to stop, if I ever was going to at all.

I agreed that the band would play as long as Ray Jr. and Karen kept their mouths shut about exactly who was going to be their musical entertainment. All along, the band's engagements had been of the type or the location that kept us from being too-public knowledge, and that was something that was fine with me. I wanted to be ready for a formal unveiling, and here it was, being handed to me.

And after Father Kulpa and Brother Mike had pronounced Ray Jr. and Karen man and wife that fine Saturday morning in late August, and once everyone had shuffled through the reception line outside church and had loaned one more fresh hanky to the sobbing, giggling bride and marveled at the strong handshake of the beaming, speechless groom, they got into their cars and drove to the cabin, where Corinne and Leeann and I were set up on the porch, ready and waiting.

They could hear us the minute they parked, I knew, our notes clear and loud and without error, announcing that this was the place for the celebration. We could see them coming through the woods now, the men loosening their ties, the women leaning on the men and picking their high heels carefully over the smooth riverbed stones that Ray Jr. had set into the ground as the walk to his home. Some of the guests carried presents, others had envelopes sticking from their pockets, others held platters of homemade desserts, because you never can have enough of those even when you have hired someone to do all your cooking for you. Some would stop to peer ahead through the trees, to see who was playing there on the front porch, to see if they could recognize the band, so they could say, oh, that's the Krakow Five—I hope they don't play all that rock 'n roll like they did at Albert's kid's wedding. Some of the guests would wait for the next person to come down the path and would motion, look, the music's started already, and there's hardly anybody here yet—wonder who's paying for such an extravagance?

One by one, they came into the yard, on which long picnic tables were lined all the way to the river's edge, bright under a big white tent that had been rented just in case of rain. They set their boxes and handbags next to the centerpieces standing in jars as plain as any you'd find on a dump, only clean and filled with pink and white coneflowers from Ray Jr.'s garden. They dropped their gifts and their cards into a wheelbarrow Karen had draped with a checkered tablecloth just for that purpose, having seen such an idea in the "100 Wedding Ideas under $100" article she'd torn from a women's magazine and tacked on Ray Jr.'s kitchen bulletin board next to the log on which, for his own personal enjoyment, he daily charted the temperature and made other notes on the weather. Then the guests walked to the house and up to the porch, and stood in front of us.

I know my music so well that I don't even need a light to play. But once the crowd arrived, I found I was unable to look up from my keyboard, staring at my hand and its life of its own, at how it really didn't need the rest of me there, finding its way up and down just fine, turning out "Wedding Bell Polka" so sweetly that I heard genuine gasps from the crowd.

Though we were lots younger than he was, Carolyn and Marilyn and Theresa and I all had helped Ray with building one or another part of the cabin he put together in every spare moment of his high school years, and I remember working with him to build that very porch, handing him the long, flat boards that he nailed in place so exactly, and once he had three of four secured in place, he stood up on them and told me that this is the place from where he would view the world. I had stepped up beside him, and I looked out and found I could see only the river in front of us, and the bridge to the left, and the high factory that grew from the other bank. But Ray, I guessed, was seeing his own world—the piece of it that he was part of and would care for and would let no harm come to if he could help it. The day of the wedding, I looked down from just about the same spot on that porch, and there was my world. It was not a yard and a newly planted lilac, or the square of green grass inside the boundaries marked by iron pipes driven far into the ground. It was people, the ones who were there when my world had been formed. The ones who were there when it took its crooked turn and kept on going. The ones who I was part of and once cared for and once would have let no harm come to if I had any say in it, the ones who now were standing there in front of me in their best clothes, their hair done and their shoes shined and their finest jewelry brought out from hiding in old Thermos bottles down the cellar and in the second nightstand drawer, pinned inside a girdle.

"Here they are," somebody yelled, and down the path, through the thick trees, came the wedding couple, hand in hand. Ray in his good suit, one of his pink wild roses pinned into the lapel, Karen holding a small bundle of the same flowers that were on the tables, the ones Ray would give to any summer visitor, always saying he had way more than one man had the right to enjoy. She was wearing white, a simple long dress, nothing frilly or ornate or veiled, nothing excessive enough to have the ladies in line at the bank on Monday talking about who did she think she was, wearing that color. They stepped onto the porch and stood at the top of the stairs, and Leeann knocked her sticks three times and we began.

I didn't give it a name. I didn't give it lyrics. I am not that good with words, only with notes, only with the notes that I had laced together and set one after the other to make this waltz for Ray Jr. who put his arms out to Karen and twirled her around the porch like this was something they did every day, and for all that I apparently hadn't known of their life, it just might have been. It was the second piece of music I had ever written, and it was the second one I played for someone at the river's edge, and like the first one it traveled with the water out to meet the Chicopee, then the Connecticut, then the Long Island Sound, where it would get all mixed up with the Atlantic Ocean and maybe travel around the world before being evaporated into the clouds and being rained all over the land, hitting everybody who didn't take cover and splashing on them some of the joy that these two people were twirling in on that day.

We did not lag between songs. I was too afraid to stop and have someone come up and ask me what did I think I was doing. We went from "Tic Toc Polka" to "Setting Sun" to the one's we'd practiced from Mrs. Dranka's book of novelty tunes: the hokeypokey, the chicken dance, the bunny hop. We did a medley of obereks, one of traditional folk songs, another of sing-alongs. People were tearing up the grass in front of the porch, circling wildly, calling out requests, shouting their approval. We gave people not two seconds to applaud between each before we continued on to another number. Soon, Corinne and Leeann were pleading with me to stop for a little while, so I did.

"We'll be back after a short break," Corinne said into her microphone, then shut it off and glared at me. "If we don't die first."

Theresa and Carolyn, whom I'd spotted watching me from the big long bench Ray Jr. chopped from the trunk of a maple that had fallen onto his driveway during Hurricane Gloria, flew up to me the next second. I hadn't seen them since they both were home three Christmases ago, and I fell into them like they were camouflage, even though Carolyn was as short as ever and Theresa not only had a hairdo as cropped as Karen's but carried not an ounce of extra weight on her, Health by Farr's new fat-burning capsules, samples of which I'd tossed over the fence to Johnny Frydryk for use on his dog-sized cat, obviously as effective as their label claimed.

"I knew you'd be here, but I didn't know it would be like this," Carolyn said, motioning to the porch and the instruments and the chairs and the drum painted with our name. "You really went and did it!"

"I thought she was kidding when she told me about this," Theresa murmured to Carolyn, like I wasn't there. "She call you, too?"

"Of course I called her," I answered for Carolyn. "I called both of you. I wanted you to do this with me."

"You were serious," Theresa said, amazed.

"I was."

"I guess so," she concluded, then whispered, "You getting paid for this?"

"We get paid," I told her. "This is our work."

Theresa motioned across the river. "You're not there anymore? Not at all?"

"Not at all."

Carolyn pushed herself in front of Theresa. "Well, I think it's fantastic!"

"Hey, so do I," Theresa said, elbowing herself back into the spot closest to me. I felt nice to be fought over.

"You gotta see the kids, they're over at the store," Carolyn said. "And Morris, he's in the tent. He has a mustache now—did you see?"

"You gotta see Benny first," Theresa ordered, not adding any particular reason why. He'd always had his devil-beard of a goatee, so that was nothing she could boast about.

"Okay, okay," I said. "but will you do me a favor first?"

"What?" asked Carolyn. "What?" asked Theresa.

"Stay up here for a little bit."

They turned to see what I was looking at nervously, how behind them had formed a line of people, all wanting, it turned out, to shake my hand and take my picture and tell me what they thought, which turned out to be a whole lot of good things about what I was doing, which they had always heard I could do, if I kept on with it. All so surprised, all so happy, they knew I'd quit my job, what were they to think but that I was home, in the dark, despondent and with no direction? They hadn't wanted to bother me in what they had seen as a difficult time, but they had prayed for me, some of them said, especially at the part in the mass where you are invited to silently submit your special petition, then everybody asks, "Hear us, oh Lord," and you desperately hope that he will.

It happed every break: Stella Muniec. Then Blind Tekla. Then Johnny Skrowronek. Then Mrs. Marcinkiewicz. Then Eddie Swist. Then Michael Zbylot. The Golases. The Gondeks. The Gulas. The Gizas. Kisses. Hugs. They all wondered why I was leaving the house so often this summer. Now they knew. Mr. Zych. Teddy. Winston. All in from Harwichport and all with tans that looked too dark to be healthy. Mrs. Dranka, and Victor and Monika, Monika thanking me for the sign that credited her needlework, as she'd already received several comments, and one request for a business card, something she has been meaning to have printed, but now, certainly, she would have to take care of.

Father Kulpa and Brother Mike, done with their masses for the afternoon. Mr. and Mrs. Lyszko, of course, and Marilyn, in from Pittsburgh with two bored-looking girlfriends from her worker's compensation office who wore clingy black cocktail dresses and were afraid of bugs and were disappointed to see there were few eligible men to meet. Then there was Babci, in the blue-green floral print my mother had sewn her for the church's seventy-fifth anniversary banquet, a madonna and child painted in a little circle of gold covering her top button.

My mother was behind her, in a suit of pink linen, its buttons covered in matching fabric. She looked at me for the longest time, then at the vest that I knew she would have stayed up overnight to get to me the day after I had asked her to make it. Behind her was Betty, in a peach linen get-up that I could tell had come from the same pattern, done in its same double-breasted style, with the same rolled cuffs, but with rounded lapels and obvious patch pockets, rather than inset ones that were like secret compartments.

"Nice. Nice suits," I said. No one was saying anything— somebody had to say something.

Then Babci spoke. " '*Jedzie* Boat,' please," she whispered with a smile as sweet as the one on her pin, and she tucked a neatly folded dollar into my hand as a tip for her request.

"Babci wants to hear her favorite," my mother said. She looked like she was going to cry any second. She grabbed me so quickly it startled me, and she hung on to me with a desperation I felt clearly, as if we had extrasensory powers and she was trying to send me a message she could not bring herself to verbalize. And I received it, leaning there in her arms, feeling the words pulse into my waiting brain: "Everything is okay."

Babci smiled and repeated. "Play my song."

"Donna." Betty spoke. "I can't get over this." She looked at

343

me with what I have to say was genuine pride, then she shook her head and fished in her little white purse, slowly bringing out a dollar, which she held out to me and said, yes, play Babci's song. I didn't reach for her money, so she said, "For a request—isn't it all right to ask for what you want?"

Donna. Donna. Donnaaaaa. Betty always asking. And I, never giving one hint of what I wanted.

"I think if you don't ask, how else is anybody going to know?" I answered, pushing back her offering. Our hands touched, and she took hold of mine, and she stared into the center of me, like I had a magic pendant hanging there. Then she looked up, "A thousand times," she said, "I've told people I have the smartest sister."

A thousand times? She had been pulling for me in stray moments that I never knew about. But that was Betty for you. What could I do? For the first time in my life, I said these two words to her: "Thank you."

"I'm just saying what's true," she said, with a shrug that underlined she had no choice but to speak about me in that way, even though that was not at all the case.

And then I turned to Leeann and called out the title as all the guests floated back into the clearing, leaving behind their drinks and their plates as they led their partners back into the music, while Babci and Betty twirled slowly, and my mother, who would not dance in public so soon after my father's passing, if she ever would again, stood to the side and clapped in time to the tune that told of a ride on a boat, of our trip, of our journey, of the good and happy landing we all hoped for on the other side.

Most everybody else who, unlike Betty, didn't say they had guests and a husband who was watching the baby and who had to get to work, hung around until it got dark, though it really wasn't that hard to see because there was a big full moon hanging over Baptist Hill, one huge lightbulb joining Ray's handmade paper lanterns in providing the illumination for the few stray dancers who clung and swayed oblivious to the guests helping to round up the recyclables and fold the folding chairs and get the yard generally in order.

"Last dance, last chance," Leeann said into the microphone, as Corinne always allowed her, and in a minute Benny and Theresa and Morris and Carolyn and Ray Jr. and Karen were moving past us, each in their own universes of tomatoes and kelp and fish-carved beds, and I'm watching them, but I can tell someone is next to me, and I look to see Winkie Papuga, smiling and smiling, saying nothing this time, just touching my hand for a moment, then letting go and blowing his nose and stepping off the porch and getting into his car and rattling over the bridge and unlocking his apartment and taking out his teeth and settling onto his daybed and clicking to the "Wheel of Fortune" and going on, I guess, with the rest of all the little actions that would make up the whole entire remainder of his life, now carrying an inkling of what he had done to mine.

I walked home in my skirt and my vest, in my whole costume, my halo of flowers still pinned to my head. I sneaked down the path when the few of us who were left had calmed down and crowded around the porch steps looking at Carolyn's pocketbook crammed with kid pictures. Except for Ray Jr. and Karen, who were headed for a week in the White Mountains, they all would be there tomorrow, and I would see them then. I carried my case down the path and up the familiar street, past the fruit store, past the entrance to Theresa's Acres. At the park, the words "Tomorrow: Larry Chesky. No BYOB or BYOF!" had been chalked onto the board." I put down my case and took a seat on it, and I shut my eyes and I waited for a message. I believe that those in heaven can see all of our lives that they want to, and I'm sure that somebody of the zillions of people who have gone up there over the ages had to be tuning in to mine this afternoon and had to have called out, "Hey, Adam! Look what your kid is doing—she's got herself an all-girl polka band, and she's making a killing at a wedding!" And my father had to have run off from his lunch with Pope John Paul I or some king from the Jagiellonian dynasty, and he had to have peered through the hole in the sky, and he had to have said slowly and with great pride, "Will you look at that! I knew if she kept on with it . . ."

But I heard nothing from up above me, only the crickets, and an owl, and the slam of somebody's back door, and the hollowness banging around in my heart that good news isn't half as good if there's no one you can run to and share it with. I lifted my accordian case and walked home so slowly you would have thought it weighed five tons.

In my kitchen I left the lights off and took a seat in the dark. A thin slice of brightness cut through the wall from Joseph Angelo's kitchen, and I could hear voices. Then his laugh, then a strange yet familiar one meeting it. I wasn't going to bother, he obviously had moved on to somebody else, probably a sister of the fireman who makes the cheesecakes or the niece of the nun who was going to sing the national anthem at Fenway Park. But then I heard the name.

So I slowly walked into the pantry, and I looked through the wall.

And what I saw, there in Joseph Angelo's kitchen, was a girl—a woman.

We were the same age.

We were the same height.

We had the same long watermelon head.

The same square shoulders.

The same dark hair.

The same smile, back when mine came as easily as hers did right then, in color now, not in the black and white that I was so used to.

Aniela. There. Three feet in front of me.

I leaned into the crack for a long time, resting my forehead against the old wood, wondering how many other strange things were going to happen in my life in this one single day before I finally got to pull the covers over myself. I had to be seeing things. I blinked, but she was still there, now seated at Joseph Angelo's kitchen table as he opened the beer she'd asked for in my father's same accent, his clipped, fast little syllables telling Joseph Angelo that she did not need what she, as had her uncle, called a "gless."

I say she looked like me, but understand that I don't mean to brag when I point out that she was rather beautiful. There was

346

something in her that was missing in me, and it wasn't the way she wore her hair now, shoulder-length layered and swept behind her ears, or how plain but lovely was the sundress she had on, ivy and blue blossoms climbing everywhere over white that I would have been afraid to wear, just knowing I would end up sitting in something and ruining it. I guess if you gave me a decent haircut and found me fashionable clothes, I could have passed for her if I were standing way down the street, but there was something more she had. I just couldn't put my finger on it.

"If I can help, good," Aniela was saying. "I just did not want to talk in front of the others, up at the house. You understand? I don't mean to be difficult."

"Whatever you're comfortable with," Joseph Angelo answered, all professional. "I'm just trying to have this all make sense."

"You have to go way back for that," Aniela said laughing. "Okay. Well, you see, Joseph (she pronounced the name like it started with a Y) I don't know—there had been a little girl in Poland?" She stopped, waiting, eyebrows high, like Joseph Angelo needed to translate what she had just said. He waved her on to continue.

"A long many years ago, when my father and his brothers and sisters were children yet."

She halted again. He nodded that he understood.

"She had been given to the family, really. You can't imagine, coming from where you do, but there are people, even to this day, who have nothing. So little of nothing that they have no hope. It was such people who gave their youngest child to my grandparents. Despite they were not doing so well themselves, my grandparents decided they had enough to share, and they said they would take this child, named Zofja."

Another pause. I used this one to scan my memory for any stories of someone with such a name, but found none.

Aniela went on: "But there were nine other children already in the family, and my *dziadek*—my grandfather?—was busy all day—he was a carpenter, just like St. Joseph, you know? And my Babci I think she was busier even than he was, from sunup to midnight, no modern things like washer, dryer. Imagine. If you want to clean something, you will need to make your own soap. They are so busy all the time that they already have the children looking after one another. You watch the one who is younger than you, that one watches the younger, so forth. Zofja was twelve when she came to the family, the age between my Stryj—my Uncle—Adam, the eldest, and my father—Czesław—the second eldest. Zofja became the charge of Stryj Adam. She was his to mind, like she now had my father, and like my father had my Aunt Ida, like my Aunt Ida had my Uncle Wacław. Like my Uncle Wacław had my Uncle Karol. Like my Uncle Karol . . ."

"I get it," Joseph Angelo said, nodding.

Aniela continued. "He did not feel inconvenienced. Zofja was attractive, and a nice girl, quiet, and seemed like she would be a lot less trouble for my Uncle Adam than my father had been—my father liked to play pranks, you know, and sometimes got into fights. Zofja enjoyed household duties and often was occupied scolding my father, who was her charge, for all he got into. Babci imagined she would make a wonderful wife one day, and some in the family believed that Babci meant a wonderful wife for Adam, and there had been some looks between the two—remember, people used to get married at sixteen. Now from what I know, my Uncle Adam did not like responsibility—as a teenager, at least. He could be quite lazy. There is a rock in the middle of the river behind the field. It is shaped like your ear. He loved to rest on it, in the sun. He went there often, including the times he should have been doing other things. Such things as his chores. Such things as his schoolwork."

She stopped once again, and the next line I knew before she said it: "Such things as watching Zofja."

Okay, Aniela said, taking in a big breath, so this is what she knows: You have to walk through deep water to get to that rock—not over your head, but at least up to your chest. Aniela herself has done it many times, but only after she grew tall enough. Zofja was a short girl, not quite near the height at which she should have been crossing by herself. But that was what she did when she spotted my father lounging on the rock.

She had a smile on her face just before, in one swift instant, the water took her—and never gave her back.

"My father, Ida, Wacław, they were in the field that afternoon, where my Uncle Adam was supposed to be, working—not lying down," Aniela said. "They saw Zofja being carried away, thrashing, kicking, screaming each time she was able to get her head above the surface. They saw my uncle leap from the rock and try to catch up with her. They ran along, but the river turned, the woods were thick, they lost sight of them both. My Uncle Adam walked into the house two days later, his clothing slashed to almost nothing, and wet and muddied, he himself all beaten from the rocks, and he never said much after that about anything."

But, Aniela added, the neighbors did, as neighbors can, and such was the commotion about the boy's lack of responsibility and the shame he had brought on the family that had promised to care for the girl that my Polish grandfather asked Stryjanka Ida to take down his words on paper and send them to his brother in America, the brother who was seeking a child for his dear wife.

I felt weighted against the counter, unable to move.

"Who told you all this?" Joseph Angelo asked.

"I don't know—a lot of people—in pieces over the years I learned it," Aniela said. "No one ever said the whole story, but as you get older, you catch on to parts. I don't think anyone here ever knew, just as we never knew that Betty was injured, not until the family came for the wedding and saw her limping even now."

"Nobody called—or wrote even—to tell you?" Joseph Angelo scratched his head. "You know, I couldn't find a thing in there about your family's reaction—not a mention of prayers or a card or anything from her old home."

"There would be nothing to find," Aniela told him. "It is the way we are. If something happens that we do not like, it is like it never was."

I felt drugged, in a trance, like it had been Harry and Jessie telling that story in their hypnotic cadences, rather than Aniela in her good English. So this was how my father came to leave home and to begin a new life in which he was one of those monks who has a secret past, and not one of the people he lived with knew or cared what he had done. It was how he had learned responsibility. And how he came to have such a lack of patience for anyone else who did what he had once done—to be human, to be a child, to make mistakes.

Aniela was the astronaut's spokesman, standing in front of all those microphones, knowing the answers to so many questions that had bugged me for half my life. She had in her big hands the five-legged sky-colored inside piece of the jigsaw puzzle that I never had been able to find back when I had the interest in locating it: the missing piece, that the same thing that had happened to my father had happened to me, and that he went and did the same thing to me that had been done to him, only without shipping me off to another part of the world.

"Donna has just been off to a whole different planet," she told all those assembled. "But she's back, and she's okay now," she would tell all those who'd assembled to listen to the reasons I had been like I had been for so long, a bead balance, affected by something you couldn't see on your hands or on your fingertips or in your history.

Joseph Angelo was silent. Aniela looked around the room. I ducked.

"The wedding," he said. "You didn't come to your sister's wedding." I should point out here that he wasn't taking notes, that he didn't have a tape recorder pointed at her. He was just asking things, and she was just answering. But he seemed to be taking under great consideration every part of what she said.

"No," Aniela said. "I did not."

"But your whole family came over."

"I did not come because I did not want to take anything for free, especially if it had to do with Elżbieta."

What? Was I hearing right?

"What?" Joseph Angelo asked for me. "You don't like her?"

"I suppose it is not her fault," Aniela said, finishing her drink, looking to the counter to see if there was more where it had come from. "My father was more the problem. I was the eldest. As I saw it, I should have been the one chosen to go, to come here as a child. I was the one who was closest to being sent out into the world. If for no other reason, I ate the most, I required the largest clothing. Wouldn't it have been better for the family to send me if they wanted to save resources? But no—*she* had to go. I got no help from anyone, I got no attention. My father kept reminding me that I was the eldest. That I was the example. Be good, generous, give everything you have to the ones below you. No child wants to hear that day after day. It could make you insane."

So Aniela, who liked to read, began to strike back. She didn't dig holes for Uncle Czesław to step into and break his ankle, she didn't serve him old meat at the dinner table. She didn't hide his spirits just before he was to sit down at his bottle on Sunday afternoon. Instead of anything like that, she studied. She got her hands on books of different languages and read every page, all so she could go up to her father and say terrible, nasty things to his face without his knowing one word of it. As for other talk, she just didn't say anything to him that she didn't have to.

"I hated him," she said plainly. "I am intelligent, you know. I could have been the doctor. I could have gone to all the schools. So I hated Elżbieta, too. Imagine. I only know her for six years, and she is a child—what did I know of her? What do I know of her now? Nothing. Of my father? I know not much more. A few years ago, I begin to wonder who I am hurting with all this hate. I make my own money now, the soap does well with the tourists, so I come now. She is my sister, right?"

"Do you like her now?"

"Look at her—have you seen her?" Aniela asked. "How could you not like her? She is like something, I don't know how to say it—an invention, something you would make out of your head. No flaws, no hatred, always something good to say."

"Yeah, I've heard that," Joseph Angelo said, and he quickly changed gears. "So why now?"

"You do not know our Babci—in Poland," Aniela said. "She sees me all my life, what I do, how I act. She comes to me often, so very nice, she says, 'Live and let live,' more than once. You don't know the things that went on in this woman's life.

But always she has that attitude, to go on, why bother with hate?"

I had heard, and had seen, certainly more than enough. I needed air and headed for the front porch. She was next to me, sitting on the steps, before I knew what was happening, smelling of Joseph Angelo's soap—her soap.

"Donna," she said. I had never thought about her voice, never would have expected it to sound so much like Betty's.

I turned and looked at her. "Aniela," I answered. "Aniela."

She laughed. "You are not surprised?"

I shook my head. "Not anymore."

"You know I am in town?"

"Nobody told me," I said, which was true.

"But you knew."

"I knew."

Aniela pushed her fingers through her hair. She wore no rings, only a silver bracelet holding a line of three amber ovals.

"That does not shock me," she said, shrugging and smiling. "After she went off to you, your father sent us a photograph of you and Elżbieta. I was astounded how we resembled one another. That made me feel good—if I could not be there to protect my little sister, it was a sign from God that someone who was just like me was here to do that . . ."

"I tried to save her," I said, and tears came to my eyes like someone had pulled a switch. Aniela put a hand on my shoulder. I had enjoyed a few drinks at Ray Jr.'s—a special *krupnik* he made with honey from the bees that live in little white cabinets out near his long row of sunflowers. But I don't think I was imagining things when I felt a great warmth from her touch, like someone had laid a heating pad there, one that was set on high.

"Donna, it is ages already," she said.

I wanted to change the subject. "What are you doing here?" I asked.

"I'm on a visit. Your friend called for me," Aniela said. "He heard I was in the town, he wanted to talk to me."

"For his book."

"No," Aniela said. "For you. As a gift, he said, for your birthday in this late August. Answers to your questions."

She was quiet for a time, for so long that the crickets beneath the stairs resumed their racket. Then she leaned into my ear: "It is none of my business, but you have something here. Don't destroy it. Love can be easy to lose, hard to find once it leaves your sight."

"Boy, you don't mince words," I said, a little embarrassed. I didn't expect any of this from her, least of all free advice on what to do with Joseph Angelo.

"*Spero,*" she whispered.

I looked at her. "What?"

"It's Italian. For hope. Isn't it a beautiful word?"

She was like looking in the mirror on the medicine cabinet. Me, but a little different, a little wavy. Kind of like what she was saying—things that were different, wavy, but familiar. She couldn't have been snooping in my accordion case—I'd had it with me all the day. Yet she knew.

"That's—that's not a bird, the word for a bird?" I asked. "Not a sparrow?"

"No," Aniela said. "It's hope. I know my Italian. I used to call my father all kinds of things that you'd have to go to Rome to understand. What I'm saying is, you have hope."

Aniela takes in every inch of my face, telling me how those are our Stryjanka Ida's lips, and that is Babci's chin, and how my Kuzynka Dorota gets that same look when she is overwhelmed. I think of how both unsettling and reassuring it is that there can be in you little pieces of people you have never met.

"How your mouth goes up on that side, our fathers' uncle, Timoteusz, he was the same way," Aniela tells me.

"Never heard of him." I am staring out into the dark, where I imagined sparrows flying optimistically, knowing the secret of their name.

"Oh," Aniela says, leaning back on the step, "he was wonderful. He had a large farm, on the road out of town that is so crooked it veers this way, then turns that way, and you nearly can fall off at some sections, and you think you are almost lost, and you see it, his big white horse, and you know you have arrived."

It is as strong and as unexpected as a hit from a diaper truck.

Suddenly I am there, on Uncle Timoteusz's farm, hopping easily onto the white horse, knowing where I want to go. I pull Aniela on with me. And in an instant I know how to fill the hole that is in my heart, I know that there are some things in this life that must be done, and there is no escaping them.

"Come with me," I tell Aniela, and soon we are moving.

I step over the one who died from blood poisoning and the one who looked like the pope, and the one who really had always loved that one, and the wife lying between them.

Just past Kolbusz and Miga and Zlotek and Shyloski, past their geranium pots and American flags and praying hands and love letters and forty-eight-hour votives flickering blue and red, I find dead Jasiu's tombstone, which I have not seen for seventeen years. Jesus is still carved into it, still pulling aside the top of his robe to expose the blinding rays of his sacred heart, still wishing for me the words he stands on top of: "*Pokój z Tobą*"—"Be at Peace." It is the same stone except for the one big huge difference that took the air out of me in an instant—my father's name now listed under dead Jasiu's, two words that might as well be written in Swahili, they look so foreign, blasted permanent and eternal onto a thing like that. It is like Betty coming to my door and telling me all over again, and I am noticing the things you would not think you would be considering at the time: how there is a pot of yellow and orange marigolds in front of the marker, how the new grass has taken, and how even though the sky is clouding over the moon, I can make out that a tiny weed with a purple flower has sprouted at the right-hand corner of the rectangle, like you would have picked that spot and planted it there.

I stand at the foot of the plot, and finally I breathe in the sweet air that we the living are so fortunate to be able to take in. I close my eyes, and I tell him I am here, and that for my side of it I will put an end to all this, that it is not too late for him to learn what I have done, to know that I am loving what I am doing, and that it first of all was done for him and done willingly and with everything in that great root cellar of love I had stocked to the ceiling in all the years I never gave him one ounce. I put my hands to keys and the buttons, and I play

"Pretty Maryśka" and "When It's Evening" and the Polish national anthem, sending the notes out across the rows and rows of stones, past them and into the vast field that farmers now tend but that one day will be the place where more people, probably myself included, will be put to rest once all we had the time to do here is done. But I am alive now, and I am here to do one more thing for him. I am here to play the tune that Ignacy Ulatowski hepled make so famous, the one with the chorus that is spelled *"Hupaj Siupaj Dana,"* but sounds like "Hoopi Shoopi Donna," and that is what I do, and just like I knew he would be there, there he is, taking my hand and spinning me around the floor, so fast I fear I will fly off, but he is holding me tightly enough to keep that from happening, and we both go on to circle the floor, making those whooping noises when we bump into the couples we know, all of us swirling in a sea of dancers and perfume and sweat and forgiveness, thinking of nothing but the music, shuffling exactly over the cornmealed floor, bowing at the end of the song in gratitude for this wonderful music here in this life that, largely, is what you make it.

I am finished, and I am somewhere else, and it isn't within five thousand miles of those couple acres of dead people. All the squares on the calendar have been checked off, I have come to the end of my crooked line, and everything before me is straight and clear. And if I've ever known any one thing for certain in my whole entire life, it was that right then, I had made myself truly happy.

In the quiet, I run my hand along my father's name. The edges of the letters are sharp, their canals deep, and lichens and mosses have yet to find them, as they have the *A* and the *L* and the *W* of dead Jasiu's line. It comes to me that you can feel rotten about things for a million years, but chances are you aren't going to last that long. Look at Adolph Zombek or Piotr Klamut or the Kostek girl. Look at my father.

I swear off my past, and from one monk to the next no one knows what that was. No matter what I do it is going to turn out all right. Even if I stop paddling or stop concentrating, I will be fine. I stand up. I step over the secret loves and the pope man and the blood-poisoned guy. I return to Aniela, who leans against my car and doesn't say a word. She walks over to hug me, hope strapped to me, big and loud and colorful and noisy between us.

"I have a story to tell you," she says. "Of your father."

"I know," I said. "So do I."

On my side of the house, the rain is hitting the windows, falling and covering everything, and a train has just passed the house, and the noise of it is getting farther and farther away, and everything is still once again, and I feel here we are all safe and all in the same place, and there is nothing but good here. And I don't have to look back fifty years later and know how lucky I am—I know it at that very point, that, if I want to, I can have it the best of anybody in the world. It's like I've arrived at where I wanted to be—even though I never knew where I was going, or what I wanted, when I set out. But here I am.

And as Aniela and Joseph Angelo joke and kid while they set the crackers onto plates and olives into a bowl and my life onto a whole new track, I am aware that even though I want to keep this all to myself, I also want to share it. And I will start with one small thing—that I know a word in Italian.

About the Author

SUZANNE STREMPEK SHEA, a former reporter for the *Springfield* (MA) *Union-News* and the *Providence* (RI) *Journal*, is the author of the highly acclaimed first novel *Selling the Lite of Heaven*. A freelance writer whose work has been published in magazines including *Yankee* and the former *New England Monthly*, she lives in Bondsville, Massachusetts, with her husband, Tommy, a columnist for the *Union-News*.